Darth Maul, merciless apprentice of evil and one of the legendary Sith, a twisted order given over to the dark side of the Force . . . champion of the nefarious Sith Lord, Darth Sidious . . . Darth Maul, a legend sprung to life from the nightmares of history, about to be unleashed . . . in an all-new tale of intrigue and mystery set just before the events of Star Wars: Episode I The Phantom Menace.

PRAISE FOR *DARTH MAUL: SHADOW HUNTER*

"Reaves writes with a creative flair, allowing readers to experience an almost cinematic sensation as they move through the story. The language is colorful, the action scenes are dynamic, and the dialogue is realistic. . . . *Shadow Hunter* is a very good *Star Wars* novel that reads as easily as a comic book. . . . Reaves does an excellent job."
—*Winston-Salem Journal*

"Fast-paced . . . Exciting . . . Reaves does an excellent job of creating suspense . . . A great read for those that really enjoy the tales from the darker side of the *Star Wars* universe."
—WritersWrite.com

By Michael Reaves

HELL ON EARTH
VOODOO CHILD
NIGHT HUNTER
STREET MAGIC
THE BURNING REALM
THE SHATTERED WORLD
DARKWORLD DETECTIVE

With Steve Perry:
THE OMEGA CAGE
DOME
HELLSTAR

With Byron Preiss:
DRAGONWORLD

DARTH MAUL
SHADOW HUNTER

MICHAEL REAVES

THE BALLANTINE PUBLISHING GROUP • NEW YORK

A Del Rey ® Book
Published by The Ballantine Publishing Group
Copyright © 2001 by Lucasfilm Ltd. & ™.
All Rights Reserved. Used Under Authorization.

All rights reserved under International and Pan-American Copyright Conventions. Published in the United States by The Ballantine Publishing Group, a division of Random House, Inc., New York, and simultaneously in Canada by Random House of Canada Limited, Toronto.

"Darth Maul: Saboteur" was originally published in e-book form by Del Rey/The Ballantine Publishing Group, a division of Random House, Inc., in 2001.

Del Rey is a registered trademark and the Del Rey colophon is a trademark of Random House, Inc.

www.starwars.com
www.starwarskids.com
www.delreydigital.com

ISBN 0-345-43541-9

Manufactured in the United States of America

First Hardcover Edition: February 2001
First Mass Market Edition: December 2001

10 9 8 7 6 5 4 3 2 1

For my daughter Mallory
"The Force is strong in this one."

ACKNOWLEDGMENTS

Sharecropping in someone else's field can often be an onerous task. In this case, however, it was a pleasure, and this is due in great part to the help I had from the many people who have helped create and maintain the *Star Wars* cosmos. Thanks are due to my editor, Shelly Shapiro, who got me the gig; to Sue Rostoni and the rest of the gang at Skywalker Ranch; to Ron Marz; to Brynne Chandler; to Steve Sansweet for his enormously helpful *Star Wars Encyclopedia*; to Steve and Dal Perry; and, of course, to George Lucas for creating what is without a doubt the most entertaining galaxy in the entire universe.

DARTH MAUL
SHADOW HUNTER

AN EVEN LONGER TIME AGO
IN A GALAXY FAR, FAR AWAY . . . .

PART I

MEAN STREETS

Space is the perfect place to hide.

The Neimoidian freighter *Saak'ak* cruised ponderously in the uncharted deeps of Wild Space. It displayed its colors proudly, its cloaking device disabled, with no fear of detection. Here, parsecs away from the civilized Galactic Core and its surrounding systems, it could safely hide in plain sight. Even the Neimoidians, those past masters of paranoia, felt secure in the vast endless abyss between the disk and one of the spiral arms.

Yet even here the leaders of the Trade Federation could not entirely let go of their natural tendency toward subterfuge. They sought duplicity and guile the way a young grub seeks the safety and warmth of its sleeping niche in the communal hive. The *Saak'ak* was a good example of this. It was, to all appearances, merely a commercial vessel, its horseshoe shape designed to carry large amounts of cargo. Not until an unwary enemy had come within firing range would the heavy durasteel armor plating, blaster turrets, and military-strength communications arrays become visible.

By which time, of course, it would be too late.

Aboard the *Saak'ak*'s bridge all was silent save for the muted beeps and chimes of various life-support monitors and the almost inaudible susurrus of the air filtration system. Three figures stood to one side of the huge transparisteel viewport. They wore the flowing robes and mantles of the Neimoidian aristocracy, but their body language, as a fourth figure appeared in their midst, was deferential, if not outright cringing and servile.

The fourth figure was not really there with them in any physical sense. The robed and hooded form was a holograph, a three-dimensional image projected from an unknown source light-years distant. Intangible and immaterial, the mysterious stooped image nevertheless dominated the three Neimoidians. Indeed, they could not have been any more thoroughly cowed had he been physically present with a blaster in each hand.

The figure's face—what little was visible of it in the shadows of the hood—was grim and unforgiving. The cowled head moved slightly as he looked at each of the Neimoidians in turn. Then the figure spoke, his voice a dry rasp, his tone that of one accustomed to instant obedience.

"There are only three of you."

The tallest of the three, the one wearing the triple-crested tiara of a viceroy, responded in a stammering voice. "Th-that is true, Lord Sidious."

"I see you, Gunray, and your lackeys Haako and Dofine. Where is the fourth one? Where is Monchar?"

Federation Viceroy Nute Gunray clasped his hands in front of him in what was not so much a supplicating gesture as an attempt to keep them from nervously wringing each other. He had hoped he would grow used to dealing with the Sith Lord over time, but so far that had not happened. If anything, these meetings with Darth Sidious had become even more gut-twisting and upsetting as the deadline for the embargo grew ever closer. Gunray did not know how his seconds in command, Daultay Dofine and Rune Haako, felt—discussing one's feelings was anathema in Neimoidian society—but he knew how he felt after each encounter with the Sith Lord. He felt like squirming back into his hive mother's birth chamber and pulling the cloacal flap in after him.

Especially now. Curse Hath Monchar! Where was the misbegotten rankweed sucker? Not on board the *Saak'ak*, that much was certain. The ship had been searched from the center sphere to the air locks at the outmost ends of each docking bay arm. Not only was his deputy viceroy nowhere to be found, but a scout vessel with hyperdrive capability was missing, as well. Put these two facts together, and the chances of Viceroy Gunray winding up as fodder for one of the fungus farms back on Neimoidia was beginning to look distressingly good.

The holographic image of Darth Sidious flickered slightly, then regained its none-too-stable resolution. A glitch, most likely caused by some solar flare on a star between here and whatever mysterious world the signal was originating from. Not for the first time Gunray found himself wondering on what world or ship the real Sith was standing, and not for the first time he flinched hastily away from the thought. He didn't want to know too much about the Neimoidians' ally in this undertaking. In fact, he wished he could forget what little he already knew. Collaborating with Darth Sidious was about as safe as being trapped in a cave on Tatooine with a hungry krayt dragon.

The hooded face turned to glare directly at him. "Well?" Sidious demanded.

Even as he opened his mouth, Gunray knew that it would be futile to lie. The Sith Lord was a master of the Force, that mysterious and pervasive energy field that, some said, knitted the galaxy together just as surely as did gravity. Sidious might not be able to read another's inmost thoughts, but he certainly could tell when someone was lying. Even knowing that, however, the Neimoidian could no more stop himself from dissimulating than he could stop his sweat ducts from oozing oily perspiration down the back of his neck.

"He was taken ill, my lord. Too much rich food. He—he has a delicate constitution." Gunray closed his mouth, keeping his lips firmly pressed together to stop them from trembling. Inwardly he cursed himself. Such a pathetic and obvious prevarication; even a Gamorrean would be able to see through it! He waited for Sidious to command Haako and Dofine to turn on him, to strip him of his vestments and rank. He had no doubt that they would do it. For the Neimoidians, one of the most difficult concepts to understand in the galactic lexicon of Basic was the word *loyalty*.

However, to his astonishment, Sidious merely nodded instead of showering him with vituperation. "I see. Very well, then—the four of us shall discuss the contingency plans should the trade embargo fail. Monchar can be briefed on them when he recovers." The Sith Lord continued speaking, describing his plan to hide a large secret army of battle droids in the cargo bays of the trade ships, but Gunray could hardly pay attention to the specifics. He was stunned that his desperate ruse had worked.

The viceroy's relief was short-lived, however. He knew that at best all he had done was buy some time, and not much of that. When Sidious's hologram again materialized on the bridge of the *Saak'ak* he would once more demand to know where Monchar was— and this time he would not accept illness as an excuse.

There were no two ways about it—his errant lieutenant would have to be found, and quickly. But how to do this without arousing Sidious's suspicions? Gunray felt certain at times that the Sith Lord was somehow able to peer into every compartment, niche, and cubicle on the freighter, that he knew *everything*, no matter how trivial or inconsequential, that took place on board.

The viceroy silently commanded himself to maintain control. He took advantage of Sidious's attention being momentarily focused on Haako and Dofine to surreptitiously slip an antistress capsule between his lips. He could feel his lung pods expanding and contracting convulsively within him, on the verge of hyperventilation. An old saying characterized Neimoidians as the only sentient species with an entire organ devoted solely to the task of worrying. As Nute Gunray felt the anxiety that had been momentarily quelled threatening to build up once more in his gut sac, the adage did seem to have an unpleasant ring of truth to it.

Darth Sidious, Master of the Sith, finished relaying his instructions to the Neimoidians and made a slight, almost negligent gesture. Across the room a relay clicked and the holographic transmission ended. The flickering blue-white images of the Neimoidians and the section of their ship's bridge captured by the split-beam transceivers vanished.

Sidious stood motionless and silent on the transmission grid, his fingers steepled, his mind meditating on the eddies and currents of the Force. Those of lesser sensitivity were oblivious to it, but to him it was like an omnipresent mist, invisible but nonetheless tangible, that swirled and drifted constantly about him. No words, no descriptions could begin to convey what it was like; the only way to understand it was to experience it.

He had learned over long years of study and meditation how to interpret each and every vagary of its restless flow, no matter how slight. Even without that ability, however, he would have known that Nute Gunray was lying about Hath Monchar's whereabouts. An old joke about the viceroy's kind summed it up nicely:

How can you tell if a Neimoidian is lying?
His mouth is open.

Sidious nodded slightly. There was no doubt of

Gunray's dishonesty; the only question was *why*. It was a question that had to be answered, and soon. The Neimoidians were weaklings, true enough, but even the most cowardly creatures would rear up on their hind legs and bite if sufficiently motivated. They were plotting behind his back. To believe otherwise was to be hopelessly naive, and though a great many crimes could be laid at Darth Sidious's feet, naïveté was certainly not one of them. Given how potentially important the Naboo embargo and subsequent economic machinations could be, there was really only one thing to do.

Sidious made another slight gesture. The Force rippled in response, and the transmission grid beneath his feet glowed again. A holograph of himself was once more sent racing through the void to another remote location. It was time to bring a new player into the game—one who had trained and studied for years for precisely this kind of assignment. The one who comprised the other half of the Sith order. His protégé, his disciple, his myrmidon.

The one Sidious had named Darth Maul.

The dueling droids were programmed to kill.

There were four of them, top-of-the-line Duelist Elites from Trang Robotics, all armed in different ways: one with a steel rapier, one with a heavy cudgel, the third with a short length of chain, and the last with a pair of double-edged hachete fighting blades as long and wide as a human's forearm. They had been programmed with the skills of a dozen martial arts masters, and their reflexes were calibrated just a hair faster than human optimum. Their durasteel chassis were blaster-resistant. They had come factory-equipped with behavioral inhibitors that prevented them from delivering a death blow once their opponent had been beaten, but these inhibitors had been nullified by their new owner. A mistake against one would be fatal.

Darth Maul did not make mistakes.

The Sith apprentice stood in the middle of the training chamber as the four droids circled him. His breathing was calm, his heartbeat even and slow. He was aware of his body's reactions to the danger—aware and in control.

Two of the droids—Rapier and Chain, he silently named them—were within his field of vision. The other two—Cudgel and Hachete—were not, being behind him. It did not matter; through his awareness of the Force he could sense their movements as plainly as if he had eyes in the back of his head.

Maul raised his own weapon, the double-bladed lightsaber, and triggered the power control. Twin lances of pure energy boiled forth, hissing and crackling in crimson loops that began and ended at the two flux apertures on either end of the device. Any Jedi Knight could wield a single-bladed lightsaber; only a master fighter could use the weapon first designed by the legendary Dark Lord Exar Kun millennia ago. Unless one was in perfect attunement with it, the weapon could be as deadly to the user as to the opponent.

Rapier lunged at full extension, its metal knee joint bent almost to the floor. The needle point flickered toward Maul's heart, almost too fast to see.

The dark side blossomed in Darth Maul, the power

of it resonating in him like black lightning, augmenting his years of training, guiding his reactions. Time seemed to slow, to stretch.

It would have been easy to chop the blade itself in half, as few metals could resist the frictionless edge of a lightsaber. But there was no challenge to that. Maul spun toward the point, twisted around the outside, and snapped his hands horizontally at chest level. The left blade of the lightsaber sheared through Rapier's sword arm. Both arm and weapon clattered to the floor.

Maul dropped to his left knee as, from directly behind him, Cudgel's full swing whistled over his head, barely missing his dorsal horn. Without looking, guided by the vibrations of the Force, he thrust backwards with the right blade, then forward with the left—*one, two!*—skewering both Cudgel and Rapier in their abdominal compartments. Sparks spewed from shorted circuitry, and lubricating fluid sprayed in a reddish oily mist.

Using the momentum of the forward thrust, Maul dived over the collapsing droid before him, flowing smoothly into a shoulder roll. He came up twirling his lightsaber overhead, then stepped down solidly into the teräs käsi wide stance called Riding Bantha. Even as he did the movement, part of him was monitoring his body's state. His breathing was slow and even, his pulse elevated by no more than two or three beats per minute from its resting rate.

Two down, two to go.

Chain charged, its weapon whirling over its head like the propeller of a gyrocraft. The heavy links lashed toward him. Maul spun on his right foot and shot his left leg out in a powerful side kick, slamming his boot into the droid's armored chest, stopping it cold. He dropped into a squat, spun the lightsaber like a scythe, and sickled the droid cleanly at the knees. Lower legs gone, it collapsed as Maul again twisted himself and his weapon, flowing into the form known as Rancor Rising. He brought the right blade up between Chain's mechanical thighs, hard, using his leg muscles to augment the strike as he pushed up from the squat to a standing position.

The force of his strike bisected Chain from its crotch right through the top of its head. There was a hard metallic screech as the droid came apart in two halves. Its feet and lower legs hit the floor slightly before the upper halves landed atop them.

The acrid smell of burned lubricating fluid and circuitry washed over Maul. What was, seconds ago, a functional piece of high-tech equipment was now a barely recognizable pile of scrap metal.

Three down, one to go.

Hachete moved to Maul's left, whirling its razor-edged blades in defensive movements—high, low, left, right, a blinding pattern of edged death waiting to blind the unwary and cut him down.

Maul allowed himself a twitch of his lips. He pressed the lightsaber's controls. The humming died as the energy beams blinked out. He bent, keeping his eyes on the droid as he put the weapon on the floor and shoved it away with his boot.

He settled himself into a low defensive stance, angled toward the droid at forty-five degrees, left foot forward. He watched the flickering arabesque of death as

Hachete edged toward him. A droid like this knew no fear, but Darth Maul knew that to put his weapon down and face a live opponent barehanded would certainly terrify anybody brighter than a dueling droid. Fear was as potent a weapon as a lightsaber or a blaster.

The dark side raged inside him, sought to blind him with hatred, but he held it at bay. He held one open hand high, by his ear, the other by his hip, then reversed the positions, watching. Waiting.

Hachete stole forward another half step, crossing and recrossing the blades, looking for an opening.

Maul gave the droid what it was looking for. He moved his left arm wide, away from his body, exposing his side to a thrust or a cut.

Hachete saw the opening and moved in, fast, very fast, snapping one of the blades out to cut while bringing the other blade over for backup.

Maul dropped, hooked his left foot around the back of the droid's ankle, and pulled as he kicked hard at the droid's thigh with the other foot.

The droid fell backwards, unable to maintain its balance, and hit the floor. Maul sprang up, did a front flip, and came down with both boot heels driving into the droid's head. The metal skull crunched and collapsed inward. Lights flashed and the hard-shell photoreceptors shattered.

Maul dived again, rolled up in a half twist into the förräderi stance, ready to spring in any direction.

But there was no need—these four were done. It would take a technician days to repair Hachete, Cudgel, and Rapier. Chain was beyond repair, useful only for parts.

Darth Maul exhaled, relaxed his stance, and nodded. His heart rate had accelerated perhaps five beats above normal at most. There was the faintest sheen of perspiration on his forehead; otherwise his skin was dry. Perhaps sixty seconds had elapsed from start to finish. Maul frowned slightly. Not his personal best, by any means. It was one thing to face and defeat droids. Jedi were a different matter.

He would have to do better.

He picked up his lightsaber, hung it from his belt. Then, his muscles warmed up now, he went to practice his fighting exercises.

He had barely gotten more than a few meters, however, when a familiar shimmering in the air in front of him brought him to a stop. Before the hooded figure's image had time to solidify, Maul dropped to one knee and bowed his head.

"Master," he said, "what do you wish of your servant?"

The Sith Lord regarded his apprentice. "I am pleased with the way you dealt with the Black Sun assignment. The organization will be in disarray for years."

Maul nodded slightly in acknowledgment. Such offhanded praise was the most he ever got in recognition of his work, and that only rarely. But praise, even from Sidious, did not matter. All that mattered was serving his master.

"Now I have another task for you."

"Whatever my master wishes shall be done."

"Hath Monchar, one of the four Neimoidians I am dealing with, has disappeared. I suspect treachery. Find him. Make sure he has spoken to no one of the impending embargo. If he has—kill him, and everyone he has spoken to."

The holographic image faded away. Maul straightened and headed for the door. His step was firm, his manner confident. Anyone else, even a Jedi, might have protested that such an assignment was impossible. It was a big galaxy, after all. But failure was not an option to Darth Maul. It was not even a concept.

STAR WARS: DARTH MAUL: SHADOW HUNTER 2.

Coruscant.

The name evoked the same image in the mind of nearly every civilized being in the galaxy. Coruscant: Bright center of the universe, cynosure of all inhabited worlds, crown jewel of the Core systems. Coruscant, seat of government for the myriad worlds of an entire galaxy. Coruscant, the epitome of culture and learning, synthesis of a million different civilizations.

Coruscant.

Seeing the planet from orbit was the only way to fully appreciate the enormity of the construction. Practically all of Coruscant's landmass—which comprised almost all of its surface area, its oceans and seas having been drained or rerouted through huge subterranean caverns more than a thousand generations ago— was covered with a multitiered metropolis composed of towers, monads, ziggurats, palazzi, domes, and minarets. By day the many crosshatched levels of skycar traffic and the thousands of spaceships that entered and left its atmosphere almost blotted out views of the endless cityscape, but at night Coruscant revealed its full splendor, outshining at close range even the spectacular nebulae and globular clusters of the nearby Galactic Core. The planet radiated so much heat energy that, were it not for thousands of strategically placed CO_2 reactive dampers in the upper atmosphere, it would long ago have been transformed into a lifeless rock by a rampant atmospheric degeneration.

An endless ring of titanic skyscrapers girded Coruscant around its equator, some of them tall enough to pierce the upper fringes of atmosphere. Similar, if shorter structures could be found almost anyplace on the globe. It was those rarefied upper levels, spacious and clean, that constituted most peoples' conception of the galactic capital.

But all visions of soaring beauty and wealth, no matter how stately, must be grounded somewhere, somehow. Along the equatorial strip, below the lowest stratum of air traffic, beneath the illuminated skywalks and the glittering facades, lay another view of Coruscant. There, sunlight never penetrated; the endless city night was lit only by flickering neon holoprojections advertising sleazy attractions and shady businesses. Spider-roaches and huge armored rats infested the shadows, and hawk-bats with wingspans of up to one and a half meters roosted in the rafters of deserted structures. This was the underbelly of Coruscant, unseen and unacknowledged by the wealthy, belonging solely to the disenfranchised and the damned.

This was the part of Coruscant that Lorn Pavan called home.

The meeting place had been suggested by the Toydarian; it was a dingy building at the back of a dead-end street. Lorn and his droid, I-Five, had to step over a Rodian sleeping in a pile of rags near the recessed entrance.

"I've often wondered," the protocol droid said as they entered, "if your clientele all subscribe to the same service—the one listing the most disgusting and disreputable places in the galaxy to meet."

Lorn made no reply. He had wondered the same thing on occasion himself.

Inside was a small lobby, most of its space taken up by a ticket booth made of yellowing plasteel. In the booth a balding human male lounged in a formfit chair. He looked up incuriously when they entered. "Booth five's open," he grunted, jerking his thumb at one of a series of doors lining the lobby's circular wall. "One credit for a half hour." He looked at I-Five, then said to Lorn, "If you're taking the droid in, you gotta sign a release form."

"We're here for Zippa," Lorn told him.

The proprietor glanced at them again, then shifted his bulk and pressed a button with a grimy finger. "Booth nine," he said.

The holobooth was even smaller than the lobby, which meant it was barely big enough to contain the four who were now crowded into it. Lorn and I-Five stood behind the single contour couch that faced the transmitter plate. Zippa hovered slightly above the plate, facing them, the sound of his rapidly beating wings providing a constant background buzz. The dim light darkened his mottled blue skin to an unhealthy shade of purplish-black.

Behind the Toydarian stood another, bulkier form; Lorn could tell that it was nonhuman, but the light was too faint for him to guess its species. He wished that Zippa would stop hovering: whatever the being behind the Toydarian was, it stank like a silage bin at high noon, and the breeze generated by Zippa's wings wasn't helping matters any. It was obvious that Zippa hadn't been any too fastidious about bathing lately, as well, but fortunately the Toydarian's body odor wasn't offensive; in fact, it reminded Lorn of sweetspice.

"Lorn Pavan," Zippa said, his voice somehow sounding faintly of static, as if it were tuned just a hair off true. "Good to see you again, my friend. It has been too long."

"Good to see you again, too, Zippa," Lorn replied. Thinking, you really had to hand it to the old crook. Nobody could fake sincerity like he could. In reality, the best thing that could be said about Zippa was that he would never stab you in the back unless it was absolutely . . . expedient.

Zippa changed the angle of his wings slightly, rotating to one side as he gestured to the shadowy mass in the corner. "This is Bilk, an . . . associate of mine."

Bilk stepped forward slightly, and Lorn could now see him well enough to recognize him as a Gamorrean. That explained the stench.

"Pleased to meet you, Bilk." He gestured at I-Five. "This is my associate, I-FiveYQ. I-Five, for short."

"Charmed," I-Five said dryly. "Now, if you don't mind, I'll shut off my olfactory sensor before it overloads."

Zippa turned his bulbous gaze toward the droid. "*Chut-chut!* A droid with a sense of humor! This I like. You want to sell him?" The Toydarian drifted closer and slightly higher, the better to evaluate I-Five's worth. "Looks pretty cobbled together. Are those Cybot G7 powerbus cables? Haven't seen them used in years. Still, he might be worth something as a curiosity. I'll give you fifty creds for him."

Lorn kicked the droid in his lower left servomotor coupling before I-Five could voice an indignant protest. "Thanks for the offer, but I-Five's not mine to sell. We're business partners."

Zippa stared at Lorn for a moment, then broke into a wheezing laugh. "You got a weird sense of humor, Lorn. I never know when you're kidding. Still, I like you."

Bilk suddenly narrowed his beady eyes and rumbled deep in his throat, leaning truculently toward I-Five. Probably only just now realizing that the droid's earlier remark had been an insult, Lorn surmised. Gamorreans weren't the brightest species in the galaxy, not by several decimal places.

Zippa drifted in front of his hulking bodyguard. "Relax, Bilk. We're all good friends here." He turned back toward Lorn. "My friend, this is your lucky day." The Toydarian dug knobby fingers into a pouch and pulled out a palm-sized crystal cube, which glowed a dull red in the semidarkness of the booth. "What I have here is an authentic Jedi Holocron, reliably chronon-dated to be five thousand years old. This cube contains secrets of the ancient Jedi Knights." He held the cube at Lorn's eye level. "For an artifact such as this, you must agree that no price is too great. Nevertheless, all I am asking is a measly twenty thousand credits."

Lorn made no attempt to touch the object that the fence held before him. "Most interesting, and certainly a fair price," he said. "*If* it is what you claim it is."

Zippa looked affronted. "*Nifft!* You doubt my word?"

Bilk growled and cracked one set of knuckles against the horny palm of his other hand. They sounded like bones snapping.

"No, of course not. I'm sure you believe what you say is true. But there are many unscrupulous vendors out there, and even someone with your discerning eye might conceivably be taken in. All I'm asking for is a little empirical proof."

Zippa twisted his snout into a grin, exposing teeth scrimshawed with the remnants of his last meal. "And how do you propose we get this proof? A Jedi Holocron can be activated only by someone who can use the Force. Is there something you're not telling me, Lorn? Are you perhaps a closet Jedi?"

Lorn felt himself go cold. He stepped forward and grabbed Zippa by his fleekskin vest, jerking the surprised Toydarian toward him. Bilk growled and lunged at Lorn, then stopped cold as a hair-thin laser beam scorched his scalp between his horns.

"Settle down," I-Five said pleasantly, lowering the index finger from which the beam had fired, "and I won't have to show you the other special modifications I've had installed."

Ignoring the face-off between the droid and the Gamorrean, Lorn spoke in a low voice to Zippa. "I know that was intended as a joke—which is why I'm letting you live. But don't ever—*ever*—say anything like that to me again." He glared into the Toydarian's protruding watery eyes for a moment longer, then released him.

Zippa quickly assumed a position just behind Bilk, wings beating harder than ever. Lorn could see him swallow the surprise and anger he was undoubtedly feeling as he smoothed away the wrinkles in his vest. Inwardly, Lorn cursed himself; he knew it was a mistake to let his temper get the best of him. He needed this deal; he couldn't afford to antagonize the Toydarian fence. But Zippa's remark had taken him by surprise.

"Touched a nerve, looks like," Zippa said. During the altercation he had held on to the Holocron; now he stuffed it back into his belt pouch. "I didn't know I was dealing with someone so . . . temperamental. Maybe I should find another buyer."

"Maybe," Lorn replied. "And maybe I should just take the cube and pay you what it's worth—which I figure is about five thousand creds."

He saw Zippa's cavernous nostrils flare. The Toydarian couldn't resist bargaining, even with someone who had laid hands on him. "Five thousand? *Pfah!* First you assault me, then you insult me! Twenty thousand is a fair price. However," he continued, stroking his stubbly, practically nonexistent chin, "it's obvious that you've had some sort of bad experience with the Jedi. I am not without compassion. In recognition of your past tragedy I might be persuaded to lower my price to eighteen thousand—but not a decicred lower."

"And I am not without some remorse for my behavior. As a gesture of apology, I'll raise my offer to eight thousand. Take it or leave it."

"Fifteen thousand. I'm cutting my own throat here."

"Ten thousand."

"Twelve." Zippa leaned back in midair, folding his spindly arms in a gesture of finality.

"Done," Lorn said. He had been ready to go as high as fifteen, but of course there was no reason for Zippa to know that. He pulled a thick wad of Republic credits from a belt compartment and began counting them. Most transactions uplevels were handled by electronic credit chips, but few people used the chips down here. Zippa brought the Holocron back into view and handed it to Lorn simultaneously with Lorn handing him the bills.

Lorn accepted the cube. "Well," he said, "it's been a pleasure doing—" He left the sentence unfinished when he saw that Bilk was now pointing a blaster directly at I-Five's recharge coupling. Zippa, his smile now decidedly unpleasant, floated forward and plucked the Holocron and the remainder of the credits from Lorn's hand.

"I'm afraid in this case the pleasure is all mine," the Toydarian said as both Lorn and I-Five raised their hands. Then Zippa's smile vanished, and the next words came out in a sinister hiss. "No one *ever* threatens me and lives to tell about it." One three-fingered hand made a pass before a sensor plate, and the booth door slid open. "I'll tell the proprietor that booth nine will be needing some extra cleaning," he said as he exited. "Hurry up, Bilk—I want to find another buyer for this item."

The booth door closed after Zippa's departure. It was impossible to tell if the piglike snout of the Gamorrean was smiling, but Lorn was pretty sure it was. "What's the galaxy coming to when you can't trust a Toydarian fence," he said to I-Five.

"Disgraceful," the droid agreed. "It just makes me want to . . . *scream*."

Lorn still had his hands raised, and now he quickly jammed his two index fingers into his ears as deeply as he could as a deafening high-pitched screech came from I-Five's vocabulator. Even with his ears plugged, the volume was excruciatingly painful. Bilk, caught with no defense, reacted exactly as they had hoped he would: he howled in pain and reflexively clapped both hands over his ears, dropping the blaster in the process.

I-Five stopped the scream, caught the weapon before it could hit the floor, and in another second was aiming it at Bilk. The Gamorrean either didn't notice this fact or was too enraged to care. Snarling, he lunged at Lorn and the droid.

The particle beam punched through Bilk's armored chest plate, seared its way through various internal organs, and exited between the shoulder blades. The beam's intense heat instantly cauterized the wound, stopping any visible bleeding—not that that mattered much to Bilk. He dropped to the floor like a sack of meat, which was essentially what he had become.

Lorn waved his hand over the exit plate, and the panel snapped open again. "Come on—before Zippa gets away!" he shouted to the droid as he charged through the lobby. The proprietor barely glanced up as they dashed by.

They both emerged into the dim light of the dead-end street, Lorn now holding the blaster, which I-Five had tossed to him. But there was no sign of Zippa. No doubt he had heard I-Five's scream, realized Bilk's probable fate, and let his wings carry him out of sight as fast as possible.

Lorn slammed a fist against the graffiti-scarred wall. "Great," he groaned. "That's just *great*. Fifteen thousand credits *and* the cube gone. And I had someone on the hook to pay *fifty* thousand for an authentic Holocron."

"Perhaps if you hadn't committed that slight blunder earlier . . ."

Lorn turned and glared at I-Five, who continued, "But now may not be the most appropriate time to discuss it."

Lorn took a deep breath, let it out slowly. Dusk was falling fast. "Come on," he said. "We'd better get out of this sector before the Raptors find us. That would be the perfect end to the day."

"So," I-Five said as they started walking, "was it a real Jedi Holocron?"

"I didn't get a chance to examine it closely. But from the cuneiform on it, I'd say it was even rarer than that. I think it was a Sith Holocron." Lorn shook his head in disgust—mostly self-disgust. He knew I-Five was right; his burst of temper had probably precipitated Zippa's reneging. He'd dealt with the Toydarian before and never been double-crossed. Stupid, stupid, *stupid*!

But there was no point in self-flagellation. He was out of credits, and this was a bad part of Coruscant to be in with no assets. He needed a hustle, and he needed it soon—or he might very likely wind up as dead as Bilk.

Not at all a comforting thought.

Darsha Assant stood before the Jedi Council. This was a moment of glory that she had dreamed about ever since she had begun her Padawan training. For nearly her entire life the world within the Jedi Temple had been, to all extents and purposes, her only world. During those years she had studied, had practiced weapon and bare-hand forms, had sat in meditation for hours on end, and—in many ways the most difficult task of all—had learned to sense and manipulate, to a small degree, the power of the Force.

And now she was close to the culmination of her training. Now she stood in the topmost chamber of the spire known as the Jedi Council, with its spectacular view of the planetary city spreading away in all directions to the far horizon. Seated in twelve chairs around the perimeter of the rotunda were the members of the council. Though she had seen them but rarely during her years of training—indeed, this was only the fourth time she had been in the Council Chamber—she knew their names and histories well from her studies. Adi Gallia. Plo Koon. Eeth Koth. The ancient and venerable Yoda. And, of course, Mace Windu, a senior member of the council. Darsha felt more than a little giddy just being in the presence of this august company.

At least she was not standing there alone. Behind her and slightly to one side was her mentor, Anoon Bondara. Master Bondara epitomized what Darsha hoped to become one day. The Twi'lek Jedi Master lived in the Force. Always still and complacent as a pool of unknown depth, he was nevertheless one of the best fighters in the order. His skill with a lightsaber was second to none. Darsha hoped that one day she might be able to exhibit a tenth of Anoon Bondara's adeptness.

Darsha had entered the order at the age of two, so like most of her comrades she had no real memories of any place other than the cloistered hallways and chambers of the Temple. Master Bondara had been parent and teacher to her for as long as she could remember. She found it hard to conceive of a life in which her Jedi mentor was not involved.

Yet now she was taking a big step into just that sort of life. For today she would be given the final assignment of her Padawan training. If she completed it successfully, she would be deemed worthy to assume the mantle of a Jedi Knight.

It was still so hard to believe. She had been orphaned in infancy on the planet Alderaan and was being raised as a state foundling when Master Bondara happened across her in his travels. Even as an infant she had shown strong Force tendencies, so she was told, and she had been brought to Coruscant in hopes of qualifying for training. Darsha knew she had been phenomenally lucky. As an orphan raised by the state, her best hope would have been some obscure midlevel government job. She would have been just another one of the countless departmental drones necessary to the smooth functioning of a planetary government, had she not been discovered by someone who recognized her potential.

But now—to stand on the verge of becoming a Jedi! To be one of the ancient order of protectors, one of the guardians of freedom and justice in the galaxy! Even now, after all these years of preparation, she could hardly believe it was true—

"Padawan Assant."

Master Windu was speaking to her. The dark-eyed human's mellifluous voice was quietly pitched, yet its power seemed to fill the large room. Darsha took a deep breath, reaching for the Force to calm and steady her. Now was definitely not the time to appear nervous.

The Jedi Master wasted no time in pleasantries. "You are to go alone to the area in the Zi-Kree sector known as the Crimson Corridor, where a former member of Black Sun is being kept in a safe house. He is to receive the council's protection in return for information regarding a recent shake-up in the higher echelons of that criminal organization. Your job is to bring him back to the Temple alive."

Darsha was afire with eagerness, but she knew it

would be unseemly to show it. She bowed slightly. "I understand, Master Windu. I shall not fail." Evidently she was not entirely successful in maintaining her equanimity, because she saw a slight smile tug at the senior member's lips. Well, so be it—being too enthusiastic was certainly not a crime. Mace Windu raised his hand in a gesture of dismissal. Darsha turned and exited the rotunda, followed by Anoon Bondara.

As the doors slid noiselessly shut behind her, Darsha faced her mentor. The question on her lips as to how soon she could begin her mission remained unasked, however, when she saw the look of worry in Master Bondara's eyes.

"Master, what is it?" For a moment she was certain that there was disappointment in the Twi'lek's gaze, as well; that Darsha had said or done something before the council to dishonor herself and her mentor. The fear sliced through her like a lightsaber's deadly edge. But the Jedi's first words relieved her of that concern.

"It is a most . . . *arduous* mission," Master Bondara said. "I am surprised at Master Windu's choice of this particular test."

"Do you doubt my ability to accomplish it?" The thought that her mentor might lack faith in her was even more distressing than the possibility of having unknowingly embarrassed herself before the council.

Master Bondara hesitated, then looked her squarely in the eyes and smiled. "I have always taught you to be honest in your feelings," the Jedi said, "for they are the surest conduit to knowledge, both of the self and of the Force. Therefore, I cannot be less than honest with you. As part of your trials, you must go alone—

and I am concerned that the mission may be too difficult and dangerous a test. The Crimson Corridor is rife with gangs, criminals, street predators, and other dangers. Also, several assassination attempts have already been made on the Black Sun member's life. But " The Twi'lek's lekku twitched in a way that Darsha had come to recognize as a fatalistic shrug. "—the council's decision is final, and we must accept it. Be assured that my concern in no way reflects my opinion of your abilities; assign it rather to the frets and misgivings of advancing age. I am sure you will acquit yourself well. Now come—we must prepare for your departure."

Darsha followed her mentor as the latter moved down the corridor toward the turbolift. Master Bondara's words had dampened her enthusiasm slightly. What if he was right? What if this was too dangerous an assignment? She had heard stories of the dangers in the infamous Crimson Corridor. And she would be on her own for the first time, without Master Bondara or even another Padawan as backup. Could she do it?

She squared her shoulders. Of course she could! She was a Jedi—or would be as soon as she completed this assignment. Mace Windu must have thought her capable of it; he would not have assigned it otherwise. She had to trust in the living Force, as Master Qui-Gon Jinn, another of her tutors, had often said. She was not going into danger alone; she had the Force with her. It would not make her invulnerable, but it certainly gave her an advantage few others had. With the Force she could accomplish things most people viewed as nigh unto miraculous: She could leap twice her own height in a one-gravity field, she could slow her rate of descent in a fall, she could even telekinetically move items a dozen meters and more away. And she could also cloak herself in its essence, hiding in plain sight, so to speak.

Granted, her ability to do these things weren't on the same level of expertise as her mentor's. Nevertheless, she was better off with the Force than without it, that was for sure. She would not fail. She would accomplish her mission, and when she returned to the Temple the title of Jedi Knight would be waiting for her.

The *Infiltrator* emerged from hyperspace well inside the Coruscant system and continued sublight toward the capital world. Darth Maul kept the ship cloaked, though he would drop that as he neared his destination—extended cloaking took too much power. His coordinates and entry code had been given to him by his lord and master, and would clear him through the orbital security grid to land at any spaceport on the planet. Still, the less noticeable he was, the better. Even a single raised eyebrow at the sight of the *Infiltrator* resting on a landing pad was too much.

The ship had been provided for him by Lord Sidious only recently, and he was still getting used to it. It handled well and easily, however. He approached Coruscant over the south pole. He was not concerned about being spotted, even though Coruscant had the most sophisticated and far-reaching system of detection arrays of any world in the galaxy. The *Infiltrator* boasted a state-of-the-art stygium crystal cloaking device and thrust trace dampers capable of confounding even Coruscant's warning grids.

He chose as his landing site a rooftop pad on an abandoned monad in an area of the city awaiting urban demolition and renewal. He left the cloaking device activated and deployed his speeder bike through the cargo hatch. The bike was a stripped-down model, designed for maximum speed and maneuverability. Maul continued his journey across the cityscape on it.

Lord Sidious had been able to learn that Hath Monchar maintained an apartment on Coruscant in a well-to-do section of the city several kilometers south of the Manarai Mountains. Maul did not know the exact address, but that did not matter. He would find the missing Neimoidian, even if he had to search the entire planetary city.

It was impossible even to conceive of a time when he had not been in thrall to Darth Sidious. He knew that he had come originally from a world called Iridonia, but knowing that was like knowing that the atoms composing his body had originally been born in the primordial galactic furnaces that had forged the stars. The knowledge was interesting in a remote, academic way, but no more than that. He had no interest whatsoever in learning any more about his past or his homeworld. As far as he was concerned, his life began with Lord Sidious. And if his master ordered an end to that life, Maul would accept that judgment with no argument.

But that would not happen as long as he served Lord Sidious to the best of his abilities. Which, of course, he would. He could not even imagine a situation or circumstance that would prevent him from doing so.

Faintly, from behind him, came the wail of a siren. Maul glanced back over his shoulder and saw he was being pursued by a police droid on a speeder similar to his own. The sight did not surprise him; he knew he was breaking several traffic laws due to his speed and course. Just as he knew there was no way the droid was going to catch him.

Maul pushed the speeder bike to maximum velocity, rocketing through the ferrocrete labyrinth on a plane between two levels of skycar traffic. The speeder had no stealth capabilities, but that did not matter; his speed and his control were more than sufficient to leave the pursuing droid behind. He knew the droid was comlinking ahead, calling for reinforcements to surround him and bring him to a stop.

He couldn't let that happen.

There was a break in the lower traffic flow ahead. Maul altered the speeder's thrust angle and dived through it, descending several stories until he dropped through a fog layer that hovered perhaps thirty meters above the ground. They could still track him, of course, but he knew that, as long as he was not endangering any lives other than his own, he would not be as high a priority to them. Besides, he had almost reached his destination.

He arrived without further incident and parked the speeder bike in one of the local lots, paying for the rest of the day in advance. Then he stepped onto a slide-walk that carried him toward one of the many outposts of the Coruscant Customs Bureau.

Several times he noticed people looking at him; his appearance was capable of turning heads even on so cosmopolitan a planet as Coruscant. It would take considerable concentration to blind these crowds to his presence by using the Force, though it could be done. But it did not matter who saw him at this point. If all went according to plan, he would be off Coruscant in less than a day, his mission completed.

He had one thing to his advantage: Even though there was a bigger variety of alien races and species here than practically anywhere else in the galaxy, there still weren't a lot of Neimoidians to be seen, due to the recent tension between the Republic and the Trade Federation. Maul entered the imposing structure of the Customs Bureau and moved quickly to a data bank terminal. Using a password provided by Lord Sidious, he instituted a HoloNet search that turned up a record of a recently arrived Neimoidian. The image matched the one of Hath Monchar given to him by his master. The name was different, but that was not surprising.

Maul ordered a new search parameter, trying to track Monchar though debit card use. There was no record of any transactions—again, not surprising. The Neimoidian would be too canny to be caught that way. No doubt he used only cash while on Coruscant.

A line had begun to form behind him; other people wanted to use the terminal he was monopolizing. He could hear grumbling voices as citizens and tourists grew increasingly impatient. He ignored them.

He hacked into the planetwide security grid that monitored the spaceports and surrounding environs, calling up the last twenty-four hours of a constant collage of images taken by stationary and roving holocams. He ordered the system to search its files for Neimoidians.

He found several images, one of which was promising. It wasn't much to go on—a blurred image of a Neimoidian entering a tavern not far from there, a few hours earlier—but it was better than nothing.

Maul smiled faintly. His hand brushed the grip of the double-bladed lightsaber that hung from his belt. He noted the address of the tavern, then turned and left the building.

Nute Gunray pushed the plate of fungus aside in irritation. It was his favorite dish: black mulch mold marinated in the alkaloid secretions of the blight beetle, seasoned to perfection, with the spores just beginning to fruit. Normally his taste and olfactory nodes would be quivering in ecstasy at the prospect of such a gastronomic experience. But he had no appetite; indeed, had not been able to look at food since the Sith Lord's last appearance on the bridge, when Sidious had noticed that Hath Monchar was missing.

"Take it away," he snapped at the service droid hovering respectfully nearby. The plate was removed, and Gunray stood, stepping away from the table. He faced one of the transparisteel ports, looking gloomily out at the infinite vista of the star field.

There was still no news of Monchar, and no clue as to where he had gone. If the viceroy had to guess— and guessing was all he had at this point—he would say that his deputy viceroy had decided to go into business for himself. There were plenty of ways that the knowledge of the impending blockade could be converted into currency, enough currency to begin a new life on a new world. Gunray felt fairly confident that this was Monchar's plan, largely because he had thought of doing it himself more than once.

That didn't make it any less of a problem, however. Unless Monchar could be returned to the *Saak'ak* before Sidious contacted them again . . .

He heard the panel to his suite chime softly. "Come," he said.

The panel slid open, and Rune Haako entered. The settlement officer of the Trade Federation forces crossed the room, sat down, and arranged his purple raiment with meticulous precision, smoothing the pleats assiduously before looking at Gunray.

"I assume there has been no further word of Hath Monchar?"

"None."

Haako nodded. He fiddled with his collar for a moment, then adjusted his bloused sleeves. Gunray felt a flash of irritation. He could read Haako like a data file; he knew the attorney had a suggestion to make regarding the situation, and he knew also that this circuitous approach to it was designed to put Gunray on the defensive. But protocol demanded that he show nothing of what he felt; to do so would be to acknowledge that Haako had the upper hand in the situation.

At last Haako looked up, meeting Gunray's eyes. "Perhaps I might suggest a course of action."

Gunray made a slight hand gesture designed to convey no more than polite interest. "By all means."

"In my offices for the Trade Federation I have had occasion to encounter a number of people with singular attributes and abilities." He adjusted the crossed points on his cowl. "I refer specifically to a certain human female named Mahwi Lihnn. For a prearranged fee she searches for and retrieves people who have strayed from their duties or who have committed crimes."

"You are speaking of a bounty hunter," Gunray said. He saw Haako restrain himself from smirking, and realized belatedly that by admitting knowledge of the term used for someone of such crass abilities he had lost face before his subordinate. He didn't care, however—he was too excited at the possibility the attorney's suggestion presented. "We could hire this Mahwi Lihnn to track down Monchar and bring him back before Sidious convenes with us again."

"Just so."

Gunray noted the veiled contempt in Haako's tone. He adjusted his own collar and took his time replying. His initial excitement at a potential solution to the problem had calmed slightly, and now he decided to show Rune Haako that one did not lightly play games of position with a commanding viceroy of the Federation. "And you . . . *know* this personage?" he inquired, his tone and expression conveying just the right amount of disdain that anyone of Haako's station would admit to having had actual social intercourse with such a low individual.

Haako's look of smugness wavered. His fingers plucked nervously at a bit of filigree. "As I said, in the course of my duties as attorney and diplomatic attaché for the Federation . . ."

"Of course." Gunray infused the two words with equal parts pity and haughtiness. "And the Trade Federation is most grateful to you for your willingness to fraternize with such . . . *colorful* . . . characters, in hopes that their abilities may one day somehow be of use." He watched Haako's lips purse together as though the barrister had bitten into a rotten truffle, and continued. "To be sure, desperate times call for desperate measures. Though I regret having to ask this of a person of your stature, I hope you can find it within yourself to once again contact this Mahwi Lihnn, in order that we may satisfactorily resolve the Monchar situation."

Rune Haako muttered an acquiescence and left. After the door closed, Nute Gunray nodded in satisfaction. Not bad, not bad at all. He had managed to implement a possible solution to the question of Monchar's disappearance, and at the same time had taken that insufferable prig Haako down a peg. He listened in pleasure to a faint rumbling in his gut sac that signified the return of his appetite. Perhaps he would give his dinner another try.

"Had th' Hutt *primed* for this," Lorn said. "Was ready t'part with a *great deal* o' cash for a real Jedi Holocron. Would've paid *twice* as much for one from th' Sith." He gazed dejectedly into the depths of his glass, swirling the remaining blue-green Johrian whiskey that had recently filled it. "Fifty thousand credits, th' cube was worth. Now've lost it *and* the fifteen thousand. All I had."

"It does put us in somewhat desperate straits financially," I-Five said.

The two were sitting at the bar near the back of the Green Glowstone Tavern not far from one end of the infamous Crimson Corridor section of the city. They were regular patrons, and the droid's presence there no longer caused much controversy, despite the sign at the entrance that proclaimed NO DROIDS ALLOWED in Basic and several other languages.

" 'S all *my* fault," Lorn muttered, more to the drink-stained counter than to I-Five. "Hadn't lost m'temper . . ." He fixed the droid with a somewhat bleary gaze. "Dunno why y' stay partners with me."

"Ah, now we come to the maudlin stage. Will this take long? I may want to put myself in cyberostasis until it's over."

Lorn grunted and signaled for another refill. "Y'can be a real *bastard*, y'know that?" he told I-Five.

"Let's see . . . according to my data banks, the primary definition of *bastard* is 'a child born of unwed parents.' However, a secondary usage is 'something of irregular or unusual origins.' In that respect, I suppose I qualify." When the bartender came over to fill Lorn's glass again, I-Five put his hand over it. "My friend has had enough neurons destroyed by various hydroxyl compounds for today. It's not like he has an overabundant supply in the first place."

The bartender, a Bothan, glanced at Lorn, then shrugged and moved on down the bar. A Duros wearing spacer's togs and sitting nearby looked at them, seeming to register the droid's presence for the first time. "You let your *droid* decide how much you can drink?" he asked Lorn.

" 'S not *my* droid," Lorn said. "We're partners. *Business* associates." He pronounced the words carefully.

The Duros flickered nictitating membranes over his eyes in a sign of surprise and disbelief. "You're telling me that droid has citizenship status?"

"*He's* not telling you anything," I-Five said as he turned to face the Duros, "largely because he's so drunk he can barely stand. *I'm* telling you to mind your own business. My status in galactic society is not your concern."

The Duros glanced around, saw that the rest of the tavern's patrons were rather pointedly ignoring the exchange, shrugged, and went back to his drink. I-Five pulled Lorn off the bar stool and aimed him in the direction of the door. Lorn walked, weaving, across the room, then turned and faced the tavern.

"I *was* somebody, once," he told the group, most of whom didn't bother to look up. "Worked uplevels. Penthouse suite. Could see th' *mountains*. Damn Jedi—*they* did this to me." Then he turned and walked out, I-Five following.

Outside, the air was chill, and Lorn could feel a small amount of sobriety returning. The sun had set, and the long twilight of the equatorial regions had begun.

"Guess I told 'em, didn't I?"

"Absolutely. They were riveted. I'm sure they can't wait for the next thrilling installment. In the meantime, why don't we go home before one of the colorful locals decides to see how fast alcohol-soaked human tissue burns?"

"Good idea," Lorn agreed as I-Five took his arm and started walking.

They passed sidewalk vendors offering bootleg holos, glitterstim, and other illegal items for sale. Beggars of various species, wrapped in tattered cloaks, pawed at them for alms. They entered the nearest kiosk entrance to the underground, descending a long-broken escalator that ended in a winding corridor. It had been warm on the surface; down here it was like a sauna. The mingled body odor of various unwashed beings moving through the passageway, combined with the fungal reek permeating the walls, verged on hallucinogenic. Why can't they all smell like Toydarians? Lorn wondered.

They turned down a narrow side passage, its walls and ceiling a complex pattern of pipes, conduits, and cables. Flickering luminescent strips at irregular intervals provided dim illumination. Granite slugs oozed along the floor, requiring Lorn to pay attention to where he stepped—no small task in his condition. Eventually they reached the third in a series of recessed metal doors, which he opened after several tries with his keycard.

The windowless cubicle, a cell carved from the city's massive ferrocrete foundation, was designed for single occupancy, but since Lorn's roommate was a droid, they were not particularly cramped for space. There were a couple of chairs, an extensible wall cot, a tiny refresher, and a kitchenette barely big enough for a nanowave and food preserver. The compartment was spotlessly clean—another advantage of having a droid around.

Lorn sat on the edge of the cot and stared at the floor. "Here's all you need to know about the Jedi," he announced.

"Oh, please—not again."

"They're a bunch of self-serving, sanctimonious elitists."

"I have this entire rant recorded, you know. I could play a holo at fast speed; it would save time."

" 'Guardians of the galaxy'—don't make me laugh. All they're interested in guarding is their way of life."

"If I were you—a hypothetical situation the mere mention of which threatens to overload my logic circuits—I'd stop obsessing over the Jedi and start thinking about where my next meal is coming from. I don't require nourishment, but you do. You need something hot to peddle—fast."

Lorn glared at the droid. "I never should have disconnected your creativity damper." He brooded for a while longer, then said, "But you're right—no point dwelling in the past. Got to look ahead. What we need is a plan—right now." And with those words he fell backwards onto the cot and began to snore loudly.

I-Five stared at his recumbent companion. "Random evolution should never have been entrusted with intelligence," the droid muttered.

Darth Sidious was also thinking about the Jedi.

Their fire was dying in the galaxy; of that there was no doubt. For more than a thousand generations they had been the self-appointed paladins of the commonweal, but that was now coming to an end. And the pathetic fools, blinded by their own hypocrisy, could not see the truth of this.

It was right and fitting that this be so, just as it was right and fitting that the instrument of their downfall be the Sith.

The few pedants and scholars who even knew the name thought that the Sith were the "dark side" of the Jedi Knights. This was, of course, far too simplistic an evaluation. It was true that they had embraced the teachings of a group of rogue Jedi thousands of years ago, but they had taken that knowledge and philosophy far beyond the insular didacticism they had been given to start with. It was easy and convenient, as well, to demarcate the concept of the Force into light and dark; indeed, even Sidious had used such notions of duality in the training of his disciple. But the reality was that there was only the Force. It was above such petty concepts as positive and negative, black and white, good and evil. The only difference worthy of note was this: The Jedi saw the Force as an end in itself; the Sith knew that it was a means to an end.

And that end was Power.

For all their humble posturing and protestations of abdication, the Jedi craved power as much as anyone. Sidious knew this to be true. They claimed to be the servants of the people, but over the centuries they had increasingly removed themselves from contact with the very citizens they ostensibly served. Now they prowled the cloistered hallways and chambers of their Temple, mouthing their empty ideologies while practicing hubristic machinations designed to bring them more secular power.

As one half of the entire existing order of the Sith, Darth Sidious craved power, as well. It was true that he was operating covertly toward that end, but he was doing so out of necessity, not sophistry. After the Great Sith War, the order had been decimated. The lone remaining Sith had revived the order according to a new doctrine: one master and one apprentice. Thus it had been, and thus it would be, until that glorious day that saw the fall of the Jedi and the ascendancy of their ancient enemies, the Sith.

And that day was fast approaching. After centuries of planning and collusion, it was now almost here. Sidious was confident that he would see its culmination in his lifetime. There would come a day in the not too distant future when he would stand, triumphant, over the last Jedi's body, when he would see their Temple razed, when he would take his rightful place as ruler of the galaxy.

Which was why *no* loose ends, no matter how inconsequential, could be permitted. Perhaps Hath Monchar's absence had nothing to do with the Trade Federation's looming blockade of the planet Naboo. That was conceivable. But as long as the slightest chance existed that it did, the Neimoidian had to be found and dealt with.

Darth Sidious looked at a wall chrono. It was now slightly over fourteen standard hours since he had given Maul the assignment. He anticipated hearing from his apprentice shortly. The stakes were high, very high, but he had every confidence that Maul would perform the task with his customary ruthless efficiency. All would continue as planned, and the Sith would rise again.

Soon.

Very soon.

The Crimson Corridor was in the Third Quadrant of the Zi-Kree sector. It was one of the oldest areas of the vast planetary metropolis, overbuilt with skyscrapers and towers constructed long ago. The buildings towered so tall and so thick that some areas of the Corridor received only a few minutes of sunlight a day. Darsha remembered hearing legends of inbred subhuman tribes living in the near-total darkness of its depths for so long that they had gone genetically blind.

But darkness was the least of the dangers in the Corridor. Far worse were the things, both human and nonhuman, that lived in the darkness and preyed on the unwary.

Darsha piloted her skyhopper down through the miasmal fog that lay like a filthy blanket over the lowest levels. Why, she wondered, would anyone pick a neighborhood like this for a place in which to conceal informants? The answer was, of course, that it was the last place anyone would look.

The safe house—a barricaded block of ferrocrete and plasteel—was in a street that was not wide enough for her to set the skyhopper down. She landed in the closest intersection, got out, and instructed the autopilot to take the craft up twenty meters and remain in hover mode there. That way it was more likely to be there when she got back.

There were a few glow sticks in protective wired cages set here and there on the buildings, but after centuries of use they were so weak that they did little to relieve the gloom. As soon as Darsha disembarked from her vehicle she was set upon by beggars supplicating for food and money. At first she tried the ancient Jedi technique of clouding their minds, but there were too many of them, and most of them had brains too addled by privation and various illegal chemicals to respond to the suggestion. She gritted her teeth and pushed her way though the forest of filthy waving arms, tentacles, and various other appendages.

The mingled revulsion and sympathy she felt was

almost overwhelming. For nearly as long as she could remember, Darsha had been coddled and cozened in the Jedi Temple, protected from direct contact with the dregs of society—an ironic situation, since the Jedi were supposed to be the protectors of all levels of civilization, even those considered untouchable by most of the upper classes. True, elements of her training had taken her to various rough neighborhoods, but nowhere else had she seen anything that even remotely compared with this. It horrified her that such poverty and neglect could exist anywhere, let alone on Coruscant.

She made it to the recessed entrance of the safe house and pounded on the reinforced door. A slit opened, and a sentry cam extruded from it. "Your name and business?" it asked in a rasping voice.

"Darsha Assant, on the Jedi Council's business."

An emaciated Kubaz sought to pluck her lightsaber from its hook on her utility belt. She seized his hand and bent the thumb backwards. He squealed and backed hastily away, but others took his place immediately. The only reason they did not drag her back into the street was that there were too many to crowd into the narrow aperture where she stood.

The security cam quickly ran a laser scan over her face. "Identity confirmed. Please hold your breath."

Darsha did so—whereupon hidden nozzles surrounding the door sprayed a pink mist at the crowd of mendicants. A chorus of indignant shouts, squeals, bleats, and other protests rose from them as the airborne irritant drove them momentarily back. The door slid quickly up, and a metallic arm grabbed Darsha and pulled her inside.

She found herself in a narrow corridor that was almost as dark as the street. The security droid who had taken her arm now led her down this passageway and around a corner, into a small, windowless room. The light was not much better here; Darsha could barely make out a hunched form sitting on a chair. Bald and humanoid, he looked like a Fondorian to her.

The droid said, "This is the Jedi who will take you to safety, Oolth."

Though she knew it was foolish, Darsha felt a little thrill at being called a Jedi, even by a droid.

"About time," the Fondorian said. He stood quickly. "Let's get out of here before it gets dark—not that it ever really *stops* getting dark around here." He moved toward the room's entrance, than stopped and looked back at Darsha. "Well, come on," he said testily. "What're you waiting for?"

"I'm just trying to decide how best to get back to my skyhopper," Darsha replied. "I don't relish the idea of wading through those poor beings out there again."

"*We'll* be the 'poor beings' if we don't get moving. This is Raptor territory. They make those scum out there look like the Republic Senate. Now let's go!"

Darsha moved toward the hallway; Oolth stood aside to let her pass. "I'm the one who needs protecting; you go first."

Whatever good he was to the council, Darsha was sure Oolth the Fondorian wasn't valued for his bravery.

She pushed past him and strode back to the outside door.

The cam's monitor was mounted by the door; it showed a few street people still loitering around the area. Most of them, however, had apparently gone looking for someone else to importune. If Darsha and Oolth moved quickly, they could probably get back to the intersection where her vehicle was without too much trouble.

"All right," Darsha said. She took a deep breath and reached for the Force to calm herself. She was a Jedi Padawan with a job to do. Time to get on with it. "Let's move out."

The door panel slid open. Darsha quested with the Force and felt no sense of anybody nearby who posed a danger. Thus reassured, she started down the street with Oolth. The vagrants seemed to materialize from out of the shadows, clustering around them again. Oolth shoved at them as they crowded in. "Get away from me! Filthy creatures!"

"Just keep moving," Darsha said to him. She had refused the droid's offer of escort because she didn't want to draw any more attention than absolutely necessary. If she had to, she could activate her lightsaber; she had no doubt that just the sight of the energy blade would send the majority of the street people fleeing. But she hoped it wouldn't be necessary. They were almost to the intersection.

And then her heart, already pounding from nervous tension, suddenly tried to batter its way up her throat.

Her skyhopper was still where she had parked it, hovering twenty meters up in the air. Clustered on the street beneath it was a heterogeneous assortment of beings, about a dozen in all. Among the species Darsha recognized were humans, Kubaz, H'nemthe, Gotals, Snivvians, Trandoshans, and Bith. All of them appeared to be in the late adolescent stage of their particular species, all were dressed in colorful and motley styles, and all looked extremely dangerous.

Oolth the Fondorian gasped, and whispered in a strangled tone, "The Raptors."

Darsha had heard tales of the street gangs that terrorized many of the more run-down sectors of Coruscant's surface. The Raptors were reputed to be the worst, by far. She had hoped to complete her mission quickly enough to avoid an encounter with them. So much for that idea.

Several grappling hooks had snagged into the two-person craft, and from them dangled ropes. Three members of the gang—a human female and two male Bith—had climbed aboard and were busily ransacking the vehicle. They tossed down various items—a holo-projector, an aquata breather, a pouch of food capsules, and medical supplies—to the gang members below. Even as Darsha watched, one of them managed to disable the autopilot, causing the craft to settle gently to the street. This was greeted by a cheer from the rest of the gang.

Oolth grabbed her robe and tried to pull her into the shadows of the narrow street. "Quick—before they see us!"

She shook off his grasp. "I can't let them strip the skyhopper. It's our only way out of here. Wait here until I've dealt with them." Then, forcing herself to project a confidence she did not in any way feel, Darsha strode toward the Raptors.

She hadn't taken more than a few steps before her approach was noted. The raucous chatter and laughter quickly subsided; no doubt, Darsha thought, because they were having a hard time believing someone could be this suicidal.

She stopped a few meters from them. There was no one else on the street now, save for the Fondorian cowering somewhere behind her. No one in their right mind wanted to be around when the Raptors were on the prowl.

"That's my skyhopper," she said, relieved to find that her voice was not shaking. "Please return the things you stole and move away from it."

The Raptors looked at each other in astonishment before breaking into the various sounds that constituted laughter for each species. One of the human males—lean and wiry, sporting an improbable mane of green hair standing straight up in an electrostatic field—swaggered toward her.

"New around here, I'm guessing," he said, causing more sniggering—this time with a distinctly unpleasant edge—to erupt from his compatriots.

Darsha reviewed her options quickly. There weren't many. She was one against a dozen, and while her knowledge of the Jedi fighting arts improved the odds somewhat, she was still not at all confident in her ability to come out ahead in a battle. She was on their turf, after all, and for all she knew, there might be a dozen more of them lurking in the shadows.

But there were alternatives to fighting. The mind

trick she had tried earlier on the beggars hadn't been completely successful, but it had turned away a few of them. It might serve now to confuse the Raptors long enough to allow her to reach the vehicle. Of course, she still had to get Oolth in the craft with her, but one problem at a time.

She raised her right hand, fanning the fingers in a gesture designed to focus their attention while she reached out mentally for the Force. "You're not interested in me," she said, using the soft but compelling tone she had been taught, "or my vehicle." She could see by their confused and uncertain expressions that it was working, could feel their wills beginning to vibrate in resonance with hers.

Green Hair was either the leader or something close to it, because when he nodded and said slowly, "We're not interested in her, or her vehicle," the rest of the gang mumbled the same words in ragged unison.

Darsha took a few steps forward, making the hypnotic gesture again. "You might as well go now," she told Green Hair. "There's nothing interesting going on here."

"We might as well go now. There's nothing interesting going on here." The rest of the gang again echoed him.

Darsha kept moving slowly but steadily forward. She stepped past Green Hair and was now in the midst of them, only a step or two away from her craft. She had them now; she could feel their minds, some struggling feebly, others willingly surrendering to her suggestive power amplified by the Force. Another moment and she would be in the skyhopper.

A scream echoed down the dark street.

Startled, Darsha whipped around, staring back toward the source of the cry. It was Oolth the Fondorian, staggering out into the middle of the narrow thoroughfare, shaking and kicking his leg frantically to dislodge a large armored rat that had clamped its jaws onto his shin. Even as she realized who it was, she realized, as well, that her tenuous mind-lock on the Raptors had been shattered by the unexpected sound. Blinking and shaking their heads as if awakening from slumber, the Raptors realized that their prey had obligingly delivered itself right into their midst.

Darsha had no choice now but to fight. She reached for her lightsaber, but before she could seize it they were upon her.

STAR WARS DARTH MAUL SHADOW HUNTER

Hath Monchar was afraid.

This was not a particularly surprising state of affairs to anyone who knew the deputy viceroy of the Trade Federation. Even among Neimoidians, Monchar was considered remarkably timid. Which made it all the more amazing that he had done what he had done.

Monchar was afraid, yes, but underneath that was another emotion, one far less familiar to him than fear. This emotion was pride—a nervous and fragile pride, it was true, but pride nevertheless. He had taken a chance—a big chance. He had dared to steer his life in a new and, with any luck, more profitable direction. He had a right to feel proud of that, he told himself.

He glanced around at the patrons of the tavern he was sitting in. It was a different establishment than the one he usually frequented when on Coruscant. That tavern was in the affluent Kaldani Spires monad, where he had an apartment. He was not staying in his apartment on this visit, however. That would make him too easy to find. Instead he had rented a cheap domicile near the Galactic Museum under an assumed name. He had seriously considered buying a holographic image disguiser that could change his appearance to that of another species, as well. His paranoia had warred with his parsimony for quite some time on that one, and finally the stinginess had won out, though just barely.

Hath Monchar had come to Coruscant because the capital world was the best place to move information quickly and anonymously. That was what he had to sell—information. Specifically, information about the upcoming blockade of Naboo and the fact that the man behind it all was a Sith Lord.

It was a dangerous scheme, to be sure. If his coconspirators found him, Monchar knew they would quickly give him up to Darth Sidious's tender mercies. The mere thought of being in the Sith Lord's clutches was enough to make the Neimoidian start to hyperventilate. Even so, Monchar couldn't resist the opportunity to make a quick fortune.

He took another gulp of the agaric ale he was drinking. Yes, the risks were high, but so was the potential for profit. All he needed was to contact the right person as an intermediary—someone who knew the people who would pay handsomely for the news he had. All it would take was a bit more fortitude on his part. He had come this far; he was not going to stop now, not with his goal nearly in sight.

Hath Monchar signaled the Baragwin bartender.

One more flagon of ale ought to give him the fortitude he needed.

Mahwi Lihnn had been a bounty hunter for going on ten standard years, ever since she had been forced to leave her homeworld after killing a corrupt government official. During that time she had traveled nearly the length and breadth of the galaxy on various assignments. She had pursued fugitives from justice on such diverse worlds as Ord Mantell, Roon, Tatooine, and dozens of others. Oddly enough, however, she had never been to Coruscant, and she was looking forward to seeing the capital of the galaxy.

The assignment from the Neimoidian viceroy's lieutenant seemed straightforward enough. Lihnn did not anticipate any great trouble in finding the missing Hath Monchar, even on a crowded world like Coruscant. As her ship descended on autopilot toward the landing pad at the eastern spaceport, she reviewed her equipment and weaponry. Her garb looked like no more than a simple utilitarian tunic and pants, but they were made of densely woven shell spider silk, a material capable of resisting even a vibroblade's thrust, as well as reflecting low-power particle beams and lasers. It was armor that did not look like armor—to the uninitiated. Experts would spot it, of course, but she didn't expect to run into any opposition. She wore twin DL-44 blasters on each hip, and a small disruptor pistol in a concealed ankle holster. Strapped to each wrist was an MM9 wrist rocket, and in her right hand she wore a palm flechette shooter. On her utility belt she carried, among other things, a set of stun cuffs, a stun baton, and three glop grenades.

Mahwi Lihnn believed in being prepared.

Her first stop after disembarking from her ship was the Kaldani Spires Residential Apartments. She seriously doubted that Monchar would be foolish enough to stay in an apartment registered to him, but one never knew. More than once Lihnn had saved herself needless trouble and time by looking in the most obvious places for her quarry.

As she entered the lobby the security droid on duty asked whom she wished to see. "Hath Monchar," Lihnn told him. The droid checked a monitor screen, then informed her that Monchar was not in; indeed, was not even on Coruscant. Lihnn nodded pleasantly and clapped the circuit disruptor she had pulled from her belt onto the droid's chassis. The droid stuttered for an instant before its photoreceptors went dark.

Lihnn took the lift tube up to the five hundredth floor and strolled down the corridor to Monchar's apartment, where she used an electronic lock breaker to void the security system. Once inside, she quickly checked the rooms. The droid had been telling the truth; Monchar was not there. Furthermore, the apartment appeared to have been vacant for some time.

The large suite was decorated in what was, to a Neimoidian, the epitome of tasteful decor; to Lihnn it looked and smelled like a fetid swamp. She did some more investigating, hoping to find a clue to Monchar's whereabouts. In this she was disappointed.

At last she left, going back down to the lobby and pulling the circuit disruptor off the security droid.

Before it could reaccess its memory banks sufficiently to realize what had happened, Mahwi Lihnn had left and was strolling along one of the skywalks fifty stories above the surface.

It would certainly take some time to search a city the size of a planet for one person. Fortunately, Lihnn felt fairly sure that such a search wouldn't be necessary. Even though Monchar was smart enough not to stay in his apartment, she was willing to bet that the Neimoidian was somewhere in the general vicinity. This was the part of Coruscant with which he was most familiar, so it made sense that he would be holed up not too far away.

Lihnn stopped at an observation deck and enjoyed the view for a few minutes. The descriptions she had read and the holos she had seen did not do justice to the stupendousness of the real thing. The last census put the population of Coruscant at somewhere in the neighborhood of a trillion living beings. Even if she could investigate one person every second, she would still need the life span of a hundred Tatooine Sarlaccs to get to them all. But there were ways to narrow the search.

Paranoid as Monchar no doubt was, he still had to eat. Lihnn pulled a portable HoloNet link from a pocket and consulted it, entering search parameters for restaurants in the area that specialized in the disgusting swill Neimoidians called food. As she had thought, there were not all that many. She glanced at her chrono and saw that it was almost the hour when most species eat their evening meal. She would go check out a few of these restaurants. It was worth putting up with the smell if it meant an early resolution to this case.

Darth Maul signaled for an air taxi. Even though his speeder was not far away, he did not wish to risk anyone connecting him to it, now that he was close to his quarry. The taxi pilot—a Quarren—looked somewhat dubiously at his passenger as Maul got into the backseat, but said nothing as he was given the address. The taxi rose rapidly straight up through two strata of traffic, its lift repulsors humming barely within the threshold of Maul's hearing, then veered north in a long arc toward a cluster of towers in the distance.

The taxi landed gently at a terminal within fifty meters of the tavern. Maul entered, stepping immediately to the shadows near the door while he looked about. His vision adjusted far more quickly to extremes of light and darkness than did most species; he was able almost at once to see the tavern's dim interior and its customers.

He saw humans, Bith, Devaronians, Nikto, Snivvians, Arcona—a cornucopia of species, all drinking or otherwise imbibing various substances capable of altering their brain chemistry. He did not see Hath Monchar. For that matter, he did not see any Neimoidians at all.

Maul approached the bar. The bartender was a tall gaunt Baragwin, his folds of facial dewlaps as leathery and creased as a bantha's skin. "I am looking for a Neimoidian," Maul said to him. "He would have been in here within the last few hours."

The Baragwin sent a ripple running through his dewlaps from top to bottom—the equivalent of a human shaking his head. "Many beings come in here," he said, his voice absurdly high and flutelike coming from such a massive head. "They come, they drink, they talk, they go. I do not recall seeing a Neimoidian recently."

Darth Maul leaned forward. "Think again," he said softly. He could easily use the Force to get whatever information might be had from this weak-willed creature, but there was no need. He knew he could get what he wanted by intimidation.

The Baragwin's nasal polyps began to quiver—a sign of nervousness. "Upon further reflection I do seem to remember a representative of that species imbibing here perhaps an hour ago."

"Did he speak to you or anyone else?"

The Baragwin's polyps were vibrating almost too fast to see now. "No. That is . . . he—he ordered agaric ale."

"And did he speak of anything else?"

"Yes. He inquired of me how one might contact someone proficient in the buying and selling of sensitive information."

Maul leaned back. "And you told him—what?"

"I gave him a name."

"You will now give me that name."

The Baragwin rippled his dewlaps from bottom to top in acquiescence. "Lorn Pavan. A human—Corellian, I believe. He is well known in this city sector as one who traffics in such merchandise."

"And where might I find this Lorn Pavan?"

"I do not know."

Maul leaned forward again, his yellow eyes blazing. The Baragwin backed up hastily. "I speak the truth! He comes in here occasionally, always accompanied by a protocol droid called I-Five. I know nothing more."

That was interesting news, Maul reflected. It should help to narrow the search; personal droids were not that common in this area of Coruscant. "Describe this Lorn Pavan."

"Tall. Muscular. Black filamentous cilia on his scalp, but none on his face. Brown ocular pigmentation. The females of his species would probably characterize him as 'handsome.' "

Maul nodded, then raised his right hand in a focusing gesture as he mentally reached for the Force. He had to make sure that this next question was answered truthfully, because the answer would determine whether or not he had to kill the Baragwin.

"Did the Neimoidian speak at all to you about the nature of the information he wished to sell?"

The dewlaps quickly undulated downward. "He did not. I have told you all that I know."

Maul sensed no negative vibration in the Force as the Baragwin spoke. He turned away without another word and exited the tavern.

He was glad that he did not have to kill the Baragwin—not out of any moral sense, or even out of pity for the pathetic creature; his relief stemmed purely from having avoided the inevitable difficulties brought on by killing someone in a public place. Nevertheless, if the Force had told him the Baragwin was lying, he would have struck him down without a second thought and dealt with the consequences. Darth Sidious had told him to kill everyone with whom Hath Monchar had shared knowledge of the blockade, and Maul would follow his master's commands, as always.

He strode along the outdoor concourse, pondering his next move. Though the walkway was crowded, his passage was not impeded, as most of the pedestrians gave him a wide berth. Which was as it should be. Darth Maul had nothing but contempt for the masses. Of all the uncounted trillions of sentient beings that populated the galaxy, only one was deserving of respect: Darth Sidious. The only man who dared to dream of conquering not just a world or a star system, but an entire galaxy. The man who had taken the young Maul from a backwater planet and raised him to be his successor. He owed Darth Sidious everything.

It had not been an easy path that he had been set upon. To be a truly superior being, apart from and above the senseless herd, required absolute devotion and dedication. He had had to learn self-sufficiency, both in body and in mind, almost from the time he had learned to walk. His master would accept nothing less than the absolute best that Maul could offer. When he was younger, if he had flinched during his training when the edge of a weapon found his flesh, or when an incorrect block or defensive maneuver resulted in a cracked bone, his punishments had always been swift and inevitable.

He had soon learned to think of pain as his teacher. From fearing it, he had actually come to welcome it, because he knew it would test his willpower and his courage; it would make him stronger. To be content, to be comfortable, was to be complacent. No one learned anything from pleasure. Pain, on the other hand, was a most efficient instructor.

He returned to the problem at hand. Perhaps tracking down the human Lorn Pavan would lead him in turn to his primary target. In all probability the Corellian would have to be killed, as well. The longer the Neimoidian was alive, the more likely his information would be disseminated. Still, Maul was not worried. If he had to wipe out this entire city sector in order to contain the news about the blockade, he would do it without a qualm. Lives, even hundreds of lives, did not matter.

The first blow came from behind, half stunning Darsha and causing her to drop to her knees. A booted foot impacted against her side, driving her breath from her. Half-blinded by pain, Darsha reached for the Force as the Raptors closed in, felt its power enfold her, cloak her like an invisible shield. She stood, thrusting out one arm in a warding gesture, and felt the reverberating ripples flowing outward, hurling back her surprised attackers. For a brief moment she stood clear of them, and she used that moment to draw and activate her lightsaber. The yellow energy blade boiled out from the hilt's projector, extending to its full length.

"She's a Jedi!" one of the Raptors, a Trandoshan, shouted. He seemed surprised, but not particularly awed or impressed.

"She's still dead meat," Green Hair said. But none

of his gang seemed particularly anxious to be the first within reach of the lightsaber.

"You should have listened to me," Darsha said as she moved slowly until her back was against the sky-hopper. "I don't want to hurt any of you. Walk away now, while you can."

She saw Green Hair and the Trandoshan exchange a glance—just a flicker of eye movement. It was enough to warn her, however, and even if it had not been, she had already sensed the disturbance in the Force coming from behind her. Darsha spun and raised the blade in a high defensive movement just in time to intercept a stocky Gotal who had leapt over the craft, aiming a vibroblade at her. The lightsaber sheered effortlessly through the Gotal's wrist, sending the blade, still clutched in the severed hand, arcing back to land in the empty vehicle. The Gotal shrieked and fell in a heap on the pavement, clutching his cauterized stump.

There was a moment of utter stillness, save for the Gotal's whimpers. Events hung in delicate balance, Darsha knew. Would they swarm over her to avenge their comrade, or flee in fear?

It was Green Hair who decided which course to take: He turned and ran up the street. The rest of the gang members promptly followed his lead, two of them dragging the wounded Gotal with them. In a matter of seconds the street was completely deserted save for Darsha and Oolth the Fondorian.

Darsha moved quickly to Oolth, who was lying on his back, moaning and still kicking feebly in an effort to dislodge the armored rat. Darsha touched the tip of the lightsaber's blade to the creature's neck, right at

the soft juncture between the head and body cara-
paces, and the rat released its grip and bolted toward
the shadows.

Darsha deactivated the lightsaber and pulled Oolth
to his feet. "Let's go—before they come back with
reinforcements."

"What took you so long? That blasted rat nearly
gnawed my leg off!"

A pity it wasn't your head, Darsha thought. "Just be
grateful I was able to chase them away. Now let's get
out of here." She helped him climb into the passenger
side of the skyhopper, then settled herself behind the
controls.

And realized that they weren't going anywhere.

"Come on—what're you waiting for? Lift off!"

"I can't." She pointed at the console, where the activated vibroblade, still gripped by the Gotal's severed
hand, had sunk to the hilt in the panel. Sparks and
smoke were still faintly visible, and she could hear the
faint hum of the weapon's high-frequency oscillation.
"It's cut through the controls for the stabilizer vanes.
We'll spin like a corkscrew if we try to fly in this."

Oolth stared at the blade, then at her. "I don't *believe* this. Some Jedi you are! You managed to disable
your own ship!"

Darsha bit back on several scathing replies that came
to mind, saying instead, "It's just a setback. I've got my
comlink; I'll just call the Temple for—"

She left the sentence unfinished, for as she was
speaking she was reaching into her tunic for her comlink. The moment her fingers touched it she realized it
was unusable, as well. The plaeklite casing was shat-

tered, no doubt by that kick she had received from one of the Raptors. It had probably protected her from a broken rib; although, all things considered, at this point she would rather have had the injury.

Before she could explain this latest reversal to Oolth, the windshield in front of her suddenly cracked in a starburst. Simultaneously she heard the muffled report of a projectile weapon. Someone, most likely one of the Raptors, was shooting at them.

Darsha made a quick decision. They would have to abandon the skyhopper. They had to get uplevels as quickly as possible. She glanced about them and realized that such an action was easier said than done. Most of the buildings were blocked off above levels ten or twelve; the inhabitants of the upper stories didn't even acknowledge the existence of those lower floors. But they couldn't stay here. As if to underscore that fact, another bolt from the hidden sniper whistled past her ear. They couldn't even take the risk of trying to get back to the safe house.

The last light of day was fading fast; soon it would be full night. Darsha stood up. "Out of the ship— fast!" She jumped to the pavement, pulling her ascension gun from her utility belt. She fired the grappling hook straight up at maximum length, hoping to strike a ledge or projection above the fog layer.

Another blast struck the windshield. Oolth screeched in fear and leapt out of the skyhopper. "What are you doing? We have to get out of here!"

"That's exactly what we're doing," Darsha said as she felt the vibration down the length of the cable, which meant the hook had found purchase. "Hang on to me!" She grabbed the Fondorian around his waist and thumbed the winding mechanism.

The liquid cable reservoir was good for a maximum of two hundred meters, and the tensile strength of the monofilament line would easily support them both. Darsha knew that if they could make it up to the first traffic skylane—around level twenty—they could find an air taxi and get back to the Temple, or at least find a working comm station from which to call for help.

Another bolt caromed off the wall directly beneath them as they rose quickly up past the first level, then the second, then the third. Darsha's arm felt like it was being pulled from its socket. She looked up and estimated that the fog was hovering at around level ten. Once they were enveloped, they would be safe enough from the sniper.

A massive shadow flitted past her, followed by several more. In the dimming light she wasn't sure what they were at first. Then she saw one clearly, and recognition sent a chill of fear through her.

Hawk-bats.

She had never seen one this close before. Their eggs were considered a delicacy; she'd eaten them more than once for the morning meal in the Temple. Ordinarily hawk-bats weren't considered dangerous, but she had heard stories of people occasionally being attacked by flocks of the creatures. Evidently they were very territorial, and danger fell to anyone who ventured too close to one of their rookeries.

Which, apparently, was just what she had done.

Suddenly they were enveloped in a shrieking, flapping nightmare of wings, beaks, and talons. Distracted,

Darsha buried her head in her shoulder as best she could to protect her eyes. She tried to summon the Force, to use it as a shield against the creatures, but the fierce buffeting of their wings made holding on to the ascension gun the best she could manage.

She kept her thumb pressed on the winding control—their best hope now was to get past the hawk-bats' territory.

Oolth tightened his grip around her chest until she felt in danger of suffocating. He shouted with pain and fear as the winged furies strafed the two of them. The claws on the edges of their leathery wings tore at Darsha's clothes; her vision was full of beaks and angry ruby eyes.

Oolth screamed again, louder this time. She glanced down and saw that one of the hawk-bats had landed on his shoulder and was savagely pecking at his face. The beak scored his cheek, drawing a line of dark blood across his skin.

Darsha felt his grip loosen. She saw another hawk-bat clinging to Oolth's arm, stabbing at his hand with its beak.

"Hang on!" she shouted. "We're almost through this!"

Oolth cried out again, louder than all his previous cries. Darsha looked down at him, saw that one of the hawk-bats had hooked its cruel beak into his right eye. Mad with pain, the Fondorian let go of her, raising both hands to push away his winged tormentor.

"*No!*" Darsha shouted, trying to hang on to him with her free hand. But his weight was too much; his shirt tore, leaving a swatch of it in her grip as he dropped with a trailing cry down into the darkness.

Darsha knew there was no point in trying to go after him, even if there was any way it could be accomplished; she was seven or eight levels up now, and the fall had undoubtedly been fatal. A moment later she entered the fog level, but the hawk-bats showed no sign of lessening their attack. Already her skin was cut and torn in a score of wounds. At this rate she wouldn't survive to reach the upper levels.

Only one course of action promised even a faint hope of survival. Each level that slipped by her had a line of dark windows. Darsha released the winding control and drew her lightsaber. As her ascent slowed and then stopped, she swung the energy blade, melting a large hole through the transparisteel of the window next to her. She got a foot on the ledge beneath it and tumbled through, releasing the ascension gun as she fell forward into darkness.

She turned the fall into a shoulder roll, holding the lightsaber away from her as she had been taught to avoid self-inflicted injury. She came to her feet, the weapon held ready to defend herself against the hawk-bats.

But apparently there was no need; none of them pursued her into the building. Slowly Darsha abandoned her fighting stance. She looked around, trying to take stock of her surroundings.

It was fully dark outside now; the broken window was merely a patch of lesser darkness. The lightsaber's coherent light beam didn't vouchsafe much in the way of illumination. Darsha listened, both with her ears and with the Force. No sound, and no sense of danger. For the moment she seemed to be safe.

Of course, that depended on one's definition of *safe*. She was trapped in the abandoned lower levels of a building in the infamous Crimson Corridor. She had no comlink and no transportation. Worse still, she had failed in her mission. The man she had been sent to save now lay dead in the street far below.

If this was "safe," Darsha thought grimly, maybe she ought to consider another line of work.

Assuming she made it back alive.

Lorn awoke feeling like a herd of banthas had stampeded over him.

He risked opening one eye. The light in the cubicle was very dim, but even so it felt like a blaster beam had fired straight into his eye and up the optic nerve to his brain. He groaned, hastily shut the eye, and wrapped both arms around his head for good measure.

Somewhere in the darkness he heard I-Five say, "Ah, the beast awakes."

"Stop shouting," he mumbled.

"My vocabulator is modulated at a median level of sixty decibels, which is standard for normal human conversation. Of course, your hearing *might* be a trifle oversensitive, given the amount of alcohol still in your bloodstream."

Lorn groaned and tried, unsuccessfully, to burrow into the sleeping pad.

"If you're going to continue such behavior," I-Five

went on remorselessly, "I suggest having a few healthy liver cells removed—if indeed you have any left— and cryogenically stored, since you may need that particular organ cloned in the near future. I can recommend a very good MD-5 medical droid of my acquaintance—"

"All right, all *right*!" Lorn sat up, cradling his aching head in his hands, and glared at the droid. "You've had your fun. Now make it go away."

The droid feigned polite incomprehension. "Make it go away? I'm just a lowly droid, how could *I* possibly—"

"*Do* it—or I'll reprogram your cognitive module with Bilk's blaster."

I-Five gave a remarkably humanlike sigh. "Of course. I live to serve." The droid paused for a moment; then there issued from his vocabulator a low trilling tone. It warbled up and down the scale, seeming to resonate in the small cubicle.

Lorn sat on the bed and let the sound wash over him, let it reverberate in his head. After a few minutes the headache began to lessen its iron grip, as did his nausea and general malaise. He wasn't sure exactly how the wordless song of the droid accomplished it, but something about the vibrations made it the best hangover cure he had ever come across. But no cure comes without a price, and Lorn knew that the price of this one would be having to put up with I-Five's smug superiority for most of the day.

It was still worth it. When I-Five finally let the sound trail off, Lorn felt remarkably better. He wouldn't be doing any zero-g calisthenics at the null-grav spa over at Trantor Center today, but at least he could think of doing them someday soon without feeling like throwing up.

He looked at I-Five and found himself wondering once again how a droid with only one fixed facial expression and limited body language could manage to look so disapproving.

"And are we all better now?" I-Five inquired with mock solicitousness.

"Let's just say I'm willing to hold off on that reprogramming—for today at least." Lorn stood up, somewhat carefully, as his head still felt like it might topple off his neck if he moved too quickly.

"Your gratitude overwhelms me."

"And your sarcasm underwhelms me." Lorn went into the refresher, splashed cold water on his face, and ran an ultrasound cleaner over his teeth. "I might actually be able to be in the same room with some food," he said as he came out.

"Time enough for that. First I think you should have a look at these messages that came in while you were comatose."

"What messages?" It was too much to hope that Zippa had decided to sell him the Holocron after all. Nevertheless, he knew I-Five wouldn't have bothered keeping the communication unless it was important.

"*These* messages," the droid replied patiently, and activated the message unit.

A flickering image of an enormous, blubbery body formed in midair over the unit. Lorn recognized Yanth the Hutt.

"Lorn," the image said in a deep voice, "I thought we were going to meet sometime today, to discuss a certain Holocron you wished me to look at. It's not polite to keep buyers waiting, you know."

The image dissolved. "Thanks," Lorn said to I-Five. "If you're not too busy later, I've got a scraped knuckle you could rub some salt into."

"I think your attitude may change when you see the next message."

The second image materialized above the projector. It wasn't Zippa or Yanth; that much was immediately evident. After a moment Lorn recognized the species—a Neimoidian. That in itself was surprising; the masters of the Trade Federation were rarely seen on Coruscant, given the current strained relationship between their organization and the Republic Senate.

The Neimoidian glanced around furtively before leaning in close and speaking softly. "Lorn Pavan—your name was mentioned to me as someone who can be . . . discreet in handling sensitive information," he said in the gurgling tones of his kind. "I wish to discuss a matter that could be very profitable to both of us. If you are interested, meet me at the Dewback Inn at 0900. Tell no one of this." The three-dimensional image winked out.

"Play it again," Lorn said.

I-Five complied, and Lorn watched the message a second time, paying more attention to the Neimoidian's body language than to what he was saying. He wasn't all that familiar with Neimoidian mannerisms, but it didn't take an interplanetary psychoanalyst to see that the alien was as nervous as a H'nemthe groom. Which could mean trouble, but which could also mean profit. In his present line of work Lorn seldom saw the second happen without having to wade through the first.

He pressed a button that deleted the second message, and glanced at I-Five. "What do you think?"

"I think we have seventeen Republic decicreds in the bank, and whatever change might have fallen under the sleeping pad. I think the rent is due in a week. I think," I-Five said, "that we should talk to this Neimoidian."

"I think so, too," Lorn said.

The time of the evening meal was almost over. Mahwi Lihnn had by now investigated four restaurants whose menus included Neimoidian cuisine. Only one of them was occupied by a Neimoidian at table—a female. Lihnn had questioned her, but she had professed no knowledge of a countryman named Hath Monchar. She had, however, told Lihnn of another eatery in the area that her kind had been known to frequent. It was a small tavern called the Dewback Inn, one of the few drinking establishments in the sector that featured agaric ale, a beverage most Neimoidians were extremely fond of.

Lihnn decided to check it out.

It had not been terribly difficult to find Lorn Pavan's dwelling cubicle. As Darth Maul approached it, he saw the door open. A human and a droid—the latter one of the protocol series—emerged. Maul quickly faded back into the shadows of the underground thoroughfare and watched them pass. Both matched the descriptions he had been given by the Baragwin bartender.

Excellent. With any luck, they would lead him to his prey.

He followed them at a safe distance, making use of shadows and concealment when it was available and trusting to the cloaking power of the Force when it was not. The human and his droid had no idea they were being followed. He would tail them until they contacted the Neimoidian, and then he would take what action was appropriate.

Maul could feel the dark side surging within him, filling him with impatience, urging him to complete this assignment as quickly as possible. *This is not what you were trained for,* he thought. *These are not prey worthy of your abilities.*

He tried to dismiss these thoughts, for they were heretical. His master had given him this assignment; that was all that mattered. But he could not help chafing at this duty. There was no real challenge to his abilities in it. He had been bred and trained to fight and kill Jedi, after all, not rank-and-file beings like these.

The Jedi—how he hated them! How he loathed their hollow sanctimoniousness, their pretense of piety, their hypocrisy. How he longed for the day when their Temple would be a ruin of smoking rubble, littered with their crushed corpses. If he closed his eyes, he could see the apocalypse of the order as vividly as if it were reality. It *was* reality, after all—a future reality, but nonetheless valid. It was destined,

ordained, predetermined. And he would be instru-
mental in bringing it about. It was what his entire life
had been designed for.

Not tracking some pathetic failure through the
slums of Coruscant.

Maul shook his head and snarled silently. His purpose was to serve his master, no matter what the assignment was. If Darth Sidious knew he was having
such doubts, the Sith Lord would severely punish him,
such as he had not been punished since he was a child.
And Maul would not resist, even though he was now a
grown man. Because Sidious would be right to do so.

The human and his droid emerged from the underground thoroughfare and proceeded along the narrow
surface streets. It was late at night, but the planetary
city never slept. The streets were crowded no matter
what time of day or night it was. This was fortunate,
in that it made it easier for Maul to keep his quarry in
sight without being noticed.

It would not be much longer, Maul told himself. He
would bring this job to a successful conclusion—and
then, perhaps, Darth Sidious would reward him with
a task more worthy of his abilities. Something like the
Black Sun assignment. That had been a challenge he
had enjoyed.

Pavan and his droid turned down another street,
this one so narrow and bounded by tall structures that
there was barely room for two lanes of foot traffic. They entered a doorway under a hanging sign
decorated with a rampant dewback.

This was their destination, then. Despite his near-perfect control of his nervous system, Maul felt his pulse quicken slightly in anticipation. If all went as planned, soon this onerous chore would be over. He entered the tavern.

9

Lorn looked around the dingy, ill-lit interior. The Dewback Inn was even less reputable looking than the Glowstone, and that was saying something. There weren't many customers, but each one that he noticed looked like he or she or it had seen their share of combat. Lorn noticed a Devaronian with one horn missing, a piebald Wookiee—half of whose hair had apparently been singed off—and a Sakiyan whose bald head was stitched with ridged keloid tissue, among others.

I-Five surveyed the room, as well. "It just keeps getting better," the droid said.

Lorn noticed a sign above the bar that read NO DROIDS ALLOWED in Basic. He also noticed several of the patrons looking suspiciously at I-Five. "I think you'd better wait outside," he told the droid. "Sorry."

"I think I can deal with the rejection." I-Five went back outside.

Lorn saw a Neimoidian sitting alone at a corner table, looking very uncomfortable. As he started to make his way through the tables he heard the door open behind him, and out of the corner of his eye he glimpsed a cloaked and hooded form entering. The newcomer had a sinister aspect about him—but then, with the possible exception of the Neimoidian, so did everyone else in the room, so Lorn didn't give the new arrival much thought.

As he drew near the Neimoidian's table he felt his arms seized abruptly in an iron grasp. "Hey!" He tried to pull free, but his assailant—a Trandoshan— was far stronger than he was. His struggles alerted the Neimoidian, who looked up.

"Are you Lorn Pavan?" he asked.

"That's me. Call off your bullyboy."

The Neimoidian made a gesture. "Release him, Gorth."

The Trandoshan let Lorn go. Lorn pulled back a chair and sat down, rubbing his arms, both of which had gone somewhat numb from the reptilian being's grip.

"I do apologize," the Neimoidian said, his gaze darting here and there about the bar as he spoke. "You can understand my desire to have some protection in a place like this. Gorth comes highly recommended."

"I can see why," Lorn said. "Let's get down to business. What do you have?"

As Darth Maul slipped into the rathole called the Dewback Inn, he kept his cowl up and moved to the darkest corner. When one of the weak minds surrounding him caused its owner to idly cast a glance in his direction, he used the Force to squelch or redirect that interest. As always when he wished it in such dens of mental weakness, he was effectively invisible.

He had spotted his prey immediately. The urge to simply step up and sever the Neimoidian's head from his body was tempting, but he knew that would be foolishness. He would have to kill the big Trandoshan bodyguard first, and probably the Corellian, as well. Slaying three people, even in a pit such as this, would not go unnoticed. Calling attention to one's self in a public place would be bad; his master had impressed that upon Maul at an early age. The Sith were powerful, but there were only two of them. Stealth was therefore one of their greatest strengths. Even as weak-minded and chemically besotted as most of the patrons of this place were, there were simply too many to control completely. He could not wipe the memories of a cold-blooded assassination from several dozen heads, nor could he be sure of destroying all of them. And here and there burned an intellect too strong to be swayed by simple mind-control techniques. These he could feel; they stood out like photonic lamps on a darkling plain.

And besides all that, he had to question the Neimoidian thoroughly to find any others the traitor might have tainted in his flight.

Nevertheless, Maul had his target in sight now. That was what was important, and it would now be only a matter of time before he was able to close the assignment. He would wait for a propitious moment to deal with him.

The human dealer in information was speaking with the doomed Neimoidian, and likely that sealed the man's fate, as well. Later, when he questioned Hath Monchar, Maul would determine precisely what had passed between the man and the Neimoidian. If this Lorn Pavan had come to discuss other matters and knew nothing of Monchar's treachery, he would be allowed to keep his insignificant life. But if he had become party to the subversion, then the human would die. Quite simple.

Mahwi Lihnn trekked through the back streets and alleys, searching for the Dewback Inn. She was certainly not overimpressed with this area of Coruscant. The surface streets in this sector were all twisted turnings and narrow byways, teeming with gutter scum looking for an easy mark. Lihnn, armed to the teeth as she was, did not present such an easy target, and the strong-arm thieves and head-bashers watched her pass but stayed on their own ground, smart enough to recognize danger when they saw it. Lihnn wasn't particularly worried about her safety; she had been in much worse places than this and survived. It was largely a matter of attitude. She projected confidence and an air of danger as she walked, an aura that made it clear that, at the first sign of trouble from any of this riffraff, the troublemaker would find his-, her-, or itself a smoking corpse on the greasy walkway, to be quickly picked over by the rest of them.

She came to an intersection, hesitated briefly, then

chose the right fork. Another person could easily get lost and stay lost in this maze, but Mahwi Lihnn had honed her sense of direction in scores of such places around the galaxy, and she knew she would eventually arrive at her destination. She always got where she was supposed to go, and she always came out on top when she got there. She was, quite simply, the best at what she did.

As Hath Monchar would soon find out.

After climbing a few flights of stairs Darsha Assant reached the lowest inhabited levels of the building. Here she found what passed for a pharmacy at the end of a squalid corridor. She had lost her regular credit tab along the way, though she still had her emergency tab. It was good for only a small amount—not nearly enough to rent a speeder, unfortunately, but sufficient to purchase enough antibiotic synthflesh bandage to treat and seal her wounds and even hire a taxi, if it didn't have to go far. Her robes were in pretty sad shape, as well, but the emergency fund was not up to covering replacements for those. No matter—she had more important things to worry about than her wardrobe.

Feeling somewhat better after she smoothed the healing synthflesh into place, she looked for a quiet spot—preferably one with walls to protect her back and sides—to ponder what she should do next.

There was no way to sugarcoat her situation. She was, quite simply, ruined. She had lost her charge; the hawk-bats were no doubt picking clean the Fondorian's bones by now. She had lost her transportation to a common street gang. Her comlink was shattered. The mission, in short, had been a complete and utter disaster. Master Bondara had been right to wonder about her ability.

Darsha sat down on a graffiti scarred bench and sought to center herself as she had been taught. It was no use; the stillness that a Jedi should always operate from was nowhere to be found. Instead she felt grief, sadness, anger—but most of all, she felt shame. She had disgraced herself, her mentor, and her heritage. She would never become a Jedi Knight now. Her life as she had known it, as she had expected it to be, was over.

Maybe it would have been better to have died, to have been eaten by the hawk-bats. At least she would not have to face Master Bondara, not have to see the disappointment in her mentor's eyes.

What was she going to do?

She could find a public comm station—some of them would work, even down here—and call for help. The council would send a Jedi—a *real* Jedi, she thought bitterly—to come and fetch her. She would be escorted back as if she were a child, taken into custody so that she could do no more damage.

She envisioned entering the Temple with such an escort. That would be all that was needed to make her shame complete.

Darsha clenched her jaw muscles. No. That wasn't how it was going to go. She had failed her mission, true enough, but she still had her lightsaber, and she still had some pride, if only a trace of what it had been. She would *not* call for help. She could find some way to return to the council under her own power. She owed that much at least to Master Bondara—and to herself.

She took a deep breath, let it escape slowly, and once again sought calmness in the Force. Her path as a Jedi Knight was done. There was no way to change that. But she could deliver herself to that judgment without begging for help.

She stood, took another deep breath, and blew it out. Yes. At the very least, she could do that much.

Lorn could not believe his luck. Finally, it looked like things were taking a turn for the better. Carefully, so as not to reveal his enthusiasm, he said to the Neimoidian, "And you say you have recorded all this information— the details of the impending blockade, and the fact that the Sith are behind it—on a holocron?"

"That is correct," Monchar replied.

"And may I, ah, see this crystal?"

Monchar gave Lorn a look that was plain to read, even given the differences between Neimoidian and human facial expressions: *What am I, stupid?* Aloud, he said, "I would not carry it around on my person in such places, even with Gorth as a protector. The holocron is safely stored and guarded elsewhere."

Lorn leaned back. "I see. And you would want to sell it for—how much?"

"Half a million Republic credits."

Lorn grinned. The way to play this was cool and easy. "Half a million? Why, sure. You have change for a million-cred note?"

The Neimoidian gave Lorn a fishy smile in return. "I'm afraid not."

Lorn had played this game before, and he knew it was time to palaver. "All right," he said. "If it is what you say it is, I might be willing to go two hundred and fifty thousand."

"Don't insult me," Monchar replied. "If it is what I say it is—and I assure you, it is—the information on that crystal is worth twice what I am asking—more, in the right hands. We will not dicker like a couple of bantha traders, human. Half a million credits, period. You'll stand to make that much and more off it if you have the wits of a Sarconian green flea."

That was true, Lorn knew. Of course, if he could lay his hands on half a million creds, he wouldn't be sitting in this dive trying to negotiate stolen data. But there was no way he could let a deal like this pass. He might never see another like it. "All right. Half a million. Where shall we make the exchange?"

The Neimoidian touched a button on a wristband, and a small holographic projection lit up just above the surface of the table, no bigger than Lorn's thumb.

"Here is the address of my cubicle," Monchar said. "Meet me there in an hour. Come alone."

One hour! Lorn kept his expression carefully non-committal. "I, ah, might need a little longer than that to raise the funds."

"One hour," Monchar repeated. "If you cannot procure funding by then, I will seek others who are more capable. I am told there is a Hutt, Yanth by name, who would be most interested in this commodity."

"I know Yanth. You don't want to deal with him. He's shifticr than a crystal snake."

"Then bring me the money and we will consummate this transaction."

Lorn memorized the address and nodded. Monchar shut the holo off.

"Okay. No problem," Lorn said. "I'll see you in an hour." He stood and wended his way toward the door.

Outside, I-Five was waiting. "Well?" the droid said, as they walked down the narrow street.

Lorn explained quickly as they walked. "So we've got an hour—actually, fifty-five minutes—to raise five hundred thousand credits." He looked at the droid. "Any thoughts?"

"It is an excellent opportunity, to be sure. In fact, it might well be the chance of your lifetime, though I expect to have better opportunities myself, since I will probably outlive you by a factor of seven-point-four to seven-point-six, at a conservative estimate, disallowing major accidents, natural disasters, or acts of war—"

"We're on the chrono and you're discussing actuarial tables. The big question is, where are we going to get half a million credits in less than an hour?"

"That is indeed the question."

"We could find a card game. I'm good at sabacc."

"But not consistently—if you were, we wouldn't be in this situation. And since we have no money of which to speak, who in all of the underground would give us enough of a marker to buy into a sufficiently high-stakes game?"

"Offhand, I'd say . . . nobody," Lorn admitted.

"And how long would it take to win such an amount, assuming you could get into such a game? Even if you cheated and were not caught, could you do it in fifty-two minutes—not counting, of course, transit time to the Neimoidian's domicile?"

"All right, sabacc is not a viable option. I assume you've got a better idea?"

I-Five cleared his speaking circuits in what sounded almost like a human cough. "There is only one viable option: Bank fraud."

Lorn stopped to stare at I-Five. A Givin blundered into him, muttered an apology, and kept going. Without taking his gaze from I-Five, Lorn grabbed the Givin's exoskeleton, pulled him back, and retrieved his wallet. He then shoved the pickpocket away. "I'm listening," he told the droid.

"I have been considering this idea for some time," I-Five said. "Keeping it in reserve as a final contingency plan. If we effect it, we will be forced to flee Coruscant, and it would be unlikely that we could ever return, unless we wished to radically change our appearances and spend the rest of our lives looking over our shoulders."

"If we had a million credits in our account, that would take us a long, long way from here," Lorn said. "And I'd be happy to leave. We could set up shop on some outlier world where the Republic doesn't have a presence, make a few smart investments, live like kings. Tell me about this plan."

They continued to walk while I-Five elaborated. They wouldn't really be able to steal the money, but the droid was confident he could jack into the data flow of one of Coruscant's many banking firms and manage a phantom transfer of funds into their personal account. The auditor droids would catch it almost immediately, so timing would be critical. But if all went well, Lorn would be able to show Hath Monchar an unencumbered credit tab that was worth half a million. Much more than that, the droid explained, would kick in automatic inquiries, and if they tried to transfer the funds after the audit, the bank would catch that, too. The real trick would be to have the Neimoidian accept the credit tab as payment and make the transfer to his account before time ran out.

"The window will be narrow, and it will close quickly," I-Five concluded. "But in theory it can be done."

Lorn felt a warm rush of excitement. They might actually pull this off. And if they did, they could walk away with a holocron worth a million creds and leave the Neimoidian holding an empty bag. Which would be too bad for him, but that's how life was in the real galaxy. Lorn wouldn't stay awake nights worrying about it, that was for sure.

"Let's do it," he said. "If it doesn't work, we won't be any worse off than we are now."

"Save for the distinct possibility of you occupying a cell in a Republic asteroid prison for thirty years, and me having a complete memory wipe."

"You worry too much."

"And you don't worry enough."

But Lorn knew I-Five would take the risk. Droids were supposed to be programmed with more integrity and honesty than humans or other natural-born species, but it didn't always work quite like that. I-Five had somehow evolved a greed circuit along the way, and the glitter of credits called to him as much as it did Lorn. Which was one of the reasons they got along so well.

Lorn felt an excitement he hadn't known in years as he contemplated it. It *would* work, and they would use the money to build a new life out on the Rim. There were plenty of worlds where, with enough money, one could disappear into a new identity and live a life of ease with no questions asked.

A new life—a *real* life this time. Maybe not the one he had before, but certainly a better one than this hardscrabble existence he was suffering through now.

Of course, it would mean leaving behind any possibility of ever seeing Jax again.

So what? a savage voice in the back of his head asked. *Like there's any chance at all of that now? That's in the past. It's time you started living again.*

Yes. Far past time, in fact.

He looked at I-Five, and though there was no expression on the droid's metallic countenance, he felt certain that I-Five knew exactly what he was thinking.

"What are we waiting for?" he asked the droid. "The Hutt's still expecting us to bring him a holocron; why disappoint him? Let's find a dataport and make it happen."

The gods of fortune smiled upon Mahwi Lihnn. Just as she arrived at the Dewback Inn she saw the Neimoidian depart in the company of a hulking brute of a Trandoshan. The big reptiloid with Monchar sported a pair of blasters, one on each hip, and moved like a bodyguard, which undoubtedly he was.

Lihnn reviewed her options. This was too public a place to take out the guard and collect Monchar, so she'd just have to follow them until circumstances were more viable. She stepped into a narrow aperture between two buildings and let them pass. She was about to fall in behind at a safe distance when someone else emerged from the inn—a robed and cowled figure, bipedal and human-sized, who slipped into the shadow of a doorway across the alley. Lihnn didn't get a look at the face, but whoever he was, he was obviously interested in Monchar.

Lihnn quickly moved behind a stanchion and out of sight.

A footpad bent on robbery? she wondered as she watched. Whoever he was, he had to be pretty sure of himself if he was willing to take on an armed bodyguard.

Sure enough, the robed figure followed the Neimoidian and the Trandoshan, keeping to the dimly lit areas and moving with a stealth that Lihnn had to admire. If this fellow could shoot half as well as he could tail, he could drill the Trandoshan and be on the Neimoidian in a hurry.

Lihnn frowned and loosened her own DL-44s in their holsters. This job was threatening to become complicated. She decided the best course was to take out the bodyguard and the mysterious robed tracker as quickly as possible. If she had to, she could use a glop grenade on Monchar, seal him up in a gel bubble, and haul him back to Gunray like that, though she didn't think it would be necessary. She'd never met a brave Neimoidian, never even heard of one, and she didn't think Hath Monchar would prove the exception to the rule.

Darth Maul melded with the darkness, becoming a shade among shadows, a ghost in the fetid gloom. It was always night this deep in the ferrocrete canyons. Artificial lights were few and far between at best, and there were many places where lights were burned out, stolen, or shattered by vandals. He had plenty of cover, and the lumbering pair in front of him had no idea they were being followed. Now and again the bodyguard would glance around to assure himself that no threat drew close, but it was obvious that he was an oaf, without skill or much training. Maul did not need to use the dark side to hide from such a being.

As he surveilled the Neimoidian and his guard, however, Maul felt a small prickling of something— not real danger, but a kind of disquiet—touch his awareness. He looked about and listened carefully, but did not see any cause for this. He expanded his consciousness, let the dark currents of the Force extend outward from him—and became aware of another presence behind him, hidden from normal sight and hearing.

Probably just another of the many predators in this dreary place, looking for prey. Now that he was aware of the presence, Maul dismissed it. He felt no real concentrations of the Force emanating from the hidden watcher, and thus whoever he was and whatever his reasons for being here, he did not pose a threat.

The Neimoidian and his guard took a convoluted path, turning and twisting back, until finally they arrived at a block of small cubic living units stacked a dozen high and twenty wide, and probably that many deep. The pair entered the building through a locked durasteel door that Monchar opened with his thumbprint.

Maul waited a few moments, then approached the door.

Mahwi Lihnn was a bit slow in arriving at the domicile. Though she couldn't put her finger on the exact reason why, she felt sure the robed stalker tailing the Neimoidian had somehow known he was being tailed in turn. Lihnn didn't think she'd been seen, and she'd moved with as much stealth as she could muster, which was considerable. But the feeling had persisted, and as a result she had dropped back. She was trusting that the lurker in the cowl wouldn't lose Monchar, and so she let the Neimoidian and his bodyguard get far enough ahead that she couldn't see them. It was risky business to track a tracker and not the primary subject, but she didn't see that she had much choice.

Given all that, by the time she got closer, the Neimoidian and the bodyguard were already inside—or so she assumed—and the tracker in the cowl was just arriving at the door.

There came a sudden flash of light, the source of which was hidden by the tracker's body. Lihnn ducked back behind a garbage bin as the light strobed. When she looked again the door was wide open and the cowled figure was nowhere in sight.

Lihnn pulled her left blaster, keeping her right hand clear to use the palm flechette shooter—the quieter, and therefore preferable, weapon. She hurried across the dim street.

When she reached the door she paused in surprise. Where the locking mechanism had been on the durasteel plate was a still-smoking semicircular hole, its glowing edges carved as cleanly as if done by laser surgery. The lock and handle lay on the ground, also smoldering from whatever tool had cut them free. Lihnn knew of only a couple of devices that could excise a thick slab of durasteel so fast and smoothly: a plasma torch, which was much too big to hide under a cloak and haul around, or a lightsaber.

And the only people she knew of who used lightsabers were Jedi.

Lihnn swallowed dryly, her belly suddenly roiling. If the Jedi were somehow involved, the risk factor had just shot off the scale. A Jedi Knight was nobody to mess with. You'd get only one shot at taking out a Jedi who was paying attention; after that you'd likely be sliced apart real quick. Lihnn had once seen a Jedi knock a blaster bolt out of the air using a lightsaber. That required inhumanly fast reflexes.

For a second she seriously considered turning around and heading for the spaceport. Haako hadn't said anything about Jedi.

But—no. She was a professional, trained and adept. She couldn't have word getting around that she had backed away from a job, no matter what the reason. She didn't know for certain that the cowled stalker was a Jedi. Besides, for all their battle skill, she had heard that Jedi did not kill unless there was absolutely no alternative—although she would hate to be in a position where she had to rely on that.

She was just going to have to take it very slowly and carefully from here on.

Very slowly and carefully.

Lorn and I-Five walked down the narrow street toward their destination, keeping to the middle so as to avoid being surprised by a robber looking for a quick knockover. Lorn had a small blaster in his tunic's pocket, gripped in his right hand—which, he noticed, was somewhat sweaty. The idea of living on a planet where you didn't have to worry about such things every time you stepped outside was most appealing. And seeing things under the natural light of a sun was a novel concept, too. They'd been down here far too long. It was definitely time for a change.

"So the scam-transfer went all right?" he asked I-Five.

"For the seventh time, yes, it went all right. We have precisely one hour and twenty-six minutes before it's discovered and rectified by the auditor droids. Perhaps another four minutes before they are able to pinpoint the location of the credit tab and, depending on how busy the local police are, anywhere from six to fourteen minutes before they arrive to take the bearer of the tab into custody for attempted grand theft and illegal use of communication protocols THX-one-one-three—"

"Spare me the details. We have less than an hour and forty-five minutes to get this deal done and be on our way. How much farther is this place?"

"At our present rate of speed we'll arrive in two-point-six minutes. Plenty of time to accomplish our task, as well as fence the holocron to the Hutt."

"Assuming the Neimoidian doesn't want to have a drink and chat about Republic politics and the latest hi-lo ball scores."

"Since you are to negotiate alone, I trust you will find some way to skip the small talk. Time's running out and the fake ID I utilized on the transfer won't slow the authorities for more than another few minutes after they collect the credit tab. That's assuming

Hath Monchar doesn't give your name to the arresting officers—which would be a dangerous assumption, for if I were him, I would do so instantly, and so would you to anybody who cheated you thus. In which case we will be in bantha excrement up to our eyeballs and photoreceptors, respectively. So decline liquid refreshment and idle chitchat and get the deal done; that's my considered advice."

Finding the Neimoidian was child's play for Maul. Walls could not stop the dark questing fingers of the Force. When he arrived at the correct domicile, he sensed that there were four beings behind the door. Monchar, of course, and the bodyguard he had seen accompanying him. The dull ripples of the other two rumbled with suppressed violence. More guards, no doubt.

No matter. Be there three guards or thirty, the result would be the same. It was time for Hath Monchar to pay the penalty for attempting to double-cross Lord Sidious.

Darth Maul pulled his double lightsaber from his belt and held his thumb upon the ignition button. He took a deep breath and centered himself in the swirls and eddies of the dark side. Then, his power and concentration thus augmented, he thrust forward his free hand as though hurling an invisible ball.

The door shattered inward.

Mahwi Lihnn moved through the building's dimly lit halls with great care, ready to shoot anything that moved. A door opened and an old human woman started to step out, saw Lihnn with her finger tightening on the trigger, and launched herself back into the room, slamming the hinged door behind her.

Lihnn managed to keep from blasting her, though just barely.

This could be a problem, she reflected. There were hundreds of rooms in this hive, and no way that she could search them all. Her plan had been to follow the cowled one to their common destination, but her few moments of shock at discovering the way the other had breached the entrance had been enough to let her quarry vanish into the warren. Lihnn knew she could wander around here for days and not find the Neimoidian. Maybe she should go back outside and set up a watch on the building's exit?

The problem with that was she wasn't sure of the cowled one's intent in pursuing Monchar. Lihnn's mandate from the Trade Federation was clear: Bring Hath Monchar back alive. If she didn't find the Neimoidian soon, she might wind up with a corpse on her hands, which would not make Haako at all happy.

There didn't seem to be much choice but to continue her search.

As soon as he was through the door, Maul triggered his lightsaber. The bright beams lanced out to their full lengths.

He took in the room: The Neimoidian sat in a chair against the far wall. A pair of Squid Heads scrabbled for their holstered blasters. The Trandoshan bodyguard already had his out, and now he fired it.

Maul spun the lightsaber and angled it slightly.

Stopping the blasterfire was easy. Redirecting it properly was a bit more difficult, but certainly not impossible. The bolt bounced from the potent energy lance and ricocheted into the nearest Squid Head, striking him on the thorax. The Quarren collapsed.

Maul allowed himself a slight frown. The deflected beam was two centimeters lower than he had aimed. Poor control on his part.

A second blaster bolt from the Trandoshan seared its way at him, and another quick shift, guided by the dark side, caught that bolt and returned it to the sender. The Trandoshan took the deflected beam in the face. He went down, twitching in his death throes, his face a blackened ruin of flesh and scales, at the horrified Neimoidian's feet.

Better.

Maul leapt at the remaining Quarren, who had his blaster halfway up. The Squid Head fired a panicked round, far too low to do any damage save to the floor. Then the lightsaber arced, and with a snap of his wrists, Maul lopped the Quarren's tentacled head from his neck.

The battle had begun and ended far too quickly for the Neimoidian to even think about running. He cowered in the chair, hands uselessly raised to ward off danger. He didn't even have a weapon.

Maul shut the lightsaber off and hooked it back on his belt. He spared a contemptuous glance at the three corpses. His dueling droids had given him a better fight than these three had. Pitiful.

He turned toward the terrified Neimoidian. Slowly he raised his gloved hands and slipped his cowl back and off, revealing his frightening visage. He smiled, showing his teeth, adding to the effect.

A pungent reek became noticeable over the stench of death in the room. The Neimoidian's bladder sac had let go its contents.

"Hath Monchar," Darth Maul said. "We have things to discuss, you and I."

As Lorn and I-Five reached the cube complex, the droid said, "Approximately one hour and thirty-three minutes left. Speed is of the essence. As it is, even assuming the meeting with the Hutt goes smoothly, the police will probably be searching for us while we're en route to the spaceport."

"Don't worry about me, just you be ready to—Hey, what happened to the door?"

"It appears to have had a disagreement with somebody," I-Five said. "Not a big surprise in this neighborhood. In any event, that's not our concern, is it? Now hurry!"

Lorn nodded and entered the building. In the small lobby he paged the lift tube to take him to the fourth level, where the Neimoidian supposedly had a residence. Monchar must be low on funds to be staying in a dive such as this—or perhaps trying very hard not to be noticed. Either way, the quicker Lorn could make the exchange and leave, the happier he'd be. He kept his grip on the blaster in his pocket and tried to look nonchalant as he waited for the lift tube to arrive. Nonchalant was hard to pull off at this juncture. The credit tab in his wallet felt like it was made of fissionable material. It wasn't every day he tried to scam a million-credit deal.

Caught in the power of the dark side, the Neimoidian struggled to breathe. Maul's left hand, raised before him, tightened into a fist, and the Neimoidian's throat constricted even more.

"Ready to talk?" Maul asked.

The Neimoidian could not speak, but he managed a nod. The crimson sclera of his eyes had darkened several shades due to blood congestion.

Maul relaxed his fist and his concentration. Hath Monchar collapsed on the floor, wheezing as he tried to suck in a breath.

"Who else knows?"

"No—no one, except a human, Lorn Pavan."

Maul sensed the truth of Monchar's words. This was good. All he had to do was kill the Neimoidian, then find the human and kill him. And then this dreary chore would be at an end.

"Where can I find the human now?"

"I don't know."

Maul's hand clenched again. Monchar choked, gasping once more for air. Maul released him.

"*Where?*"

"He—he's coming here to buy the holocron!"

"When?"

"Any time now!"

Maul smiled. He had all the information he needed.

"Excellent. You have been most cooperative, Hath Monchar."

Monchar looked up from his supine position. There

was an instant of hope in his eyes, but it died when he read his fate in Maul's expression.

Maul drew his lightsaber. "Time to die," he said.

"Wait!" The Neimoidian's voice was a bleat of fear. "I can pay you—every credit the human gives me will be yours! *Please*—"

"Stand up," Maul said. "You can at least meet your fate without groveling."

But Monchar was too palsied with terror to comply. Maul felt a wave of disgust for the cringing creature. With his free hand he made a sharp upward gesture, and the Neimoidian was lifted like a puppet on strings. He hung, helpless, in the Force's grasp.

"*Nooo*—"

Darth Maul lit one blade of the lightsaber and swung it laterally, cutting off the Neimoidian's final wail, along with his head. He then released the lines of Force that held the twitching body and watched it crumple.

There was a durasteel safe on the floor behind the body. Maul opened it with a careful swipe of his lightsaber. Ah—there was the holocron crystal of which Monchar had spoken. He extinguished his lightsaber, hung it on his belt, and bent to pick up the holocron. Before his fingers touched it, however, he sensed that he was not alone.

"Don't move!" came a voice from the door even as he realized this. "You so much as breathe deep and I'll fry you where you stand!"

Maul glanced at the doorway. A tall human female in shell spider silk armor stood there, aiming a pair of blasters at him.

Maul realized that this was the same being he had sensed following him earlier. His lips twitched in annoyance. He tried a quick mental probe, but the bounty hunter—for surely that was what she was—was too sharp, her attention too focused, to fall for mind tricks.

Maul considered his options. He would never reach his lightsaber fast enough, even as quick as he was. He might be able to dodge a single blast, maybe even two, but hemmed in as he was in this small cubicle against a woman who could likely put a dozen bolts into the air from two semiautomatic blasters in half a second, he would have to have a distraction.

Near his feet lay the Trandoshan's blaster. It would serve nicely.

Using his control of the Force, Darth Maul gripped the weapon in a dark tentacle of energy and hurled it at the bounty hunter's face, hard.

The woman was fast. She dodged the blaster, firing a bolt at it. She missed and recovered, but the distraction had served its purpose. Before the weapon had bounced off the wall and landed on the floor, Maul had the lightsaber in his grasp. He thumbed on both blades as the next blaster bolt and half a dozen more came his way in rapid succession. The Sith apprentice's hands were a blur as he let the dark side take him over completely, giving in to its power and allowing it to control and manipulate him.

Blaster bolts struck the lightsaber's spinning blades and were deflected into the walls, the ceiling, the floor. No time to aim, though a bolt or two did hit the bounty hunter without apparent effect. Her armor was apparently state-of-the-art.

The bounty hunter dropped her useless blasters and reached for one wrist, where she wore a rocket launcher. The fool! Maul thought grimly. If a rocket exploded in here, it would kill them both!

There was no time to try to stop her. Maul slipped along the lines of the Force, moving at unnatural speed as he spun toward the nearest wall, a cheap plastic panel, twirling the lightsaber in a cutting pattern. The plastic shredded easily before the blades' superhot plasmatic edges, and Maul ran through the wall, leapt over a chair in the next room—which, fortunately for its tenants, was deserted at the moment—and stabbed downward with one blade of his lightsaber, shearing a ragged oval in the floor. He dropped through the ceiling of the cubicle below just as the rocket struck the wall of the Neimoidian's room and exploded.

Lihnn had never seen anybody move like the man with the horned and tattooed head. He wasn't dressed like a Jedi, but his expertise with the double-bladed lightsaber far exceeded the skill of any Jedi Lihnn had ever heard of. He knocked blaster bolts away as if swatting flies! And if he could do that, Lihnn couldn't stop him. He would use that double-bladed lightsaber to slice her apart.

Desperate, she reached for her wrist launcher. Her only chance was to hit the horned one squarely and hope that the explosion would be contained enough by the other's body to allow Lihnn to survive. But as she triggered the launcher the tattooed man seemed to disappear in a blur. All of a sudden there was a hole in the wall where an instant ago it had been solid.

Too late, Lihnn tried to stop the rocket from firing, but the reactionless motor flared and the missile leapt from her wrist. She tried to jump back into the hallway.

Lorn was almost to the room where he was supposed to meet the Neimoidian when a sudden explosion hurled him backwards a good three meters, impacting against the wall of a T intersection. As the shock wave lifted him he caught a glimpse of what looked like an armored human flying across the hall just ahead of him and smashing halfway through the wall. Then he hit the far wall himself and didn't think about anything for a time.

He was out for only a minute or two; when the corridor swam back into focus the smoke was still swirling and debris was still settling. There was a ringing in his ears that was a result of either the blast or the dozens of residential alarms activated by it, or both. Lorn managed to get to his feet, pulled his blaster, and edged unsteadily forward. All he could see of the body was a pair of legs, unmistakably female, sticking out of a hole in the wall, so thinking of her as dead seemed a pretty safe bet.

He turned and peered into the blackened cube. What looked like the remains of four bodies lay scorched and smoking on the floor. He took a few steps into the chamber. One of the smoldering corpses looked like Monchar, but it was hard to be sure—given that it was headless.

Lorn felt his guts churn, both at what he saw and what it meant: Hath Monchar wouldn't be making any more deals with anybody. He was quite seriously dead, and Lorn and I-Five might as well be, too, if they didn't get off Coruscant in the next hour or so. The whole bank-fraud escapade had been for nothing!

Damn!

Lorn turned to run. Even in this sector an explosion like the one that had just happened would bring the security forces in to investigate. He had to get out of there, and fast. But as he started to move he noticed a glimmer of light in a corner of the room and reflexively glanced at it.

What he saw brought him skidding to a stop.

Could it be? It seemed too much to hope for. But when he bent down and looked closer, he realized that maybe the game wasn't over yet.

The holocron crystal lay in the half-open safe, which had no doubt protected it from being destroyed by the explosion. Lorn grabbed it up, holding it tightly in one hand and the blaster in the other, and now he did run, as fast as he could, down the corridor, past the confused and frightened faces of tenants who had cautiously emerged to investigate, and toward the stairwell. There was still a chance—a very slim chance—that he and I-Five could yet turn this fiasco into a winning situation. But doing so meant getting far away from here as fast as possible.

The building Darsha had entered was a monad—a kilometer-high, totally self-contained habitat. More than just an apartment complex, the huge structure, like countless others sprouting from the surface of Coruscant, contained virtually everything its tenants needed: living quarters, shops, hydroponic gardens, and even indoor parks. Many people, she knew, literally lived their entire lives in buildings like these, in some cases holocommuting to offices halfway around the planet without ever venturing outside.

She had never understood the attraction of such a life before. Now, however, she found herself in sympathy with such people in at least one respect: she had no desire to leave the building either. But her reluctance did not rise out of nascent agoraphobia; rather, it stemmed from the fact that to leave meant returning to the Jedi Temple, where she would have to face the council and admit her failure.

However, there was no other alternative. The council had to know of the Fondorian's death, and quickly. It was her duty to report her failure, no matter how shameful it was.

She had to climb four more flights of stairs before she reached a level that had a working lift tube. This she took up another ten levels, where she encountered a border checkpoint, complete with an armed guard droid, separating the downlevels ghetto from the functioning upper section of the monad. The droid eyed her disreputable appearance with some suspicion, but let her pass when it realized she was a Jedi.

When Darsha emerged from the building, she was in a much more familiar world. She walked out onto a transparent skybridge and looked down through the permacrete floor. The sleek sides of the buildings all around her fell away into darkness and fog. Beneath that fog was the abyss she had just escaped. If she was given a choice between returning to it or returning to the Temple to admit her defeat, she honestly wasn't sure which she would take.

But there was no choice, was there? Not really.

She made her way to an air taxi stand, aware of the stares that her torn clothing and bandaged wounds drew. *Truly I am still trapped between worlds*, she thought.

Just enough credit was left on her emergency tab to hire an air taxi that would take her back to the Temple. As Darsha settled into the vehicle's backseat, she felt suddenly overcome by lassitude. It was all she could do not to fall asleep as the taxi made its short journey. She recognized the drowsiness as not so much a reaction to the trials she had just undergone but as an attempt to escape what lay ahead.

All too soon the commute was over. Darsha paid the driver and entered the Temple. As far back as she could remember, passing through the doors had been a source of comfort to her. It meant a return to sanctuary, to safety, to a place where the cares and worries of the rest of the world were left behind. She did not feel this way now. Now the high walls and soft lighting induced anxiety and claustrophobia.

She shook her head and squared her shoulders. Might as well get it over with. At this time of day she would most likely find Master Bondara in his quarters. She would report to her mentor first; then, in all likelihood, they would both go to the council.

Darth Maul had made an error.

The enormity of that knowledge weighed upon him like a giant planetoid. He had underestimated the bounty hunter because the woman had not been strong in the Force. Such a mistake had almost cost him his life—and how ignominious would *that* have been, to die at the hands of a common bounty hunter, he who had been trained to fight and slay Jedi!

He could not make such dangerous assumptions.

He would not make them again.

He knew what his next move had to be. Hath Monchar was dead, but there was still the human to deal with. As Maul emerged from the building the police and firefighting droids were already starting to arrive. He could not cloud the cognitive circuits of droids as easily as he could organic brains, and so he had to move quickly into the shadowy surface streets to avoid questioning.

He found a deserted blind alley a few blocks away and activated his wrist comm. A moment later the image of Darth Sidious appeared before him.

"Tell me what progress you have made," Sidious said.

"The tergiversator Hath Monchar has been killed. He has shared his knowledge with one other—a human named Lorn Pavan. I know where the human lives. I go now to find him and kill him."

"Excellent. Do so as quickly as possible. You are certain that no one else knows of this?"

"Yes, Master. I—" Maul stopped suddenly in shocked realization. The holocron!

As always, Sidious immediately knew that something was wrong. "What is it?" the Sith Lord demanded.

Darth Maul knew he would have to admit failure. He did not hesitate. The concept of lying to his master never even occurred to him. "Monchar possessed a holocron that he said contains the information. I had an opportunity to acquire it, but I—failed to do so." It would be pointless to try to exculpate himself by telling Sidious of the bounty hunter's unexpected appearance and the subsequent explosion that he had barely escaped. The only important fact was that the holocron was not in his possession.

Maul saw Darth Sidious's eyes narrow in disapproval. "You disappoint me, Lord Maul."

He felt that censure spear him like an icy shaft. No trace of it showed on his face. "I am sorry, my master."

"Your tasks are now twofold: Destroy this Lorn Pavan and find the crystal."

"Yes, my master."

Sidious regarded Maul steadily for a moment. "Do not fail me again." The hologram vanished.

Darth Maul stood silently for a moment in the perennial darkness of the city's surface. His breathing was steady and even, his body motionless. Only one trained to sense the whorls and verticils of the Force would get a sense of the dark storm that raged within him.

His master had *rebuked* him. And rightly so. That crystal could be the ruination of all Darth Sidious's carefully laid plans. And he, Darth Maul, heir to the Sith, had left it behind when he had fled for his life.

Fool!

Maul's nostrils flared as he drew in a deep, shuddering breath. He had no time for self-recrimination. The Neimoidian's cubicle was no doubt already overrun with police droids searching for a clue to the explosion. They would hardly overlook an information crystal lying in an opened safe.

There was, of course, the possibility that it had been destroyed in the explosion, but he couldn't count on that. He would have to go back and find out what had happened to it, even if every police droid on Coruscant was packed into that tiny room.

And after he had found the holocron and disposed of the human, then he would have to face whatever punishment Darth Sidious would undoubtedly devise for his lamentable failure.

Maul strode out of the alley and back toward the domicile.

Lorn found I-Five just venturing into the first floor of the building—or trying to, as the stampede of panicked tenants had filled all the exits. Though the droid's metallic face was expressionless as always, he still somehow managed to project concern, followed by relief as he saw Lorn.

"Let's get out of here," Lorn muttered to the droid. "Fast."

"That sounds like a remarkably astute idea."

Walking quickly, they soon put several city blocks between themselves and the debacle. Then I-Five said, "It appears that all did not go entirely according to plan."

"Ever a master of the understatement." Lorn explained what had happened. "I have no idea who the dead woman was. I have no idea what caused the explosion. I have no idea who killed the Neimoidian and his goons. What I *do* have is this." He pulled the holocron from a pocket.

I-Five took it and looked closely at it. "It appears to be encoded," the droid said. "It definitely contains some sort of information. Whether it's the details of the trade embargo of Naboo or a recipe for Alderaan stew is impossible to tell without activating it."

"It better well be what Monchar said it is." Lorn glanced at his wrist chrono. "We've got barely enough time to make the meeting with the Hutt and then get to the spaceport."

"I would predict another half hour or so of grace.

Most of the local law enforcement will be more interested in the explosion than in catching us. Nevertheless, I agree that a hasty retreat is called for. I took the liberty of using our temporary wealth to secure two berths on the next spice transport bound for the Rim. Once we have the money from the Hutt we can pay the fare in cash."

Lorn nodded. I-Five was right; the important thing was to unload the holocron and get offworld as quickly as possible. It was likely that whoever had terminated Hath Monchar was looking for the crystal, and Lorn most definitely did not want to make his acquaintance. In his mind's eye he could still vividly see the Neimoidian's headless body lying on the floor of the apartment, along with his bodyguards. One of them had been decapitated, as well.

He stopped abruptly, paralyzed by shock. I-Five looked at his face, then quickly dragged him out of the stream of foot traffic. "What is it?"

"No blood," Lorn said.

I-Five said nothing. He waited.

"Whoever did Monchar cut off his head. One of the Quarren bodyguards got the same treatment. But there was no blood to speak of. You understand? No blood. That means—"

"Cauterization. Fusion of the tissues by sudden intense heat." I-Five paused, and Lorn knew the droid had reached the same conclusion that he had. "Perhaps a quick lateral movement of a blaster on continuous fire—"

"The particle beam from a hand blaster—even a DL-44 — isn't that hot, and you know it. On a straight line, yeah, it can seal as it burns, but to cauterize something the size of a neck would take several seconds. It would have to have been done after Monchar was dead, and what's the sense of that?

"There's only one weapon capable of doing it instantaneously. The same weapon that was used to cut the lock out of the durasteel door."

"A lightsaber." I-Five glanced about as if to assure himself that no one was listening. "Are you saying a Jedi killed Monchar?"

"Much as I hate to admit it, executions aren't their style." Lorn's mouth was suddenly very dry; he had to swallow several times before he could continue. "Which leaves only one other logical choice."

"The Sith? Impossible. The last one died over a thousand years ago."

"That's what everyone believes. But it's the only conclusion that makes any sense. The Jedi have kept the details of lightsaber manufacture secret for millennia. To create and use one, you have to be adept in the Force. And the Sith were the only other order of Force-sensitives the galaxy has ever known."

"And why couldn't it just as easily be a rogue Jedi? One who has succumbed to some kind of psychosis—a failing organic beings are often prone to, I've noticed. I think you're jumping to conclusions," I-Five said.

"No, I'm not." Lorn grabbed the droid and pulled him along as he started to walk faster. "I'm jumping on that spice transport and getting off this overbuilt rock—and so are you." He spied a public trash disintegrator across the street and changed course, with

I-Five still in tow. "And we're getting rid of this holocron, right now."

They stopped before the disintegrator receptacle. Lorn pulled the information crystal from a pocket, but before he could throw it in, I-Five grabbed his arm.

"Now I *know* you're crazy," the droid said. "That holocron is our only chance to build a new life. And how will we pay our passage on the spice freighter? We can't just—"

Lorn shoved the droid up against the graffiti-frescoed wall of a large hydro-reclamation processor. Pedestrians of various and sundry species passed them, paying little or no attention to the altercation.

"Listen to me," Lorn said through clenched teeth. "If I'm right, there's a Sith out there. He's probably looking for this." He held up the holocron. "He can't be bought off, scared off, or thrown off the trail, and he'll stop at nothing to get it. I don't fancy having *my* neck cauterized."

"Let's say you're right," I-Five said. "Let's say Monchar's mysterious assassin is a Sith. Let's say he wants the crystal, and he knows we have it. Let's say he corners us before we reach the Hutt and demands we give it to him. Which will make him happier with us—handing him the crystal, or telling him we destroyed it?"

Lorn paused, trying to quell his panic. He knew he wasn't using his brain—at least, not the part parked directly behind his forehead. He was thinking with the organ's hindquarters, the primal fight-or-flight component.

But fight-or-flight—or, more precisely, just *flight*— was the only option that made any sense in this case. In his previous life Lorn had researched the Sith thoroughly, and he knew they were fanatics, pure and simple. If a Sith was on their trail, the only prudent thing to do was to put half a galaxy between them and their stalker as quickly as possible.

Nevertheless, he had to admit that I-Five's argument about keeping the holocron had a certain logic. After all, fencing it to the Hutt might be sufficient to throw the Sith off their trail. It was reasonable to assume he was after the holocron, not them.

And all this was based on the assumption that Monchar's killer was in fact a Sith. It was a big galaxy, after all, and Coruscant was the biggest melting pot of all the inhabited worlds. It was possible that there existed someone, neither Jedi nor Sith, who had somehow gotten hold of a lightsaber and could make it work. After all, it probably didn't require being a master of the Force to simply slice an energy blade through someone's neck.

But none of this made Lorn feel any easier. Neither he nor I-Five had managed to survive these past four years in the rancid underbelly of Coruscant by taking chances. As he had told the droid more than once, it wasn't a question of being paranoid, it was a question of being paranoid *enough*.

Still, there wasn't a whole lot of choice. They could keep the holocron and stay on Coruscant in the hope that giving it up would dissuade Monchar's murderer from beheading them, as well. Or they could sell it and use the credits to flee—and hope they were not pursued.

Neither alternative seemed to offer much in the way of living to a ripe old age.

Lorn sighed and released the droid. "All right," he said. "Let's go meet the Hutt."

12

Alone in his secret chambers, Darth Sidious meditated on this latest set of circumstances.

In many ways Darth Maul was an exemplary acolyte. His loyalty was unquestionable and unshakable; Sidious knew that, if he were to command it, Maul would sacrifice his life without a second's hesitation. And his skills as a warrior were nonpareil.

Nevertheless, Maul had his flaws, and by far the largest of these was hubris. Though he had said nothing when given the assignment, Sidious knew Maul felt that such a job was beneath his skills. There were times—many times—when Sidious could see Maul's aura pulsing with the dark stain of impatience. He wondered sometimes if he had inculcated too much hatred of the Jedi and their ways in his apprentice. Maul did tend to focus on their destruction at the expense of the larger picture.

Even so, Sidious had every confidence that Maul

would accomplish the task he had been set. Complications and setbacks were to be expected, and would be dealt with. All that mattered was the grand design, and it was proceeding apace. Soon the Jedi would be put to the slaughter. That should make his impetuous subordinate happy.

Soon. Very soon.

Master Anoon Bondara sat in silence for several minutes after Darsha finished her report. They were, quite possibly, the longest minutes of the Padawan's life. The Twi'lek Jedi sat with head bowed and fingers steepled, looking at the floor between them. There was no way to read his body language, to tell what he was thinking. Even his lekku were motionless. But Darsha had a pretty good idea that, whatever her mentor's thoughts were, they did not bode well for her continued career as a Jedi.

At last Master Bondara sighed and raised his gaze to meet Darsha's. "I am glad you are still alive," he said, and Darsha felt a surge of gratitude and love for her mentor that was almost overwhelming in its intensity. Her safety had been more important to Master Bondara than the mission.

"Now tell me," the Twi'lek continued, "did you see the Fondorian die?"

"No. But there was no way he could have survived such a fall—"

Master Bondara held up a hand to stop her. "You did not see him die, and I assume you did not feel any upheaval in the Force that could have meant his death."

Darsha thought back to the nightmarish events of

several hours previous. Scanning the waves of the Force for such a ripple of disturbance hadn't exactly been uppermost in her mind at that moment. Would she have felt such an agitation, preoccupied as she had been with trying to save her own life? Her mentor would have, of that she was sure. But was she that finely attuned to the Force?

"I did not," she said slowly, then felt compelled to add, "but, given the circumstances—"

"The circumstances were hardly optimal, I'm sure," Master Bondara said. "But as long as the slightest chance exists that Oolth is still alive, we must pursue it. The information he had is that important."

"You want me to go back and verify his death?" The thought of returning to the Crimson Corridor was enough to make her dizzy with revulsion. Nevertheless, if that was what had to be done, she would do it.

Master Bondara stood, his attitude and posture decisive. "We shall go together. Come." He strode toward the door of his quarters, and Darsha hastened to follow.

"But what about the council? Should we not tell them—"

The Jedi stopped before reaching the door and looked back at the Padawan. "Tell them what? There is nothing definitive to report as yet. Once we know for certain whether the Fondorian is alive or dead, then shall we make our report." He turned back to the panel, which slid open before him, and started down the corridor. Darsha followed, only gradually beginning to realize that there might be a chance, however infinitesimal, that her mission had not ended in failure. It was the lightest and most frangible of straws; nevertheless, as long as it hovered before her, she could do nothing else but grasp at it.

Maul kept his cowl up and his lightsaber clipped as he reentered the building. Fortunately there was a human officer at the checkpoint, asking those coming and going to state their business. It was ridiculously easy for Maul to cloak himself in the Force and thus slip by the dim-witted fellow.

The forensics droids were laser-scanning the cubicle when he arrived. There were a couple of criminologists, one Mrlssi and one Sullustan, as well. He stayed in the hallway and listened to what scraps of conversation he could. He heard no mention of a holocron being found. Carefully he probed and prodded first the Mrlssi's mind, then the Sullustan's, and detected nothing about the crystal in their thoughts. Still cloaked in the dark side, he stole past the entrance of the cubicle, glancing at the open safe as he did so. The holocron was not there. Maul pondered the possibilities. If it was gone, then someone other than the security forces must have taken it. And who might that have been? Obviously, the buyer Monchar had been expecting momentarily—the human known as Lorn Pavan. He was going to enjoy taking that one's head.

Darth Maul turned and headed for the exit.

Now he had a double incentive to find the human and his droid. The first place to check, of course, would be their pathetic subterranean cubicle. It was not far from here; only a few minutes' walk.

Which, with any luck, would be the same few minutes Pavan had left of his life.

On the whole, Lorn did not consider himself to be overly xenophobic—after all, given the way he had been making his living for the last half decade, to be prejudiced against other species was not only bad for business, it could be downright dangerous.

But he hated dealing with Hutts.

On a purely physical level, everything about the giant invertebrates repulsed him: their huge, reptilian eyes, their slithering method of locomotion, and, most of all, their slimy mucosal skin. Just having to be in a room with Yanth sent a wave of horripilation over him that he was hard put to quell.

Yanth was young as Hutts go—less than five hundred standard years old. Even so, he was smart and cagey, and working his way up through the underworld ranks rapidly. Though Lorn could barely stand to be in the same room with the overgrown slug, he had to admit a reluctant admiration for the young Hutt's amoral cunning and craftiness. No one could figure the angles as quickly and completely as Yanth could.

Now he reclined on a dais in his subterranean headquarters, desultorily puffing on a chakroot hookah while he examined the holocron crystal. A couple of Gamorrean bodyguards stood nearby, watching Lorn and I-Five.

"Why did you not go directly to the Jedi with this?"

he asked Lorn, his rumbling basso profundo setting off unpleasant vibrations in the human's gut. "They would seem the logical ones to approach."

Lorn saw no reason to elaborate on his own personal distaste for the Jedi to Yanth. "They claim to have very little discretionary funds for this sort of thing," he said. "Besides, I wouldn't put it past them to use their mind tricks to force me into handing it over for free." He glanced surreptitiously at his chrono and said, "So, are you interested or not? I can always take it directly to the Naboo representative here on Coruscant."

Yanth waved a pudgy hand in a placating gesture. "Patience, my friend. Yes, I am interested. But—and please don't take this as a reflection on you—I would be a fool not to test its authenticity before handing you a stack of credits."

Lorn kept his face carefully expressionless. If Yanth suspected the time crunch they were in, the Hutt would have no compunctions about using it as leverage to gouge a cheaper price. On the other hand, time was most definitely running out. "And just how do you plan on doing that?" he asked the Hutt.

Yanth simply smiled and slid several facets of the crystal aside at various angles, manipulating it much as one might a child's geometric puzzle. After a moment a beam projected from the holocron's uppermost surface, resolving into a midair display of glowing words and images that slowly curtained up the length of the holographic frame before vanishing. Lorn was too far away to read the text—not only that, but he was behind the display, so that the words and alphanumerics appeared reversed to him. The text seemed to be in Basic, however, and the images looked like schematics for Naboo N-1 starfighters and Trade Federation ships.

Yanth rotated a facet, and the images cut off. "Opening one of these holocrons can be somewhat tricky," he said. "Neimoidians as a species are not overly clever."

I-Five said, "Excellent. Now you know the article is genuine. We are asking a million credits."

"Done," Yanth replied, much to Lorn's surprise. "It is worth ten times that." The Hutt turned to a control console near at hand and pressed a button.

Lorn permitted himself another glance at his timepiece. They could still reach the spaceport, if everything continued to proceed smoothly. In another hour Coruscant, the mysterious Sith killer, and the police would be vanishing into the void behind them.

Darth Maul neatly and quickly excised the lock on the underground cubicle with one blade of his lightsaber, as he had earlier at Hath Monchar's building. He stepped inside quickly, letting the door slide closed behind him. Harsh glow lamps flickered on automatically, illuminating a living space even smaller and tawdrier than the one the Neimoidian had rented. The compartment was empty; the only possible place where someone might hide was the refresher, and it was the work of only a few seconds to make sure that was empty, as well.

Maul stepped to a section of wall that held a vidscreen and message unit. He activated the latter. An image formed in midair; the image of a Hutt. He recognized the creature: Yanth, an up-and-coming gangster in the Black Sun organization—one of the few who had survived the slaughter Maul had recently unleashed.

The Hutt's image spoke. "Lorn, I thought we were going to meet sometime today, to discuss a certain Holocron you wished me to look at. It's not polite to keep buyers waiting, you know."

Maul turned and strode out of the cubicle, moving quickly.

13

All too soon, Darsha Assant found herself back in the underbelly of Coruscant.

When she had escaped the area earlier that day, she had estimated that by now she would have been stripped of her rank and reassigned to the agricultural corps. She had envisioned herself in the process of packing her belongings and saying her good-byes. That she might instead be returning to the scene of her disgrace with her mentor had certainly never occurred to her.

And yet, here she was, seated beside Anoon Bondara in the latter's four-person skycar, heading back toward the Crimson Corridor and the monad where she had lost the Fondorian and nearly lost her life, as well.

The ways of the Force were nothing if not unpredictable.

"That's the one," she said, pointing toward the

tower that rose up ahead, stark against the afternoon sun. "Down there."

Master Bondara said nothing as he angled the skycar out of the flow of traffic. They slipped into a vertical descent lane and began dropping.

The mist that seemed always present around the hundred-meter mark, demarcating the thriving upper levels from the slums below, wrapped around them momentarily and then faded away, to be replaced with an aerial view of the dark streets. Though it was still daylight above, down here it was at best a dim perpetual twilight.

She watched the wall of the building slip past, and pointed out to her mentor the ascension gun's grapnel, still hooked to a ledge. They followed the cable into the miasmic depths.

When they were ten meters above the pavement, Master Bondara turned on the landing lights. The section of street below them was illuminated. Darsha, looking over the side, could see shadowy figures, long conditioned to prefer darkness to light, scuttling away.

There was no sign of the Fondorian. In all probability his body had been dragged away by scavengers. There was, however, a smear of purplish blood on the pavement and, nearby, the body of a hawk-bat, its neck broken in the fall. Master Bondara trained one of the lights on that and looked at it. His lekku slumped slightly, along with his shoulders. And, watching him, Darsha realized that her last hope of salvaging the mission was finally, irrevocably dead.

"What shall we do now?" she asked him softly.

He was silent for a long moment. Then he sighed

and said, "Return to the Temple. We must report what has happened to the council."

So there it was, she thought. Oddly enough, now that she knew hope was dead, she did not feel the crushing sorrow that she had anticipated. Instead she felt a surprising sense of relief. The worst had happened, and now she would find a way to deal with it. As with most looming disasters, the reality was almost anticlimactic compared to the dreadful anticipation.

Up to this point her concern about the mission had left little room for her to feel sympathy for Oolth the Fondorian. Now, however, looking at the stain of his blood on the walkway, she felt compassion well within her. He had been an obnoxious poltroon, and no doubt a conscienceless criminal, but few people deserved a death as horrible as his had been.

Master Bondara fed power to the repulsors, and the skycar began to rise.

Lorn watched as one of the Hutt's flunkies delivered a large case to his master. Yanth opened it, and Lorn grew dizzy at the sight. It was filled with crisp Republic credit standards in thousand-denomination notes. Yanth turned the case toward him, displaying the wealth, and Lorn could feel his fingers twitching with the desire to take possession of it. He hadn't seen that much hard cash in—he had *never* seen that much cash in one place before.

"One million nonsequential Republic credits," Yanth said, as casually as if he was discussing the weather. "You take them—I keep this." He held up the holocron. "Everybody's happy."

Lorn didn't know or care about everybody, but he was sure of one thing—*he* was happy. He watched, still hardly able to believe this was happening, as I-Five stepped forward to take possession of the money that would transform their lives. He glanced at his chrono. Just enough time to get to the spaceport, if they left now.

I-Five was reaching for the case when the door behind them suddenly flew open. A Chevin bodyguard staggered backwards into Yanth's sanctum, a force pike dropping from his nerveless fingers. It clattered across the floor to the foot of the dais. The leathery-skinned being looked down at his chest, in the middle of which was a smoking hole, and then collapsed.

Through the door stepped a nightmare.

Lorn stared in shock at the apparition. The Chevin's killer was almost two meters tall and dressed entirely in black, including hooded cloak, boots, and heavy gauntlets. He carried a lightsaber unlike any Lorn had ever seen: It boasted not one but two energy blades, emanating from either end of the hilt. But as intimidating as his weapon was, it was his face that struck true horror into Lorn's heart. The killer pulled back his hood, revealing a countenance that was a sinister variegation of red and black tattoos around gleaming yellow eyes and blackened teeth. From the bald scalp sprouted ten short horns, like a demonic crown. He stared balefully at the others in the room, then spoke in a guttural voice.

"None shall survive."

Lorn was completely frozen to the spot, unable to

offer any resistance, as the killer stepped toward him. His eyes shone like twin suns as he raised the lightsaber.

I-Five grabbed the case full of money from Yanth and hurled it between Lorn and his attacker just as the latter swung the lightsaber in a flat arc that would have separated the Corellian's head from his neck. The case intercepted the blade's swing; the plasmatic edge sliced through the case, scattering burning credits everywhere. The force of the blow was so strong that it probably would still have decapitated Lorn, but its momentum was slowed just enough to give the droid time to dive forward, knocking his friend out of harm's way. Lorn felt the heat as the blade's incandescent tip seared through his hair.

The Sith—for there was no doubt in Lorn's mind that he was facing one of those legendary Dark Lords out of the mists of the past—recovered almost instantly and swung around to attack again. But by this time both Gamorrean guards had pulled their blasters and were firing. The Sith spun the double-bladed weapon before him, deflecting the blasterfire back at the guards. That was all Lorn had time to see before I-Five yanked him to his feet and pulled him through the doorway.

They fled down the narrow corridor that led from Yanth's sanctum, passing several more dead guards and two piles of melted, twisted metal that had once been droids. Yanth's headquarters was beneath a nightclub he owned called the Tusken Oasis; Lorn and I-Five stumbled up a short flight of stairs and burst out into a blue-lit chamber full of sabacc tables, dejarik game boards, and scantily clad females of various species dancing on pedestals. They hurtled through the room and out the entrance.

"Where are we going?!" Lorn shouted as they ran down the street.

"Away from there!" I-Five shouted back.

Lorn wanted to protest that it wouldn't make any difference; he had looked into the eyes of the Sith, and he had seen his doom there, as plainly as the tattooed whorls that surrounded those eyes—an implacable fate that would hunt him down no matter how far and how fast he ran. But he had no breath in him to speak, no breath left for running either, but the fear of what he had seen in those eyes kept him running anyway.

Maul saw his quarry slip past him, but could do nothing to stop their flight while his attention was occupied by the two Gamorreans. Using one hand to spin the lightsaber in a blazing pattern that blocked the particle beam bursts, he gestured with his free hand, plucking the invisible lines of the Force and sending reverberations that caused the blasters to fly from the surprised guards' grips.

Before they had time to recover from their surprise, Maul leapt forward, skewering first one and then the other with quick, deadly thrusts. The lifeless Gamorreans sagged to the floor, and Maul wheeled quickly about to deal with the Hutt.

Despite his bulk, Yanth could move quickly when he had to. He slithered off the dais and grabbed up the force pike dropped by the Chevin. He hurled it at Maul, who slashed it in two with a sweep of his own weapon. The generator in the pike's shaft shorted out in a shower of sparks.

Yanth had not waited to see the results of his attack. His massive bulk moved rapidly, slithering through the singed and blackened credit notes that littered the floor, the holocron crystal still clutched in one hand. He had almost reached the exit when Maul leapt, executing a twisting forward flip that covered the length of the large chamber and deposited him directly in front of the Hutt.

Before Yanth could recover from his surprise, Darth Maul plunged one of the lightsaber's blades deep into the Hutt's chest. The stench of burning flesh and blubber filled the room. Yanth died with a croaking gurgle, the gelid mass of his body sagging bonelessly to the floor.

Maul deactivated both blades. He reached out with his free hand, and the holocron leapt from the dead Hutt's grasp into his own. Stuffing it into a belt compartment, he turned and ran from the room. At the top of the stairs he plunged recklessly through the gambling chamber, hurling guests and workers aside with savage Force-laden gestures.

He reached the street and paused, looking first one way, then another for his prey. Pavan and the droid were not in sight. Maul gritted his teeth. They would *not* be permitted to slip away again! One way or another, he was determined to end this chore. It had already gone on far too long.

He sought the dark side once more, bade it illuminate the path his quarry had taken. Then he began to move, shoving his way through the hapless press of street people.

Though his appearance alone was enough to cause most of the hard cases on the street to give him a wide berth, his progress was still too slow. *Enough of this!* Maul thought. He unleashed the dark side, using the Force like a battering ram against those who got in his way.

Maul angled to the middle of the narrow avenue. His speeder bike was parked not far away; he could activate the slave circuit by remote control and have it here within a few minutes at most. But there was an even quicker way to overtake them. He called upon the Force, moving easily five times faster than a human could travel at a dead run. There was no way they could escape him now.

Within moments he was in sight of his quarry. Another few seconds and he would catch up to them—and then the lightsaber would do its work once more, slashing through metal and flesh, and at last bringing this dreary task to an end.

He grinned and lengthened his gargantuan stride even further, sailing over the fire-blackened husk of a parked landspeeder. Pavan and the droid looked back and saw him coming; he could see the fear in the human's face. It was most satisfying to witness.

One more leap, and both of them would be his.

And then an invisible hammer struck him in midleap, pounding him to the ground. What was this? Who *dared* to interfere? Maul looked up, saw a skycar settling to the ground alongside Pavan and the droid. The repulsor beams from its undercarriage had struck him down when the vehicle passed directly over him. The skycar was less than five meters away; he could see the driver and his passenger clearly.

They were Jedi.

Darsha had sensed the disturbance in the Force at the same time as Master Bondara. They had almost reached the cloud level when they felt the dark vibrations from below; they stared at each other simultaneously in shock, and then the Twi'lek put the skycar in a steep dive back down toward the street.

Neither spoke; Darsha wasn't sure how the blast of hatred and destruction reverberating from below had affected her mentor, but she had been left shaken and nauseated by the intensity of the empathic burst. Someone down there was well-versed in the use of the Force and powerful to boot. There had been several deaths already, and more intended, no question about it. She didn't know who had died or who was in danger, but they could not ignore such a strong and savage use of the Force. They had to find out who was responsible, and stop him, her, or it if they could.

Master Bondara leveled off at twenty meters above street level, moving as fast as was prudent through the urban maze. The skycar's headlights illuminated the narrow thoroughfare, and as they rounded a corner they saw, perhaps a hundred meters ahead, the one who had to be responsible for the pulsation they had felt: a tall biped in dark robes, covering ground in a series of gigantic strides that had to be Force-assisted.

Who—or what—could he be? Not a Jedi, that much was certain. He wielded the Force with the surety of a Master, but no Jedi ever gave off such darksome emanations.

There was only one explanation—but even as the thought occurred to her, Darsha felt her mind flinching away from it. It *couldn't* be. It was impossible.

She had no time to wonder about it. Up ahead they could see the two who were the dark one's targets; that much would be obvious from their terror-stricken flight.

The dark one would reach his prey in one more gargantuan leap. Darsha could think of only one way to stop him, and it was evident from the direction in which Master Bondara was taking the skycar that he had thought of the same tactic.

The skycar passed right over the robed figure at a height carefully calculated to deliver a force from the repulsors sufficient to stun but not kill. It worked; as the vehicle lurched and moved on, Darsha looked behind them and saw the mysterious assailant lying in the street, the fuliginous robes a darker blot against the general darkness. Then Master Bondara brought the skycar to a stop near the two fugitives. Darsha noted with surprise that one of them was a droid.

"Get in," Master Bondara said to the human. "He's unconscious, but I don't know how long he'll be—"

"Not long," the droid said, and pointed back toward the pursuer.

Darsha glanced back and saw to her astonishment that the dark one was already rising to his feet. She could scarcely believe he had recovered from the repulsors' hammering so fast.

"Get in!" Master Bondara shouted. "Now!"

The human, who had been staring at Darsha and her mentor with a strange expression—mingled relief and revulsion—seemed to wisely decide that they were by far the lesser of two evils. He vaulted into the skycar's backseat, followed by the droid. Darsha cast another glance behind her and saw the dark one leaping toward them. This close, she could see his face, and a more fearsome visage she could not recall ever having encountered. Then her neck was jerked painfully as Master Bondara hit the ascent control and the skycar rocketed upward.

But not swiftly enough. The vehicle shuddered from a blow delivered to the stern undercarriage, and then lurched to one side. As Master Bondara fought the controls, Darsha saw a black-gloved hand catch the cockpit's rear gunwale.

He must have used the Force to help him jump, she thought, as the skycar was already a good ten meters off the ground. Even as the thought went through her mind, she thrust out both hands in a pushing gesture, hurling an invisible but nonetheless powerful blow concentrated at that hand. It lost its grip, and the craft jerked again as the dark one fell back to the street.

"Let's get back uplevels!" she shouted. But even as the words left her, she saw the look on Master Bondara's face.

"We can't," he said.

Darth Maul's fury at seeing Pavan and his droid snatched from his clutches yet again was almost mitigated by the realization that the Jedi had entered the picture. Finally, a foe that might be worthy of his attention—someone who could truly test his mettle! Shrugging off the effects of the repulsor field, he charged after the rising skycar, igniting his lightsaber and slashing at the drive mechanism that made up part of the vehicle's undercarriage. His blow did some damage—that he could tell by the way the craft pitched to one side. Gathering the Force around him, Maul leapt and managed to seize the gunwale with one hand. Before he could heave himself into the cockpit, however, he felt the younger Jedi strike out at him with considerable power, enough to cause him to lose his hold and plummet back to the street.

He landed lightly, the Force cushioning his fall. Even before his boots touched the ground he had his wrist comm activated and was speaking into it the code command that would activate his speeder bike and bring it homing in on his signal. As he did this, he watched the skycar stabilize and then shoot forward. In the space of a second it had rounded a corner and disappeared from view.

No matter, he told himself as he awaited the speeder bike's arrival; the skycar would be easy enough to track via the Force, especially with the Jedi on board. Pavan and his droid had had more than their share of luck this day. But now their luck had most definitely run out.

"The vertical adjustment on the repulsor array has been damaged," the Jedi piloting the craft said.

"What does that mean?" the woman asked. She was younger than her companion; younger than Lorn, too.

"It means," I-Five said, before the Jedi could answer, "that while we can move laterally and descend, we can't rise above this level."

Lorn glanced over the side. It was hard to estimate their altitude in the pervasive gloom, but it looked to him that they were about twenty meters above the street. The skycar was moving at a fast clip. There was little air traffic at this level, which was fortunate, given the limited room for maneuverability granted by the narrow, twisting streets.

He looked at the Jedi. He was a Twi'lek who appeared to be in his mid to late forties. Lorn could not recall having seen him around the Temple. Of course, that meant nothing; there were plenty of Jedi with whom he had had little or no contact.

The irony of it all would have made him laugh, if it wasn't still so blasted terrifying. To be rescued from the deadly grasp of a Sith by a Jedi! Still, he had to admit it was providential that they had come along when they did. Since it looked like he and I-Five wouldn't be heading offworld any time soon, the Jedi Temple was probably the safest place for them now— though it galled him to admit that, even to himself.

So much had happened within the last few minutes— and practically all of it disastrous—that he hadn't even begun to come to grips with it yet. The Jedi shot around another corner, and Lorn felt inertia press his body against the low-powered tractor field designed to prevent injury in the case of accidents.

"Take it easy!" he said. "There's no way he can catch up with us on foot now."

"He's not on foot," the woman said tensely.

Darth Maul leapt onto the speeder bike as it flashed past him. He wrapped both hands around the acceleration grips on the handlebar and opened them up. The repulsor engine's hum climbed as the speeder shot forward. Maul leaned into the turns as the speeder zoomed around corners.

There was no need to activate the heads-up tracking display. The Jedi and his quarry gleamed like twin beacons in his mind; he could feel them in the skycar ahead of him. The speeder bike was moving at half again their speed. He would overtake them in mere minutes.

Maul grinned savagely. It would be the work of a moment to dispose of Pavan and the droid. Then he would see just how good the Jedi were. It had been far too long since he had felt his lightsaber clash against another, had heard the grating scream of energy blades in conflict, had smelled the ozone tang. Far too long.

*   *   *

"Why is the Sith after you?" Master Bondara shouted over the slipstream's howl.

Though Darsha had come to the same conclusion, it was still shocking on a very deep level to hear Master Bondara articulate her thoughts. She had learned much about the Sith during her studies, of course, but all of the lectures and data seemed unanimous in the conclusion that the ancient dark order was no more. And yet, what else could he be, this creature of the night who even now pursued them? He was adept in the use of the Force, but it was quite obvious he was not a Jedi. That didn't leave a whole lot of choices.

She saw the human and the droid look at each other, and realized they had come to a silent agreement about something. Then the droid spoke.

"We are information brokers," he said, and something—or rather, the absence of something—in the timbre of his voice surprised Darsha. She could hear none of the built-in obsequiousness that droids, particularly those of the protocol series, evidenced as a rule. He had a confidence in his tone and manner that was startling enough for her to notice, even given the duress of the moment.

"I am known as I-Five, and my associate is Lorn Pavan," the droid continued. Darsha saw Master Bondara glance quickly at Pavan, and then return his attention to piloting.

He knows the name, she thought.

"We were recently contacted by a Neimoidian named Hath Monchar, who wished to sell us a holocron containing details of a trade embargo to be imposed on the planet Naboo by the Trade Federation."

Master Bondara said nothing in reply for a moment. Then he asked, "Is this in retaliation for the new tax recently imposed by the Republic Senate on the Trade Federation?"

"Yes," Pavan replied. "The Federation fears the new tax will cut into their profits."

"Naboo is highly dependent on imports to maintain its way of life," Master Bondara said. "Such sanctions could prove devastating to its people." He steered the skycar around another corner. Pedestrians, knowing the potential danger from the repulsor beams of a vehicle traveling this low, scattered left and right. "That doesn't explain why the Sith is trying to kill you," Master Bondara continued.

Darsha admired the Jedi's equanimity; he might have been having this conversation in one of the quiet, comfortable reading chambers of the Temple instead of in a damaged skycar traveling a dangerous route at maximum velocity.

"You can see why the Neimoidians don't want this information to get out," I-Five said. "We're not sure why or how the Sith are involved. But Hath Monchar was killed by the one who's now pursuing us."

"What happened to the holocron?" Darsha asked.

"We were in the process of selling it to a Hutt named Yanth," Pavan replied, "when the Sith broke in. My guess is that the Hutt is dead, and the Sith either destroyed the crystal or has it with him."

"This information must be brought to the council

immediately," Master Bondara said. "You two will be kept safe until the threat of the Sith has been dealt with."

Darsha glanced at Lorn Pavan and saw mingled frustration and resignation in his expression.

"Jedi," he muttered to himself. "Why did it have to be Jedi?"

She looked behind them. Their circuitous route had brought them into a somewhat less dark area of the city now, and she could plainly make out the shape of a speeder bike behind them. Even without the Force to confirm it, she would have been sure that it was the Sith pursuing them.

"Here he comes," she said. "He's gaining fast." She saw that Pavan's face had gone pale, but that he didn't seem to be panicking. Good; the last thing they needed to deal with was another Oolth the Fondorian.

She looked at Master Bondara and saw his jaw muscles clench in determination.

"Take the controls," he told her.

His order surprised her, but his tone of voice brooked no questioning. She slid over as Master Bondara pushed himself up and back, then swung his feet over the back of the padded crossbar separating the front and rear seats. She looked at the rear vidscreen and saw that the Sith was not more than five meters behind her. He drew his lightsaber, activating the twin crimson beams.

"Get them back to the Temple!" Master Bondara shouted at her. Then, before Darsha could even realize what he intended, much less protest or try to stop him, the Jedi stood up on the rear seat between Pavan and

I-Five. He activated his lightsaber, took two steps up onto the rear engine compartment—and leapt from the speeding skycar.

The Twi'lek Jedi's leap, guided by the Force, landed him squarely behind Maul on the rear engine housing of the T-shaped bike. The action took Maul by surprise; he had not expected such a courageous, if foolhardy, deed.

Unexpected as the move was, however, Maul was still able to block the slash of the other's lightsaber with his own energy blade. He quickly activated the speeder's autopilot, then twisted around in the saddle, thrusting his weapon at the Jedi's chest. The Jedi blocked the blow and countered with another.

Maul knew the battle could not continue this way. The speeder bike's autopilot was not sophisticated enough to chart a safe course at high speed through the torturous windings of the surface streets. He grabbed the handlebar and jerked the speeder toward a docking platform on a nearby building, about thirty meters above the street. They shot by the skycar, which had slowed after the Jedi left it, and rose toward the shelf. As the ledge came within range of the autopilot's sensors, the speeder slowed, then settled down to a landing on the extruded slab of ferrocrete.

The Sith and the Jedi leapt from the speeder bike onto the platform to continue their battle. The docking ledge was only about ten meters by fifteen, barely enough room to maneuver in. Maul knew he had to dispatch the Jedi quickly, before Pavan once again vanished into the labyrinth of Coruscant's downlevels. He pressed the attack viciously, blocking and thrusting, the twin radiant blades spinning a web of light about him.

The Jedi was obviously a master of the teräs käsi fighting arts, as well, judging by the smooth way he parried and counterattacked. Still, within the first few moments of the engagement, Darth Maul knew that he himself was the superior fighter. He could tell that the Jedi knew it, too, but Maul also knew that it didn't matter. The Jedi was committed to stopping the Sith, or at the very least slowing him down enough to let the others get away, even if it meant giving his own life to do so.

Maul bared his teeth. He would *not* lose his quarry again! He doubled his efforts, pressing the attack hard, hammering away at the Twi'lek's defenses. The Jedi gave ground, but Maul was still unable to slash through his guard.

Then he heard something: the distinctive sound of the skycar's damaged engine. He let his awareness expand on the ripples of the Force, and what he sensed brought a dark smile of satisfaction to his face.

The skycar—with his prey—was returning.

*   *   *

Darsha could not believe it at first when Master Bondara leapt from the skycar onto the Sith's speeder bike. Her first action was reflexive; she slowed the skycar, intending to go to her mentor's aid.

"What are you doing?" Pavan shouted. "He said head for the Temple!"

"I'm not going to abandon him to that monster!" Darsha shouted back. She saw the speeder bike shoot past them, then rise and head for a docking ledge that protruded from a dilapidated building.

"He knows what he's doing," the droid told her. "Are you prepared to make his sacrifice meaningless?"

Darsha knew the droid's words made sense, but she didn't care. After all, she had made one mistake after another in the past several hours; why stop now? She had gone far past the point of worrying about the consequences of her actions; all she knew was that she could not leave Master Bondara to battle the Sith alone. It was hard for her to conceive of a situation in which her mentor could be bested in combat, but if anyone was capable of it, she had the feeling the Sith was that one.

She slowed the skycar and brought it around, heading back toward the landing ledge—and realized she had a problem. The damaged repulsor array had fixed the vehicle's ceiling, and the platform was a good ten meters above them. Her ascension gun was still, as far as she knew, attached to the monad, nearly a kilometer from her present position.

It would be no problem to leap ten meters straight up; in training exercises she had used the Force to help her perform jumps higher than that. To assay such a leap onto a narrow platform and into the midst of a raging lightsaber duel was a considerably more complex undertaking, however. It would do Master Bondara no good for her to get herself killed by the Sith.

Still, there was no other choice. Her mentor might sense the skycar's presence and leap back into it, but there was no guarantee he would be able to do so in the heat of battle. Darsha brought the skycar to a hovering stop below and to one side of the ledge. Above her, the two dueling figures were hidden by the ferrocrete slab, but she could see the variegated flashes and hear the angry buzzing and screeching of the lightsabers as they clashed. She had to take action, now. She stood, pulled her lightsaber from its belt hook, and prepared to leap.

And the world suddenly dissolved in a burst of blinding light and a deafening roar.

Darth Maul had seen the grim realization in the eyes of his foe: the knowledge that the Twi'lek could not defeat his adversary. Once defeat was conceded in the mind, its reality was inevitable. It was only a matter of time.

He pressed his attack to an even higher intensity, driving the Jedi back toward his speeder bike, intending to pin him between the dual-bladed lightsaber and the bike. With his movements thus constricted, it would be mere moments before the Twi'lek's tentacled head was separated from his neck.

But then he saw the desperation in the other's face suddenly give way to realization, and then to triumph. Quickly, before Maul could intuit what was intended, the Jedi whirled toward the speeder bike, raised his lightsaber—and plunged it to the hilt into the bike's repulsor drive housing.

Maul realized his suicidal intention, but too late. The superheated energy blade melted with lightning swiftness through the housing and sank into the bike's power cell core. Maul turned and leapt from the platform, reaching for the dark side, enfolding himself in it even as the power cell exploded, the heat and pressure wave vaporizing the Jedi in a microsecond and then expanding, reaching hungrily for him, as well.

The landing platform shielded the skycar from the main force of the explosion; otherwise the three passengers would not have survived. Even so, the shock wave hurled Darsha from her standing position back over the rear of the craft. She would have plunged to the street below had Lorn not grabbed her wrist as she fell past him. I-Five lunged for the controls and fought to stabilize the vehicle, which was pitching and yawing wildly. For an instant that felt like an eternity Darsha hung over the abyss, too stunned to use the Force to help lift herself to safety—and then Lorn managed to pull her back into the rear seat compartment.

But the danger was not yet over; the explosion had caused the platform to break free of its supports. It began to collapse, sagging away from the building wall. As it did so, Darsha caught a glimpse of the Sith's dark form hurtling from the ledge into the darkness below. The buckling platform clipped the skycar's side, sending it spinning out of control toward the street, as well.

I-Five fought with the controls and managed to level out as the vehicle reached the ground. The spectators drawn to the scene by the explosion scattered in panic as the skycar pancaked to a rough landing.

Darsha, half-stunned, was vaguely aware of an insistent beeping that was rising in frequency and tone. Even as realization of what the beeping signified penetrated her dazed brain, she felt herself seized in a powerful grip and pulled from the wrecked skycar. As she stumbled across the litter-strewn pavement she realized the droid was dragging her and Lorn Pavan away from the vehicle.

"Hurry," she mumbled. "Power cell's on overload . . ."

"A fact of which I am quite aware," I-Five replied. He stopped before a kiosk. A sign on the door read KEEP OUT in Basic, but the droid ignored this and blasted the lock with a laser beam that shot from his left index finger.

Within the kiosk was a narrow, dimly lit stairwell. The three of them hurried down it as, behind them, the alarm beeps reached a crescendo. A moment later a second, more powerful explosion rocked the area. Darsha felt the stairwell shift and shudder as if in the throes of a temblor. The light went out, she felt herself falling—and then she knew no more.

PART II
LABYRINTH

Nute Gunray was in his suite on board the *Saak'ak*, trying to enjoy a mildew rubdown and failing utterly, when his private comlink chimed. His masseuse had slathered his naked form with liquefied green mold and was industriously kneading the muscle nodules of his upper back, which were so tight with tension that he could hear them crackle.

At his grunted acknowledgment, the image of Rune Haako formed near the massage table. The barrister did not look happy, but that in itself meant little; Neimoidians as a species rarely looked happy.

"I have news," Haako said in a low voice.

"Come to my quarters," Gunray replied, and the holoimage flickered out.

Whatever news Haako had for him was best heard in person, in the privacy of his sanctum. Even though there was supposedly no one on board the freighter who was not loyal to him and his cause, the viceroy was taking no chances. He knew very well just how easily the allegiance of his cohorts and underlings could be bought.

He dismissed the masseuse, donned a vermilion robe, and paced restlessly, awaiting Haako's arrival. The intricacies of protocol dictated that he be sitting at ease in a couch or chair, his nonchalant attitude conveying the impression that, no matter what news Haako might be bearing, it could not possibly be important enough to cause him any concern. But he was beyond caring about such formalities at this point. There had been no word for nearly forty-eight hours from the bounty hunter they had engaged, and no news of Hath Monchar's whereabouts or plans. At any moment he expected to see the holographic presence of Darth Sidious materialize again before him, demanding that he once more assemble his gang of four to continue discussions concerning the Naboo blockade. And what would happen when Gunray was still not able to account for Monchar's absence? He winced as the mere thought of such a conversation with Sidious caused his gut sac to fill with acidic bile. He knew he was building a world-class ulcer in his lower abdomen, but there didn't seem to be much he could do to stop it.

The door panel slid open, and Haako entered. A moment later Daultay Dofine entered, as well. Gunray steeled himself; one look at his compatriots' hunched postures and furtive miens assured him that he was not about to hear good news.

"I have just heard from the consular representative at our embassy on Coruscant," Haako said. His willingness to skip the preamble of verbal fencing and get right to the subject was ample evidence that his concern was just as great as Gunray's. "One of our people has been killed there."

Gunray had to will his salivary glands to moisten his palate before he was able to speak. "Was it Monchar?"

"At this point, we don't know for certain," Dofine said. "There was evidently an explosion, although the investigation is unclear as to whether that was the cause of death. Genetic ID verification is pending."

"However," Haako continued, lowering his voice and peering about as if he expected Darth Sidious to appear at any moment, "a piece of singed cloth that was once part of a miter of the office of deputy viceroy was found at the scene."

Nute Gunray closed his eyes and tried to imagine what life as a mulch farmer back on Neimoidia would be like.

"In addition," Dofine said, "several other bodies were discovered at the scene of the explosion. One has been conclusively identified: the bounty hunter Mahwi Lihnn."

Mulch farming probably had its good points, Gunray told himself. For one thing, the possibility of having to deal with the Sith in his new occupation was very unlikely.

"I think we must admit the conclusion that Hath Monchar is no longer among the living," Rune Haako said. He began to wring his hands as though he was twisting the life out of a swamp toad he planned to have for a snack.

"This is a disaster," Dofine whined. "What will we tell Lord Sidious?"

What indeed? the viceroy of the Federation wondered. Oh, there was no shortage of lies that they could come up with—but would Sidious believe any of them? That was the all-important question. And the answer, much as Gunray hated to admit it, was, almost certainly not. The Sith Lord's cowled face rose unbidden before his mental vision, and he could not help but shudder. Those eyes, hidden deep in that hooded cloak, could penetrate subterfuge and dissimulation as easily as X rays penetrated flesh and illuminated the bones within for all to see.

But what other option was there? Though the thought of doing so galled him on a very fundamental level, Gunray knew that they could simply admit the truth: that Monchar had absconded, to where and for what reason they did not know—although anyone with the brains of an oxygen-starved Gamorrean could extrapolate *that* fairly quickly. But the truth had its own built-in hazards, chief among which was the fact that it had not been presented when Sidious first noticed Monchar's absence.

Veracity and prevarication seemed equally dangerous here. It was a Neimoidian's worst nightmare: a situation from which it was impossible to worm one's way out. Gunray looked down and saw that he was wringing his own hands every bit as industriously as were Rune Haako and Daultay Dofine.

Only one thing was certain. Soon—very soon—they would have to tell the Sith Lord *something*.

*   *   *

Jedi Master Yoda entered the conference ante-chamber, a smaller room off to one side of the Council Chamber. Mace Windu and Qui-Gon Jinn were already seated at the pleekwood table. Behind them a floor-to-ceiling transparisteel window offered a panoramic view of the endless architectural welter that was Coruscant and its continuous streams of air traffic.

Yoda moved slowly toward one of the chairs. He leaned on his gimer-stick cane as he walked, and Windu had to suppress a smile as he watched Yoda's progress. While Yoda was easily the oldest member of the council, being well over 800 standard years of age, he was by no means as decrepit as he sometimes pretended to be. Though it was true that he had slowed slightly in the years that Windu had known him, Yoda's skill with a lightsaber was still second to none on the council.

Windu waited until his colleague was seated before he spoke. "I have not deemed it necessary to call a general meeting of the council concerning this yet," he said. "Nevertheless, it is a problem that in my opinion warrants discussion."

Yoda nodded. "Of the Black Sun matter you speak."

"Yes—specifically of Oolth the Fondorian, and the Padawan Darsha Assant, who was sent to bring him here."

"Has there been any word at all from her?" Qui-Gon Jinn asked.

"None. It has been almost forty-eight hours. The mission should not have taken more than four or five at the most."

"Anoon Bondara is missing, as well," Yoda said reflectively. "Coincidence I doubt it is."

"You think Bondara has gone in search of Assant?" Windu asked. Yoda nodded.

"Understandable," Jinn said. "Assant is his Padawan. If he felt she was in danger, he would look into it."

"Of course he would," Windu replied. "But why did he not inform any of us as to his intentions? And why has there been no communication from either of them?"

There was silence for a moment as the three Jedi Masters pondered the questions. Then Yoda said, "Some infraction on her part, perhaps he knew or suspected. Want to protect her from repercussions, he would."

Jinn nodded. "Anoon has always been one to chafe at rules and restrictions."

Mace Windu glanced at Jinn and raised an eyebrow. Jinn smiled slightly and shrugged.

"This makes sense to me," Windu said. "It feels right. But, however noble Anoon Bondara's intentions, we cannot have him and Assant acting without the knowledge or consent of the council."

"Agreed we are on this matter," Yoda said. "Send an investigator we must."

"Yes," Windu said. "But who? With the current state of affairs in the Republic Senate, all our senior members are on standby alert, and may continue to be for some time."

"I have a suggestion," Qui-Gon Jinn said. "Dispatch my Padawan. If Black Sun is involved, he will be able to sense it."

"Obi-Wan Kenobi? Potentially strong in the Force he is," Yoda mused. "A good choice he would be."

Mace Windu nodded slowly. Yoda was right. Though not yet a full-fledged Jedi Knight, Kenobi had amply demonstrated his skills in battle and in negotiation. If anyone could find out what had happened to Bondara and Assant, he could.

The senior member of the council stood. "We are decided, then. Qui-Gon, you will explain the situation to Kenobi and send him on his way as soon as possible. There is something about all this . . ." Windu was silent for a moment.

"Yes," Yoda said soberly. "No accident this was."

Qui-Gon Jinn said nothing; he merely nodded his agreement, then stood. "Obi-Wan will leave for the Crimson Corridor immediately," he told Windu and Yoda.

"May the Force be with him," Yoda said softly.

There is no emotion; there is peace.
There is no ignorance; there is knowledge.
There is no passion; there is serenity.
There is no death; there is the Force.

The Jedi Code was one of the first things Darsha Assant had learned in the Jedi Temple. As a child, she would sit cross-legged on the cold floor for hours at a time, repeating the words over and over, meditating on their meaning, letting that meaning seep into her bones.

There is no emotion; there is peace.

Master Bondara had taught her that this did not mean one should repress one's emotions. "One of the few things that all intelligent species in the galaxy share is the ability to have feelings. We are creatures of emotion, and to deny those emotions is profoundly unhealthy. But one can feel anger, for example, without being controlled by it. One can grieve without being crippled by grief. The peace of the Force is the foundation upon which the structures of our feelings are built."

There is no ignorance; there is knowledge.

"Chance," the Twi'lek Jedi had told her, "favors the prepared mind." Certainly the Jedi were among the most prepared in the galaxy as far as that went. She had never seen anyone as awesomely well-educated as Masters Windu, Bondara, Yoda, Jinn, and the many others she had studied under or otherwise come in contact with. She had doubted her ability to hold her own in conversations with them, or even with her fellow Padawans like Obi-Wan and Bant. So she had studied assiduously, almost obsessively, taking advantage of the incredible wealth of wisdom and lore available in the Temple's libraries and data banks. And she had found that the more she knew, the more she wanted to know. Knowledge was as addictive in its own way as glitterstim.

There is no passion; there is serenity.

At first she had thought this was merely a restating of the code's first precept. But Master Bondara had explained the difference. Passion, in this context, meant obsession, compulsion, an overweening fixation on something or someone. And serenity was not merely a synonym for peace; rather, it was the state of tranquility that could be reached when one was able to let go of such fixations, when one could be at peace with one's emotions and had replaced ignorance with knowledge.

Master Bondara had taught her so many things, had helped her forge her life into something far beyond anything she had thought it was her potential and destiny to be. She owed him so much, and now she would never be able to repay him.

There is no death; there is the Force.

Darsha knew that if she had truly internalized the first three maxims of the Jedi Code, she would be able to take comfort from this last one, as well. But it was obvious that she had not reached that stage yet. Because she could find no peace, no serenity, in the knowledge that her mentor was dead.

All she could do was grieve.

She had been in a state of half awareness, her only real emotion that of sorrow, for an unknown amount of time before she was jolted back to consciousness by a building vibration and roar that seemed to be hurtling toward her. She opened her eyes in time to see a huge transport vehicle thunder by, only a meter or so from where she lay. The sound of its passing was deafening; then it was gone, the roar dopplering swiftly away to silence.

Or rather, relative silence; there was an omnipresent background drone of machinery and ventilation equipment. She looked around, saw Lorn Pavan seated against a wall about a meter away, and I-Five standing next to him. They were in a large tunnel, dimly illuminated by photonic wall sconces set at wide intervals.

She realized where they were—in one of the countless service conduits that stitched Coruscant's lowest levels, like the skein of blood vessels under living skin. Through these tunnels flowed an endless automated stream of vehicles hauling goods and materials from spaceports and factories to millions of destinations all over the planetwide metropolis.

"How did we get down here?" she asked. Even as the question left her lips she dimly recalled being dragged from the wreckage of the skycar and down the stairwell by the droid as the craft's power cell exploded. He had undoubtedly saved both of their lives.

Pavan jerked a thumb at I-Five. "Thank Wonder Droid here," he said. "Hadn't been for him, we'd both be hash for the armored rats. Sometimes he's almost worth having around."

"Please, don't gush," the droid said. "It's embarrassing."

Darsha struggled to her feet. The planet skewed nastily on its axis for a moment, and the lights dimmed even more than they already were, but then things steadied again. She checked for her lightsaber and was relieved to find it hanging where it should be from her utility belt.

"Where's the stairwell?" she asked. "I have to see if . . ." *If Master Bondara is still alive,* she finished to herself. She could not bring herself to say it out loud, for fear that one of them might tell her what she already knew.

Pavan pointed to an alcove about two meters away. "But the stairwell won't do you any good. The skycar's explosion brought about a ton of real estate down on it. We'll have to find another way out."

Darsha nodded. "Then we'd better get going. There has to be another access stairwell along this route."

"Why not just call for help?" Pavan asked. "You've got a comlink, haven't you?"

"I had one, but it was damaged earlier." It occurred to her only now that she should have replaced it when she had been back at the Temple.

Pavan raised an eyebrow. "First time I've seen a Jedi who wasn't prepared for everything." There was a faint note of sarcasm in his voice.

Darsha bit back the retort that rose to her lips. It wouldn't take much to put him on her list of least favorite people; after all, he was indirectly responsible for Master Bondara's death. On the other hand, he had saved her from falling out of the skycar. "Don't *you* have a comlink?" she asked.

Pavan looked uncomfortable and didn't reply.

"Yes, he does," I-Five said. "It's in fine working order, too—except that the power pack is depleted and he can't afford to replace it."

Darsha said nothing to that; her silence was ample indication of how she felt.

Pavan stood up. "Might as well get moving," he said, "before another—"

His words were drowned out by the passage of another transport. They shrank back against the curved wall of the tunnel as it hurtled by them. The automated conveyances were sleek, massive bullets that all but filled the shaft, moving in excess of a hundred kilometers an hour, propelled by repulsor drives.

As it disappeared into the distance Darsha said, "Let's hurry. We'll be deaf inside of an hour if we stay here."

They moved quickly, single file, down the narrow

sidewalk. It didn't matter which direction they went at this point; the goal was just to get out of the transport tube as fast as possible. The droid led the way, as his photoreceptors were best able to adjust to the dim light.

They saw another recessed doorway ahead as the rumbling approach of a third transport began to build behind them. The door was locked, but I-Five's finger blaster quickly removed that obstacle, and they hurried through it just as the freight vehicle blasted by.

Other than the fact that there were now no convoys thundering past, their new location was not much of an improvement. The transport tube had at least been reasonably clean and lit. Best of all, while it hadn't led back to the surface, it had remained horizontal.

Now, however, they found themselves in another stairwell, only this one led down rather than up. There seemed to be little choice but to follow it. There were no lights; the only illumination came from a phosphorescent lichenlike growth on the walls, and this light was barely enough to let them see each other and the next few steps. The ferrocrete walls wept with a slimy discharge, and there was a faint scent of decay in the air.

At last they reached the bottom of the stairwell, which opened into a small chamber lit by one flickering photonic sconce. In the wall opposite the stairwell were openings to three branching tunnels. Signs mounted above each one supposedly gave directions, but they had been reduced to illegibility by successive layers of graffiti.

"My locator was in my comlink," Darsha said. "I have no idea which way to go."

"Fortunately, I have a built-in global positioner," I-Five said. "To orient ourselves toward the Jedi Temple, we would be best served by taking that one." He pointed to the leftmost tunnel.

"That's a good argument for taking the right-hand tunnel," Pavan muttered. Darsha looked at him; he met her eyes for a moment and then looked away.

"I'm trying to get you back to a safe haven," she told him. "If you'd rather take your chances with our friend up there, that's fine with me. I can tell the council about the impending blockade as easily as you can."

He turned back to look at her again. "Hey, the Sith was probably vaporized along with your Jedi buddy," he said. "And good riddance to both of 'em."

Darsha felt herself go cold with anger. Without taking her gaze away from his, she said, "I-Five, what do you think the chances are that the Sith's dead?"

"Given the fact that, in our brief peripheral acquaintance with him, he has already survived several attempts on his life and killed quite a few beings, as well, I wouldn't count him out until I saw his dead body," the droid said. "And even then I'd want him frozen in carbonite just to make sure."

Darsha nodded. "I agree. But you're entitled to your opinion, Pavan. Maybe it'll be safer if we all go our separate ways; after all, *you* seem to be the one he's looking for."

Even as she said this, she realized it was a mistake. She didn't need to see the look that passed between the droid and Pavan to know that she couldn't play one off against the other. Whatever bond they had was strong enough to unite them, even in a situation like this.

I-Five said to Pavan, "She's right about you being the primary target. Sanctuary from the Jedi may be your only option. Are you willing to accept that?"

"Of course," Pavan replied with a scowl. "I'm not stupid. But that doesn't mean I have to be happy about the situation."

"True," Darsha said. "But you could at least try being congenial. If we're going to be stuck with each other for a while, we might as well try to make it pleasant." She turned to face the left-hand tunnel, took a few steps toward it, then turned back to him and added, "Anoon Bondara died saving your life. I don't want to hear any more disparaging remarks about him."

Neither Pavan nor I-Five made any reply to that as she started down the tunnel. After she had taken a few steps they fell in behind her.

There is no emotion; there is peace. Well, maybe someday. After all, she wasn't a full-fledged Jedi yet, and the way things were going, it didn't look like she ever would be. But some truths you didn't need the Force to see. Like the fact that one Anoon Bondara was worth a fleet of Lorn Pavans.

18

Lorn didn't like the Jedi Padawan. This fact would hardly be surprising to anyone who knew him even casually—which was how pretty much everybody knew him, these days—as he was not reticent about his feelings when the subject of the Jedi Knights arose. He had stated on more than one occasion to anyone who would listen that he considered them on a par with mynocks in terms of parasitic opportunism, and a notch or two beneath those energy-sucking space bats on the general scale of galactic evolution.

"Shooting's too good for them," he once told I-Five. "In fact, dumping them all in a Sarlacc's pit to marinate in gastric juices for a thousand years is too good for them, but it'll do until something worse comes along."

He had never told anyone why he felt this way. In his present circle of acquaintances only I-Five knew, and the droid would never divulge the secret of Lorn's bitterness to anyone.

And now, thanks to a truly ironic twist of fate, here he was almost literally stun-cuffed to a Jedi and dependent on her to save him from the murderous intentions of a Sith—a member of an order sprung from the Jedi millennia ago. It seemed that, no matter which way he turned, the self-styled galactic guardians were there to complete the ruination of his life that they had started.

Lorn felt the bitterness growing within his breast as he trudged along through the subterranean tunnel following I-Five and Darsha Assant. It certainly hadn't taken her long at all to settle into that sanctimonious holier-than-thou attitude that he despised so much. They were all alike, with their sackcloth fashion sense and their austere asceticism, mouthing empty platitudes about the greater good. He much preferred dealing with the street scum; they at least were villains without the taint of hypocrisy.

Lorn was under no illusions about the treatment he would receive when he once again entered the Jedi Temple. Forget about any sort of reward; he and I-Five would be lucky to get protection against the Sith while the council debated how they could best make use of this windfall of information. He had no doubt that they would find a way to make it serve their purposes, as they were able to do with everything they came in contact with.

Everything and *everyone*.

This underground passage they were traveling was no more dark and torturous than the labyrinth of his memories and hatred. He wondered for the dozenth time why he hadn't just let Assant fall when the speeder bike explosion had hurled her from the sky-car. He couldn't even excuse it on the grounds that he had needed her to pilot the vehicle; I-Five was perfectly capable of that. No, it had been that most pernicious of impulses, one that Lorn thought he'd managed to eradicate within himself long ago: a humanitarian motive.

The memory of what he had done bothered him immensely. He had made it a policy during the last five years to stick his neck out for nobody, with the exception of I-Five. The mordant droid was the closest thing to a friend that he had. What made him such a good friend, in Lorn's opinion, was very simple: he asked for nothing back. Which was good, because Lorn had nothing to give. Everything that had made him human had been taken from him five years ago. In a very real way, he realized, he was no more human than the droid who was his companion.

He forced his thoughts away from memories; he knew of no more certain way to plunge himself into a black depression. This he could not afford to do; he had to keep his wits about him if he was going to get out of this situation alive. He couldn't count on the Jedi for help; he trusted them about as far as he could throw a ronto. He refocused his attention, not without some effort.

The weak glow of the ancient photonic sconces had petered out about half a kilometer back. The only light source they had now was the droid's illuminated photoreceptors, which were capable of casting twin bright beams as strong as vehicle headlights. They revealed what was directly before or behind them, depending on where I-Five turned his head, but from all other sides the darkness pressed in avidly. Lorn was becoming claustrophobic. It wasn't just the pervasive gloom; he could *feel* the incalculable weight of the structures overhead pressing down on him. Coruscant was a tectonically stable planet—that and its location had been the main reasons for it having been chosen the galactic capital—but even though there had not been a major quake anywhere on it for thousands of years, he found himself vividly imagining his probable fate should one occur while he was wandering around in the bowels of the planet.

It was hard to tell in the gloomy murk, but judging by the echoes of their footsteps, the tunnel seemed to be widening out somewhat. For the last couple of hundred meters they had been passing what seemed to be branching passageways—nothing more than clots of darkness in the walls—and Lorn's imagination had no problem supplying those side tunnels with all kinds of nasty inhabitants. Armored rats the size of skycars was one image he could happily have done without. Life on the upper levels of Coruscant was a joy to experience, because such problems as environmental pollution had been largely eradicated centuries before. But there was always a price to be paid for the benefits of technology, and while the upper levels didn't have to pay it, the lower levels did. Down here below the planet's city scape it was one huge, pulsing malignancy of industrial waste and carcinogenic chemicals. The more sensational news programs on the HoloNet were always full of stories about dangerous mutations being found in the sewers and drainage systems—stories that, at the moment, Lorn had no problem whatsoever believing. He was sure he could hear ominous slithering sounds from either side, the slow step-and-drag of some murderous bipedal beast following them, the stealthy breathing of something huge and hungry about to pounce. *Stop it,* he told himself sternly. *It's nothing but your imagination.*

"Did you hear that?" Assant asked.

The three stopped. I-Five probed the darkness in various directions with his eye beams, which revealed nothing more than ancient, moss-covered walls. "My audioreceptors are set at maximum. I hear nothing that might indicate danger. In addition, my radar detects no movement in the vicinity."

"Maybe you've got radar," Assant said, "but I've got the Force, and right now it's telling me that we're not alone."

"Impossible," Lorn said. The Jedi were always playing the Force as a hole card, using it as an excuse to justify all kinds of actions and opinions. Not that Lorn had any doubt that the Force existed and could be manipulated by them; he'd seen too many examples of it. But he felt that their use of it was largely just another way to justify questionable actions.

He continued, "You think something that lives down here could have access to a radar jammer?" He was about to enumerate several sarcastic reasons why this was a ludicrous idea when something whistled out of the darkness and struck him in the head, and he lost interest in the conversation for a while.

Darsha jerked her lightsaber from its clip and activated it. She had no idea what sort of threat was impending, but whatever it was, it was all around them. She and the droid positioned themselves back-to-back, with Pavan's unconscious form lying between them. I-Five had both hands up, the index fingers extended, like a child pretending to point a pair of blasters. He swiveled his head slowly through 360 degrees, illuminating their surroundings. There was a branch corridor on their left and two more on their right. Nothing moved. There was no indication of where the weapon that had laid Pavan low had come from. It was a curved throwing stick; she could see it lying on the floor at her feet.

"We're too exposed here," she said in a low voice. "Pick up your friend and let's at least get our backs against a wall."

The droid did not answer. Keeping his left finger blaster extended, he reached down with the other arm and hooked it around Pavan's waist, lifting the unconscious human as easily as Darsha might lift a small child. They began to move cautiously toward the nearest wall.

The attack came from the one direction they had not expected: above.

Without warning, a net of fine mesh dropped down on them. Darsha sensed it settling from overhead and slashed at it, only to have the lightsaber's blade screech and emit a shower of sparks. She realized too late that the net was charged with some kind of power field. She felt a bolt of energy slam through her, and then for the second time in as many hours darkness engulfed her.

19

Discipline.

Discipline is all. It conquers pain. It conquers fear. Most important of all, it conquers failure.

Discipline is what allowed Darth Maul to survive a thirty-meter fall into a pile of rubble and debris: the discipline of his teräs käsi fighting skills, which gave him complete control over his body, allowing him to utilize midair acrobatics to direct his fall and so avoid striking ornamental projections, ledges, and other potentially lethal obstructions; the discipline of the dark side, which let him manipulate gravity itself, slowing his descent enough to hit the ground without becoming a lifeless bag of broken bones and ruptured organs. Even half stunned by the unexpected explosion of his speeder bike, Maul was able to aim his falling body in such a way as to survive.

But even someone in as superb shape as Maul could not come out of such an explosion and a fall completely unscathed. After the impact he lay, semiconscious, in the debris, remotely aware of a second explosion some distance away as the skycar blew up.

He lay there, and he remembered.

There is no pain where strength lies.

To Darth Maul, it seemed that his master had always been there, a part of his life—implacable, indomitable, inexorable. Since before Maul learned to walk, discipline had been his guiding beacon. Darth Sidious had molded him from a weak, puling child into the ultimate warrior, sculpting his body and his mind as a seamless weapon. Maul was willing to die for him, without question and without hesitation. Lord Sidious's goals were the goals of the Sith, and they would be achieved, no matter what the cost.

Maul's entire existence had consisted of training, of exercise and instruction. Early in his life, before his voice had deepened, Maul had learned the intricate movements and forms of the teräs käsi fighting style, the patterns of movements based on the hunting characteristics of various beasts throughout the galaxy: Charging Wampa, Rancor Rising, Dancing Dragonsnake, and many more. He had practiced gymnastics in environments ranging from zero-g to gravity fields twice that of Coruscant's. He had mastered the intricate and dangerous use of the double-bladed lightsaber. And all for one purpose: to be the best possible tool of his master's will.

But he had not learned just how to fight. His master's teaching had encompassed far more than that. He had also learned stealth, subterfuge, intrigue.

What is done in secret has great power.

One of his earliest memories was that of being taken to the Jedi Temple. Both he and Sidious had been disguised as tourists. His master's command of the dark side had been sufficient to cloak them from being sensed by their enemies, as long as they did not enter the building. That had been unlikely anyway— the Jedi Temple was not open for tourism. They had stood there for the better part of the day, Darth Sidious pointing out to him the various faces of their foes as the latter came and went. It had been thrilling to Maul to realize that he could stand in the presence of the Jedi, could listen to his master whisper to him of their ultimate downfall, without them having any inkling of the fate that ultimately awaited them.

That was the great glory and hidden strength of the Sith: the fact that there were only two, master and apprentice. Their clandestine operations could take place practically under the very noses of the Jedi, and the fools would not suspect until it was too late. The day of the Jedi's downfall would be soon—very soon.

It could not happen soon enough for him.

Anger is a living thing. Feed it and it will grow.

The Twi'lek he had fought had not been the first Jedi he had crossed lightsabers with, but he was not far from having that honor. It had been exhilarating to know that he, Darth Maul, was better in combat than his hated foes. He longed to battle one of the truly great Jedi warriors: Plo Koon, perhaps, or Mace Windu. That would be a true test of his skill. And he had no doubt that such an opportunity would come to him.

His hatred of the Jedi was strong enough that it alone would bring such a confrontation into existence.

Soon.

He came to his senses, realizing he was lying in a pile of trash not far from where the Jedi had engineered his own doom and nearly that of Maul's, as well. A Devaronian scavenger was about to appropriate his lightsaber, which lay nearby. Maul glared at the encroacher, who lost no time in making himself scarce.

Maul seized his lightsaber and rose to his feet. His muscles, bones, and tendons screamed in pain, but pain meant nothing. The only important question was, was his mission finally complete?

A hundred meters down the street lay the wrecked remains of the skycar. Maul investigated it. It had been smashed beneath large chunks of ferrocrete and durasteel that would take too long to move, even with the aid of the Force. He opened his senses, trying to determine if his enemies' bodies lay beneath the rubble. What the Force told him made him clench a fist in fury.

The skycar was empty.

It was possible that the explosion had flung them clear before the debris collapsed. If so, their bodies might have been dragged away by those who scrounged the streets. But he wasn't certain that was what had happened. Given the kind of luck the Corellian had had so far, Maul knew he would have to see Pavan's dead body—preferably after his head had parted company with his shoulders, thanks to Maul's lightsaber—before he would feel comfortable reporting to Lord Sidious that the problem was at last resolved.

Maul was actually starting to feel something of a grudging respect for this Lorn Pavan. Although some of the hustler's continued avoidance of his fate could be ascribed to luck, some, the Sith apprentice had to admit, was due to Pavan's survival instincts. Of course, he would not have lasted as long as he had downlevels if he had not had a roachlike ability to sense and avoid danger. Nevertheless, Maul was slightly impressed. Not that it mattered. His quarry's skill at staying alive would just make Maul's inevitable triumph all the more satisfying.

He began to search the area, questing along the filaments of the dark side, seeking the route they had taken. He saw the kiosk almost immediately. Even without the Force to guide him to it, he knew this could be the only logical escape route. Unfortunately, the skycar's explosion had covered the underground entrance with debris.

Maul was running out of patience. Five meters farther up the street he spied a ventilation grid that appeared to open onto the same underground conduit as the kiosk. He lit one end of his lightsaber and jabbed it into the grid. The blade sliced easily through the metal slats. In a second the grate had dropped down into the conduit, and Darth Maul followed it.

He landed lightly. The entire tunnel was shaking as with the roar of some titanic beast. Maul looked up to see a driverless freight transport bearing down on him at better than one hundred kilometers an hour.

Anyone else, even a trained athlete raised in a heavier

gravity field, would have been crushed to paste. But Maul seized the Force, let it whip him up and to the side as if he were attached to a giant elastic band. The metal behemoth missed him by millimeters.

Maul found himself standing on the narrow lip of a walkway that ran along one side of the conduit. He looked about, questing with his eyes and his mind. Yes—they had escaped down here. The trail still remained.

They could run, but they couldn't hide.

Darth Maul resumed the hunt.

Lorn's first thought as he returned to partial consciousness was to wonder why someone had gone to the trouble to kidnap him off Coruscant and drop him on one of the galaxy's gas giant worlds—Yavin, possibly. Obviously this was what had happened, because gravity and atmospheric pressure were slowly crushing him into a boneless putty. His head, particularly. And whatever it was that he was breathing, it wasn't anything close to a comfortable oxygen-nitrogen mixture.

Or maybe he'd been parked in a too-close orbit around the event horizon of a black hole, and the tidal forces were pulling him apart. That would explain why his head hurt so abominably, and why he couldn't feel his hands and feet.

Lorn blinked, then saw dim light the color of verdigris. He realized he was lying on a cold stone floor, his arms and legs bound. The light, faint and sickly though it was, was still too much for his headache to deal with. *Must've* really *tied one on this time*, he thought. *Maybe I-Five's right about those liver cells, not that I'd ever admit it to him.*

But something was still wrong with this picture. He knew he could be a fairly obstreperous drunk on occasion, but he'd never reached the point of obnoxiousness where he'd had to be trussed up. Hmm. Maybe he'd better open just one eye again—carefully, of course—and take another look around.

Staring at him from no more than a handbreadth away was a face unimagined in his worst nightmares.

Lorn gasped and instinctively jerked backwards, trying to get away from the monstrous apparition. The sudden movement set off a thermal detonator that someone had unkindly implanted in his skull, and the pain was so amazingly intense that for a moment he forgot about the *thing* that had been inspecting him.

But only for a moment.

It moved closer to him, staring at him—no, Lorn corrected himself, not staring: you had to have eyes to stare. Just about every component of its face was repulsive in the extreme, but the eyes were unquestionably the worst. Worse than the dead bluish-white skin and the stringy, mosslike hair, worse than the wide lipless gash of a mouth, like a cavern entrance filled with yellowed stalagmites and stalactites, worse even than the skull-like nub of a nose, with two vertical slits for nostrils.

The eyes were definitely worse than all that.

Because it didn't seem to have any. From the heavy ridges at the sloping base of the forehead down to the gaunt cheekbones, there was nothing but albino skin. Behind that skin, where the orbital sockets should have been, Lorn could see two egg-shaped organs moving restlessly, swiveling independently of one another. Occasionally they were occluded by darker hues, as if membranes beneath the skin were sliding over them.

Lorn had dealt with a large variety of alien species in the past few years. One grew used to seeing all kinds of creatures on the streets and skywalks of Coruscant. But something was terribly, obscenely *wrong* about this monster's appearance—him and the others like him, for now that Lorn's eyes had adjusted to the wan light, he saw that there were at least a dozen, maybe more, hunkered down in a semicircle around him.

He backed up still farther, scrabbling on his heels and elbows—not an easy task considering that his head still felt large enough to warrant its own orbit. The creatures moved closer to him, shambling grotesquely on bent legs and knuckles. Lorn glanced around desperately, looking for I-Five, feeling the beginnings of a scream welling in his throat. He saw Darsha Assant lying about two meters away from him on the filthy stone floor, and I-Five an equal distance on the other side. The Padawan seemed to be unconscious, but she was breathing normally as far as he could tell. He noticed with no great surprise that her lightsaber no longer dangled from her utility belt. I-Five was lying with his face turned toward Lorn, and the human could see that the droid's photoreceptors were dark. His master control switch had been turned off.

They were in a large chamber, the ceiling supported by groined pillars. The light—what there was of it—

emanated from more of that phosphorescent lichen covering the walls. The place looked like a junkyard; pieces of broken equipment and machinery were lying here and there. It smelled like a charnel house.

Looking closer, he saw that scattered among the technological debris were what looked like gnawed bones of various species.

Lorn carefully adjusted his position, getting his legs underneath him. His head was still screaming like a Corellian banshee bird, but he tried to ignore the pain. If he could reach I-Five and flip the master switch on the back of his neck, the droid could probably make short work of these subterranean horrors. Their ears seemed to be abnormally large; no doubt they relied primarily on hearing to guide them through the darkness. One good screech from I-Five's vocabulator should send them stampeding back into the shadows where they belonged.

He was fairly certain he knew what they were now, although the knowledge gave him little comfort. Quite the opposite, in fact. Occasionally, since his fall from grace had landed him on the mean streets of Coruscant, he had heard rumors of devolved humanoid creatures called Cthons, lurking deep within the underground labyrinths of the planetary city. Dwelling in darkness for thousands of generations had robbed them of their eyes, so the story went. Supposedly they retained some rudimentary working knowledge of technology, which would explain the electroshock net they had used to capture Lorn and his comrades.

Supposedly also they were cannibals.

Lorn had never given any credence to the stories before now. He had assumed they were just tales used to scare recalcitrant children into obedience, just another of the many stories that sprouted like mushrooms on the downlevels streets. But now it was obvious that this particular rumor was all too real.

The Cthons moved closer. One of them positioned himself—or herself; though they were all naked save for ragged loincloths, their skins were so loose and flabby that it was hard to determine what sex any individual was—between Lorn and I-Five.

This is the way it ends, Lorn thought, feeling surprisingly little fear. *What a unique career arc: To go from being a prosperous business affairs clerk in the employ of the Jedi to a fugitive about to be devoured by mutant cannibals in the bowels of Coruscant. Didn't see that one coming.*

The Cthons moved closer still. One reached out a pale, hirsute arm toward him. Lorn tensed. He would fight, of course. He would not be led like a nerf to the slaughter. He could at least do that much.

I'm sorry, Jax, he thought as they closed in on him.

Obi-Wan Kenobi activated the descent repulsor array and dropped out of the airstream traffic flow. As his skycar descended in a tight spiral down toward the blanket of mist that marked the inversion layer, the young Padawan watched the lights in the monads and skyscrapers all around him blinking on. It was just before sunset, and the cerise light faded fast as he descended.

He glanced at the instrument panel, reassuring himself that he was homing in on the coordinates for the safe house in the Crimson Corridor. He noted some deterioration in the appearance of the buildings as the skycar dropped deeper—peeling paint, a few broken windows—but it wasn't until he passed through the mist that he noticed a real change. Now shattered and lightless windows gaped like wounds on all sides, and the few skywalks stretching between the structures were deserted, their railings sagging or broken.

It's a different world, he thought. Descending through the cloud layer was almost like making a hyperspace jump to some decrepit outlying planet. Obi-Wan had known that slums like this existed here and there on Coruscant's surface, of course; he just hadn't realized that one lay this close to the Jedi Temple—less than ten kilometers away.

Once through the mist, the skycar's head- and groundlights activated, and he could see fairly clearly. The vehicle came to a hovering stop a few centimeters from the cracked surface of the street. The area was relatively deserted, save for a dozen or so mendicants of various species who fled as his skycar touched down. That was odd, Obi-Wan thought; one would expect them to crowd around, begging, instead. Perhaps it had to do with the fact that this was Raptor territory after dark.

He looked around and saw Darsha's skyhopper parked not far away, in the shadow of a building. He deactivated the safety field and vaulted over the skycar's edge.

When Master Qui-Gon had told Obi-Wan that Darsha Assant was missing, the Padawan had volunteered to search for her before his mentor could tell him to. He and Darsha were not close friends, but she had been in several of his classes and he had been quite impressed with the way she had excelled in her studies. He had mock-dueled with her twice: he had won one match, she the other. They had even shared a mission once. She was bright, and she knew it; she was quick-witted, and she knew that, too. But she didn't come across as conceited. Obi-Wan thought that Darsha had the makings of a fine Jedi Knight in her. And it wouldn't take much coaxing to get him to admit that she was pleasant to look at, as well.

Even if she had been someone he couldn't stand to be around, he would have accepted without question the assignment to search for her. It was, after all, his duty. But Darsha, he felt, was special, even among the Jedi. He hoped she had not come into harm's way. Now, however, looking at her skyhopper, he found that hope fading fast.

For the craft had been gutted. There was little left of it except the frame; the drive turbines, the power generators, the repulsor engines, and just about everything else that wasn't too heavy to carry had been stolen. The instrument panel had a huge gash in it, as if some kind of vibroblade had punched through it, although there was no weapon in sight.

Obi-Wan checked the craft's interior carefully, using a small but powerful glow light. He found no evidence of foul play in the vehicle, but he did see a few spots of blood on the ground nearby. It was impossible to tell if it was human blood or not.

Something flickered at the edge of his vision.

Obi-Wan froze, then slowly turned to look. He saw nothing threatening in the vespertine shadows. Nevertheless, there had definitely been movement—stealthy, furtive movement. He had been thoroughly briefed on the dangers of street gangs and predators, both human and nonhuman, in the Crimson Corridor. It did not take an overactive imagination to assume that one of these threats might be lurking nearby, ready to strike. If there was a whole gang of footpads sizing him up, he would be hard put to defend himself, even with a lightsaber.

Fortunately, the lightsaber was not the only defense at his disposal.

Obi-Wan Kenobi reached out for the Force. It was there for him, as it always was. He let his awareness expand outward along its invisible corrugations, a psychic radar that searched and probed the darkness. If danger existed, the Force would find it.

His mind touched that of another: a will that felt weak and serpentine, more used to striking furtively from the shadows than in direct confrontation. A human mind.

Before the lurker was fully aware that he was being probed, Obi-Wan seized his will. The Force, Master Qui-Gon had told him more than once, can have a strong influence on the weak-minded. Though Obi-Wan was by no means anywhere near as accomplished a practitioner as his tutor, it didn't take much more than the skill of a novice to influence a mind as weak as this one.

"Come here," he said, his tone quiet and authoritative.

From out of the dusk emerged a young human male—probably around sixteen or seventeen standard years old, Obi-Wan estimated. He was wearing mostly rags and leather, topped by a ten-centimeter-high thatch of green hair held in place by an electrostatic field. The Padawan could feel the sullen guilt and fear in the other's mind—the fear that his captor somehow knew that he and his gang had assaulted the other Jedi.

"Where is she?" Obi-Wan asked.

"I—I don't know who you're—"

"Yes, you do. The Jedi Padawan who owned this skyhopper. Tell me quickly, or—" Obi-Wan let his hand drop, to rest suggestively on the lightsaber hilt hanging at his belt. He wouldn't go so far as to actually use it, but even a veiled threat could work wonders.

He could feel Green Hair's fear and hatred, like an acid in his brain. It was difficult to keep his composure.

"All *right*—we messed with her a little, but we took the hint when she chopped off Nig's hand, y'know? I mean, she wanted the ship so bad, she could have it, right?"

"Where did she go?"

Green Hair shook his head and shrugged. Obi-Wan listened to the Force and knew he was telling the truth.

"Was there a Fondorian male with her?"

"Him?" Green Hair grinned crookedly. "The hawk-bats got *him*. What was left, the street trash dragged off."

Obi-Wan felt despair pushing in on him, as bleak as the downlevels darkness that surrounded them. It appeared that Darsha's mission had been a total failure that might very well have culminated in her death. He would, of course, comb the area, ask any other locals he could find, and try to sense her through the Force, but given the time that had passed and the inhospitable environment he was searching . . .

"There was some more Jedi," Green Hair said abruptly. "I didn't see it, but I heard about it."

"Heard about what?"

"Some o' my bloods saw somebody on a speeder bike chasin' another in a skycar. He caught up with 'em and there was this big brawl. The speeder blew up an' the 'car crashed over on Barsoom Boulevard. Big blowup. That's what I heard."

Obi-Wan frowned in puzzlement. The Jedi Green Hair spoke of could only be Darsha and her mentor, Anoon Bondara.

He questioned Green Hair more thoroughly, making sure he would be able to find the crash site, then released him from thrall. The boy lost no time in making himself scarce. Obi-Wan got back in his skycar and headed for the location, more puzzled than ever. Even under careful questioning and mind-probing, Green Hair had stuck to his story: Two robed and cowled figures had been seen first in a high-speed pursuit and subsequently on a docking ledge, battling each other with all the ferocity of a couple of Tyrusian manglers. The battle had culminated in two big explosions as both the speeder bike and the skycar had blown up.

Obi-Wan shook his head as he piloted the skycar down the dark and narrow streets. Speculation was fruitless at this point. With any luck, all would be made clear when he reached the crash site.

Very little had been disturbed since the crash of the skycar; in this part of town it might be months before a droid cleanup crew was assigned to deal with the wreckage. But few of Obi-Wan's questions were answered by investigating the torn and twisted hulk of the skycar, or the nearby pile of debris that was once a docking ledge. So much rubble was piled on Master

Bondara's vehicle that Obi-Wan couldn't even tell if bodies were still in it or not. The Force did not seem to indicate that a Jedi had died here, but it had been several hours since the occurrence, and what perturbation remained in the energy field was subtle and hard to read. Possibly Master Qui-Gon Jinn could read it, but Obi-Wan was not that skilled yet.

Still, he sensed something disturbing here. The sense of a powerful evil, a corruption. Obi-Wan glanced about him nervously. The street was mostly deserted and quiet, but it wasn't a peaceful silence. Instead it bore a feeling of trepidation, of lurking danger. The temptation to snatch his lightsaber up and activate it was almost overwhelming. The combination of few street lights, towering buildings, and omnipresent cloud cover made it impossible to see more than a meter or two in any direction. An entire army could be surrounding him, invisible in the breathing darkness, poised to attack.

Obi-Wan shook his head, attempting to banish the sudden surge of uneasiness. *There is no emotion; there is peace.* Giving in to paranoia would not further his mission. He had to operate from the assumption that either Darsha or Master Bondara or both were still alive. Based on that assumption, he had to find an eyewitness to the battle who could give him a better account of what had happened. Facts were what he needed, not speculation and hearsay. *There is no ignorance; there is knowledge.*

He knew this was true. Nevertheless, it was hard to quell the anxiety he felt as he started toward a nearby tavern to ask some questions of the locals.

*　　*　　*

Two hours later Obi-Wan was more baffled than ever.

He had found few people who were willing to talk with him without being prodded by the Force, and what little he had learned was confusing and contradictory. One thing was for certain: A lot had been happening in this neighborhood recently, even by the rough-and-tumble standards of the Crimson Corridor.

He had found no one who would admit to being an eyewitness to the battle, but several had seen the high-speed chase between the skycar and the speeder bike. Some had said there were Jedi involved, some said one or none. Some swore a droid was piloting the skycar. Some were certain a Jedi had been riding the bike, others were not. He had also learned that a black-clad figure—possibly, according to one, the figure who had been on the speeder bike—had been somehow implicated in yet another explosion, this one in a block of cubicles a few streets away. Several people had been killed in that blast, including a human bounty hunter. There had also been a fracas at a nightclub owned by a local Black Sun vigo, one Yanth the Hutt, in which a cowled character had been somehow implicated.

None of this seemed to make any kind of sense.

He had spoken to one witness who seemed certain that the two Jedi in the skycar had been a Twi'lek male and a human female. That would be Anoon Bondara and Darsha, Obi-Wan surmised. But he still had no clue as to whether they had survived the explosions. His informant said they had been riding with a human male and a droid.

After some consideration, Obi-Wan decided his best bet would be to investigate the nightclub. If Yanth, the owner, was a member of Black Sun, he might know more about all this than the street rabble.

"I've got a bad feeling about this," he murmured to himself as he headed for the nightclub.

21

As from a far distance, Darsha heard the sounds of a struggle. It seemed to rise and fall, the sounds breaking over her like oceanic waves as her mind struggled to find its way back to consciousness. She wished dimly that whatever was going on would stop, so that she could slip back down into the depths of the black well out of which she was reluctantly rising. She had been through a lot of pain and fear lately, and she felt she deserved a rest.

But the altercation didn't subside; instead it grew louder. Now she recognized one of the voices: it was Lorn Pavan's. The other voices seemed to be nonhuman—mostly grunts and guttural bellows.

It was obvious that he was in some kind of trouble. In her semiconscious state Darsha didn't see any real reason why she should come to his aid. She didn't like him, and he'd made it perfectly clear that he wasn't overly fond of her. There didn't seem to be any personal animosity involved on his part; he just despised Jedi in general. In a way, that was even more insulting. Darsha would rather someone base their dislike on her personality, not on an abstract that she represented. She could deal with enmity easier than bigotry.

It was becoming painfully obvious, however, that the struggle she was hearing wouldn't resolve itself anytime soon. And suddenly, in a rush of returning wakefulness, Darsha remembered what had happened: the attack by unseen foes in the tunnels, the electroshock net that had trapped them. She had been knocked out by the net's power field. Wherever she was now, it couldn't be any place healthy.

Darsha opened her eyes and managed to raise her head enough to see what was going on, even though doing so sent a stab of pain like a blaster bolt through her skull. What she saw kicked her adrenal glands into overdrive. Pavan was struggling with several creatures—hard to tell in the dim light exactly what they were, other than bipedal and definitely subhuman. He had apparently managed to knock one of them unconscious; the limp form lay on the mossy stone floor next to the droid, who seemed to be out of commission, as well.

Darsha pushed herself up to a kneeling position. The movement attracted the attention of several of the creatures who were circling Pavan, looking for an opening. They turned and shambled toward her, their snarling mouths stretched wide. She saw the undulating skin that covered their eye sockets, and the horror of the sight caused her heart to stutter.

Darsha gathered the Force to her. Still on her knees,

she thrust out both arms, fingers splayed wide, hurling twin waves of invisible power toward them. The unexpected surges struck them, causing them to stagger back. They howled in mingled fear and anger, an eerie ululation that reverberated in the chamber.

Darsha took advantage of the momentary respite to stagger to her feet. She reached instinctively for her lightsaber, and wasn't really surprised to find it missing from its belt clip. She had no time to look for it, because now several more of the subhumans were lumbering her way. Though they moved slowly, it was hard to avoid them, given how many there were in the relatively small chamber.

Pavan, who had two of them hanging on to each arm, saw she was awake. "Cthons!" he shouted to her. "They're cannibals!"

His words sent a chill of fear and repugnance down Darsha's spine. Like most people who lived on Coruscant, she had heard the legends of the sightless subhumans, but had never considered them based in reality. Fear gave her new strength and focus, and once again she drove them back by throwing Force waves at them. But they were stronger than they looked, and extremely tenacious; though battered off their feet by her power, they picked themselves up and came back for more, moaning and howling.

Pavan was doing worse than she was, having only his fists and feet to fight with. The Cthons were dragging him toward one of the darker recesses of the chamber.

"I-Five's been deactivated!" he called to her. "He can help us!"

Yes, of course! Darsha thought. She'd had firsthand experience of how strong the droid was when he'd carried both her and Pavan to safety after the skycar's crash. She looked at I-Five and could just see in the dim light that the master switch on the back of his head was in the off position.

Could she reactivate him? She wasn't sure. There was no way she could reach him physically, and she wasn't at all confident in her control of the Force, particularly under these circumstances. It was one thing to use it like a bludgeon against an enemy, but quite another to flip a small switch several meters away.

She pushed the doubts away. She *had* to do it—or she and Pavan were quite literally dead meat.

She focused her mind on the droid, felt the tenuous, intangible connection between her thoughts and the cool metal of the control switch. She pushed against it with her mind, feeling the resistance.

A Cthon grabbed her from behind.

Darsha bit back a cry of shock and surprise. She felt her attenuated mental grip on the tiny nub of dura-steel almost slip free, and with all the power of her will she *thrust* the Force tendril against it. Then the Cthon yanked her backwards, and she felt its clammy fingers, like the hands of a corpse, reach up and close about her neck.

A shrill screech, unlike anything she had ever heard before, suddenly filled the air. It was more than just unpleasant; it was actively painful. It drilled into both ears and expanded in the center of Darsha's head like something alive and voracious. The Cthon released her and she staggered forward, clapping her hands over her ears. That helped somewhat, but not nearly enough.

But it was obvious that the stridency was causing the Cthons far more pain than she was feeling. Which made sense, certainly; here in the eternal darkness the creatures would have grown over generations to depend on their ears far more than their vestigial eyes. Their shrieks and moans of agony were barely audible above the continuing screech, which Darsha now realized was coming from I-Five.

The reactivated droid was standing. He moved quickly, pushing through the dazed group of sub-humans toward Lorn Pavan while the earsplitting sound continued to emanate from his vocabulator. The Cthons who had been dragging Pavan away were writhing in pain like their comrades, leaving him free.

Darsha followed in the droid's wake. I-Five grabbed Pavan and headed for the dark aperture of a tunnel in the chamber's far wall. No matter where it led, it had to be someplace better than where they were now.

But the chances of their reaching it were not looking good. Though obviously still in pain, the Cthons were starting to rally, no doubt motivated by the sight of their dinner making an escape. Darsha hurled more invisible blows to either side, clearing a path for the three of them. But a large group was gathering ahead to block their escape.

Darsha looked about desperately for something to use as a weapon—and saw her lightsaber lying perhaps five meters away on a mound of mingled offal and techno-trash. With a gasp of surprise and gratitude, she reached out for it with her hand and her mind. The device flew from its position across the intervening space. A Cthon somehow sensed it sailing through the air and made a clumsy leap that almost intercepted it. He sprawled on the ground at her feet, and Darsha felt the lightsaber smack into her hand. She thumbed the activator button and heard the satisfying *thrum* as the yellow blade boiled out to its full length.

She gripped the weapon in both hands, weaving it in a figure-eight defensive pattern. It was hard to concentrate, as I-Five was still emitting his painful siren cry and her head was feeling like it would come apart at any minute. She hoped that some of the Cthons would at least get hit by the shrapnel.

Against the combined threats of her lightsaber and the droid's howl, the subhumans had no choice but to fall back. The three entered the tunnel at a dead run, I-Five in the lead and Darsha bringing up the rear. Their former captors' enraged cries followed them, but that was all.

The phosphorescent lichen that covered the chamber's walls continued only a short way into the underground passage and then died out, save for sporadic patches that did little or nothing to relieve the darkness. I-Five illuminated his photoreceptors, revealing a brick-lined tunnel barely high enough for Lorn to stand upright. It did not run in a straight line, but instead meandered gently, first left, then right.

I-Five shut off the screeching sound once they were out of sight of the Cthons' chamber. They dropped from a run to a fast walk. Darsha had to hustle to keep up with the long-legged strides of the other two, and each time her boots contacted the hard pavestones she felt a new spear of pain go through her head. She wished devoutly that one of the Force's attributes was an ability to cure headaches.

As if reading her mind, the droid began making another sound: a low trilling that was as unlike the discordant noise of before as it was possible to be. It seemed to somehow penetrate her bones and muscles—indeed, her very cells—and subtly vibrate them, flushing away the toxins and pains that had filled them. After a few minutes the sound ceased, leaving her feeling, if not in top shape, at least markedly better.

After walking for another few minutes, I-Five stopped. Pavan and Darsha stopped, as well, the latter deactivating her lightsaber as she did so.

"My sensors indicate no one is following us," the droid said.

"Let's keep moving anyway," Pavan replied. "You were wrong before, remember?"

"Don't be so hard on him," Darsha said. "After all, he just saved our lives again."

"Much as I crave validation, I feel constrained to point out that you saved us this time," said I-Five. "I couldn't have done anything if you hadn't reactivated me." Though the droid was speaking to Darsha, he was looking at Lorn Pavan.

Pavan hesitated a moment, scowling. Then he looked at Darsha and said, "He's right. Thanks."

It obviously had taken a herd of wild banthas to drag the words out of him. Why did he hate Jedi so much? Darsha wondered. Aloud, she said, "No problem. You saved my life back in the skycar. Now we're even."

Pavan gave her a look that seemed equal parts gratitude and resentment. He said to I-Five, "Let's find the fastest route back to the surface. Even the Raptors look friendly compared to what lives down here."

The droid nodded and started walking again. The two humans followed. Neither of her companions spoke further, which suited Darsha just fine. She strode along behind Lorn Pavan, wondering once again what caused his intense antipathy toward her and her order.

She could simply ask him, of course. The only reason she hadn't done so yet was because there hadn't been any time to; they'd been on the run from the moment they'd met. But her instincts told her that now would not be a good time to bring it up, so she kept quiet. Maybe after they emerged from these labyrinthine catacombs—if they ever did—she would broach the subject. For now it seemed best to just let it lie.

"I'm surprised the Cthons gave up so easily," Pavan said abruptly to the droid. "They didn't even follow us into this tunnel."

"I've been wondering about that, as well," I-Five said. "Two possibilities come to mind—neither of them particularly pleasant to contemplate. The first is that they may be planning another trap of some sort."

"That's what I was thinking," Pavan replied. "What's your second scenario?"

"That there may be something up ahead that even the Cthons fear."

Pavan did not reply. They trudged on through the bowels of the planetary city, and Darsha mulled over the droid's words. They certainly didn't paint a cheerful picture of the immediate future. Something even worse than the Cthons?

Darth Maul followed his instincts. They led him a short distance along the transit tube and down a stairwell, and from there into a dark tunnel. He moved swiftly but cautiously. He knew that this deep in the guts of the planet there lived creatures that even a Sith Lord would have a hard time dealing with. But they would not keep him from overtaking his quarry and completing his mission.

He would kill Pavan first, for two reasons: because he was the primary target, of course, but also because Maul would then be free to take his time killing the Jedi. He did not anticipate her putting up much of a fight. His impression was that she had been naught but an apprentice to the Twi'lek he had killed, and thus not much of a potential opponent. But she was still a Jedi, and he could toy with her for a bit before delivering the fatal blow. He felt he deserved some entertainment as partial recompense for all the trouble they had put him to.

The subterranean course he followed was as dark as a coal sack nebula. Even Maul, whose eyes were far more sensitive to light than a human's, could barely see enough to make his way. But he was not depending on vision so much as on the perturbations in the Force to guide him. Now he could sense them ahead—he would not go astray.

Nevertheless, he felt impatient. He wanted to run, to rapidly close the distance to his prey, to be done with all this. But only fools rush into unknown and hostile territory, and Darth Maul was no fool.

He had pushed his hood back the better to hear anything that might warn him of a threat. Then he paused abruptly, listening to faint vibrations.

He knew he was not alone.

The dank and miasmal air was still, and even the disturbance he sensed in the Force was of the most subtle nature. Still, he had no doubt that he was being watched. The almost nonexistent light told him that he was standing in a wide part of the tunnel, with several side passages opening into it. It was from these that he suspected the attack would come.

Moving very slowly, he dropped his gloved hand to the lightsaber dangling at his belt.

He did not expect the assault to come from above, but he was not taken by surprise when it did. He sensed the electroshock net dropping down from overhead, and knew that if he tried to slash it with his energy blade, the power surge would reverberate back down his arm and through him with devastating effect. So instead he dived forward, executing a smooth shoulder roll that carried him beyond the reach of the mesh. He came to his feet and spun about, lighting both ends of his weapon as he did so.

And then they were upon him.

Darth Maul once again abandoned himself to the dark side, letting it guide his movements and power his strikes. He stood in the center of a maelstrom of hulking silhouettes, visible only in brief stroboscopic flashes as the whirling energy blades struck them down. He recognized them from his studies of Coruscant's indigenes: Cthons, degenerate subterranean humanoids, considered by many scholars to be apocryphal. His master would be most interested to learn that they actually existed. Assuming, of course, he did not slay them all.

By the time they broke off the attack and retreated, howling, into the side tunnels, there were several fewer in existence than had been moments before. Maul had killed, as best he could count in the darkness, nine of the loathsome creatures.

He moved on, continuing to follow the trail and wondering if Pavan and the Jedi had encountered the Cthons, as well. If they had, he felt it strongly possible that they had not survived. Perhaps his job had been done for him. That would be a disappointment, as he would then be deprived of the pleasure of the kill, but at least the mission would be at an end.

Of course, he could not assume that this was the case, not until he found definite evidence. The human had certainly proven harder to kill than he had anticipated so far.

He pressed ahead through the everlasting night, alert for the possibility of more attacks.

*   *   *

As Lorn followed I-Five through the dark tunnel, he considered various possible solutions to his situation. There didn't seem a lot of them. In all his years as a businessman, information broker, and even working for the Jedi, he certainly hadn't come across anything this challenging before. Pursued by the Sith—who weren't even supposed to exist—into the deepest pits of the city where flesh-eating cannibals stalked him . . . it was a challenge, no doubt about it.

Assuming that they made it back aboveground and were able to return to the civilized levels of society, what should his next move be?

He knew that the Padawan planned on taking him straight to the Jedi Temple so that he could share his information with Mace Windu and the other council members. But that event was not anywhere near the top of Lorn's list of desires. Certainly the Jedi would be best at protecting him from the Sith—assuming their tracker had not been killed in the explosion—but as far as he was concerned it would be a solution almost as bad as the problem. To be a resource held and *used* by the Jedi? It was a sickening thought, one that awoke far too many memories Lorn had worked hard to put away. So instead of giving in to the feelings that threatened to overwhelm him, he considered his other obvious option: *Run.*

The key question was how to get on board a ship that could take him and I-Five far enough away to avoid being tracked by both the Sith and the Jedi. The spice transport I-Five had arranged passage on had already left, but there was certainly no dearth of ships at the spaceports. Once they were off Coruscant it would be easier. It was a big galaxy, after all. There couldn't be that many Sith out there, or there would have been rumors that the Jedi would have picked up by now. And if there were only a few, Lorn reasoned, it wouldn't really be in the Sith's interests to spend much time tracking down one low-life information broker.

So that was the plan: get on a fast ship, maybe a smuggler, and leave Coruscant behind. He didn't know how he was going to pay for passage yet, but he would figure something out. They could hightail it out to some backwater planet like Tatooine, hole up in the Dune Sea or the Jundland Wastes for a while, become part of the scenery. After a few years he could maybe open a tavern in some place like Mos Eisley. It wasn't a particularly thrilling life to contemplate, but at least it was a life.

Of course, I-Five might not be too happy about all that sand. Droids tended to need a lot of oil baths in environments like Tatooine's. Lorn looked thoughtfully at his partner walking ahead of him, the droid's metallic shell catching the reflected light from his photoreceptors. He would need to discuss this plan with him, see if I-Five had any new angles about the money end of it. The droid always seemed to have the right idea to complement Lorn's own. Of course, to do this he would have to get a few moments away from the Jedi.

Darsha. Her name was Darsha.

With an uncomfortable start, Lorn realized that he was feeling a little guilty at the thought of running out on her. He'd hated the Jedi with an all-inclusive passion for so long, it was hard to see any of them as individuals. After all, she had saved his life. It was difficult to get past the fact that she was a Jedi, but deep down he knew she was more than that: she was a person. Even likable, hard though that was to believe. And admirable in a number of ways, as well. Considering that her mentor had been killed in that explosion, she was carrying her grief fairly well. She'd saved all of them back there from the Cthons, too, no question about that.

But not because she liked you. Only for the information.

Lorn nodded to himself. He had to keep in mind that the Jedi did nothing that did not serve their own interests. Nothing. He would be doing himself no favors to walk into their clutches.

No, the best way out was to run. But to book passage on even a garbage scow was financially out of the question at this point.

And then he remembered—Tuden Sal! A few months past he'd given the owner of a successful chain of restaurants a tidbit of data that had helped the Sakiyan keep his liquor license. At the time Lorn had been flush and had charged only a few drinks—well, more than a few—but Sal had promised him a favor if the day ever came that he needed one.

As far as Lorn was concerned, that day was here. Tuden Sal was known to have strong contacts with several smuggling organizations, including Black Sun. He would know how to get them off Coruscant. Lorn felt revitalized by the possibility. This was a good plan—if he could just stay alive long enough to make it happen.

Ahead of him the droid slowed down. There was a change that Lorn could feel in the air. The echoes of their footsteps seemed to be hollower, more distant.

I-Five confirmed it.

"For those of you who are interested, the cavern we have just entered is roughly seven hundred standard meters wide, two hundred meters across, and festooned with stalactites starting forty or fifty meters above our heads. The ledge we are on, unfortunately, ends within seven meters, culminating in a drop that is—" The droid paused. "—currently not measurable with my modest sensory capabilities."

Terrific, Lorn thought.

Darsha heard Lorn Pavan release a long-suffering sigh. "Let me guess," he said, "we have to jump across."

"Not unless you've suddenly gained greater levitation powers than our Sith friend," the droid replied.

Darsha reached out with the Force. She sensed nothing other than the usual low-level life signs found everywhere.

"It feels empty," she said.

"Well, thank you, Mistress of the Force, but pardon me if I don't stop worrying," Pavan replied sarcastically. "It seems like your track record with that skill is still a little on the nebulous side."

She glared at Pavan. "It so happens that even Jedi Masters—which I am not—can be taken by surprise by things that are not Force-sensitive. Creatures who

make very little ripples in the psychic flow are sometimes as good as invisible." Abruptly she remembered
Bondara's leap toward the Sith, and fell silent.

After a moment, I-Five said, "The good news is that
there seems to be a bridge."

Darsha moved forward to stand next to the droid.
To keep her balance, she inadvertently put her hand
on Pavan's shoulder, felt him tense and move away.

What was it with him? she wondered. What did he
feel the Jedi had done to him to make him hate her and
her kind so? Darsha remembered the look on Master
Bondara's face when Pavan had introduced himself.
Her mentor had known the man's name. What did
that mean? She wasn't usually the prying type, but as
soon as she got back to the Temple she'd do her best to
find out.

Sure, she thought. As if there would still be a place
for her in the Temple after all this. Fail the graduation
exercise, get her Master killed, and wind up nearly
eaten by a bunch of blind monsters. What kind of Jedi
was that?

Not a very good one, she had to admit.

Darsha shook her head slightly, trying to banish
encroaching despair. *There is no emotion, there is
peace*. She had made mistakes, that was for sure, had
probably lost any chance of ever becoming a Jedi. But
until Master Windu or another member of the council
officially reassigned her, she would continue to do her
duty as best she saw it. She would get Lorn Pavan to
the Temple because his information would be valuable to the council, could help maintain order against

the misuse of power. It was what a Jedi would do, and so it was what she would do.

Thankfully, Pavan was not at all like Oolth the Fondorian. That one had been nothing but bluster and cowardice. Pavan was hard to read, but his actions so far had been those of a loyal, brave individual. The only thing that made him difficult to get along with was his hatred of the Jedi.

I-Five turned his photoreceptors up a few notches brighter and aimed them down at the bridge.

Several large ropes, gray and dusty with age, stretched out from the end of the tunnel beyond the limited light put out by the droid. Across the ropes had been laid an odd assortment of flat objects: boards, pieces of sheet metal, and other odds and ends. About the only thing they had in common was that they were all more or less flat and laid out in the direction the group wanted to go.

Lorn stepped out and jumped on one of the ropes. His balance was excellent, she noted, and he seemed to have a natural grace as he leapt. He saw her watching and pushed off extra hard on the last bounce, doing a quick somersault in midair.

"Ropes seem strong enough to me," he said, landing in a perfect double-foot plant. He waited a moment before answering her unasked question. "I used to dabble in zero-g sports when I, uh, had a better lifestyle."

The droid broke in. "If you two are finished playing primitive mating games, maybe we could see about traversing this bridge. There may be a Sith pursuing us, if you recall."

"Excuse me?" Lorn said. *"Mating games?"*

Darsha felt indignant as well. "Your droid has a point. We need to keep moving." *Mating games, indeed,* she thought as she stepped onto the bridge. Not likely.

23

Lorn wished he had a weapon.

Ahead of him, I-Five was armed with his finger blasters, as well as a few other tricks, and behind him Darsha had her lightsaber.

It wasn't that he felt they were in any particular danger at the moment, but a weapon—any weapon—would have given him a better sense of control over his own safety. While it was true that being unarmed did make him very alert, that didn't count for much with a sensor-equipped droid and a Force-sensitive Jedi for companions. Lorn felt he might as well be blind compared to them.

The going was slow; there were no handrails on the bridge, and it didn't look like the planks, lids, and other objects they were walking on had been attached very firmly to the support ropes. Indeed, he got the opinion that they had been added *after* the trestle had been formed. By the Cthons, perhaps? It was impossible to say. The bridge, Lorn noted, was of a very strange construction. In addition to the thick support cables that ran along either side of the odd planks they walked on, there were vertical cables every few meters, some coming from the roof of the cavern, as might be expected, but others stretching from the bridge supports down into the darkness below.

What could all this be for?

He voiced the question.

"Based on the depth of the excavation," I-Five said, "I postulate that this could have been used as an access point for the underground oceans."

Possible, Lorn thought. Most of Coruscant, except for a few park areas, was built-over landmass. The water had to go somewhere.

"But why this bridge? I mean, it's a pretty primitive construction. Why not have a better way of getting around?"

The droid paused and looked over its shoulder, photoreceptors gleaming. "Perhaps the Cthons are responsible. Why can't you just be grateful that it's here where and when we need it?" I-Five resumed his progress forward.

Lorn raised an eyebrow. "Who pissed in *your* power supply?" he muttered.

He heard a chuckle from behind him. Great. Shot down by his own droid, and a *Jedi* got the laugh.

"I've got to ask," Darsha said. "How did you two wind up working together?"

"I'm impressed. You managed to come up with a topic even less interesting than his," I-Five said.

"Perhaps *you* aren't in need of a distraction," Darsha said, "but I sure could use one after the last few hours."

The woman had a point. Lorn, somewhat to his surprise, was the one who answered.

"I acquired I-Five a few years back when I first got started selling information. He was a protocol droid belonging to a rich family who left him with the children. The children were spoiled. They used to do things like make him jump off the roof to see how high he would bounce."

The memory surprised him with its intensity. He recalled the smell of the junk dealer's shop, a mixture of hydraulic fluid and the ozone of cooking circuits. It had been a humid day, and he was tired. He'd been fired from the Jedi Temple only a few days previously—not that *they* had called it that, of course.

There is no emotion; there is peace.

He'd read the words a thousand times when he had studied his enemies, fought their power over his life and Jax's. The words had never made sense before, and they didn't now.

"I figured that he might have some interesting secrets tucked away that I could use, so I bought him and brought him back on-line."

Lorn remembered the first words the droid had spoken. They had hit him with their utter hopelessness and helplessness, reminding him of his own.

"I am I-FiveYQ, programmed for protocol." There had been a pause after the initial main sequence had activated, and then the droid had asked, "Are you going to hurt me?"

Fury had blossomed in Lorn when he heard those

words. He, too, had been broken into pieces recently, hurt savagely by those he had always been told would protect him.

The Jedi.

Darsha watched Lorn go quiet. Something seemed to have disturbed the man in the telling of his story, something that she felt reticent to press him on. She decided to ask the droid instead.

"So he fixed you up, and you talked him into being your partner?"

I-Five answered after a pause.

"Lorn had been treated badly recently by his . . . employers. He felt that I was a kindred spirit, at least in potential. He had a friend who was handy at reprogramming droids install a top-of-the-line AI cognitive module, and deactivated my creativity damper, as well. As a result, I am as close to full sentience as any droid can be."

Intrigued, Darsha had to ask. "Who were his employers?"

I-Five glanced at Lorn before replying. "The Jedi."

She had suspected as much. That explained Master Bondara's recognition of the name. But why and how had the order treated Lorn so terribly? As far as she knew, they always dealt fairly with all employees who were non-Jedi. It didn't make any sense.

"How long have you trained at the Temple, Padawan Assant?"

It was plain, at least, that I-Five was a better droid than the one assigned to watch over the Fondorian in the safe house. That one hadn't recognized her as a Padawan.

"I've lived at the temple practically all my life. My formal training started when I was four," she said. And probably ended as of today, she added silently.

"I have been in business with Lorn Pavan for five standard years."

Then the droid went silent and left Darsha to her own thoughts. She realized that he had given her a clue to the mystery of Lorn's past.

She cast her thoughts back five years earlier. A new student had come to the temple back then, a two-year-old. Darsha remembered it because of the boy's high midi-chlorian count. She hadn't heard all the details of course, but the temple was a small pond, and ripples of any discord traveled quickly across its surface. Apparently the boy had been the son of a temple employee, who had been fired after he agreed to let his son be trained—why, she wasn't sure.

She gave Lorn a measuring look. If he were that student's father, and if his son had been taken from him without his consent, to be raised by the order—well, then it was certainly no wonder that he hated the Jedi.

She tried to imagine how she would feel in his place, but could not.

She looked at Lorn again and knew her suspicion was right. It certainly explained the man's attitude toward her and Master Bondara. She felt a great upsurge of pity for him then, so much so that she had to look away from him lest he read it in her expression.

She turned her focus back to their surroundings. It

still rankled her that she hadn't noticed the Cthons before they had attacked, and she had vowed to herself not to let something like that happen again. Seeking out life-forms around her with the Force was a task with varying degrees of difficulty. Intelligent, Force-sensitive beings were usually easy to spot, of course, while lower-level forms—insects and animals, for example—did not broadcast nearly much of a blip on her mental radar. It was true that her mastery of the Force was nowhere near perfect, but that was no excuse for not doing the best she could. Her Twi'lek Master had once explained to her that sensitivity and fine-tuning came with time. "As a Padawan," he had said, "I could push boulders around with ease, but seeds were next to impossible."

The thought reminded Darsha that it was time to check on possible pursuit again. Ever since they had entered the underground tunnels she had periodically scanned behind them for any signs of the Sith. She had not sensed his approach before the Cthon attack and was still hoping that he had been killed along with Master Bondara. But she couldn't take the chance of becoming complacent. She closed her eyes, keeping a slight cognizance of her immediate surroundings with the Force, and cast her awareness backwards, along the path they had traced across the old bridge, across the ledge, back into the tunnel.

A cold pillar of darkness formed in her mind as her awareness reached the tunnel. Power and energy seemed to radiate off of it like electricity from a thundercloud.

He was right behind them!

"Lorn, I-Five—the Sith is behind us, almost to the bridge!"

There was no response from either of them. Darsha opened her eyes and for a moment forgot about the imminent threat of the Sith.

They had found the reason why the Cthons had not pursued them.

Darth Maul advanced along the dark passage as fast as he dared. His sense of the Jedi and her companions grew stronger. Events had stretched out much longer than they should have; it was well past time to put an end to this.

Even so, he realized he was letting his eagerness overcome his caution. He deliberately slowed his pace, forcing patience. It would not do to be caught in some trap deep underground, to have half of the Sith in the galaxy lost due to carelessness.

He probed the darkness with renewed caution, sensing nothing dangerous ahead. The path of the Jedi was very fresh now; he could sense her presence. Not much farther.

And then he felt her find him. A clumsy probe it was, weak and hesitant. He was disappointed by it. It would be no real challenge to face someone so little steeped in the ways of the Force. Definitely not in the same class as her Master, the Twi'lek who had destroyed his speeder bike. He had been a worthy adversary. Not as good as Maul, of course, but that was to be expected.

He saw a faint light up ahead as he came around a curve in the tunnel. The echoes of his footsteps changed, and he realized he had reached a larger open space. He sent mental investigative tendrils of the Force outward, finding the boundaries of the ledge he stood on and the bridge just ahead. He sensed the Jedi on the bridge, perhaps halfway across, with Lorn Pavan and his droid just ahead of her, and beyond them.

Maul frowned. There was an odd quality ahead of them in the darkness—an empty spot in the mental topography of his probe. The light, which he now realized had to be from the droid's photoreceptors, gave him a brief glimpse of something huge and oddly insubstantial, like a weaving pillar of smoke ahead of the three on the middle of the bridge. Whatever it was he saw produced no corresponding vibration in the Force.

This was most odd.

Curious, he tried again. And again his probe met with nothingness. No, not exactly nothingness—the sensation was almost like encountering a surface so slick that one could find no purchase on it. It was like trying to see something that radiated only ultraviolet light. A strange phenomenon, but one he paid little attention to, because he now noted that the Jedi and Pavan were coming back along the bridge toward him.

He was surprised—pleased, but surprised. Surely the Padawan knew she could not defeat him. What, then, was her purpose? Had the other human continued ahead he would have been certain it was a delaying tactic, such as the Twi'lek had attempted earlier. But no—Pavan was accompanying the Jedi, along with his droid.

Once again Darth Maul admitted to being impressed by his prey. They were brave enough to come back and face him, and smart enough to realize, finally, that it was pointless to keep running. Naturally they would die, but perhaps he would grant them some small measure of mercy, would be a trifle quicker in killing them than he had originally planned.

The woman had activated her lightsaber. As if that would make the slightest bit of difference, he thought.

He stepped forward onto the bridge and walked out to meet them.

Darsha had never seen anything like the creature that faced them on the bridge. It was *huge*, a great long body that stretched back at least as far as a hoverbus. As she watched, segment after segment wound over the side of the bridge, which shuddered in response as the motion brought the creature up from underneath and onto the structure with them. Its skin was composed of segmented overlapping plates, dotted here and there with small nodules that were perhaps two centimeters in diameter. Its head was capped by two great black eyes and a pair of curved mandibles, each easily as long as her leg. Below them were an array of small, clawed arms, and below that a series of short, thick legs.

The most amazing thing about it, however, was that its chitinous exoskeleton and internal organs seemed to be completely *transparent*. Apparently it had no internal skeletal structure, though how a creature that size could exist without the support of bones in a one-gravity field was beyond her understanding. Darsha saw a flash of reflected light from within its midsection, a few segments back from the head, and stared in disbelief. Momentarily illuminated by I-Five's photoreceptors was a pile of bones—human bones—that shifted in the thing's gut as it heaved more of its quaking mass up onto the bridge. Also in the monster's digestive tract was a more recent acquisition—a partially digested Cthon. Thankfully, the droid's light failed to show it in great detail.

"Why didn't this thing show up on your sensors?" Lorn hissed at I-Five as the two backed hastily away from the giant beast.

"Perhaps you forget it was the *less*-expensive unit you had installed? Not the one with the extra sensitivity hi-band—something about saving money, as I recall . . ."

Those two would probably die arguing, Darsha thought as she backpedaled carefully, trying to keep her balance on the swaying bridge. The big question as far as she was concerned was why the Force hadn't warned her of this thing's presence. While it was true that sentient beings were on the whole easier to sense than nonsentient ones, a living creature this size and this close would have made a noticeable dent in the energy field even if it had a brain the size of a jakka seed.

As she retreated, Darsha sent a questing mental beam toward the creature—and felt it disappear. There was no psychic reverberation at all.

How could that be?

Her surprise nearly caused her to topple into the abyss. Her eyes told her the monster was there before them, her body felt the bridge swing and vibrate as it raised more of its bulk up out of the depths, but as far as sensing it via the Force, she felt nothing.

This was *impossible*. Maybe she wasn't an adept in the same league as Masters Yoda or Jinn, but she'd have to have zero point-zero midi-chlorians in her bloodstream not to get some kind of reading on something that huge!

The creature reared up, some of its legs quivering in the light of I-Five's photoreceptors. There was a sound, a kind of dry rasping, which it seemed to make by rattling its segmented chitinous plates. It towered over them and opened its mouth.

Darsha activated her lightsaber as the droid fired both finger blasters, hitting several pairs of legs and scarring the creature's torso. It shrieked and slammed the upper length of its body back down on the bridge, nearly shaking the group off. They had to drop prone to keep from falling—which was lucky, because the stream of fluid that arced from the dark rictus of its mouth passed over their heads instead of coating them. Even as she clung to the metal plank beneath her, it was clear to Darsha that the stuff being spat by the monster was the same substance that made up the gray silken material of the bridge.

This thing had made the bridge.

Something about all this seemed familiar, but she couldn't recall how or why. A vagrant stream of the silk drifted toward the Padawan, and without thinking, she moved her lightsaber to intercept it. The silk burned as it hit the yellow energy beam, vaporizing into a cloud of smelly vapor.

The three got to their feet and started moving quickly back down the bridge toward the tunnel. Behind them the monster hitched itself forward, its multiple legs clinging to the silken bridge.

Well, I-Five's blasters hadn't worked, Darsha told herself. Let's see how well it stands up to a lightsaber.

Lorn was *really* wishing he had a weapon right about now. Forget hand blasters—he was far past desiring something that small. Maybe a tripod-mounted V-90, or a few plasma grenades. As long as he was wishing, how about a ship-mounted turbolaser—with him safely inside the ship.

Where had this creature come from? One minute they were walking along the bridge, the next it was just *there*.

Retreat was the obvious choice. But just before this thing reared its ugly head, hadn't he heard Darsha say something about the Sith being right behind them?

Talk about being trapped between the Black Hole of Nakat and the Magataran Maelstrom.

At that moment he realized what the creature was.

When Lorn had worked for the Jedi he'd had access to a lot of literature about them and many related topics. After he'd learned that Jax was off-limits to him he'd spent weeks studying everything he could about the Jedi: their history, their powers, their strengths and weaknesses. He hadn't found anything that could help him, but he had come across some interesting and esoteric bits of knowledge—including, in one old text, stories about a supposedly extinct species of giant invertebrates that could, after a fashion, hide from the Force. What had it been called?

Taozin—that was it.

Apparently they *weren't* extinct.

At that moment Darsha dived past him and I-Five toward the monster, her lightsaber flashing.

"Darsha! Stop! It's a taozin!"

Darsha came out of her forward roll near the base of the creature, lightsaber extended. She thrust forward, angling the cut of the weapon to carve out a huge chunk of the monster's belly. *Let's see how hungry you are after your prey bites back,* she thought.

She executed the move as perfectly as she ever had in practice; Master Bondara would have been proud. The only problem was that it didn't work.

She watched in disbelieving shock as the yellow glow of her blade *diffused* as she sank it into the creature, losing its coherency and radiating in all directions. Darsha dodged back, narrowly avoiding the backsplash of her own weapon. The blade regained its congruency as she withdrew it from the creature's abdomen. The beast spasmed and roared angrily, its translucent flesh rippling in reaction; the strike had evidently hurt it, though not nearly as much as she had anticipated.

Darsha was so astonished by the result of her attack that she almost let the beast seize her with those sharp mandibles and pull her into the mouth that gaped overhead. At the last moment she scrambled back, waving the lightsaber to evaporate the gout of wet silk that it vomited toward her. At least the energy blade was good against that. She noted that the silk expellant became opaque only after it left the thing's mouth.

She realized belatedly that Lorn had called out something to her a moment ago. It hadn't registered at first, but now it did.

A taozin?

She remembered a few references to the beasts in her first history class. Thought to be extinct, they had been one of the few living creatures ever encountered that could not be perceived through the Force. Apparently someone had imported one to Coruscant some time in the past.

There was an old Jedi adage that Master Bondara had been fond of quoting: Any enemy may be defeated—at the right time.

This, Darsha realized, was not the right time.

She retreated toward Lorn and I-Five, who had gained another few meters. The taozin sprayed more webbing at them. Darsha pushed with the Force, deflecting the flow of sticky fluid when she could and vaporizing it with her lightsaber when she couldn't. There was nothing else to do but keep retreating— back into the clutches of the Sith.

Lorn, I-Five, and Darsha moved away from the taozin as fast as they could without dislodging the planks and plates that made up the bridge. These were held in place only by the stickiness of the web support cables, so the three couldn't break into a full run.

Fortunately, for all its many feet, the creature wasn't terribly fast. It lurched along behind them, launching webbing from time to time, which Darsha managed for the most part to deflect. As they retreated, I-Five spoke to Lorn in a low voice, pointing at the varied surfaces they were walking on.

"Help me remove some of these."

Lorn blinked. Did I-Five think the taozin might fall through the cracks? He started to question the droid's instructions, but then shrugged. Apparently his companion had a plan, which was more than Lorn had at the moment. It wasn't like he had anything better to do; why not spend the last few minutes of his life dismantling a bridge?

Darsha saw what they were doing and slowed her pace slightly, giving them more time to work. It went surprisingly quickly, considering that Lorn had no tools. I-Five used his finger blasters to sever the largest connecting points between each item and the supporting web, and they began tossing the various pieces over the side.

Lorn estimated that they were about three-quarters of the way back to the ledge. For an instant he entertained the crazy hope that maybe Darsha was wrong and the Sith actually wasn't behind them. Which would give them a little more space in which to retreat, although eventually they would reencounter the Cthons. That hope was quickly extinguished, however, when he glanced over his shoulder and saw the twin crimson blades of the Sith's lightsaber glowing behind them. So much for that idea. Their nemesis was there waiting for them.

He turned back to I-Five. "If you're going to do something, now would be a good time."

The droid glanced back at the Sith and shook his head. "Not yet. We need to be closer to the edge."

Lorn resisted the temptation to point out that he personally was already far closer to the edge than he cared to be. Instead he grabbed the corner of the next support piece—it looked like the cowling of a vaporator unit—and tugged it free of the bridge. Maybe he would jump before he let the Sith get him. He tossed the cowling over the bridge and watched it sail out of range of I-Five's photoreceptors. There was no sound of it hitting bottom. A plethora of ways to die were available here, none of them pleasant: eaten by a monster, decapitated by a lightsaber, or falling to smash against the planet's bedrock.

Lorn gritted his teeth and pulled another support free.

Even with the aid of the Force, Darsha could barely manage to keep dodging fast enough as the taozin fired barrage after barrage of silken webbing at her. She had given up trying to influence it with the Force; its eerie invulnerability to that form of attack was evidently quite complete.

Despite the desperate straits she found herself in, however, Darsha had never felt so deeply *in* the Force. So much at peace, so . . . *calm*. The logical, rational side of her mind kept reminding her that she was trapped in a tightening vise, but for some reason that just didn't bother her. All that mattered was reacting to the monster's attack, letting the Force guide her movements, letting it fill the vessel that she had become. A constant current of challenge and opposition, attack and defense. As insane as it sounded, given the situation, she felt good. Better than good, in fact; she felt *great*.

Master Bondara had told her it would be like this. "When you are one with the Force," he had once said, "you are as nothing. A calm in the storm, a pivot to the lever. Chaos may rage around you, yet you are still. You will experience it someday, Darsha, and you will understand."

A distant part of her mind was sad that she could not tell him now, could not share the joy of discovery with him—but another part of her was somehow certain that he already knew.

She kept the lightsaber moving, keeping the taozin at bay. Although the blade was less than fully effective against the creature, it still respected the weapon's incandescent bite. She swung it again, grazing the thing's exoskeleton and shaving a couple of those small skin nodules off. They hit the bridge's surface and stuck to the webbing.

Whatever the droid's idea was, it had better be quick. Darsha could feel the presence of the Sith without seeking him now.

Darth Maul felt surprise as the Padawan and Pavan approached closer. Neither was facing him; instead, they were backing away from some huge, incredible creature.

Once it was close enough for him to see clearly, he recognized what it was. Darth Sidious had insisted that he read and reread every scrap of information available on the Jedi, as well as all data that related to them, no matter how obscurely. Knowledge of the enemy was power, his master had told him, and the Sith are the acme of power. An obscure HoloNet article on beasts that had, through various quirks of mutation and natural selection, become invisible in the Force had told him about the taozin.

They were supposed to be extinct—but then, so were the Sith. Sidious's apprentice sent a strong tendril of power molded from the dark side toward the creature—and felt the mental probe pass *through* it, as light penetrates transparisteel.

Fascinating.

Darth Maul stepped back a pace; his presence had drawn the creature's attention. It fired a thin runnel of webbing at him, and he let his connection to the Force take over, his lightsaber easily vaporizing the stream.

The creature paused and spat webbing at the Sith, who was just a few meters behind them now. I-Five pulled a final object from the bridge's surface, then spoke to Lorn and Darsha. "Now is the time," he said. "Hold on tightly to me."

The droid waited to be sure both humans had done as he said, and then jumped over the side of the bridge, hooking one of his arms around the main support rope nearest him.

"Cut the support," he said to Darsha.

Darsha understood what his plan was now. It was a bold one, she had to give him that. He and Pavan had ripped away enough of the detritus that coated the bridge's webbing to render its supports unstable. When the Padawan's lightsaber bit through the thick support cable, the section of the structure they were clinging to collapsed. As the three began falling, I-Five fired upward, his finger blasters striking the juncture of every remaining plate and the support rope they were clinging to. Their momentum increased, and suddenly they were past the tail of the taozin, swinging in a very long arc toward the opposite side of the chasm.

In the distance they heard the Sith shout—in rage, it sounded like—as they kept falling. After a second or two I-Five no longer had to shoot to separate the support cable from the bridge decking. Their weight and momentum ripped the strand away for them as they fell.

"If you can slow our acceleration," the droid said to Darsha, "it will perhaps make this fall survivable."

Darsha closed her eyes, knitting her brow in concentration, and reached out for the Force once more. After a few seconds she could feel their speed decrease.

I-Five said, "I calculate that we will reach the other side of the cavern in about—"

The trio hit the rock wall on the opposite side of the cavern. Even with Darsha's use of the Force to slow them, the impact was considerable. Darsha gasped, the wind knocked out of her. She barely managed to keep her grip.

"Well, about now," I-Five finished.

"Thanks," Lorn managed, "for your accurate-as-usual timing."

"You're welcome."

They'd made it across. Now all they had to do was climb up the cable.

As he fanned the vaporized webbing away from his vision with one gloved hand, Darth Maul saw his quarry jump over the side of the bridge and cut the support strand away, turning it into an escape route. For a moment the Sith apprentice stood absolutely still, realizing how he had been outwitted. He let his rage boil out of him in a frustrated shout. The Force-dampening energy of the taozin had prevented his sensing their escape until they were already gone. It was astounding, the amount of good fortune his prey were experiencing.

He was really going to enjoy completing this mission.

Just now, however, he had more pressing matters to attend to. Between the weight of the taozin and the dismantling by his quarry, the bridge was beginning to fall apart. The Sith jumped nimbly over to the remaining support cable and began to move toward the opposite side of the cavern. He could easily cross the remaining distance before his prey climbed up out of the chasm. His athletic skills and connection to the Force made the thin support rope seem as wide as a walkway.

But the taozin had other ideas. It wound around the remaining support cable, blocking his path. Its head—now below the cable—fired another stream of webbing up at him.

Again he vaporized the arcing reticulation. The creature attacked again, but in a different way this time, using its legs to vibrate the strand on which the Sith stood.

Darth Maul began to fall backwards, but he did not panic. He reached out, grabbing the support cable with his free hand, careful to keep his lightsaber away from it. He now hung directly in front of the creature, only a couple of meters away from its sharp mandibles.

He knew now that he wouldn't be catching up to Pavan and the others within the next few minutes. He spun his lightsaber over in a perfect execution of Slashing Wampa and cut the remaining bridge support that he clung to. He and the taozin fell away in opposite directions, he slamming against the wall on the opposite side from the three fugitives while the taozin disappeared into the abyss.

Unfortunately, disposing of the creature had also disposed of his only route across the cavern. Darth Maul climbed up the support cable to the ledge from whence he had come.

He gritted his teeth. Even with the Force to aid him he could not leap across a chasm this wide. He would have to retrace his route back up to the surface, which was frustrating beyond bearing. He knew he would find them again. There was no place in the galaxy he could not follow them, and he would not fail, however long it took. But to be so close and to fail yet again—it enraged him.

They would pay for this in full.

Obi-Wan Kenobi shouldered through the doors of the Tusken Oasis and for a few seconds felt as though he had returned uplevels. The club was lavishly decorated and well kept. Statues of beasts from various galactic mythologies intertwined in a lusty wall frieze that stretched around the big room, and photonic crystal fixtures glowed with multicolored lights, offsetting the overall darkness. The predominant color at the moment was blue, but as the Padawan watched, it cycled higher up the spectrum toward violet. A quartet of Bith musicians were playing something lively in the corner, their large, bulbous heads bobbing in time to a melody from their leader's omni box.

Only after looking more closely at the patrons of the club was he reminded that he was still below levels in the Crimson Corridor. Gamorrean bodyguards carrying blasters mingled with their gambling clients, and many patrons without paid protection carried their own weapons. There was enough firepower in the room to start a small revolution.

As Obi-Wan let his senses ride the currents of the Force and expand into the club—feeling its pulse, so to speak—he sensed a wrongness, an out-of-step sequence. *Something* had happened here not too long ago, of that he was sure. He spotted a Twi'lek's lekku wiggling over the heads of some of the patrons near the band, and for a moment he thought he'd found Anoon Bondara, but a closer look told him it was not the Jedi after all.

He moved toward the large bar at the back of the room and noticed that he was being watched. Several Rodians at the end of the bar followed him with their black, featureless gaze, snouts quivering. Each wore cut-down versions of Stalker armor suits and might as well have been stamped with the words *Black Sun Enforcer*. As he neared the back of the room a Kubaz crunching on still-wriggling insects from a bowl on the bar looked up, noticed the cowled figure approaching, and promptly hopped off his barstool, heading for one of the exits.

The bartender was of a species that Obi-Wan did not recognize. Its dark blue head had no neck, instead flowing smoothly into large shoulders from which draped six muscular arms resembling serpents. At the end of each arm was a pair of digits. Two arms were currently mixing a large drink while another tapped information into a datapad. As Obi-Wan approached the bar, he saw the remaining three arms drop down below the level of the bar.

It didn't take the skills of someone like Yoda to guess that a weapon was being readied down there. His source regarding the Hutt's establishment had apparently been correct. He faced the bartender and slowly moved his hands up to slide back the cowl covering his face. The bartender looked at him with an expression that, on a human face, would have been called a scowl. "Whar' ya wan'?" it croaked in thickly accented Basic.

"I'm looking for some information."

"Don' hav'ny," the bartender rumbled, a fourth arm slithering furtively down under the bar to join the other three. Obi-Wan could feel the tension building.

Be in the moment; be aware only of the present.

He had heard Master Qui-Gon's admonition so many times, it seemed almost as though his Jedi mentor was standing next to him. The Padawan knew that his tendency to look to the future sometimes blinded him to the present. In his current situation, he felt it prudent to take Qui-Gon's advice.

Obi-Wan reached out with his mind and felt what could not be seen. The bartender was close to activating a blaster under the bar, which was pointed straight at the Padawan's abdomen. The two Rodians had split up and were flanking him now, just out of lightsaber range. He could sense their weapons being readied, as well.

What were they waiting for?

Then he noticed the bartender's four eyes glance over at a tiny pair of crystals inset in the bar's surface near the datapad, seemingly part of the design. One was lit; it glowed red. Near it was a green crystal, unlit. As he watched, the red crystal winked out and the green crystal lit up.

Events slowed and perception stretched then, as Obi-Wan Kenobi reached for the Force and his lightsaber simultaneously. He dropped flat to the floor as the bartender fired its weapon, sending pieces of the beautiful wooden bar exploding outward to shower the apprentice with splinters. He ignited his lightsaber and swung it up in a shallow arc, the superhot blade slicing almost without resistance through the bar and the blaster it concealed without touching the bartender's prehensile limbs. He rose to his feet quickly, almost levitating with the aid of the Force, and continued the arc, twisting to face the Rodians, who had raised their weapons. He gestured, and one of the blasters leapt out of its surprised owner's hand and seemingly flung itself across the room. His partner fired, a particle beam burst that was deflected by the cobalt-hued energy blade, sending its trajectory off into the ceiling somewhere. Obi-Wan gestured again, and the second Rodian's blaster flew over to land at his feet.

All around him, the club's habitués had stopped their gambling to watch, many dropping instinctively into defensive postures, weapons ready, or hiding behind their bodyguards. Sensing the immediate danger was over, they turned back to their games of sabacc, dejarik, and other pursuits.

Obi-Wan turned around and faced the bartender, his lightsaber already deactivated.

"Like I said—I just want some information. No trouble."

Although he couldn't read the being's face, Obi-Wan noted that the color of the bartender's head had altered to a much lighter shade of blue and that it seemed to be having trouble with its respiration. He sensed movement behind him: the Rodians were moving in again. He turned to face them.

"That's enough, boys," someone said. "Our Jedi guest isn't here to cause a problem. Are you, friend? . . ."

"Kenobi. Obi-Wan Kenobi. And, as I mentioned to your bartender, all I'm looking for is information." The Padawan turned to face the new arrival, who was a short, muscular human with a large braid of hair trailing down his back. There was an aura of power about him—not Force related, just sheer animal prepotency.

"I'm looking for information, too, Jedi Kenobi," the man said. "Perhaps we can help each other. My name is Dal Perhi."

Perhi led Obi-Wan down a short flight of stairs and along a corridor, apologizing as they walked.

"Sorry about the rough stuff—but we had to be sure you really were a Jedi. The fact that you didn't even have to harm any of our boys speaks for itself. The Jedi are known, after all, for valuing life."

There was more than a touch of sarcasm to his tone. Obi-Wan smiled tightly.

"And the Black Sun are not. You realize if I hadn't been a Jedi, I would likely be dead now."

The gangster nodded. "As I said, a simple precaution.

You'll see why in a minute. Just part of doing business, Jedi Kenobi."

"Are you taking me to see Yanth the Hutt?"

The gangster glanced at the Padawan. "Good guess."

They reached the end of the corridor and passed through a pair of wide doors that looked as if they had been melted in the center. As they entered the room, Obi-Wan immediately noted several Gamorrean guards lying on the floor. He was no forensic specialist, but it seemed as though they had been shot with blasters. He stepped over a broken force pike and followed Perhi toward a large shape on the floor ahead.

He knelt down and examined the wound that had killed the Hutt. It looked almost as if it might have come from a lightsaber. That wasn't possible, of course. It had to be a blaster burn.

He looked over at the Black Sun representative. Could it be that his organization was having one of its periodic in-fighting episodes? A coup in the making?

"I was hoping, Jedi Kenobi, that you might be able to shed a little light here. Isn't there some—" Perhi gestured vaguely. "—mystic way you can tell who did this?"

It was interesting, Obi-Wan thought, the mythologies of various organizations. Among the Jedi there might well be those who wondered about the mysterious Black Sun, exaggerating their reach, their connections, their dangerousness. Certainly the opposite was true here. Perhi obviously felt there was some cabalistic way his Jedi guest could learn what had happened here.

"Give me a minute," Obi-Wan said.

The gangster nodded and stepped back.

Obi-Wan knelt on the floor and allowed his senses to expand, meditating on the apparent events. The sense of corruption he'd felt before on the street came back strongly, as did the disturbances caused by many other beings—but it was all too muddled. Too much time had passed, too many people had been in and out. A Master such as Mace Windu could probably make sense of it—but Obi-Wan was not a Master. He wasn't even a Jedi Knight yet.

He shook his head. "I'm sorry. Perhaps if I'd been here earlier—"

The gangster nodded. Obi-Wan sensed his disappointment, though Perhi hid it well. "Not your fault. Thanks anyway."

Obi-Wan was surprised to find that he felt slightly relieved. After all, if he'd found it was Darsha or Master Bondara who had perpetrated this carnage . . . But in all probability it was not.

But who could it have been?

"No one saw who did this?" he asked Perhi.

"No. You'd think there'd be at least one witness, but everyone says they couldn't get a good look at him, even when he ran right by them."

Obi-Wan nodded. That could be the natural reticence to get involved usually found in people on the far side of the law—or in fear of retribution.

He walked toward the exit, followed by Perhi.

"Jedi Kenobi?"

"Yes?"

"I've never had the pleasure of seeing one of you

work until today. What you did up there in the bar—
are all Jedi that good?"

Obi-Wan stopped and turned to face Perhi. "No,
they're not."

The gangster seemed to relax slightly—but his expression changed as Obi-Wan continued.

"I'm only an apprentice. I have yet to take the Jedi
trials. My Master is far more skilled than I. As a student, I'm afraid I'm a bit of a disappointment to him.
In terms of fighting skills, I'm probably least among
the Jedi."

The Padawan had the satisfaction of watching the
gangster pale slightly. Then he turned and left Yanth's
underground office, and the Tusken Oasis. With any
luck, he had given Dal Perhi something to think
about.

As he returned to the street, Obi-Wan mentally reviewed what he knew so far. Not much, unfortunately.
He debated reporting back to the council, but decided
to wait until he had something more than hearsay and
supposition to offer. So far, all he knew for certain was
that Darsha Assant had lost the informant she was assigned to protect. Her skyhopper had been gutted by a
street gang, and her Master's skycar had been destroyed after a supposed brawl with a cowled figure.
He had seen the vehicles, but no body for the informant, no Darsha, and no Master Bondara.

Add to that the fact that a Black Sun vigo, Yanth the
Hutt, had been killed by a cowled figure. There had
been a sense of corruption pervading the location,

similar to what he had experienced at the crash site of Bondara's skycar.

Obi-Wan had two theories, which unfortunately were mutually contradictory. Theory number one: Darsha loses her informant to Black Sun attackers and trails them to the Tusken Oasis, where she is attacked and defeats an entire roomful of guards, along with Yanth the Hutt. She calls for help, and her master comes to aid her. They flee and . . . vanish.

There were holes in that theory that he could fly a Dreadnought through. Darsha was good in a fight, but if she was *that* good, she would never have lost her informant in the first place. Also, it didn't explain the sense of wrongness that lingered over the site of the skycar crash and the murders.

Theory number two was that there was some other entity—most likely connected somehow with Black Sun—involved who had killed Yanth the Hutt and his bodyguards. Obi-Wan liked the second theory better for several reasons, not the least of which was that he didn't want to believe any Jedi capable of the crimes he'd been investigating. But neither theory explained where Darsha and her Master were, or why they hadn't been heard from for so long.

Obi-Wan sighed. He hadn't exhausted all his leads yet. There was still the block of cubicles to investigate. He checked the address he had been given and started to walk. With any luck at all, he might learn something there that would shed some light on the entire mess.

No such luck.

At the site of the cubicle explosion Obi-Wan had

learned some very interesting news—but it was news that served only to muddy the waters further. One of the local police investigating the incident had told him that Hath Monchar, the Neimoidian deputy viceroy of the Trade Federation, had been the tenant of the blasted cubicle, and that he, too, had been killed.

It seemed obvious that Black Sun was somehow mixed up in all this. There was no evidence anywhere to suggest that the crime cartel was in bed with the Trade Federation, but it was possible, certainly.

Too many questions, Obi-Wan thought. Too many questions, and not nearly enough answers.

There was light at the end of the tunnel.

Lorn, I-Five, and Darsha hurried toward it. They reached a doorway—the partially boarded-over entrance to another kiosk similar to the one by which they had entered the underground—and emerged into the tenebrous shadows of Coruscant's Crimson Corridor section.

It was like stepping into bright sunlight compared to the labyrinth they'd been trapped in for so long.

Lorn breathed a sigh of relief. It had taken longer than they had expected to find a path back to the surface, involving several dead ends and retracing of their routes, but at least they had not suffered any further attacks by more underground denizens. Apparently the only Cthons on the other side of the bridge had been the ones in the taozin's belly.

Which was fortunate, because after the effort of

climbing the long silken rope to the top of the under-ground chasm, the two humans were exhausted. But they couldn't afford to rest, or even slow down. They had to assume that the Sith was still somewhere be-hind them, still pursuing them.

Which was the worst of their problems, but by no means the only one. Lorn figured that in all likelihood the bank's security personnel were after him and I-Five by now, as well. The transaction fraud they had committed would probably have also attracted the notice of the planetary police, and very possibly a few Republic treasury agents.

It had also occurred to Lorn that Black Sun might have a few questions for him, depending on what kind of records Yanth had left of his business dealings and what the eyewitnesses at the Tusken Oasis had pieced together. In short, probably just about every orga-nized power on the planet was looking for him and I-Five.

Of course, the only pursuit he knew of for certain was the Sith's. The rest I-Five would probably charac-terize as paranoia. So what? Lorn told himself. Down-levels, paranoia wasn't a disorder; it was a lifestyle.

Darsha spoke. "My people will no doubt have sent out searchers by now. If we can get to a comm station, all we have to do is alert them to come pick us up."

Right—the Jedi. He'd forgotten about them. That made one more at the party.

I-Five said, "We are in an area with very few oper-ating public comm stations. It's likely there will be a higher quantity of functional ones some levels up."

Sharp, Lorn thought. There were stations to be

found if you knew where to look, but he didn't want to give Darsha a chance to drag them back to the Temple just yet. Back there in the tunnels, during the endless search for a way out, he'd managed to whisper a few instructions to the droid without Darsha hearing him. I-Five knew Lorn wanted to get to Tuden Sal as quickly as possible—without the Jedi Padawan.

"So we're back to the question of the day: How do we get uplevels?" Darsha asked. "Climbing is risky. I had a bad experience earlier with some hawk-bats. I found my way up a monad, but I don't see any of those nearby."

It was true: without some kind of transportation, the problem of getting uplevels in this area was a sticky one. Of course, if he could contact Tuden Sal, the man would send a transport—but the problem was circular. First he had to get to a comm station.

It was extremely frustrating. They had never been more than half a kilometer from one of the most cosmopolitan areas in the galaxy. The only problem was, it was half a kilometer *straight up*. The possibility of freedom lay only a score of levels over their heads, and yet it might as well be on one of the orbiting space stations for all that they could reach it. All things considered, Lorn thought, it was hard to see how things could get any worse.

"We are being watched," the droid said.

Even as the droid spoke, Darsha could feel them— more than one, of different species, and with unmistakably malign intent.

"Why am I not surprised?" Lorn said. "Any way to tell exactly *who* is watching us?"

Darsha reached out with her senses and felt familiar signatures. She was sure she had come across them before recently.

"It's not the Sith," she said, and saw the broker relax. And then she recognized the vibration in the Force. "It's—"

"Hey, lady—still slumming?"

It was Green Hair, the leader of the Raptor gang that had attacked her when she first touched down in the Corridor. Three of his cronies—the Trandoshan, a Saurin, and a Devaronian—were with him. Darsha almost smiled in relief. Compared to the creatures she'd faced under the surface, these punks were nothing.

Lorn seemed to feel the same way. He said, "Slide off, boys—we're more trouble than you're worth."

She could tell from the look on Green Hair's face that this was not the script he had planned on running. His purported victims were showing no fear. She had to give him credit, though—he tried again, speaking as if he hadn't heard Lorn.

"You're in our territory, and you gotta pay the toll."

Darsha almost laughed. It seemed like years ago that she'd been nervous about facing this riffraff. Her perspective had radically changed in the last thirty-six hours. Something of what she felt must have gotten across to the Raptor leader, because he looked worried for a few seconds.

"I said—" he began.

Lorn interrupted him. "What you said and what

you're gonna get are two entirely separate things. Listen up—this is how it's gonna play. You give us your money now—*all* of you. And you—" He pointed at the leader. "—are taking us on a tour."

Green Hair could not have looked more shocked if Lorn had shoved a power prod against his chest. He stood there like a statue for a few moments, his electrostatic hairdo quivering slightly in the low breeze. His mates looked uneasy, as well; this kind of confidence was not something they encountered often on their turf. They glanced at Green Hair, and Darsha did not need the Force to read what was in that look. They were waiting for him to make a decision.

It was equally obvious that Green Hair knew what was expected of him. He looked back at his crew, then at Darsha, Lorn, and I-Five. "Take 'em!" he shouted, jumping toward Lorn.

Lorn sidestepped, tripping the youth as he rushed by. I-Five hammered the green head with one metal fist, and the boy went down. The Trandoshan lunged forward, a vibroblade extended. The droid used his finger blaster to heat the vibrating blade to incandescence. With a scream, the Trandoshan dropped the blistering metal and bolted into the shadows, cradling his burned hand with his other one.

Darsha was deep in the Force, knowing what her attackers were going to do before they did it. It was far easier than facing the taozin. Before she was even aware of reaching for it, the lightsaber was in her grasp, its blade gleaming in the shadows as she deflected the blaster bolts that whizzed from the Devaronian's weapon toward her and her friends. She thrust out her free hand, and the Saurin's blaster leapt from his hand toward Lorn, who caught it. He thumbed the setting to stun and fired twice. The remaining two gang members collapsed on the street's cracked ferrocrete alongside their stunned leader.

The skirmish had taken no more than a few seconds. Lorn and I-Five began searching the three unconscious bodies.

"What are you doing?" the Padawan asked.

"What does it look like?" Lorn replied. "We're taking from those who don't need and giving to those who do—namely us. We've got to have credits to get uplevels."

Darsha started to say something, then thought better of it. She didn't like scavenging off the bodies, but she could see the necessity.

Green Hair stirred and moaned. Lorn prodded him with the blaster. "Up," he said. Green Hair got to his feet, not looking too happy.

"I'm sure you boys have a way uplevels," Lorn said to him. "Let's go find it."

Darsha could feel the boy's resistance. She started to make a hand motion to focus the Force on him and give Lorn's suggestion a better chance of working, but Lorn held out a palm to her. "No mind tricks, Darsha—I want him alert."

She started to say something, then shrugged. He seemed to have a plan, which was more than she had at the moment.

Lorn prodded the Raptor with his newly acquired blaster. He felt much better now that he had a weapon.

True, it wasn't much—only a BlasTech DH-17, without optical sighting arrays and with its power charge nearly depleted, but it had made a satisfying sizzle when he'd fired it during the short battle. He'd also picked up a vibroblade. These weapons might not help him if the Sith caught up with them, but they were better than facing his nemesis empty-handed.

There was another reason to celebrate. Since he and I-Five had been the only ones to check the unconscious bodies of the Raptors, Darsha had missed I-Five's find. The droid had flashed it at Lorn when she had been watching Green Hair. It was a small comlink—no doubt keyed to the Raptor who had owned it, but both Lorn and I-Five had hacked comlinks often enough that he knew getting around basic security would be no problem at all.

The three of them set out, following their unwilling guide, alert for any deception on his part. He led them toward an alley about two hundred meters from the direction he'd come.

Now if I-Five could just get a few minutes away, or have a chance to socket the comlink into his data plug, he could call Tuden Sal and set up a meeting. Things were looking better and better, Lorn told himself. He and his partner just might be able to get themselves safely offplanet after all.

Of course, it would mean dropping Darsha—a prospect that, he had to admit, he wasn't looking forward to nearly as much as he thought he would. After all, she had helped keep him alive through this nightmare. He tried to remind himself that she was doing it purely to get the Neimoidian's information into the hands of the Jedi—but at this point she knew practically as much as he did. While he might be able to supply some more details, Darsha was as capable of delivering the gist of the data to the Jedi Council as he was.

Though it galled him to admit it, the truth was that he was growing somewhat fond of her. True, she was younger than he was by a considerable factor, but there was still a certain attractive quality to her.

Remember, he told himself sternly, *she's a Jedi.*

Or a Padawan, to be pedantic. A Padawan on her first solo mission—that much he'd gleaned from listening to conversations she'd had with I-Five. Tough cut of the cards, Lorn thought, to lose her Master, her mission, and even her informants on the first trip out. Why did she keep going? What made her want to bring them back to the Temple? Couldn't she see what manipulators the Jedi were?

Lorn wanted to find out. As they walked, he dropped back a couple of paces until he was alongside her, leaving I-Five to keep tabs on Green Hair.

"Padawan Assant," he said, somewhat stiffly, "I hope you don't mind my asking, but—just what made you choose the Jedi path? They're not—I mean—" He stopped, unsure how to continue. He glanced at her and saw her watching him.

Even in this dim light, her eyes were so incredibly blue.

"Never mind," he said gruffly. He started to walk faster, to bring himself back up to I-Five, but she put her hand on his arm. He looked at it, then at her.

"I was chosen," she said. "Chosen by the Force."

She told him that she had never been part of a family. "When the Jedi came and told me I could be a part of theirs, it all made perfect sense."

Of course it did, he thought. *You weren't taken from a father who loved you by an order who then fired him because they thought it best that his son have no attachments.*

He felt angry at her answer. He wanted to somehow break that composure, shatter that maddening calm, that sanctimonious righteousness she shared with all the others of her order.

"But now you might not be able to keep on being a Jedi," he said. "Doesn't that make you angry? These people, this order that you consider your family, casting you out?"

"Do you know of the Jedi Code?"

Lorn nodded. "Yes. I've heard it plenty of times."

" 'There is no emotion; there is peace,' " she quoted. "This doesn't mean I won't be upset if I can't stay at the Temple—just that emotion does not rule me. I am joined with the Force for my entire life. Down there, facing the taozin, I had a chance to really understand what that means.

"Whether or not I become a Jedi doesn't matter now. I have felt the balance of the Force at a deeper level, and I know that I have done—and will continue to do—what I can to help maintain that balance. I'll do it with the Jedi, or on my own—but I will do it. I am at peace, even though I may suffer disappointment."

His confusion must have shown on his face, because she smiled. There was a time when a smile like that on the face of a Jedi would have infuriated him, probably would have even made him try to wipe it off with his fists.

He didn't feel that way now.

"Let me put it another way," Darsha continued. "I have achieved my goals, even if I do not complete my mission."

Lorn nodded, but did not reply. It sounded like just the kind of ambiguity all the Jedi Knights were so fond of spouting—but like the smile, it didn't anger him to hear it coming from her. He wasn't sure what that meant.

He wasn't sure he wanted to find out.

28

Darth Maul stalked the underground passage back the way he had come, his rage boiling into the darkness like superheated steam. His power in the Force was magnified by this; unlike the foolish Jedi, the Sith harnessed the intensity of their emotions, refusing to pretend that such things did not exist. Any creature foolish enough to impede his speedy progress to the surface would be sorry indeed.

He passed through the Cthons' cavern and saw no sign of the subterraneans. Doubtless his previous passage through their domain had given them ample cause to make themselves scarce. Which was just as well—though he would have welcomed the opportunity to mow some of them down given the mood he was in, time was of the essence.

The intensity of his connection to the Force brought back a memory: another day of intense focus of his power. The day he had constructed his lightsaber. Maul was not wont to revisit his past, unless doing so somehow served his master, but the satisfaction of the creation, the perfection of focus and the highly charged connection to the Force that had wrought his weapon stood out now in his memory.

The specialized furnace, which he had created from plans taken from his master's Sith Holocron, had radiated an intense heat as it shaped the synthetic crystals needed for his lightsaber. But rather than leaving the kiln chamber and allowing them to form on their own, he had remained near the device, concentrating on the metamorphosing gems, using the Force to purify and refine the lattice of the molecular matrices.

Most Jedi used natural crystals in their lightsabers; Adegan crystals were the gems of choice. Most of the other components of a lightsaber were easily obtained—power cells, field energizers, stabilizing rings, flux apertures—but not the crystals themselves. They had to be mined in the Adega System, deep within the Outer Rim Territories. The difficulty of using natural materials meant that the alignment process could take a long time—and the calibration had to be perfect, because mismatched crystals could destroy not only the lightsaber, but its creator. Finding and aligning the crystals was a Jedi test, but it was not the way of the Sith. The dark masters of the Force preferred to create their own synthetic crystals, to match the harmonics in the searing heat of a crucible and thus take their creation of the weapon to a deeper level.

Maul had sat by the furnace, focusing his hatred of the Jedi to a fiery peak and expanding his control of the Force, which he used to manipulate the molecular structures of the four gems required for his double-bladed weapon. The choice to make two blades instead of one had been an easy one. Only an expert would even think of trying to handle a double-bladed weapon, and he would be no less than an expert. The glory of the Sith required it, as did his master.

Not even the compressed ferrocrete walls of the pressurized chamber could entirely contain the intense temperature required to form the crystals. Hour after hour had passed, the searing heat washing over the apprentice. But his control had not wavered; the pain had not swayed his focus. Layer after countless layer of the crystals had been laid down, aligned, and perfected. It had taken days, days without food or water or sleep, but eventually he had sensed their readiness. Then he had deactivated the furnace and cracked it open. There, sitting in the formation crucibles, had been his four perfect crystals.

Maul grinned into the darkness. Yes, it was a good memory, an attainment that reminded him of his powers, that reassured him of his eventual and inevitable triumph. He had been thwarted thus far by an odd chain of events, but that would change soon.

He was back in the transport tube now. Ahead of him he could see light shining down from overhead, where he'd cut through the ventilation grid. Maul gathered the Force to himself and jumped straight up, rising several body lengths to shoot through the opening. A derelict human, deep in the throes of some narcotic delusion, was lying on the street nearby. He saw the Sith rise from the depths, gave out a little gasp, and passed out as Maul's boots touched the pavement.

*   *   *

Not far away, the wreckage of the Twi'lek Jedi's skycar and its attendant debris still partially blocked the streets. The Sith Lord considered how he might best locate his quarry. Once he reacquired their trail he could easily locate them. The weakness of that strategy was that he would still be following them. There had been far too much of that. Much better to get ahead of them somehow and be waiting for them.

Maul recalled the method by which he'd located the Neimoidian earlier. Perhaps the planetary net cams would be useful to him again; if he could find the most recent location where the humans had been seen, he could save time tracking them by going straight to it.

But to begin his search he needed a data terminal, and there were none to be found in this urban jungle. He was reminded of something Lord Sidious had once told him: "For every solution there are two problems."

Darth Maul considered for a moment, then activated his wrist comm and holoscreen monitor. He commed the *Infiltrator*, tapped into its main computer, and used that to access the port datalink, bypassing the regular navigation request screens until he located a menu offering access to other networks. His master's password again opened locked doors, and within a few seconds he had called up several data sources.

The first was a holomap of this section of the Crimson Corridor. Maul located his current position and tapped in the last known vectors for the humans and the droid.

The planetary data bank gave him the information he wanted. It was as he had suspected; they were heading in the direction of the Jedi Temple, using the droid's global positioner to guide them. Fortunately they still had a long way to go, not only toward the Temple, but uplevels, as well. He zeroed down to street level and identified several exits from the subterranean passages that they might have used.

Next he tapped into Coruscant's security network and called up a listing of surveillance cams near those exits. He flashed through hundreds of images from the last few minutes, finding nothing that would help him. He left the link open and shifted to check recent crimes in the area. Not surprisingly, hundreds of incidents popped up for the last few hours in the Crimson Corridor: street fights, petty theft, other common crimes. He noted in passing an oddity: a droid was being sought for scamming the banking system. But he found nothing recent that had happened in the target areas that would serve him.

Darth Maul scowled. He needed transportation; that way he could get nearer his target zones. He considered the problem.

As he did so, his comm flashed that he had an incoming message. He felt a finger of worry touch him. It could be only his master. The thought of not answering did not occur to the Sith. He toggled the secure communications mode, dumping his connection to the security net, and waited for the readout to confirm his scrambled signal.

Sidious's voice crackled over the comlink. "Time grows short, my apprentice. What is the state of your current project?"

"My master, I have obtained the holocron. I am

holding it for your inspection. There have been . . . delays in finding the human whom the Neimoidian spoke with, but they are now within my grasp. I shall not fail you."

Darth Sidious was silent for a second before he replied.

"See that you do not. When they are dead, contact me, and I will instruct you in how to deliver the holocron. Be very careful not to reveal our presence, Lord Maul—it is not yet time."

"Yes, my master."

Darth Maul moved toward the clearing where the Jedi's skycar had crashed. It would be a good location to try what he had planned. He reached out with his senses. There was no sign of Jedi anywhere close now.

Cautiously Maul shielded his strength, hooding his power in the Force lest any approaching Jedi notice. It was sensible that those of the Temple would investigate the crash of one of their transports, but it was still cause for discretion. He had little doubt that he could defeat any living Jedi, but there were many of them here on the capital of the Republic. Even he was not foolish enough to try to take them on all at once. With the Jedi searching, events were complicated that much more.

It had certainly turned out to be a much more interesting mission than he had thought it would be.

Maul settled himself in the shadows beyond the area where the skycar had crashed, and reaccessed the planetary security grid, using the same technique he had before. Few taxi drivers could be enticed to enter the Crimson Corridor, and even the security forces did not enter the zone without good cause. But good cause was something he could supply.

This time, instead of activating the menu, he scanned the current patrol routes for this quarter of the city. High above, still several kilometers away, were a pair of patrol officers on speeder bikes, circling on their regular beat. Maul noted their designations and then accessed the dispatch queue for emergency calls. He fed data directly into the dispatch computer. Eventually an audit might reveal his call to be a ruse, with no comlink recording, but it would serve for now.

The bait he chose was the droid banking crime. The police would be wary of any dangerous call-outs for the area, but they would perhaps be less concerned with a white-collar crime conducted by someone's mechanical servant. It was the best inticement he could come up with on short notice.

Having set out his lures, the Sith apprentice waited to see what he might catch. He did not have to wait long. A few minutes after he'd entered the data into the security net, two police speeder bikes came roaring in from uplevels, strobe lights flashing. From the shadows in which he crouched, Darth Maul prepared to move.

Abruptly he halted. At the edge of his perceptions was something else. He reached for it, projecting jagged tendrils of the Force to discover what lay unseen. And then, as his probe reached it, it swung lower into view, hovering above the crash site.

It was a PCBU—a droid-piloted police cruiser backup unit. The Crimson Corridor had been the site of a number of officer murders over the years, which was why the

PCBU had been developed. It carried two state-of-the-art swivel laser cannons mounted on the top and bottom of the unit, as well as a variety of sensors, scanners, and disruptors. Maul watched it approach. He had not expected the arrival of such a heavily armed craft, but it would delay his plans only slightly.

He waited until the unit had passed him, following the two speeder bikes, and then acted. He seized the Force and used it to propel himself high into the air, to land on the top of the PCBU. His lightsaber blades ignited as his feet hit the surface of the craft, and he quickly sheared the upper gun free of its mount, spinning the double-ended blade after this to cleave through the transparisteel cockpit bubble and the droid pilot. The PCBU began to descend, its autopilot taking over now that the droid was no longer activated.

Either the speeder bike patrol officers had noted the descent of the craft, or the driver of the PCBU had had time to get off a signal, because they spun their bikes around and flew toward him.

Excellent.

One speeder bike was ahead of the other. Maul deactivated one of his lightsaber's blades and hurled it toward the first of the oncoming speeders like a spear. It pierced the officer's armored chest while the Sith, again assisted by the Force, jumped from the descending PCBU toward the other officer.

By the time he had landed on the speeder his lightsaber had rejoined him, snatched back to him by a feathery runner of the Force. Within moments the second police officer was dead, and Darth Maul had his transportation. With no witnesses, there was little chance of anyone suspecting the use of the Force, and the entire operation had been accomplished quickly enough that, in all probability, neither of the two officers had had a chance to send a distress signal.

Immediately he lifted off on one of the speeder bikes, heading uplevels to get ahead of his quarry. He set the speeder into a vertical spiral and checked his wrist comm as he rose. Again, he noted nothing unusual in the target area. However, one of the cam pickup sites seemed unusually devoid of traffic. Something about it . . .

Darth Maul replayed the scene again at a slower speed. Yes, right there—a flicker of something. He watched the security cam footage play again, slowing it even more. Nothing, nothing . . . and then, abruptly, there he was.

It was unmistakably his target, the information broker known as Lorn Pavan.

The Sith checked the time stamp on the data. The image had been recorded only about twenty minutes ago. He accelerated the speeder toward the location given on the screen.

He had them now.

29

Lorn poked the Raptor leader in the back with the barrel of his blaster as they reached the alley. "Hold it," Lorn said. He turned to I-Five and Darsha. "Any warnings from the science and sorcery team?" he asked. "And don't start whining again about the cheap sensor suite I had installed in you," he added to the droid.

"Well, it *was* less expensive than the Mark Ten."

"But more expensive than the other five choices. A *lot* more expensive." Lorn glanced at Darsha as he spoke, intending to ask her if she was receiving anything on the Force bandwidth, and was somewhat surprised to see that she was smiling. What was even more surprising—downright shocking, actually—was the way he found himself reacting to that smile.

He liked it.

He liked her.

This was bad.

He knew he would soon have to break clear of her. There was just no way he was going back to the Temple. Sure, she was nice-looking, but he'd had nice-looking before, lots of times since Siena had left him. This was definitely not the direction in which his best interests lay. It was best to cut this off, right here and right now. Raise the blast shields, secure the air locks, bolt the hatches.

But instead, to his horror, Lorn realized he was smiling back.

As they walked toward the alley, Darsha enjoyed the patter between Lorn and I-Five. It was clear that they cared as much for each other as two friends would, two equals. Unusual, but at the same time it seemed quite natural.

She'd rarely had the opportunity to develop that kind of bond. The Jedi didn't discourage friendships, of course, but the intensity of her studies and the time they demanded made it difficult to cultivate anything more than casual friendships with the other Pada-wans. Probably the closest she had to a friend at the Temple—aside from her Master, of course—was Obi-Wan Kenobi, and if she had the opportunity to speak with him more than once a week, she counted herself lucky.

As she listened to Lorn and I-Five, she kept her senses alert for any potential dangers ahead or behind. The only obvious latent trouble was Green Hair; the Raptor was brimming with hatred that he had been so easily captured, and that he was being made to lead enemies to his gang's secret exit route uplevels. He would bear very close watching, but I-Five and Lorn seemed to have the situation in hand.

Behind them, she could feel no sign of the Sith, which either meant that they had finally made a successful escape, or was merely evidence of the fact that she still had a long way to go before she could stay in the Force at all times. Earlier, while fighting the Raptors, she'd stepped back into a full communion with it, every sense sharpened and honed, as she had done with the taozin. But she was not yet to a point where she could remain there. She had many years to go before she could be anywhere as good as Master Bondara had consistently been.

Lorn was arguing with I-Five about the latter's sensors. Darsha quested outward with the Force, feeling only the minimal vibrations of animal life in the alley—a few spider-roaches, armored rats, those sorts of creatures. Certainly nothing that represented much of a threat.

". . . more expensive than the other five choices. A *lot* more expensive," Lorn was saying to the droid. He glanced at her as she finished the sentence. She grinned, and was very surprised to feel a depth to his answering smile. Could he possibly be attracted to her? There was certainly no hostility in him at the moment, which was a far cry from his attitude toward her when they had first been thrown together.

It was tempting to probe his emotions, to use the Force on an empathic level to see if she was right. But even as the urge to do so came over her, she quelled it. It would be taking unfair advantage. Besides, looking at him now, Darsha realized that she didn't need to use the Force. The attraction was definitely there on his end, obvious to anyone.

How interesting.

Which begged the question: How did she feel in response?

Lorn suddenly looked away, and Darsha knew he was uncomfortable, unsure of how to deal with this new dynamic between them. A strong sense of guilt came from him: this wasn't a question of probing; she'd have to be blind to the Force not to notice. She could certainly understand where the guilt was coming from. After years of hating the Jedi, to find himself attracted to one would have to be a considerable shock.

Now was neither the time nor the place to explore this, Darsha told herself. With any luck, there would be better opportunities later. For now, she decided to save face—his and hers.

"I don't sense any large life-forms in the alley, for what it's worth," she told him.

Lorn nodded, still looking away, and prodded the Raptor again with his blaster. "Okay, killer— lead on."

Off balance a bit, still focused on the fact that she'd just noticed his attraction, Darsha almost missed the Raptor's sudden surge of anger. It reminded her that they were by no means out of the woods yet.

Lorn followed Green Hair into the alley, his mind still very much on the wordless interchange that had just taken place between him and Darsha. Had she somehow felt what he was thinking, used the Force to peer at his naked emotions? He hoped not. But let's face it, he told himself, she was a Jedi. She certainly had the ability to do such a thing, and in Lorn's experience, people who had skills tended to use them.

He tried to feel angry, to feel invaded by her action, but all he felt was curiosity—curiosity as to whether there was any attraction on her side. And *that* bothered him even more than the invasion of privacy.

I-Five broke into his thoughts. "I concur with Padawan Assant's conclusions about life-forms, but you might be interested to know that there are two active power relays in the first fifteen meters of—"

"Lorn, watch it! He's going to try something!" Darsha shouted from behind.

Sure enough, the Raptor dived toward a pile of trash just under a small architectural overhang on the left side of the alley. Lorn leapt after him, trying to see what the gang member was reaching for under the garbage. Green Hair hit the ground first, however, tearing into the trash. His palm slammed toward a large yellow activation reader. Lorn had seen readers like these before; they were capable of being utilized only when someone with the right identification pattern touched them. That pattern could be the user's DNA, a subcutaneous chip, or sometimes a skin decoration, like a tattoo. Whatever the activation mode, Lorn knew that if he didn't move fast, he would very shortly find out what the switch was for.

Lorn caught the boy's wrist and pulled his arm up behind his back, hard. Green Hair let out a cry, and Lorn grabbed his other hand, as well. He dragged the struggling youth back to where I-Five and Darsha stood.

"Got anything we can use to immobilize him?" he asked the droid.

"What a clever idea," I-Five said, handing Lorn a length of rope he had picked out of the trash. "Too bad it didn't occur to you before we were nearly vaporized."

Lorn secured Green Hair's wrists, then turned the youth around to face him. "All right, what's the switch for?"

Green Hair just stared at him, mouth defiantly clamped shut.

Lorn glanced at I-Five, who said, "I traced the circuit to an energy source high on the alley wall—about there." The droid pointed up at a rusty vent about three meters above the group. Abruptly his pointing finger deformed, the end irising open. A beam fired four times, each hair-thin line of ruby light striking a corner of the vent. Lorn smelled the tang of vaporized metal faintly over the ripe organic scents that filled the alley.

The vent cover fell off and hit the ground below with a clang, and he could see the harsh end of a tripod-mounted blaster just inside the hole. Motorized, no doubt, and cued to zap anyone not near the activation switch.

Wouldn't *that* have been a nasty surprise.

Lorn shook his head, then glanced at Darsha. "Here's a thought," he said. "Maybe we ought to try one of those mind tricks you wanted to use earlier."

Darsha gave him a wry look, then turned her attention to Green Hair. She made a subtle gesture with one hand as she said, "You will show us the way uplevels, with no more tricks."

Fascinated, Lorn watched as the Raptor's eyes defocused and he repeated, "I will show you the way uplevels, with no more tricks."

It was eerie, seeing the ease with which she controlled the boy, and Lorn found himself wondering, not for the first time, if she could do the same thing to him.

Their prisoner pointed deeper into the dark alley. "This is the way," he said woodenly.

Lorn glanced at Darsha. She nodded. Lorn took the lead.

Darsha couldn't believe she'd missed the relays. She'd been so focused on the idea of living enemies that it hadn't occurred to her to check for mechanical ones. She had to make sure that it didn't happen again.

She sent her senses questing out ahead of them, feeling for living and nonliving eyes. Just around the corner was a security cam. Lorn stepped around the bend before she could call out, but it didn't matter—she had it handled. It took a little more concentration to defeat a mechanical device, but it certainly wasn't beyond her abilities. She simply jammed the lens aperture control shut.

She, the Raptor, and I-Five caught up to Lorn in short order. He was looking at the security cam.

"Don't worry," she said, "I rascaled it."

He glanced at her. "It was live? I figured it was a dummy they'd set out to keep their trail clear."

"There were, you'll remember, two active power relays back there," I-Five said.

Lorn glanced at him, shrugged, then nodded thanks to Darsha. The gesture came from him easily and naturally. It was hard to believe that less than a day ago he'd resented her for saving his life.

They continued on. It was a twisty path that Green Hair led them down, even for Coruscant—through dark alleys and back utility routes grown vermicularly complex over the centuries. At times the way was so narrow and the darkness so complete, it was hard to believe that they had returned to the surface. Darsha kept her senses sharp, but other than an occasional mendicant or vagrant huddled shapelessly in dark corners, they met no one on the route. After another ten minutes they came to a large round tube, identified as a thermal conduit. Faded signs all around it gave warnings in various Republic languages as well as universal pictograms about the dangers of the pipeline.

Green Hair indicated an access hatch on the side of the pipe. "Through there," he said.

Lorn stared at the access hatch on the side of the conduit, then at Green Hair. "You're sure the whammy you put on him is still working?" he asked Darsha.

Darsha nodded. "He's not lying," she said. "He believes this is the route. Unless he's delusional, this is the way they use to go uplevels."

I-Five tapped the pipe. It rang hollow. "My sensors can't penetrate the insulation. It could be safe, though."

"Fine," Lorn said. "*You* open it." He stepped back and let I-Five take his place.

"I live to serve," the droid said sarcastically, gripping the access wheel. He twirled it easily and popped the hatch. No clouds of boiling steam poured out, and the droid looked inside.

"It appears to go up ten levels, at least. There's a ladder on the inside. Anyone ready?"

Lorn glanced at Darsha. Green Hair waited placidly beside them. "Do we bring Fashion Plate here with us, or leave him?" he asked her.

Darsha turned to the youth. "Are there any other traps or codes we need to know to get through the tube?"

The Raptor nodded. "Only the door access code at the other end. One-one-three-four-oh."

The Padawan looked at Lorn. "Leave him."

Lorn nodded and untied their captive. Darsha laid her hand on the youth's shoulder and spoke to him one more time. "You will forget all about us."

"I will forget all about you."

"Be on your way. If danger threatens, you will come to your senses immediately. Otherwise, you will become yourself again after an hour. Go. And," Darsha added as he turned to leave, "get a haircut."

Green Hair nodded and wandered off, still in his Jedi-induced daze. Lorn couldn't help smiling at the Padawan again. Not bad, not bad at all. He glanced at I-Five and saw the droid watching him, his blank expression somehow even more noncommittal than usual. Lorn cleared his throat and motioned the droid into the pipe. He wasn't looking forward to climbing a ladder ten stories.

Darsha followed Lorn and I-Five up the ladder. It was a long, claustrophobia-inducing climb, and on top of all the other exertions she had been through, it was fairly grueling. But the thought of finally leaving the lawless abyss that was the Crimson Corridor helped propel her upward.

There was another access hatch at the top, which I-Five popped open easily. They followed him through.

They were in a large chamber that, by the look of it, once had been a central power-dispensing agency for several blocks' worth of buildings. It was two stories high and filled with conduits of all types, a bewildering array of catwalks, and what looked like several old thermal generators. At some point the plant must have been closed down and turned into a storage facility. At the far end of the room was a thick durasteel storage chamber designed for hazardous wastes. I-Five took a look inside it.

"More junk," he reported, "including a small carbon-freezing chamber." The droid looked around the room, noticing the various containers of fuel and tanks of gas for welding stacked all over the place. "I wouldn't fire any blasters if I were you," I-Five said to Lorn.

"If I have anything to say about it," Lorn said with heartfelt intensity, "I'll never fire a blaster again."

Darsha looked at I-Five and would have sworn the droid was smiling. Across the room was a door. There were several windows in the upper walls, and through them streamed bright sunlight. She grabbed Lorn and hugged him.

"We made it!"

He looked surprised, then uncertain—then surrendered to the moment and returned the hug. Before he could say anything, however, Darsha felt her joy wash away in a flood of dread.

She could feel him before she could see him. She let go of Lorn and spun toward the door, lightsaber already in her hand.

The door opened.

The Sith was there.

Darth Maul stood in the doorway and gazed upon his quarry, feeling the surprise and horror of the two facing him ripple across the room. They were trapped. He knew it and so did they, and it made this moment all the more glorious. He grinned slowly.

He had arrived at the lower end of the conduit quickly, using the patrol speeder's strobes to clear a path through the traffic. He had missed them, of course, but a quick reconnaissance of the conduit had revealed the only logical destination of the group. All the while he had acted with just the barest awareness of the Force, cloaking himself from its embrace. He had lived within the powerful boundaries of the dark side for so long that to not do so had left him feeling naked and blind at first, but it was necessary in order to not provide any warning to the Jedi apprentice who had sided with his quarry. He had circled the building, seeing only a few high transparisteel windows and one main doorway to the interior. He could not have devised a better trap had he tried.

Still further removed from the Force than he had been in years, he had extended the tiniest tendril of awareness to the edge of the door leading into the building. There he had stood, waiting for confirmation that his prey was at its final destination.

After a time, it had come, and he had stepped back into the Force, enjoying the sensation as the dark side enfolded him. Immediately he had felt the Padawan react, and then he had opened the door.

Now Darth Maul stepped forward, igniting both blades of his lightsaber. The moment had been perfect, but like all such, it was fleeting, already over. It was time to create another, far more satisfying one: the triumph of finally completing his mission.

For a few incredibly long heartbeats Darsha was paralyzed by shock, defeated by her emotions. Fear, despair, and hopelessness clawed at her, sapping her will. She faced the ultimate enemy; the Sith was far more powerful than she in the Force. He had slain Master Bondara, one of the Jedi's best fighters.

Give up, an insistent voice in the back of her mind whispered. *Drop your weapon. Give up . . .*

But as the Sith activated his lightsaber's twin blades, years of training that had grown almost into instinct flared within her. The council of despair in her head was stilled.

She embraced the Force.

There is no emotion; there is peace.

Her fear evaporated and was replaced by quietude.

She was still conscious of the fact that the Sith was well capable of killing her, but it was a distant concern. If death was inevitable, then what mattered was how she faced it.

There is no ignorance; there is knowledge.

She had attended a lecture on battle techniques given by Master Yoda earlier this year, and the memory of it came back to her now.

Yoda had faced the assembled students and spoken, his thin reedy voice somehow carrying to the far corners of the lecture hall without benefit of amplifiers.

"Better than training, the Force is. More than experience or speed it gives."

And he had given a demonstration. Three members of the council—Plo Koon, Saesee Tiin, and Depa Billaba, excellent fighters all—had come forward and attacked him. Master Yoda had not been armed, and had not seemed to move more than a meter or so, his tread slow and measured. Nevertheless, none of the three had been able to lay a finger on him. The lesson had struck powerfully home: Knowledge of the Force was infinitely better than technique.

Now Darsha let herself sink into the Force, not trying to maintain any control over it, letting it take over as she had when facing the taozin and the Raptors. How many times had Master Bondara told her to simply relax, to let go? She did so now, feeling herself reach a deeper place in the Force than she had ever been before. How she knew this she could not say—it simply *was*. She felt her senses heighten to diamond sharpness, and every feature of the abandoned power station came into focus, both the visible and the invisible. She knew every wall, door, and piece of machinery, each particle of dust.

And she knew what she had to do.

All this, in less than a second's time.

With a small wave of her hand behind her, Darsha telekinetically pushed Lorn and I-Five backwards, sending them shooting dozens of meters into the storage chamber that she knew had been designed to be strong enough to hold dangerous, volatile waste. The hatch slammed shut. The Sith would not be able to reach them immediately, which would give her time. With a thought she scrambled the lock mechanism so that the door could not be opened, then ignited her lightsaber, its golden glow shining in the dimness of the old power station.

The twin ruby blades of the Sith's lightsaber spun as he leapt toward her, and she stepped forward to meet him.

Lorn pounded on the door of the waste-containment chamber, but it would not open.

"Darsha! Open the door!"

He tugged frantically at the latch, but the lock mechanism had been scrambled. There was a small port of yellowed transparisteel in the hatch, and through it he could see Darsha and the Sith battling, the energy blades colliding in showers of sparks.

This was madness! What had she done? She had to know she had no chance against the demon who had killed her Master. The three of them together, with I-Five's finger blasters and his own blaster, might possibly be able to take him. But there was no way she could face him alone.

She was going to die.

After her, in all probability, he would be next—but Lorn barely thought about that. All that mattered was getting that hatch open so that he could reach her, somehow help her!

He pulled the vibroblade from his pocket and tried it on the locking mechanism. No good.

"I-Five, get us out of here!" he shouted. When the droid did not respond, he turned to see why.

I-Five had powered up the carbon-freezing unit. A cloud of bilious smoke—carbonite vapor—misted the small chamber.

"What are you doing? She's going to die out there!"

"Yes," the droid said. "She is."

Darth Maul felt a change in the Force as the woman stepped forward. Interesting—she was more powerful than he had thought. It did not matter, of course. He, who had trained his entire life to kill Jedi, could certainly not fail to kill a mere Padawan. But a more challenging opponent would take more time. Still, there were no other exits from the building; his target and the droid weren't going anywhere.

He might as well enjoy himself.

Maul twirled his twin blades in an overhand arc, the better to separate her upper body from her lower.

And she caught the strike on her weapon's yellow length of plasma, deflecting the first blade, then sparking on the second to twist it past.

He changed direction, stabbing forward in the form known as Striking Sarlacc to pierce her heart.

Which was deflected by her in a downward stroke, the tip of her blade then arcing out to gut him.

But he wasn't there, having backflipped to land in a defensive posture.

Darth Maul bared his teeth at her. For a Padawan, she was a worthy opponent. No Jedi Master lived within the Force more fully than she did at this moment.

But he was going to kill her. He knew it, and so did she.

The Sith apprentice launched a simultaneous attack, using the Force to throw a rusty power-wrench and a bucket of old fasteners from a worktable at her as he launched himself forward, lightsaber dancing a variant of a teräs käsi Death Weave.

This entertainment was beginning to pall. Time to kill her and move on to his primary target.

There is no passion; there is serenity.

It was true. Every action she took was committed and well defined, but there was no emotion, no conscious thought preceding it. The Force guided her, helped her make the lightning-fast movements necessary to deflect the Sith, and even to counterattack.

But it was not enough. The Sith was the best fighter Darsha had ever seen. His movement was precise, his control of the Force that of a musician playing an intricate solo. All of which made it even more mandatory that information about him reach the Temple.

Using the Force, she deflected the tool and bucket of parts he hurled at her. Several of the latter got through, striking her legs and torso as she leapt five meters up and onto a catwalk that ran the length of the chamber. As she landed, she caught a glimpse of Lorn's stricken face, framed in the viewport of the containment unit's hatch. She barely had time to catch her breath before the Sith was there in front of her. His eyes were hypnotic, their golden hue an eerie counterpart to the bloodred and black tattoos covering his face. But they did not prevent her from deflecting his strikes as he again moved within range, his twin blades spinning so fast they seemed to merge into a crimson shield.

There was a sizzle as her blade intersected his, a flash of sparks as they separated, she to deflect, he to attack with the blade opposite.

Darsha slashed backhand, feeling a weakness in his defense.

But it was a trap, carefully laid, and he spun a ruby shaft to intersect, which would have hit her at the same time.

But she wasn't there, having propelled herself sideways to a new position a meter away, her lightsaber pointed at his chest.

And the Sith dived forward, striking left-right-left in a series of attacks that left her winded, even assisted as she was by the Force. She deflected, forcing her mind to disengage from following his technique, to relax and maintain her deep connection to the Force. Thoughts were a hazard.

He did not share that weakness; she could feel the truth of that. He had more conscious control of the power at his command, and that gave him the edge. If she tried to increase her control of the Force, she would reduce her ability to simply react—but if she did not, she could only defend.

The problem reverberated within her as she maintained her connection with the environment, her senses reaching out, her mind searching for answers.

When she found one, she tested it and realized it was her only chance.

Lorn grabbed the droid's arms and tried to pull him away from the unit's controls. He might as well have tried to pull a skyhook down from orbit. "What are you *doing*?"

I-Five did not stop working as he answered. "Trying to ensure that her sacrifice is not a futile one."

"It won't be, if you'll just blast that damned door open!"

I-Five kept talking, his voice maddeningly even. "Even my reactions are no match for the Sith's—and I am far faster than you and Padawan Assant. She is doing for us what her Master did for her—buying time."

"What good will that do? We're trapped in this chamber—"

"With a carbon-freezing unit that can be adapted to put us both in cryostasis."

Sheer surprise kept Lorn from protesting for a moment. The droid continued, "It's theoretically possible for living beings to be frozen in a carbonite block and later revived. I read an interesting treatise on the subject once in *Scientific Galactica*—"

Lorn turned, a snarl building deep in his throat, and

aimed the Saurin's blaster at the hatch lock. One way or another he was going to reach her.

"Stop!" I-Five commanded. "This chamber's magnetically sealed. The ricochet would most likely destroy us both."

Lorn spun about and pointed the blaster at I-Five. "Get over there and open that door," he said, in a voice that did not sound remotely like his own, "or I'll blow you to scrap metal."

I-Five turned his head and looked at him for a moment. Then the droid reached out and grabbed the blaster, taking it away from Lorn before the latter had time to pull the trigger.

"Now listen to me," I-Five said as he returned to his work. "We have one chance to survive this, and it's not a very good one. The Padawan has no chance. She knows this." He finished entering a final bit of data on the unit's control panel. "Get into the unit."

Lorn stared at him, then turned and looked back out of the hatch window. He couldn't see Darsha or the Sith directly, but he could see their shadows moving on the floor, cast by the light from the high windows. He realized they had taken the battle to one of the overhead catwalks.

She is doing for us what her Master did for her—buying time.

He had known her for barely forty-eight hours, and in that time he had gone from hating her and everything she stood for, to—this. This frantic pain, this frustration, this welter of emotions he had not allowed himself to feel for years. He did not love her; there hadn't been enough time for that. But he had come to feel fondness for her, to deeply respect and admire her. If all the Jedi were like her . . .

He didn't want to finish the thought. He forced himself to.

If all Jedi are like her, then what happened to Jax was the best thing for him.

"Hurry!" I-Five said. "The unit's on a timer. We have less than a minute."

Lorn pressed his face to the transparisteel, trying to get a last look at her. He failed. He could dimly hear the crackling and buzzing of the lightsabers, could see the flashes and cascades of sparks as they clashed against each other or sliced through metal as though it were flimsiplast. But he could not see her.

I-Five took him gently but firmly by the shoulders and turned him away from the hatch. Lorn let the droid lead him over to the carbon-freezing unit. He felt no fear as he stepped into it. The temptation was to not feel anything at all, to just be numb.

No, he told himself. He had lived too long that way. If these were to be his final moments—which they could very well be; the odds of the droid's plan succeeding were slim indeed—he would not live them in an emotional void.

It was the very least he could do in acknowledgment of her sacrifice.

He stepped into the open cylinder of the device. I-Five crowded in beside him. There was barely enough room for both.

Lorn looked at the droid.

"If we come out of this alive," he said, "I'm going to kill that Sith."

I-Five did not reply; there was no time. Lorn felt freezing-cold steam boiling up around him. His vision was obscured by mist, which turned to darkness—a darkness as deep and complete as death.

Darth Maul felt a slight disappointment as he realized that the Jedi was not truly as powerful as she had first appeared. Her depth in the Force was impressive, but her methodology did not match it. Both of them knew it was only a matter of time now. He focused his attacks, forcing her to use a more technique-based defense.

She leapt down to the floor, and he followed her. He felt a Force-powered pressure move toward him and deflected it, sensing several large tanks and canisters being shoved around behind him. She was growing weak. Such an attack was a sign of desperation. Soon it would be over.

He dived forward, rolling to come up alongside her, deflecting her attack as he did so. Another invisible pressure wave knocked over more equipment behind where he had been.

Pitiful.

Maul thrust upward with his blade and was met with hers, thwarted for the moment. A deliberately left weakness in his attack was not exploited, and again he felt a loss of respect for her.

It was too bad, but there would be other missions, other challenges more worthy of his skills. Someday the Jedi Temple would be in ruins, and he would be there to see it, after having killed many of the Jedi himself. But now it was time to end this.

Darth Maul readied himself for the final strike.

Darsha sent a second wave of the Force outward, tumbling over yet another tank of fuel. She had managed to move several welding cylinders and fuel cells toward each other. They were heaped together now, an extremely explosive accident waiting to happen.

How appropriate, she thought, to use Master Bondara's sacrifice as an example.

Darsha let herself think of Lorn for a moment. She hoped the droid had figured out the potential for escape that the carbon-freezing unit represented. If not, then her sacrifice would be in vain.

She had seen Lorn's face in the hutch window, his expression full of desperation and concern—not for himself, but for her. It had most definitely not been the expression of someone who hated her, or was even indifferent to her fate.

It was too bad, she thought. If they had had more time . . . If they'd been able to see this through to the end, reach the Jedi Temple together . . .

But that was not the way it was fated to be.

There is no passion; there is serenity.

She thrust at the Sith, her lightsaber thrumming, and moved into a better position. She had to get this just right, make it look like it wasn't deliberate.

She left herself open. The Sith immediately took advantage of it.

His blade pierced her side, a fiery hot jet of pain that caused her to cry out.

Darsha Assant released her lightsaber, using the Force to send it forward, still lit, to pierce one of the gas cylinders.

She had time for one last thought.

There is no death; there is the Force.

She knew it was the truth.

Darth Maul saw his opponent's strategy, realizing what she planned to do nearly too late. He jumped, using the Force to propel him upward toward one of the high windows. He smashed through it easily and landed on a nearby walkway as the explosive canisters within detonated.

Fortunately, the strong walls of the structure contained the explosion. The Padawan had been truly devious at the end; he now realized she'd been preparing the trap with her feeble Force attacks. A far more worthy opponent than he'd realized.

Her actions had cost him the pleasure of killing his primary target. Maul offered a smile to her memory. Not all could fight so well; this was to be honored.

A crowd was beginning to gather. He had to make sure his mission was complete, and that was best done quickly. He leapt back to the window he had just broken through. Smoke was pouring from it now;

through it he could dimly make out the inferno that the chamber had become. He used the Force to momentarily dissipate the clouds and saw below him the waste-containment unit that his target had hidden in. The contained pressure wave of the explosion had ripped it open; Maul could see shattered and twisted pieces of equipment.

Nothing could have survived that. He saw no trace whatsoever of either the Padawan's or Lorn Pavan's bodies; the explosion had vaporized them.

His mission at last was complete.

Still, it behooved him to be absolutely certain. After all, Pavan had proved extraordinarily hard to kill, had even survived a previous explosion. Maul had to make sure.

He asked the dark side, sending investigatory vibrations throughout the chamber, searching for any signs of life.

There were none.

Excellent.

Darth Maul dropped back down to the walkway. Paying no attention to the milling onlookers, he pulled his cowl up and walked away from the burning building.

It was time to inform his master of his success. At last.

32

Obi-Wan Kenobi sensed death as he once more neared the site of Master Bondara's wrecked skycar. It wasn't the Jedi's passing that he had noticed earlier; this was something new.

As he drew closer he saw smoke rising from the street and noticed strobes flashing from police cruisers surrounding the area. Obviously some new disaster had occurred here—one important enough to bring the local law enforcement out.

After leaving the Tusken Oasis, he had decided to return to the last place that Darsha and Master Bondara had been seen, which was in the latter's skycar. A floating barricade warned the Padawan to stay back, and for a second Obi-Wan considered doing so. This was the Crimson Corridor, after all. No doubt some unconnected crime was being investigated here, and if that was the case, he would only get in the way.

But then he felt it again—the sense of foreboding

that had so unnerved him when he'd been at the site before.

Obi-Wan maneuvered his vehicle past the barricade. A forensics droid was ready to warn him off, but when it saw that he was a Jedi Padawan, it let him through. The Jedi did not like to use their secular powers, but within the structures of the Republic they were legally empowered to cross police lines on any investigation that touched on their own.

As he landed just outside the scanning line of police lasers, two plainclothes investigators—a Mrlssi and a Sullustan, both of whom looked like they'd rather be anywhere but here—made their way to intercept him. The Mrlssi spoke first.

"Can we help you?"

Obi-Wan decided to see what response he got with part of the truth. There was no reason for them to know that two Jedi Knights had gone missing.

"I've been following reports of a criminal who has been reported operating in the area. Apparently there have been some assaults . . ." He let his statement taper off, focusing on the reactions of the pair, hoping to provoke a response. "I was led to believe that there might be some connection here."

The Sullustan looked at the Mrlssi. "Well, yeah, there might be. Come have a look."

Obi-Wan followed the two over toward a new piece of wreckage, perhaps half a block from Master Bondara's vehicle. Although it had been badly burned and the metal twisted in the heat of the fire, it was plain that a large section of the police unit had been sheared away, and there was a cut through the canopy where the pilot droid would have sat.

"Any ideas, Padawan? . . ."

"Kenobi. Obi-Wan Kenobi."

The Sullustan spoke. "Recognize the skycar type?"

Obi-Wan shook his head. "Is there any significance to it?"

The investigator nodded. "This is—or was—a PCBU: police cruiser backup unit. They're specifically designed to aid officers answering calls in places like the Crimson Corridor. SOP is to hover back ten meters, up fifteen meters from answering units."

Obi-Wan could see the problem they were wrestling with. How could someone get fifteen meters into the air to reach the PCBU without getting shot?

"Was anyone killed?" he asked, although he already knew the answer.

"Two patrol officers," the Mrlssi said.

Obi-Wan nodded to the two investigators. "This may be the work of Black Sun operatives. I will contact the Temple regarding this. You will have the full cooperation of the Jedi in this matter." So saying, he turned away, heading back to his skycar.

This matter had now grown too large to be dealt with by one Jedi Padawan. Given possible involvement with Black Sun, and now the death of two Coruscant officers, Obi-Wan knew that the only prudent thing to do was to report back to his superiors. A full-scale investigation would have to be launched, in cooperation with the security forces.

He raised his skycar up to around the tenth level— below the lowest stratum of traffic, but high enough to ensure a relatively straight course back to the Temple. Whatever was going on, he was certain now that it involved far more than just the disappearance of Master Bondara and Darsha.

Darth Sidious could feel a slight disturbance in the Force before his scrambled comlink chimed, and knew by this that his apprentice was about to contact him. He stepped to the holoprojector and activated the grid. Privacy failsafes glowed green before he spoke.

"My apprentice. Your mission is complete."

It was a statement, not a question. Sidious knew Darth Maul would not call to report failure, and there were no untoward signs in the energies that surrounded his image.

"Yes, my master. The Jedi Padawan died in combat. She fought well, for a neophyte. An explosion generated from our battle destroyed Lorn Pavan and his droid."

Darth Sidious nodded. He could feel the truth of the statement even at this distance. This was excellent news. Any leaks that could impact his plans had been sealed. Certainly there would be other challenges—he didn't trust the Neimoidians' abilities in combat any more than he did their veracity—but such obstacles would come only after his plan was too far along to be stopped.

"I will require you to bring the holocron to this location." Sidious gave Maul the coordinates and the specialized instructions his apprentice would require to get past the security droids. Darth Maul acknowledged the instructions.

"Be most wary, my apprentice. Our stealth is vital. The Jedi will be most unhappy at the loss of two of their number, and will be searching for answers. You must see that they find none."

Darth Sidious did not wait for a response; none was necessary. With a gesture he closed the relay, breaking the connection.

It was time to make other preparations. Time to finally put into motion the plan that had taken decades to set up. The strategy that would culminate in the final destruction of the Jedi.

Soon.

Very soon.

Obi-Wan pushed the skycar to the maximum safe speed, swooping through the narrow maze of streets and buildings. Suddenly his attention was distracted by a rumble and a flash of orange light two streets over.

Yet another explosion, he thought wonderingly as he headed toward its source. He didn't know what was going on, but if it didn't stop soon, this sector of the city was going to look like it had been bombed from orbit.

He brought his skycar to a stop on a landing platform and walked cautiously closer to the inferno, using the Force once more to try to discern what had happened. His senses expanded into the building, detecting no life, but picking up the residual disturbances of a powerful struggle. He could sense Darsha's presence and the same tendrils of evil that had plagued him all day. Looking around, the Padawan noticed a section of burned rubble that had been blasted from the entrance. Something gleamed in the debris, and he stepped forward to see what it was.

Shock sent waves of jangling sensations up his body, and he had to still himself, force his mind to unclench and accept what he was seeing.

He used the Force to grasp the shiny bit of metal, pulling it out of the rubble, bringing it to his hand.

It was the twisted, melted hilt of a lightsaber, its body scorched almost beyond recognition.

Almost.

In practice duels at the Temple, two Padawans traditionally exchanged salutes prior to their match, raising their lightsaber hilts to their foreheads before igniting the energy coils. Obi-Wan had noted more than once the carefully wound wire grip on Darsha's weapon, a unique design.

The same design he was looking at now.

The Force confirmed it, as if there were any doubt. Darsha Assant was dead.

Obi-Wan Kenobi stood quietly, looking at the hilt in his hand.

There is no emotion; there is peace.

How he wished it were so.

33

Lorn stared up at the brightest light he had ever seen.

He felt . . . *brittle,* as though he might crack into countless pieces if he tried to move. There was a strange ringing in his ears, an odd smell in his nostrils. His eyes refused to focus. Everything seemed dreamlike. He had no idea where he was or how he had gotten there.

Abruptly the light—which he now realized was the sun—was blotted out by a familiar face.

"Good—you're awake. How do you feel?"

Lorn moved his jaw experimentally, found that he could speak without too much difficulty. "Like a battle dog's chew-toy." He sat up, his vision still blurred, a multitude of aches trying to drag him down. "What happened?"

I-Five didn't reply for a moment. "You don't remember our recent . . . situation?"

Lorn looked around him. He and the droid were on a small setback roof about halfway up the side of a building. The last thing he remembered . . .

He turned and looked in another direction. Perhaps fifty meters away was the building they had been trapped in by the Sith. He remembered Darsha opening the door, remembered seeing the Sith framed in the doorway—but nothing more than that. He said as much to I-Five.

The droid nodded. "Loss of short-term memory. Not surprising, given the trauma of recent events and the carbon-freezing." He helped Lorn to his feet. "Can you walk?"

Lorn tested his balance. "I think so."

"Good. The authorities will no doubt be here soon, but with any luck Tuden Sal will arrive before they do."

Tuden Sal. For some reason the name triggered more flashes of memory. "You froze us in carbonite."

I-Five nodded. "The waste-treatment chamber we were in was set up to contain volatile materials for transport. It was simply a matter of readjusting the parameters for—"

It hit him then, like a stun grenade at close range. "Darsha!"

The sunlight, so much brighter than he was accustomed to, faded momentarily back to the grayness of downlevels. I-Five's mechanical hand gripped his upper arm, steadying him.

Darsha, the Jedi Padawan, the woman with whom he'd shared the last tumultuous forty-eight hours—the woman who'd come to mean, in that short and

intense time, more to him than anyone except Jax and
I-Five—Darsha was dead.

No. It couldn't be. The droid and he had managed
to cheat certain death; surely there had been some way
that she, too, might have.

He looked desperately at I-Five. Saw that the droid
knew what was going through his head. And read,
somehow, in the other's metallic, expressionless face,
the truth.

They had escaped because she had bought them
time—had bought it with her own heart's blood.

That part came back, too. She was . . . gone.

"What happened?" he asked dully.

"She managed to stack some of the flammable containers together during her battle and ignited them as
she was struck down."

Struck down.

Lorn was quiet as they made their way to the
roof's edge.

"Why aren't we dead?"

"Carbonite is extremely dense. It survived the explosion, and since we were encysted within it, so did
we. There was a process timer, which I set to thaw us
after a half hour. Then I thought it prudent for us to
relocate."

Lorn nodded slowly. "What about the Sith? Did he
survive, or did he die with—" He could not bring himself to finish the sentence.

"Unknown. If he did survive—which, were we
dealing with anyone else, I would deem extremely
unlikely—then in all probability he thinks we're dead.
The carbon-freezing lowered all biological and elec-

tronic processes to a level far too faint for even a
master of the Force to detect."

Lorn stretched his arms and twisted cautiously
from side to side. Other than a major headache, he
seemed to be experiencing no adverse effects. All in
all, he'd had hangovers that were worse.

A pinging sound came from I-Five's midsection.
"That would be our ride," the droid said, pulling the
comlink out of his torso compartment and activating
it. He confirmed their location and toggled it off.

Within seconds a large black skycar with a canopied
roof and dark windows dropped toward them, its side
doors opening when it reached their level. Lorn looked
in and saw that Tuden Sal himself had come to pick
them up.

"I'm wondering what you two have gotten your-
selves involved in this time," Sal said as the chauf-
feured skycar lifted away from the scene. He glanced
out the tinted window at the destruction below. "But
given what I see down there, I'm not sure I want
to know."

"A wise decision," I-Five said, as he leaned over to
look out the side window. "The less you know, the
less they can indict you for."

The skycar was drifting higher, heading toward a
traffic lane that would take them to Eastport, where
one of Sal's restaurants was located. I-Five tapped
Lorn on the arm and pointed out the side window.

"You may not want to see this," he said.

Lorn looked out the window and saw a tiny figure
in black striding along one of the elevated walkways
below. He felt his insides ice over as if he'd been

plunged once more into carbonite. He got only a glimpse of the figure, who was pretty far away, but it looked like—

His throat was dry; he had to swallow twice before he could speak. "Got enhancers on this crate?" he asked Tuden Sal, who was slouched on the cushioned bench across from him.

The restaurateur was a Sakiyan—short, stocky, and possessed of skin that looked like burnished metal. He nodded and tapped a control alongside the window panel. The aircar was the epitome of plushness: tiny drink dispenser, high-powered comlink, and an inter-species climate control. Instantly, in response to Sal's command, the tiny figure below became much larger, zooming to fill up half the window. His cowl was up, covering his face, and the enhancement threatened to break up the image into component blocks of digital artifacting, but Lorn recognized him nonetheless.

It was the Sith.

As he watched, the cowled killer pulled something from his belt compartment and held it up to look at. A request to Sal caused the enhancer to focus on it. Lorn wasn't surprised to see the holocron in the Sith's hand.

"Friend of yours?" Sal asked.

Lorn shook his head. "Not at all. But I'd like to keep track of him. Do you mind if we take a little detour?"

"No problem. I owe you, Lorn."

"Keep the enhancers at full, and stay as far back as you can," I-Five advised.

Sal toggled a switch and gave the droid chauffeur the instructions. They began to follow the cowled figure at the maximum visible distance, just barely keeping him in sight.

Darth Maul reined in his connection to the dark side and made his shadow within it as small as he could. His master was right: it would not do to succeed in silencing the enemies of the Sith only to reveal himself to others of them through a mistake.

The apprentice hailed a cab. With his speeder bike destroyed and the one he'd taken from the patrol no doubt dangerous to use by now, he needed transportation to take him nearer to the abandoned monad where his ship was located.

As the air taxi lifted off, its driver having been given directions, Maul kept an eye out for followers. It was unlikely there would be any, since almost all who had seen him had died, or were ten or more levels below— but his master had ordered stealth, and thus it would be.

Lorn and I-Five watched the dark figure alight from the cab and walk toward the upper entrance of an abandoned monad. They watched for a few more minutes until the Sith reappeared on the rooftop.

A few seconds later they saw him step into thin air and vanish.

"Nice trick," Tuden Sal said.

Lorn just stared, completely baffled for the moment, not sure whether to believe his eyes. Was this some new arcane power of the murdering Sith? But then he heard I-Five say, in answer to Sal's comment, "He must have a high-grade cloaking device. Probably crystal based."

Of course. Their nemesis had gotten into a cloaked spaceship. It made perfect sense, Lorn thought. The Sith had accomplished his mission; he had gotten the holocron and, as far as he was concerned, killed everyone who knew anything about it. He was no doubt preparing to leave Coruscant.

Only I'm not dead, you murderer. You think I am, but I'm not.

The question was, what was he going to do now?

For the first time since this nightmare had begun, he was safe. The Sith thought he was dead. All Lorn had to do was lie low and the demonic killer would pass out of his life forever. He and I-Five could get off Coruscant and pile as many parsecs between them and the hub of the galaxy as they deemed necessary. They wouldn't be rich, but they'd be alive.

And the rankweed sucker who had killed Darsha would get away with his crime.

Lorn knew he could go to the Jedi and tell them what had happened. They would no doubt mobilize their ranks and start hunting for the one who had killed two of their order. Even though Lorn and they had some bad history, there would be no problem convincing them to believe him—one of the few advantages of dealing with a fraternity of Force users.

But the wheels of any organization, no matter how self-consciously benign, turn slowly and ponderously. Even now, the Sith was no doubt getting ready to raise ship. Could even the Jedi find him once he fled this world?

Lorn stared out the window. Before him, spread from horizon to horizon, lay Coruscant in all its tessellated splendor. More than just about anybody else, he felt he could say that he had seen the best and the worst the capital planet had to offer. He had led a life that had been by turns dangerous, frustrating, terrifying, and heartbreaking. There had been little joy in it. Still, he was reluctant to do anything that might result in his losing it.

He had never wanted to be a hero. All he had wanted was to live a quiet, normal life with his wife and son. But his wife had left him, and the Jedi—those whom the galaxy looked upon as heroes—had seduced him into giving them his son.

He would never have called any Jedi a hero—until he met Darsha Assant.

He took a deep breath and looked at Tuden Sal. "We need a spaceship," he said.

His friend nodded. "I-Five told me. No problem. Where do you want to go?"

Lorn looked back down at the roof of the monad, where the Sith had been visible until a moment ago.

"Wherever he's going."

34

Darth Maul settled into the pilot's chair. He pressed his hand to a sensor plate on the console before him, and the hemispheric control chamber filled with various hums, tones, and vibrations as the *Infiltrator* powered up. A quick outside scan revealed nothing in the immediate area that would interfere with his launch. Maul nodded in satisfaction.

His mission was nearly over at last. It had taken far longer than anticipated and had led him into dark corners of Coruscant he had not even known existed. But now his assignment was almost accomplished. Everyone whom Hath Monchar had spoken to, every potential information leak, had been stilled. Darth Sidious's plan for the trade embargo, and eventually the destruction of the Republic, could now proceed unchallenged.

Maul pulled the holocron from one of his belt compartments and looked at it. Such a small item, and yet the repository of so much potential power. He returned it to the compartment, then activated the vertical repulsor array. He watched on the overhead monitors as the monad's rooftop fell away from the ship. The *Infiltrator*'s nav computer began plotting directional and velocity vectors that would take him to the rendezvous point specified by his master. There he would deliver the holocron to Darth Sidious, and then his mission would be complete.

Within a matter of minutes he was high above the clouds, the curve of the planet revealing itself. It would take a little time to reach his destination; the orbital shells surrounding Coruscant were nearly as congested as the traffic strata on or near the surface. Once he was in orbit he would have to disable his invisibility field; otherwise it would be too difficult to avoid a collision with one of the myriad satellites, space stations, and ships that circled the planet.

Maul took the ship off autopilot and fed minimal power to the ion drive. The autopilot was more than capable of delivering him to his destination, but he preferred to be in control.

As he settled the *Infiltrator* into low orbit, barely skimming the tenuous gases of the upper ionosphere, Maul thought about his battle with the Jedi Padawan. She had certainly been smarter and more resourceful than he had given her credit for. So had her companion, for that matter. They had led him on quite a merry chase. He mentally saluted them both. He admired courage, skill, and brains, even in an enemy. They had been doomed from the start, of course, but at least they had fought their fate instead of submitting meekly to it, like that cowardly Neimoidian who had caused all this trouble to begin with.

He wondered what his master had in mind for his next mission. Something relating to the Naboo blockade, most likely. He hoped there would be more Jedi involved. Killing the Padawan had only whetted his appetite.

The ship Tuden Sal provided for Lorn and I-Five was an ARE Thixian Seven—a four-passenger modified cruiser. The craft had definitely seen better days, Lorn thought as the skycar settled down next to the ship's berth at Eastport, but that didn't matter. As long as it could fly and shoot, that was all he cared about.

As Tuden Sal arranged for launch clearance via his comlink, Lorn turned to I-Five and said, "Give me the blaster."

I-Five returned the Raptor's weapon to him. "As long as you're not planning on trying to shoot me with it again," the droid said.

"I wouldn't have shot you."

I-Five made no reply to that.

"Listen," Lorn continued, "I don't expect you to go with me. In fact, it makes more sense for you to go to the Temple and tell the Jedi what's been happening. That way there'll be a backup plan if I fail."

"Oh, please," I-Five said. "You take on the Sith alone? You've got about as much chance as a snowball in a supernova."

"It's not your fight."

"Finally, something we agree on. Nevertheless, I'm

not letting you go up there alone. You're going to need all the help you can get. Which reminds me—" The droid pulled from his chest compartment what looked like a small white ball. He handed it to Lorn, who looked closely at it. It was semitransparent, roughly spherical, about half the length of his thumb in diameter, and apparently made of some organic material.

"What is it?"

"A skin nodule from the taozin. They're made of specially adapted cells that block receptivity to the Force."

Lorn regarded the ball askance. Now that he knew what it was, he felt revulsed by its touch. "You're saying if I have this, the Sith can't use the Force on me?"

"I'm saying it may shroud your presence long enough for you to sneak up on him unnoticed. It won't protect you from his telekinetic powers, and it certainly won't do anything about his fighting skills. But it's better than nothing. Now I suggest we raise ship." So saying, the droid turned toward the ramp of the Thixian Seven.

Lorn let him get two paces ahead of him, then reached out and deactivated the master switch on the back of I-Five's neck. The droid collapsed, and Lorn caught him, settling him to the ground. He turned to see Tuden Sal watching.

"Family squabble?"

"Something like that. I need one more favor," Lorn said. "Deliver this bucket of bolts to the Jedi Temple. He's got information they'll want to hear."

Sal nodded. He picked I-Five up under the arms and

dragged him over to his skycar. Lorn watched for a minute, then turned and boarded the ship.

Lorn could honestly say that he wasn't frightened at the thought of facing the Sith alone. *Frightened* was far too mild a word. He was *terrified*, paralyzed, totally unmanned by what he was contemplating. He knew he was pursuing a suicidal course of action, and for what? Some quixotic notion of revenge for the death of a woman he barely knew? It was madness. I-Five was right: his chances for survival were so long that the odds were up in the purely theoretical number range.

As the Thixian Seven lifted away from the spaceport, Lorn felt himself on the verge of hyperventilation. Every nerve in his trembling body was on fire with adrenaline; every brain cell still functioning after his periodic bouts of alcohol abuse was screaming at him to leave orbit and just keep on going. Instead, he instructed the nav computer to plot the possible trajectories of a ship coming from the surface grid containing the abandoned monad.

Within far too short a time the computer had identified a craft in low orbit, thirty-five kilometers away. Lorn put it on visual, since the readout said that the stealth mechanism had been deactivated. He stared at the computer-enhanced image of the Sith's vessel. With long nose and bent wings, it was a sleek craft, nearly thirty meters long; the scan readout didn't specify armament, but it looked mean.

Below him, Coruscant looked like a gigantic circuit board laid across the planet's surface. It was a spectacular sight, but Lorn wasn't in any mood for sightseeing. He settled into an orbit below and well behind his enemy's ship. He didn't know how much protection—if any—the taozin nodule would grant him, and he wasn't going to press his luck. He was going to need plenty of luck as it was.

Lorn wished I-Five was with him. He was painfully aware that since this nightmare had begun, every time his life had been in peril it had been either the droid or Darsha who had saved him. Some hero, he thought.

He missed Darsha, as well, although he didn't wish she was with him. He wished she were still alive and far away from here, safe on some friendly planet that had never heard of either the Sith or the Jedi. He wished he was there with her.

The nav computer beeped softly to get his attention, and displayed a course vector overlay on one of the monitors. The Sith's ship had changed course; it was now headed for a large space station in geosynchronous orbit over the equator.

His mouth dry as paper, Lorn instructed the autopilot to follow. He had no idea what he was going to do when he got there. All he knew was he had to try, somehow, to stop the Sith.

For Darsha's sake.

And for his own.

Tuden Sal loaded the deactivated I-Five into his skycar and instructed the droid chauffeur as to their destination. The vehicle lifted away from the spaceport, sliding smoothly into the airborne traffic lanes.

He felt sorry for Lorn. His friend hadn't told him very much about the situation he was in, but from the few hints he had dropped and from the look of the goon he was chasing, Sal figured his chances of survival were not great. That was too bad. He'd always thought Lorn had potential, even though he came across as a chronic underachiever. One rogue can always recognize another.

But in all probability, Lorn was going to die on this crazy quest of his. A shame, but it really wasn't any of Sal's business. He was far more concerned about the droid.

The Sakiyan had never really understood how Lorn could treat I-Five as an equal—even going so far as to call him a "business partner." Droids were machines—clever ones, to be sure, and able in some cases to mimic human behavior to a startling degree. But that's all it was: mimicry. Legally they were property. Though he'd become somewhat accustomed to it during the year or so he'd known Lorn and I-Five, Sal had never completely gotten over the vaguely creepy feeling it gave him to see the two of them interacting as peers.

Well, there would be no more of that. He'd had his eye on this droid for some time; the weapons modifications alone would make him a valuable asset. Since Sal occasionally had dealings with Black Sun, it was not a bad idea at all to have a bodyguard, and he was certain that I-Five would make a very good one—once the droid's memory had been wiped, of course.

He wasn't overly concerned with how Lorn might feel about this. After all, he fully expected never to see Lorn again. And even if he did, it wasn't a capital crime to steal and reprogram a droid. The most he could expect in terms of legal repercussions might be a fine, which wouldn't be nearly as much as the cost of a new droid with I-Five's special features.

No matter how you looked at it, even throwing in that clunker of a ship, it was good business.

The Temple's roof sparkled in the afternoon sun as Sal's skycar shot by it. Soon it was lost to sight among the countless other flying craft that filled the skies of Coruscant.

The *Infiltrator* settled into one of the space station's docking sleeves, and Maul heard the muffled metallic sounds of the air lock's outer hatch sealing with the station's. He deactivated the life support and artificial gravity systems—then, weightless, he made his way through the ship's dark interior to the air lock.

This point of egress to the station was in one of the outlying service modules. Darth Sidious had promised him that there would be neither human nor droid to interfere with his progress, and as Maul emerged from the air lock he saw that this was so. The lock opened into what appeared to be a service corridor—narrow and low, the walls and ceiling covered with pipes, conduits, and the like. The artificial gravity was not on in this region of the station, no doubt for budgetary reasons. No matter; Maul had operated in zero-g environments before. He pushed himself away from the lock and floated down the corridor, using the impedimenta that festooned the walls to pull himself along.

The directions Darth Sidious had given him were clear in his head; he was to proceed down this passageway to the module proper, and then take a vertical shaft up to one of the larger habitation modules. At a prearranged time—less than fifteen minutes away—he would rendezvous with Maul. Maul would then hand him the crystal.

And then his mission would be complete.

Lorn let the autopilot take care of the docking procedure; he wasn't all that good of a pilot. *I'm not all that good at anything,* he thought bitterly, except *getting those I care about in trouble.* He still had the blaster he had taken from the Raptor, but he only now remembered its power pack wasn't good for more than a few shots. Of course, a few shots would probably be all he would have time for, one way or another.

After the green light flashed, Lorn crossed into the service shaft. It had been some time since he'd experienced zero-g. When he could afford to, he used to work out fairly regularly at a spa that featured null-grav sports. He'd enjoyed the workouts; feeling like he could fly, even if only within the small confines of the spa's structure, had always been good for taking some of the weight of his existence off him.

He was under no illusions, however, that his familiarity with weightlessness gave him any kind of edge over the Sith. He had no doubt that his opponent could handle himself with consummate and deadly skill in any kind of environment. He would need an enormous amount of luck to pull this off.

Once inside the corridor, he moved very cautiously and slowly. There was no sign of his enemy anywhere ahead, and it didn't look like there was anyplace to hide here. Nevertheless, he was taking no chances. Lorn wouldn't have been surprised if the Sith suddenly materialized out of thin air in front of him at this point.

He had no idea what he was going to do once he spotted him; he hadn't had time to formulate a plan. If the taozin nodule let him get close enough to get off a shot, he had absolutely no compunctions about shooting his adversary in the back—assuming he didn't pass out from sheer terror once he had him in his sights.

He reached the end of the corridor. An access shaft

led up from here. Before following it, Lorn pulled out the blaster and checked its power supply.

What he found was not good. The weapon had enough power left for one shot at maximum setting, or three shots at the low-level stun setting. After a moment's thought, Lorn adjusted the setting to the lower level, figuring it would be better to have three chances of incapacitating the Sith rather than one chance of killing him. Assuming the stun setting would in fact stun him. By now Lorn wasn't at all persuaded that anything could harm his nemesis.

He eased himself into the shaft. It led to a larger, better-lit chamber, perhaps ten meters by ten, and fairly empty save for some equipment bins anchored to the walls.

At the other end of the chamber was the Sith.

His back was to Lorn; he was entering a code on a wall panel, preparing to open a hatch in the far wall.

Lorn rose quietly out of the tube and gripped the blaster in both hands. He braced his feet against the edge of the shaft; there would be a slight recoil in zero-g.

The taozin nodule seemed to be doing its job: the Sith was apparently unaware that Lorn was ten meters behind him and drawing a bead right between his shoulder blades. His hands were trembling, but not so much that he shouldn't be able to hit a target as broad as his enemy's back, especially with three shots at his disposal. Once the Sith was stunned, Lorn would finish him off with the lightsaber and then grab the information crystal.

The Sith pressed a wall button. A light glowed green, and the hatch started to open.

Now. It had to be now. Lorn drew a deep breath, opening his mouth wide so that the Sith wouldn't hear the intake of air. He exhaled the same way, then drew in another breath and held it.

He pulled the trigger.

The shot was true. The stun bolt nailed the Sith squarely in the middle of his back, hurling him forward to slam against the bulkhead. Lorn fired one more, which hit the Sith's lower back.

Lorn couldn't believe it. He shoved himself forward, shooting the length of the chamber toward his adversary, who was now floating limply back toward him in a slow rebound from the impact. Blaster held ready—he had one shot left—Lorn grabbed the Sith's robes, pulling the latter around to face him. As he was reaching for the lightsaber he noticed a sparkle of reflected light coming from a half-open compartment on the utility belt.

It was the holocron crystal. Lorn grabbed it and shoved it in his pocket. Then he reached for the lightsaber.

He was staring directly into the sinister tattooed face when the Sith's yellow eyes opened.

Lorn froze, mesmerized by that ferocious glare. He forgot about the lightsaber he was reaching for, forgot about the blaster still in his other hand. Then he was hurled back by a blast, unseen but nonetheless powerful, that left him gasping for air.

The Sith's lightsaber leapt into a black-gloved fist, both blades flashing into existence. One of them flickered toward him like crimson lightning. Lorn felt a blow to his right hand, saw the hand, still clutching the blaster, go spinning away in slow motion, a few globules of blood following it. He didn't feel any pain, did not in fact realize what had happened until he saw the blackened, cauterized stump at the end of his arm.

And now the Sith was spinning around, using the energy of the last blow to rotate himself into attack position again. The moment stretched for Lorn, unbelievably clear and sharp. The Sith's teeth were bared in a rictus of animal hatred. The lightsaber started a horizontal arc that would, in less than a second, shear through his neck.

He was floating in front of the open hatch. His left leg was bent, his foot grazing the side of one of the storage canisters. Lorn kicked against it, propelling himself backwards through the hatch. The energy blade slashed through the empty space his neck had occupied a moment previously.

He brought his legs up as he sailed through the hatchway. He flipped over in a back somersault, his head coming up and his left arm reaching out for the hatch controls. He saw the Sith hurtling toward him, framed in the opening. His hand slapped the button, and the hatch swung shut in the Sith's face. A red light glowed, indicating the hatchway was sealed. Lorn raked his fingers over the access panel keypad, scrambling the code.

Through the hatch's port he could see the Sith's face—a sight to chill the blood. Then, faintly, he heard the sound of metal beginning to melt and saw a faint blush of red building in the hatch's center.

The Sith was using his lightsaber to melt through the hatch.

Lorn turned and started pulling himself frantically along the corridor he was in. He didn't know where he was going, or how he was going to escape the vengeance of the monster behind him. There was no room in his head for anything—not even the pain of his severed wrist as the shock began to wear off— except raw red panic.

For possibly the first time in his life, Darth Maul had been taken completely by surprise.

He had felt no warning vibration of the Force before being hit by the blaster bolts. The astonishment this caused him was almost equaled by the shock of realizing that the attack had come from Lorn Pavan. He had been so certain of the Corellian's death back on Coruscant that awakening to see him alive and looting his utility belt had caused Maul to momentarily question his own sanity.

It was the combined shock of these two events— plus the confusing fact that, even though he could see Pavan before him, he could not sense his presence with the Force—that had slowed his reaction time just enough to let the Corellian get through the hatchway and lock it in Maul's face. Now he had to burn his way through the lock mechanism. As soon as the hatch came loose, he savagely hurled it open and shot after Pavan, using the Force to propel his weightless self in pursuit. There was no time to lose. He did not know how Pavan had escaped the explosion back in the storage facility, or how he was able to block his presence in the Force—and he did not care. In a few minutes his master would be at the rendezvous point, and Maul intended to be there, as well, holding the holocron in one hand and Pavan's severed head in the other.

This had gone on long enough.

Lorn hauled himself up another vertical shaft, moving as fast as he could with only one hand to aid him. It seemed he could feel the hot breath of the Sith on the back of his neck; he dared not look behind him in case he actually did see the latter's demonic face. To look into those yellow eyes one more time would, he felt sure, utterly paralyze him.

His one hope was to reach the space station's main section, where he could find some kind of security personnel. Surely, with enough blasters between him and the Sith, he would be safe.

It seemed impossible now that he had ever seriously intended, even for a moment, to kill the black-robed creature. That he had even managed to take the holocron away from him now seemed a miracle. Not that he would keep it for very long if he didn't find help fast.

And then he shouldered his way through one final

access port and found himself in a large solarium. As he passed through the entry, Lorn felt weightfulness return with a rush.

He looked around. Plants and dwarf trees were tastefully arranged in a small garden setting. Half of the domed ceiling was made of polarized transparisteel, affording a magnificent view of the stars and a huge crescent of the planet. And standing in the garden were several people of various species, some of whom were wearing the robes of Republic Senate members, and others dressed in the dark, formfitting attire of Coruscant guards.

He recognized one of the senators. When he had worked for the Jedi, Lorn had heard him spoken of many times, always as a man of clear-minded practicality, a stranger to corruption and intrigue. If anyone could be counted on to protect the information on the holocron and see it safely reach the sanctuary of the Jedi Temple, it would be him.

Lorn staggered forward. One of the senators, a Gran, saw him coming and reacted with a bleat of fright. Several of the guards moved in to protect their charges, drawing blasters.

"Wait!"

The command came from the senator whom Lorn had recognized. He stepped forward, his expression one of concern.

"What's the matter, my good fellow? What brings you here in this extreme state?"

Lorn pulled the crystal from his pocket and held it out. He saw the other's eyes narrow as he recognized it.

"A holocron crystal?"

"Yes," Lorn gasped, dropping it into the senator's outstretched hand. "It must reach the Jedi. Very important."

The senator nodded, and quickly tucked the holocron away in a fold of his robe. Then he noticed the stump where Lorn's other hand had been. "You're injured!" He turned to one of the guards, summoning him with a quick, imperious gesture. "This man requires hospitalization immediately! And protection from assassins, as well, by the look of it."

Lorn sagged into a chair. As the others came forward he risked a glance over his shoulder at the service port where he had entered. There was no sign of the Sith.

Relief flooded over him. The nightmare was over, at last.

He felt his consciousness starting to slip away and realized that for the first time in days he could allow himself the luxury of exhaustion. "Make sure . . . the holocron . . . ," he mumbled, but was too tired to finish the sentence.

His benefactor leaned over him and smiled. "Don't worry, my brave friend. I'll take care of it. Everything will be all right now."

Lorn managed to mumble, "Thank you, . . . Senator Palpatine." And then everything faded.

When Obi-Wan Kenobi reached the Temple he could tell immediately that something was wrong. It wasn't just the ominous reverberations in the Force that pulsed invisibly all around him; the Padawans and messengers he passed in the hallways all wore looks of concern and concentration. One of them saw him and stopped.

"Padawan Kenobi, you are to report to your Master immediately." Then he continued on his way before Obi-Wan could ask what was causing the palpable air of tension.

He found the door to Master Qui-Gon's domicile open. The Jedi was inside, loading his utility belt with field items such as an ascension gun and food capsules. He evidenced relief when he saw Obi-Wan standing in the doorway.

"Excellent. You have returned just in time."

"What's happened, Master?"

"The Trade Federation has blockaded Naboo. You and I have been selected as ambassadors to the Trade Federation flagship to settle this."

Obi-Wan felt stunned at the magnitude of this news. "Surely the Republic Senate will condemn such an action!"

"I suspect the Neimoidians are counting on the senate's past record of being . . . less than effective in such matters. In any event, we must leave immediately."

"I understand. But I must tell you—Master Anoon Bondara and his Padawan, Darsha Assant, are both dead. There is no doubt of this."

Master Qui-Gon paused in his packing and looked at Obi-Wan. The Padawan could see the sadness in his mentor's eyes.

"And the cause of this tragedy?"

"I'm still not certain, although I suspect Black Sun involvement."

"I want to hear all about it," Master Qui-Gon said, "and so will the council. But speed is of the essence now. You will make your report to them via holo transmission once we are on our way."

"Yes, Master." Obi-Wan followed Qui-Gon Jinn as the latter strapped his belt around his waist and left the room.

He would do as his Master said, of course. Obviously this new crisis superceded the events that had taken place in the Crimson Corridor. As he followed Master Qui-Gon, ObiWan wondered if he would ever know the complete story of what happened to Darsha and Master Bondara. She had had the potential to be a good Jedi Knight, and he grieved for her passing.

*   *   *

The Sith lunged for him, twin energy blades flashing.

Lorn awoke with a gasp. He stared about him, still feeling for a moment the panic of his nightmare. Then, slowly, as his eyes took in his surroundings, he began to relax.

He was in a private room in a hotel—nothing fancy, but far superior to what he had been used to for the past five years. His severed wrist had been treated with synthflesh, and he had been told by Senator Palpatine that within a few days a prosthetic replacement would be grafted on. More important, Palpatine had also told him that the information crystal had been delivered to the Jedi Temple and the assassin captured.

In short, Lorn had won.

Not completely, of course. He still mourned the death of Darsha. He was also concerned about I-Five's whereabouts: apparently the droid had never made it to the Temple. A Pyrrhic victory—but a victory nonetheless.

He had been given his choice of futures: relocation to a colony world somewhere in the Outer Rim, or a permanent address in a monad on Coruscant. Either way, he had been assured that the bank fraud charges had been dropped, and he would be awarded a stipend that would allow him and I-Five to live comfortably. He hadn't decided yet what to do, although he was leaning toward staying on Coruscant. By staying he could possibly reestablish some form of relationship with Jax. The Jedi owed him that much, at least.

Also, he owed it to himself. It was time he started to

live again—a real life, not the empty mockery he had been trapped in for so long downlevels. It might take a long time for the nightmares to subside, but eventually they would. Eventually he would know peace.

Lorn got out of the bed. In the closet was a new set of clothes, which he put on. He had no place in particular to go, but he felt like getting outside. He needed to feel the sun on his face, to breathe clean air. It had been a long time since he had enjoyed those simple pleasures.

He opened the door.

The Sith stood before him.

Lorn was too stunned to even be afraid. His enemy stepped forward, implacable, unstoppable, and activated his lightsaber. Lorn knew there was nothing he could do. The hotel room was small, barren of weapons, with only the one door.

This time there was no escape.

Surprisingly, in that moment—the final moment of his life—he found he was not afraid. Found, in fact, that he was in a place similar to that which Darsha had described when she was deep in the embrace of the Force.

He was at peace.

The information about the Sith had been given to the Jedi. The fact that the assassin was able to escape his incarceration couldn't change that. His death, Lorn realized, was in the service of a higher purpose.

He was content that it be so.

The lightsaber's blade shimmered toward him. His last thought was of his son; his last emotion was pride that someday Jax would be a Jedi Knight.

*   *   *

Looking into Pavan's eyes, Darth Maul knew what the man was thinking. Even were he not Force-sensitive, he could have read it clearly in his enemy's eyes and expression.

He said nothing.

Though Maul had no compunctions about killing anyone who stood in his or his master's way, he was not without a sense of honor. Lorn Pavan had managed, against all odds, to be more of a challenge to Maul than many of the professional killers of Black Sun. He was a worthy opponent and had earned the right to die quickly.

The lightsaber sizzled through air, through flesh, through bone.

Darth Maul turned and walked away, his mission at last complete.

Join Darth Maul
for another exciting adventure
as he continues to do
his master's bidding,
laying the groundwork
for the events to come in
STAR WARS:
THE PHANTOM MENACE.
Previously available
exclusively in electronic format.

Nearly every world in the Videnda sector had something to recommend it—warm saline seas, verdant forests, arable grasslands that stretched to distant horizons. The outlying world known as Dorvalla had a touch of all of those. But what it had in abundance was lommite ore, an essential component in the production of transparisteel—a strong, transparent metal used galaxywide for canopies and viewports in both starships and ground-based structures. Dorvalla was so rich in lommite that one quarter of the planet's scant population was involved in the industry, employed either by Lommite Limited or its contentious rival, InterGalactic Ore.

The chalky ore was mined in Dorvalla's tropical equatorial regions. Lommite Limited's base of operations was in Dorvalla's western hemisphere, in a broad rift valley blanketed with thick forest and defined by steep escarpments. There, where ancient seas had once held sway, shifts in the planetary mantle had thrust huge, sheer-faced tors from the land. Crowned by rampant vegetation, by trees and ferns primeval in scale, the high, rocky mountains rose like islands, blinding white in the sunlight, the birthplace of slender waterfalls that plunged thousands of meters to the valley floor.

But what was once a wilderness was now just another extractive enterprise. Huge demolition droids had carved wide roads to the bases of most of the larger cliffs, and two circular launch zones, large enough to accommodate dozens of ungainly space shuttles, had been hollowed from the forest. The tors themselves were gouged and honeycombed with mines, and deep craters filled with polluted runoff water reflected the sun and sky like fogged mirrors.

The ceaseless work of the droids was abetted by an all but indentured labor force of humans and aliens, to whom the mined ore served as a great equalizer. No matter the natural color of a miner's skin, hair, feathers, or scales, everyone was rendered white as the galactic dawn. All agreed that sentient beings deserved more from life, but Lommite Limited wasn't prosperous enough to convert fully to droid labor, and Dorvalla wasn't a world of boundless opportunities for employment.

Still, that didn't stop some from dreaming.

Patch Bruit, Lommite Limited's chief of field operations—human beneath a routine dusting of ore— had long dreamed of starting over, of relocating to Coruscant or one of the other Core worlds and making a new life for himself. But such a move was years away, and not likely to happen at all if he kept returning his meager wages to LL by overspending in the company-run stores and squandering what little remained on gambling and drink.

He had been with LL for almost twenty years, and in that time had managed to work his way out of the pits into a position of authority. But with that authority had come more responsibility than he had bargained for, and in the wake of several recent incidents of industrial sabotage his patience was nearly spent.

The boxy control station in which Bruit spent the better part of his workdays looked out on the forest of tors and the shuttle launch and landing zones. To the station's numerous video display screens came views of repulsorlift platforms elevating gangs of workers to the gaping mouths of the artificial caves that dimpled the precipitous faces of the mountains. Elsewhere, the platform lifting was accomplished with the help of strong-backed beasts, with massive curving necks and gentle eyes.

The technicians who worked alongside Bruit in the control station were fond of listening to recorded music, but the music could scarcely be heard over the unrelenting drone of enormous drilling machines, the low bellowing of the lift beasts, and the roar of departing shuttles.

The walls of the control station were made of transparisteel, thick as a finger, whose triple-glazed panels were supposed to keep out the ore dust but never did. Fine as clay, the resinous dust seeped through the smallest openings and filmed everything. As hard as he tried, Bruit could never get the stuff off him, not in water showers or sonic baths. He smelled it everywhere he went, he tasted it in the food served up in the company restaurants, and sometimes it infiltrated his dreams. So pervasive was the lommite dust that, from space, Dorvalla appeared to be girdled by a white band.

Fortunately, everyone within a hundred kilometers of Lommite Limited's operation was in the same predicament—miners, shopkeepers, the beings who tended the cantina bars. But what should have been just one big happy lommite family wasn't. The recurrent incidents of sabotage had fostered an atmosphere of wariness and distrust, even among laborers who worked shoulder to shoulder in the pits.

"Group Two shuttles are loaded and ready for launch, Chief," one of the human technicians reported.

Bruit directed his gaze to the droid-guided, mechanized transports that were responsible for ferrying the lommite up the gravity well. In high orbit the payloads were transferred to LL's flotilla of barges, which conveyed the unrefined ore to manufacturing worlds along the Rimma Trade Route and occasionally to the distant Core.

"Sound the warning," Bruit said.

The technician flipped a series of switches on the console, and loudspeakers began to hoot. Miners and maintenance droids moved away from the launch zone. Bruit looked at the screens that displayed close-up views of the shuttles. He studied them carefully, searching for anything out of the ordinary.

"Launch zone is vacated," the same technician updated. "Shuttles are standing by for liftoff."

Bruit nodded. "Issue the go-to."

It was a routine that would be repeated a dozen times before Bruit's workday concluded, typically long past sunset.

The eight unpiloted craft rose from the ground on

repulsorlift power, pirouetting and bringing their blunt noses around to the southwest. The air beneath them rippled with heat. When the shuttles were fifty meters above the ground, their sublight engines engaged, flaring blue, rocketing the ships high into the dust-filled sky.

The ground shook slightly, and Bruit could feel a reassuring rumble in his bones. He took a deep breath and let it out slowly. For the next hour, he could relax somewhat. He had turned from the view of the launch zone when his bones and his ears alerted him to a shift in the roaring sound, a slight drop in volume that shouldn't have occurred.

Sudden apprehension tugged at him. His forehead and palms broke an icy sweat. He whirled and pressed his face to the south-facing transparisteel panel. High in the sky he could see two of the shuttles beginning to diverge from course, their vapor trails curving away from the straight-line ascent of the rest of the group.

"Fourteen and sixteen," the technician affirmed. "I'm trying to shut down the sublights and convert them back over to repulsorlift. No response. They're accelerating!"

Bruit kept his eyes glued to the sky. "Give me a heading."

"Back at us!"

Bruit ran his hand over his forehead. "Enable the self-destructs."

The technician's fingers flew across the console. "No response."

"Employ the emergency override."

"Still no response. The overrides have been disabled."

Bruit cursed loudly. "Vector update."

"They're aimed directly for the Castle."

Bruit glanced at the indicated tor. It was one of the largest of the mines, so named for the natural spires that graced its western and southern faces.

"Order an evacuation. Highest priority."

Sirens shrieked in the distance. Within moments, Bruit could see workers hurrying from the mine openings and leaping onto waiting hover platforms. Two fully occupied platforms were already beginning to descend.

"Tell those platform pilots to keep everyone aloft," Bruit barked. "No one'll be any safer on the ground than in the mines. And start moving those droids and lift beasts out of there!"

A colossal bipedal drilling machine appeared at the mouth of one of the mines, engaged its repulsorlift, and stepped off into thin air.

"Thirty seconds till impact," the technician said.

"Jettison the shuttles' guidance droids."

"Droids away!"

Bruit clenched his hands. The two rudderless shuttles were plummeting side by side, as if in a race to reach the Castle. The technicians had already managed to shut down fourteen's sublight, and sixteen's flared out while Bruit watched. But there was no stopping them now. They were in ballistic freefall.

In the control station, droids and beings alike were crouched behind the instrument consoles—all except for Bruit, who refused to move, seemingly oblivious to the fact that concussion alone could turn the booth's transparisteel panels into a hail of deadly missiles.

The shuttles struck the Castle at almost the same

instant, impacting it above the loftiest of the mines, perhaps fifty meters below the tor's jungled summit.

The Castle disappeared behind an explosive flare of blinding light. Then the sound of the collisions pealed across the landscape, reverberating and crackling, echoing thunderously from the twin escarpments. Immense chunks of rock flew from the face of the tor, and two of its elegant spires toppled. Dust spewed from the mine openings, as if the Castle had coughed itself empty of ore. The air filled with billowing clouds, white as snow. Almost immediately the ore began to precipitate, falling like volcanic ash and burying everything within one hundred meters of that side of the mountain.

Bruit still didn't budge—not until the roiling cloud reached the control station and the view became a whiteout.

Lommite Limited's headquarters complex nestled at the foot of the valley's western escarpment. But even there a half a centimeter of lommite dust covered the lush lawns and flower gardens LL's executive officer, Jurnel Arrant, had succeeded in coaxing from the acidic soil.

The soles of Bruit's boots made clear impressions in the dust as he approached Arrant's office, with its expansive views of the valley and far-off tors. Bruit tried to stomp, brush, and scuff as much dust as he could from his boots, but it was a hopeless task.

Jurnel Arrant was standing at the window, his back to the room, when Bruit was admitted.

"Some mess," Arrant said when he heard the door seal itself behind Bruit.

"You think this is bad, just wait'll it rains. It'll be soup out there."

Bruit thought the remark might lighten the moment, but Arrant's piqued expression when he turned from the view set him straight.

Lommite Limited's leader was a trim, handsome human, just shy of middle age. When he had first come to Dorvalla from his native Corellia, he had not been above rolling up his shirtsleeves and pitching in wherever needed. But as LL had begun to thrive under his stewardship, Arrant had become increasingly fastidious and removed, choosing to let Bruit handle day-to-day affairs. Arrant favored expensive tunics of dark colors, the shoulders invariably dusted with lommite, which he wore as a badge of honor. If his nonindigenous status had been held against him initially, few had anything disparaging to say about the man who had single-handedly transformed formerly provincial Lommite Limited into a corporation that now did business with a host of prominent worlds.

Arrant glanced at the white prints Bruit's boots had left on the carpet. Sighing with purpose, he motioned Bruit to a chair and settled himself behind an old hardwood desk.

"What am I going to do with you, Bruit?" he asked theatrically. "When you asked for enhanced surveillance equipment, I provided it for you. And when you asked for increased security personnel, I provided those, as well. Is there something else you need? Is there something I've neglected to give you?"

Bruit compressed his lips and shook his head.

"You don't have a family. You don't have a girlfriend that I know about. So maybe you just don't care about your job, is that it?"

"You know that isn't true," Bruit lied.

"Then why aren't you doing it?" Arrant put his elbows on the desk and leaned forward. "This is the third incident in as many weeks, Bruit. I don't understand how this keeps happening. Do you have any leads on the shuttle crashes?"

"We'll know more if the guidance droids can be located and analyzed," Bruit said. "Right now they're buried under about five meters of dust."

"Well, get on it. I want you to devote all your resources to rooting out the saboteurs responsible for this. Do you think you can do that, Bruit, or do I have to bring in specialists?"

"They won't be able to learn any more than I have," Bruit rejoined. "InterGalactic Ore is becoming as desperate as LL is successful. Besides, it's not just a matter of industrial rivalry. A lot of the families that work for InterGal have vendettas with some of the families we employ. At least two of these recent incidents have been motivated by personal grudges."

"What are you suggesting, Bruit, that I terminate everyone and ship in ten thousand miners from Fondor? What's that going to do to production? More important, what's that going to do to my reputation on Dorvalla?"

Bruit shrugged. "I don't have any answers for you. Maybe it's time you brought this to the attention of the Galactic Senate."

Arrant stared at him. "Bring this to Coruscant? We're not in the midst of an interstellar conflict, Bruit. This is corporate warfare, and I've been in the trenches long enough to know that it's best to resolve these conflicts on your own. What's more, I don't want the senate involved. It will come down to a contest between Lommite Limited and InterGalactic, as to who can offer the most bribes to the most senators." He shook his head angrily. "That'll bankrupt us quicker than this continued sabotage."

Bruit had his mouth open to reply when a tone sounded from Arrant's intercom, and the voice of his protocol droid secretary issued from the annunciator.

"I'm sorry to disturb you, sir, but you have a priority holotransmission from a Neimoidian, Hath Monchar."

Arrant's fine brows beetled. "Monchar? I don't know the name. But go ahead, put him through."

From a holoprojector disk set into the floor at the center of the office rose the life-size holopresence of a red-orbed, pale-green Neimoidian draped in rich robes and wearing a black headpiece that aspired to be a crown.

"I greet you in the name of the Trade Federation, Jurnel Arrant," Hath Monchar began. "Viceroy Nute Gunray conveys his warmest regards, and wishes you to know that the Trade Federation was sorry to learn of your latest setback."

Arrant scowled. "How is it that whenever tragedy strikes, the first ones I hear from are the Neimoidians?"

"We are a compassionate species," Monchar said, his heavily accented Basic elongating the words.

"Compassionate and Neimoidian don't belong in the same sentence, Monchar. And just how did you come to hear of our 'setback,' as you call it? Or was it that the Trade Federation had a hand in the matter?"

The nictitating membranes of Monchar's red eyes began to spasm. "The Trade Federation would never do anything to impair relations with a potential partner."

"Partner?" Arrant laughed ruefully. "At least have the decency to speak the truth, Monchar. You want our trade routes. I don't know how much you had to pay the Galactic Senate to obtain a franchise to operate with impunity in the free trade zones, but you're not going to buy your way into the Videnda sector."

"But you could ship ten times as much lommite ore inside one of our freighters as you can in twenty of your largest barges."

"Granted. But at what price? Before long it would cost us more to ship with you than we could possibly earn back. You wouldn't be wearing those expensive robes, otherwise."

Monchar took a moment to reply. "We would much prefer that our partnership begins on solid footing. We would hate to see Lommite Limited become ensnared in a situation that allows it no recourse but to join us."

Arrant bristled and shot to his feet. "Is that a threat, Monchar? What do you intend to do, send your droids down here to invade us?"

Monchar made a motion of dismissal. "We are merchants, not conquerors."

"Then stop talking like a conqueror, or I'll report this to the Trade Commission on Coruscant."

"You're upset," Monchar said, nervously stroking his prominent muzzle. "Perhaps we should speak at some later date."

"Don't contact me, Monchar. I'll contact you."

Arrant deactivated the holoprojector and dropped back into his chair, forcing a long exhalation through pursed lips. "Scavengers," he said after a moment.

"I'd sooner see LL go under than sell out to the Trade Federation."

Into a brief succeeding silence came a persistent plopping sound from outside the office's floor-to-ceiling viewpanes. "What now?" Arrant asked, swiveling his chair toward the sound.

"Rain," Bruit muttered.

Despite its rich deposits of lommite, or the recurrent attention it received from the Trade Federation, Dorvalla was to most observers an inconsequential speck in the sweep of star systems that made up the Galactic Republic. But among the few who had been monitoring the events on Dorvalla, none had followed them as keenly as Darth Sidious, the Dark Lord of the Sith.

"This rivalry between Lommite Limited and Inter-Galactic Ore intrigues me," Sidious was saying as he moved about the cavernous den that was both his sanctuary and repository. The hood of his cowl was raised over his lined face, and the hem of his robe trailed on the gleaming floor. His voice was a rasp, absent emotion but not without instances of intentional inflection.

"I see a way that we might exploit this entanglement to our own gain," he continued. "A push here, a shove there, and both mining companies will collapse. Thus, we will be able to deliver Dorvalla to the Trade Federation—the ore, the trade routes, Dorvalla's vote in the senate—and, in so doing, gain the further allegiance of Viceroy Gunray and his lackeys."

Sidious removed his hands from the ample sleeves of his robe. "Viceroy Gunray claims to be persuaded of the worth of serving us, but I want him fully in our grasp, so that there can be no doubt of his heeding my commands. With Dorvalla secured, he will likely be promoted to a permanent position on the Trade Federation Directorate. We can then further our larger plan."

Sidious cast his hooded gaze across the room to a deeply shadowed area in which Darth Maul sat silent as a statue, his tattooed face lowered, so that all Sidious could see was the crown of vestigial horns that sprouted from his hairless skull.

"Your thoughts betray you, my young apprentice," he remarked. "You are puzzled by my steadfast interest in the Neimoidians."

Darth Maul lifted his face, and what scant light there was seemed to recoil. Where his Master represented all that was concealed and mysterious in the Sith, Maul was the personification of all that was to be feared.

"From you, Master, I cannot hide what I feel. The Neimoidians are greedy and weak-willed. I find them unworthy."

"You left out duplicitous and sniveling," Sidious said.

"Most of all, Master."

Sidious came as close as he ever came to grinning.

"Less than admirable traits, I agree. But useful for our purposes." He approached Maul. "To realize our goal, we will be forced to deal with all classes of beings, each less noble than the last. But this is what we must do. I assure you that the Neimoidians will come to play an important role in our effort to bring new order to the galaxy."

Maul's yellow eyes held Sidious's perceptive gaze. "Master, how will you help Viceroy Gunray and the Trade Federation secure Dorvalla?"

Sidious came to a halt a few meters away. "You will be my hand in this, Darth Maul."

Instantly, Maul bowed his head once more. "What is your bidding, Master?"

Sidious put his hands on his hips. "Stand, Darth Maul, and face me." He gave his apprentice a moment to comply before continuing. "Thus far your apprenticeship has been impeccable. You have never wavered in your intent, and you have executed your tasks flawlessly. Your skill as a sword master is peerless."

"My Master, " Maul said. "I live to serve you."

Sidious fell briefly silent—never a good sign. "There are certainties, Darth Maul," he said at last. "But there is also the unforeseen. The power of the dark side is limitless, but only to those who accept uncertainty. That means being able to concede to possibilities."

Darth Sidious raised his right hand, palm outward.

Before Maul could prevent it—even if he had chosen to do so—the long cylinder that was his double-bladed lightsaber flew from its hitch on his belt and went directly to his Master. But instead of grasping it, Sidious stopped the lightsaber in midflight, centimeters from his raised hand, and directed it to spin and rotate before him, leaving Maul to gaze at him in unabashed awe.

Sidious bade the lightsaber to ignite. From each end blazed a meter-long blade of rubicund fire, hypnotic in the intensity of its burning. The free-floating weapon pivoted left, then right, eliciting a thrumming sound that was as menacing as it was rousing.

"An exquisite weapon," Sidious said. "Tell me, my young apprentice, what were you thinking when you fashioned it? Why this and not a single blade, as the Jedi prefer?"

"The single blade has limitations, Master, in offense and defense. It made sense to me to be able to strike with both ends."

Sidious made a sound of approval. "You must bear that in mind when you go to Dorvalla, Darth Maul. But remember this: What is done in secret has great power. A sword master knows that when he flourishes his blade, he reveals his intent. Be watchful. It is too soon to reveal ourselves."

"I understand, Master."

Sidious deactivated the lightsaber and sent it back to Maul, who received it as one might a cherished possession. Then Sidious approached Maul and handed him a data disk. "Study this as you travel. It contains the names and descriptions of the beings you will encounter, and other information you will find useful."

Sidious beckoned Maul to follow him to the far wall of their murky lair. As they approached, a great panel drew open, revealing a lofty view of the planet-wide cityscape that was Coruscant.

"You will find Dorvalla to be a much different landscape than Coruscant, Darth Maul." Sidious turned slightly in Maul's direction, appraising him from beneath the cowl. "I suspect that you will savor the experience."

"And you, my Master, where will you be?"

"Here," Sidious said. "Awaiting your return, and the news that your mission was successful."

It had taken two days to locate and exhume the guidance droids from the crashed shuttles, and it had rained the entire time. The soup in the shadow of the Castle was three meters thick. Bruit had insisted on overseeing the search-and-recovery operation. He wanted to be on hand when the droids were analyzed.

Few of Lommite Limited's employees had access to the launch zone, and fewer still had access to the mechanized shuttles themselves. Tampering of the sort that had brought down the crafts would have left characteristic signs of the computer slicer who had effected previous acts of terrorism and sabotage. Bruit's sources had already established that the slicer was an agent of InterGalactic Ore, but the saboteur's identity had yet to be ascertained.

The team Bruit had assigned to the retrieval was a mix of beings from the relatively nearby star systems of Clak'dor, Sullust, and Malastare—that was to say, Bith, Sullustans, and transplanted Gran. All were suited up in goggles, respirators, and large-format footwear that kept everyone from sinking too deeply into the gelatinous mess the rain had made of the ore. All except Bruit, who was sporting thigh-high boots in an effort to stay clean.

"No doubt about it, Chief," one of the limpid-eyed Sullustans said, after running a series of tests on one of the R-series guidance droids. "Whoever sliced his way into this little guy is the same one who shut down the conveyors last month. I'll stake my wages on it."

"Don't bother," Bruit said. "You've only corroborated what all of us already knew." He gave his head an angry shake. "I want the launch zones shut down until further notice—off-limits to everyone. Then I want every member of the launch prep and maintenance crews brought in for questioning."

"What about the ore, Chief?" one of the Bith asked.

"We'll import temporary crews, even if we have to go to Fondor to stock the crews we need. Once we're up and running, we'll have to double the shuttle flights."

Knowing what doubling the flights would entail, everyone groaned.

"What's the boss going to say about this?" the Sullustan asked.

Bruit glanced in the direction of headquarters. Arrant already knew that the guidance droids had been located, and was waiting in his office for Bruit's report.

"I'll tell you when I get back," Bruit said.

He set off for the landspeeder he had left at the control booth, but he hadn't gone ten meters when his left boot became hopelessly cemented in the mucky soup. He grabbed the thigh-high cuff of the boot, hoping he could simply pull it free, but he lost his balance and pitched to one side, sinking up to his right shoulder. He maintained that indecorous pose for some moments, while he daydreamed of what life might be like on Coruscant.

"You were right about things getting worse," Arrant said when Bruit entered the office, muddy and in his stocking feet.

"I was also right about InterGalactic. The guidance droids show exactly what we expected to find."

A grim expression marred Arrant's handsome face. "This has gone far enough," he said after a moment. "Bruit, you know that I'm a patient man, and basically a peaceful one. I've tolerated these acts of vandalism and sabotage, but I've reached my limit. The loss of those two shuttles . . . Look. Corellian Engineering just turned to InterGalactic for a shipment we couldn't provide—no doubt, just as InterGalactic anticipated would happen."

"It won't happen again," Bruit interjected. "I've shut down the launch zones, and I'm bringing in replacement crews."

"You have one day," Arrant said.

Bruit gaped at him.

"Eriadu has placed major orders with us and Inter-Galactic," Arrant explained. "We're expected to deliver by the end of the week, which gives us just enough time to get the barges loaded and jumped to hyperspace. This is a make-or-break contract, Bruit, and Eriadu is going to award it to whichever one of us can deliver on time and without incident. LL needs to get there first, do you understand?"

Bruit nodded. "I'll have the shuttles up and running in one day."

"That's only the beginning," Arrant said carefully. "It's a sure bet you're not going to root out the saboteurs by then, so instead of that I want you to arrange for us to reply in kind to InterGalactic's actions." He waited for Bruit to absorb his intent. "I want to hit them hard, Bruit. But I don't want us to do the hitting directly."

Bruit considered it. "I suppose we could turn to one of the criminal organizations. Black Sun, maybe."

Arrant waved his hands in a gesture of dismissal. "That's your area of expertise. The less I know about it, the better. I just don't want us to be in a position where we can be blackmailed afterward."

"Then we're better off using freelancers."

"Do whatever you need to do—and no matter what the cost."

Bruit took a breath. "I've a feeling that Dorvalla isn't going to be the same from this point on."

* * *

Dressed in a lightweight utility suit and a black overcloak, its hood raised against teeming rain, Darth Maul strode down the main street of the company town Lommite Limited had assembled in the midst of what had once been a trackless tropical forest. Beneath the cloak, he wore his double-bladed lightsaber hooked to his belt, within easy reach should he need it. Dorvalla's gravity was slightly less than what he was accustomed to, so he moved with an extra measure of grace.

A grid of permacrete streets, the town was a warren of prefabricated domes and rickety wooden structures, many of them lacking transparisteel in their windows. Music spilled from the entrances to cantinas and eateries, and folks of all description meandered tipsily down the raised walkways. The place had the feeling of frontier towns throughout the outlying star systems, with the routine mix of aliens, humanoids, and older-generation droids; sterility and contamination; repulsorlift vehicles operating alongside four- and six-legged beasts of burden.

The residents, all of whom either worked directly for Lommite Limited or were there to defraud those who did, projected the same mix of autonomy from the laws that regulated life on the Core worlds and enslavement to perpetual toil and poverty.

Unlike Coruscant, where beings hustled to and fro with determination, here reigned an atmosphere of purposelessness, of accidental life, as if the pitiful beings who had been born here, or who had arrived for whatever reason, had resigned themselves to the depths. Like the bottom feeders who dwelled in the lawless bowels of Coruscant, they seemed to be going through the motions of living, rather than grasping life and turning it to their own purposes.

The revelation fascinated Maul as much as it disheartened him. He decided that he needed to gaze beyond appearances.

The air was thick with heat and humidity, and the buzzing and chirping sounds of the surrounding forest played at the edge of his hearing. He could sense the interplay of life there, the fights and flights, and the ongoing struggle for survival. And the forest had imparted some of itself to the town. For here lived beings who were not above hunting and killing to obtain the sustenance they required. A veneer of laws regulated such things, but beneath that veneer lurked a more base morality that allowed opponents to settle their matters without fear of intrusion by keepers of the peace, judicials, or even worse, the Jedi Knights.

Life was cheap.

Maul threw out his right hand and snatched a fist-sized insect in midflight. Dazed, the flitter lay in his palm, perhaps wondering on some primitive level just what make or manner of predator it had blundered into. The creature's six legs wriggled and its pair of antennae twitched. Its twin eyespots and carapaced body glowed with a faintly green bioluminescence.

Darth Maul studied the insect, then sent it on its way to rejoin the multitude that buzzed about the town.

His Master had shown him many places, but always under escort, and now he was suddenly on his own, a stranger on a strange world. He wondered if he might have found his way to a place like Dorvalla had it not been for Darth Sidious and the life he had provided. He had been raised to believe that he was extraordinary, and he had come to accept that. But every so often doubt would drift in of its own accord, and he would be left to wonder.

He shucked the mental intrusion and quickened his pace.

His Sith training allowed him to spot weaknesses of character or constitution in each of the various beings he passed. He drew on his dark-side instincts to guide him to the best means of carrying out his mission.

Maul came to a halt at the entrance to a noisy cantina. It was the sort of place where anyone who entered would be appraised by the clientele within, so he moved quickly—a blur to most; to others, just another laborer hurrying in out of the rain. He slid onto a stool at the bar, keeping his hood raised and his face in profile when the human female bartender approached.

"What can I get you, stranger?"

"Pure water," Maul growled.

"Big spender, huh?"

Maul made a negligent motion with his fingers. "You'll bring my drink and leave me alone."

The muscular, tattooed woman blinked twice. "I'll bring your drink and leave you alone."

Maul expanded his peripheral vision to take in the two adjoining rooms. He made use of the mirror behind the bar to see what his eyes could not, and he drew on the dark side to fill in the rest.

The cantina had an air of benign neglect, a smell of liquid inebriants and greasy food. The lighting was deliberately low. Flying insects of various sizes circled the illuminators, and children of several species ran in and out. Males and females fraternized openly, with a sense of levity or abandon. Music was provided by a ragtag band of Bith and fat Ortolans. Along the length of the bar Weequays conversed with Ugnaughts, Twi'leks with Gands. Maul was the only Iridonian in the place, but he was not the only sole representative of a species.

If some of the residents he had passed on the street were the hunters, the manka cats, here were the nerfs the cats fed on—the ones who gave themselves over to intoxicants and games of chance and other vices. It was the sheer absence of discipline that sickened him. Discipline was the key to power. Unflinching discipline was what had forged him into a sword master and warrior. Discipline was what enabled him to defy gravity and slow the inrush of sensory input, so that he could move between the moments.

Maul sharpened his faculties, extending the range of his hearing to monitor nearby conversations. Most were as prosaic as he had expected them to be, revolving around gossip, flirtation, petty complaints, and future plans that would never be realized.

Then he heard the word sabotage, and his ears pricked up. The customer who had uttered it was a stout human, seated off to Maul's right in a booth along the cantina's rear wall. Another human sat opposite him, tall and dark complexioned. Both men wore the gray lightweight coveralls that were standard issue for employees of Lommite Limited, but the lack of lommite dust in their hair or on their clothes made it clear that they weren't miners.

A third man, straight-backed and robust-looking, approached while Maul watched out of the corner of his eye. Maul took a sip of water and turned slightly in the direction of the booth.

"I figured I'd find you two here," the new arrival said.

The stout one smiled and made room on the padded bench seat. "Step into our office and we'll buy you a drink."

The third man sat, but declined the offer with a shake of his head. "Maybe later."

The other two traded looks of surprise. Maul read the lip movements of the taller one: "If he's not drinking, then something serious has come up."

The third man nodded. "The chief has called a special meeting. He wants us at his place in half an hour."

"Any idea what it's about?" the stout one asked.

"It has to be the shuttle crash," the man opposite him surmised. "Bruit probably has a line on the culprits."

Maul recognized the name. Bruit was Lommite Limited's chief of field operations. The three men were probably security personnel.

"Like there was any question about the culprits," the stout one was saying.

"It's bigger than that," the third man said, lowering his voice almost to the point where Maul had to strain to hear him. "Word has come down from Arrant on how we're going to respond."

The stout man sat away from the table that bisected the booth. "Well, it's about time."

"I'd say that calls for another round of drinks," his partner said.

Maul continued listening, but his eyes were no longer fixed on the men but on something he had glimpsed on the wall above the booth. It resembled the bioluminescent flitter he had captured earlier on.

This one, however, wasn't moving from its spot on the wall. The reason became apparent once Maul probed it through the Force. Not only was it a fabrication, it was also a listening device.

Maul scanned the room, then turned to face the mirror. The device wasn't very sophisticated; its large size was evidence of that. Even so, that didn't mean that whoever was eavesdropping on the security men had to be inside the cantina. But Maul suspected that they were. Without looking at it, he focused his attention on the artificial flitter and screened out all extraneous sounds—the pulsing music, the dozens of separate conversations, the noises of glasses clinking or being filled with one inebriant or another. Once he could discern the muted beeping of the device's transmitter, he listened for signs of the receiver with which it was in communication.

At a round table in the adjoining room sat a Rodian and two Twi'leks, ostensibly engaged in a game of cards—sabacc, in all likelihood. Maul watched them for a moment. Their playing was desultory. He observed their facial expressions as the security agents continued to converse. When one of the men said something of interest, the Rodian's faceted eyes would flash and his short snout would curl to one side. At the same time, the Twi'leks' head-tails would twitch and their pasty faces would flush ever so slightly.

The Rodian's left ear was sporting an earbead receiver, while the Twi'leks' receivers took the form of dermal patches, disguised as lekku tattoos.

Maul was certain that the trio were in the secret employ of Lommite Limited's onworld competitor, InterGalactic Ore. He recognized the Rodian from

RECEIPT

9/23/2020   07:08 AM
SOUND TRANSIT
Puyallup
TVM #   43

VISA/MC/AMEX SALE
CARD/EXP: 1779 22/ 4
AUTH # :   012218
BANK REF#:   8283
SALES AMT: $40 00

E-Purse
841721- 43

the disk Sidious had given him. It was possible that they were the saboteurs themselves.

His eyes darted back to the listening device and the security men. Creatures of habit, they probably occupied the same booth night after night, completely unaware that their conversations were being monitored. Such carelessness exasperated Maul to the point of fury. The men were deserving of whatever harm would surely come their way.

The three security men left the cantina on foot and wended their way to a ribbon of trail that wove through a dense stand of forest. Maul followed from a discreet distance, keeping to the shadows when Dorvalla's moon came up, full and silver-white.

The trail eventually arrived at a tight-knit community of flimsy dwellings, many of them raised on stilts to keep them above pools of runoff water left by the rain. The humidity was oppressive.

The dwelling that was the trio's destination was an elevated cube with a metal roof angled to channel rainwater into a ferrocrete cistern. The cube's only door was accessed by means of a ladderlike stairway. A rusted landspeeder with a cracked windscreen was parked in a muddy front lot.

Maul kept to the trees while a thickly built human responded to the stout agent's raps on the door frame.

"Come on up," the man said. "Everyone else is already here."

Bruit. Darth Maul waited until the three agents were inside, then he hurried from the shadows and planted himself under an open side window. Not content with his choice, he ducked beneath the house and clambered up one of the stilts to wedge himself between the floor joists of the front room. In the room above, someone was pouring liquid into several glasses.

Maul extracted a miniature recording device from the breast pocket of his utility suit and placed it against the underside of the rough-hewn floorboards.

"Here's the long and short of it," Bruit said while the glasses were being filled. "Arrant has decided that we need to level the playing field. We're going to strike at InterGal at Eriadu. Our shipments will reach the planet, and theirs won't."

Someone whistled in astonishment.

"Does the boss realize what he's letting loose?" perhaps the same man asked. "This is going to lead to a shooting war."

"This comes straight from Arrant," Bruit said. "He's been in the trenches before. Those are his words, and this is his show."

"His show and our livelihood," someone pointed out. "There has to be a better way of settling this. What about petitioning the senate to intervene?"

"A cure that can be worse than the disease," another answered, much to Maul's amusement. "The senate will defer to committees run by corrupt bureaucrats. It will take months for it to get to the courts."

"No senate, no courts," Bruit said. "That much has already been decided. It's up to us."

"So what happens at Eriadu?"

"We've been able to learn the hyperspace route InterGal's ships are going to take. They'll arrive by way of Rimma 13, and are scheduled to decant from hyperspace at 1400 hours, Eriadu local time. The folks we're employing to execute the strike will be able to calculate the precise reentry coordinates."

"Who are we employing?"

"The Toom clan."

Expressions of dismay flew from all corners.

"Cutthroats," someone said.

"Exactly," Bruit said. "But we need to team up to accomplish this, and Arrant's willing to spend the necessary credits. By using them, no one will suspect us, and Arrant doesn't care, because he doesn't want to know any more than he has to. He wants to keep his hands clean while I make the connections. Besides, the Tooms have the means to get the job done."

"And no scruples to stand in the way."

"Have they agreed to terms?"

"At first contact," Bruit said. "Although I have to say that I sometimes wish I could see both Lommite and InterGal brought down, so that someone with real foresight could build a better organization from the dregs."

Several glasses clinked together.

"So what's our part in this, Chief, if the deal has already been struck?"

Bruit snorted. "We need to prepare ourselves for InterGal's counterpunch."

Maul peeled the recorder from the floorboards and dropped down to the loamy soil below the house. He remained still for a long moment, crouched in the darkness, listening to sounds of distant laughter and the stridulations of profuse insect life. Then he thought back to Coruscant, and the question his Master had put to him regarding his double-bladed lightsaber.

It made sense to me to be able to strike with both ends, Maul had answered.

With a note of approval, his Master had said, You must bear that in mind when you go to Dorvalla.

Maul reached within his cloak and unclipped the long cylinder from his belt. One end, then the other, Maul told himself. Both, to effect a single purpose.

Maul waited until the moon was low in the sky before he went to Lommite Limited's headquarters at the base of the escarpment. The incidents of sabotage had caused the complex of buildings to be placed on high alert. Armed sentries, some accompanied by leashed beasts, patrolled, and powerful illuminators cast circles of brilliant light over the spacious grounds. A five-meter-high electrified stun fence encompassed everything.

Maul spent an hour studying the movements of the sentries, the periodic sweeps of the illuminators, the towering fence, and the motion detector lasers that gridded the broad lawn beyond. He was certain that infrared cams were scanning the grounds, but there was little he could do about those without leaving evidence of his infiltration. A probe droid would have been able to tell him all he needed to know, but there wasn't time and he wanted to do this personally.

To test the possibility that pressure detectors had been installed in the ground, he used the Force to propel stones over the fence. As they struck specific places on the lawn, he waited for some response, but the guards stationed at the entry gates simply continued to go about their business.

When he was satisfied that he had committed the results of his reconnaissance to memory, he shrugged out of his cloak and leapt straight up over the fence, landing precisely where some of the rocks he had tossed rested. Then he sprang to a series of other sites that ultimately carried him to the wall of the principal building, moving with such speed the entire time that whatever holorecordings were being made wouldn't show him unless they were played in slow motion.

He reached one of the doors and found it locked, so he began to work his way around the building, testing other doors and windows, all of which were similarly secured.

He tested the building's flat roof for motion and pressure detectors as he had the lawn. Vaulting to the top, he was confronted with an expanse of solar arrays, skylights, and cooling ducts. He moved to the nearest skylight and ignited his lightsaber. He was ready to plunge the blade through the transparisteel panel when he stopped himself, and peered more intently at the panel. Embedded in the transparisteel were monofilament chains, which, when severed, would trip an alarm.

Deactivating the blade, he reclipped his lightsaber and sat down to think. It was unlikely that Lommite Limited's central computer was a stand-alone machine. It would have to be accessible from outside locations. Bruit would have remote access. Maul berated himself for not having recognized that fact earlier. But it wasn't too late to rectify his oversight.

Maul returned to Bruit's dwelling just before sunrise. Unlike the headquarters complex, the stilted house had no security. The chief of field operations either didn't have enemies or didn't care, one way or the other. Perhaps Bruit was that resigned to fate, Maul thought. It scarcely mattered, in any case.

He circled the house, occasionally chinning himself on the windowsills to peer inside. In a rear room Bruit was sprawled atop a knocked-together bed, half in, half out of a net tent that was meant to keep nocturnal insects from feasting on his blood. He was fully clothed, snoring lightly, and dead drunk. A half-emptied bottle of brandy sat on a small table alongside the bed.

Maul gritted his teeth. More carelessness, more lack of discipline. He couldn't summon any compassion for the man. The weak needed to be weeded out.

Maul let himself in through the unlocked door and scanned the front room. Bruit was a man of few worldly possessions, and not a particularly orderly one. His dwelling was as chaotic as his life appeared to be. The confined space smelled of spoiled food, and lommite dust coated every horizontal surface. Water dripped from a sink faucet that could have easily been repaired. Arachnids had woven perfect webs in all four corners of the room.

Maul searched for Bruit's personal computer and located it in the bedroom. It was a portable device, not much longer than a human hand. He called the machine to him and activated it. The display screen came to life and a menu presented itself. It took only moments for Maul to find his way to Lommite Limited's central computer, but for the second time that night he found himself locked out.

The computer was demanding to see Bruit's fingerprints.

Maul might have been able to slice his way inside the central computer, but not without leaving an easily followed trail. What is done in secret has great power, his Master had said.

Maul gazed at Bruit. With a scant motion of his left hand, he caused the man to roll over onto his back. Born of some uneasy dream, a prolonged groan escaped the human. Maul gestured for Bruit's right arm to rise, wrist bent, with the palm of his hand facing outward. Then he stealthily carried the computer to Bruit's hand, easing the display screen into gentle contact with the outstretched fingers. When the machine had toodled an acknowledgment, Maul dropped Bruit's arm and rolled him back onto his side.

By the time Maul left the bedroom, the directories for the database were scrolling onscreen. Maul pinpointed the files relating to the imminent Eriadu delivery and opened them.

The cantina was doing a brisk lunchtime business when Darth Maul stole through the entrance and took a seat at a corner table in the smaller room. Outside, a gloomy downpour was inundating the town. He kept the dripping hood of his cloak raised, and he angled himself away from the crowd, ignoring the few second glances he received.

Two of Lommite Limited's security men occupied their usual booth, feeding their faces with fatty foods and talking with their mouths full. Not far from where Maul was seated, the Rodian and the two Twi'leks he had identified the previous evening as agents of InterGalactic Ore were gathered around a card table. Shortly the three were joined by a dark-haired human female, who placed a stack of company credits on the table and joined the sabacc game in progress. Maul recognized the piece of cuff jewelry that adorned the woman's left ear as a receiver.

He waited to act until the four of them were engaged in monitoring the security agents' conversation. Then, with a slight motion of his hand, he Force-summoned the listening device to peel itself from the wall above the booth, zip into the small room, and alight at the center of the card table.

The Rodian sat back, startled, clearly failing to recognize the artificial bug as their own device. "A new player joins the game."

One of the Twi'leks raised his open hand to shoulder level. "Not for long."

The Twi'lek's long-nailed hand was halfway toward smashing the flitter when the human female grabbed hold of his wrist and managed to deflect the downward strike.

"Hold on," she whispered urgently. "I heard your voice."

"That's because I said something," the Twi'lek said.

"In my earpiece," the woman said, gesturing discreetly. "And now I'm hearing my voice."

"I'm hearing your voice," the Rodian said, confused.

"What in the name of . . ."

The Twi'lek allowed his voice to trail off, and all four of the agents sat back in their stiff wooden chairs, gazing in astonishment at the listening device.

"It's ours," the woman said finally.

The Rodian glanced at her. "What's it doing here?"

Maul called on the Force to move the bug.

"It's crawling around, is what it's doing," one of the Twi'leks said, with a measure of distress. He glanced over his shoulder at the preoccupied security men, then at his comrades.

Maul activated the remote control he had tuned to the frequency of the insect transmitter.

"This comes straight from the Toom clan," the bug sent to the earpieces and dermal audio patches worn by the conspirators, all of whom traded wide-eyed looks.

"Here's the long and short of it. Arrant has decided to move against InterGalactic Ore shipments. No petitioning the senate. He's letting loose a shooting war. That much has already been decided."

Absorbed in what she was hearing, the woman used her right forefinger to tilt the ear cuff for clearer reception.

"The Toom clan has a way of settling this—a cure for the disease. InterGal can level the playing field by employing us to strike at Eriadu. We of the Toom clan wish to see LL brought down. Someone with real foresight could build a better organization from the dregs.

"We've been able to learn the hyperspace route Lommite Limited's ships are going to take to Eriadu, and the precise reentry coordinates. They'll arrive by way of Rimma 18, and are scheduled to decant from hyperspace at 1300 hours, Eriadu local time.

"We've been in the trenches. This is our livelihood. We can intervene and execute the strike. The Tooms have the means to get the job done. No one will suspect us. We have no scruples about what happens.

"To team up to accomplish this, be willing to spend the credits necessary. Contact us."

Maul had spent all morning adulterating the recording he had made during the meeting at Bruit's dwelling, and modifying the resequenced phrases to sound as if they had been uttered by a single individual. The result appeared to be having the desired effect. The four agents were continuing to stare at the bug they themselves had installed. The woman's mouth was slightly ajar, and the Twi'leks' head-tails were twitching.

Maul was pleased to hear the Rodian say, "This has to go directly to the top—and I mean now."

The Toom clan had a motto: "Pay us enough and we'll make worlds collide."

They had started out as legitimate rescue workers and salvagers, using a powerful Interdictor ship to retrieve ships stranded in hyperspace. By mimicking the effects of a mass shadow, the Interdictor had the ability to pull endangered ships back into realspace. While the rewards for such work were substantial, they were never substantial enough to satisfy the desires of the clan, and over the course of several years, the group had launched a second career as pirates, employing their Interdictor against passenger and supply ships, or hiring themselves out to criminal organizations to interfere with shipments of spice and other proscribed goods.

However, unlike the Hutts and Black Sun, both of which could usually be relied upon to honor the terms of any agreement, the Toom clan was motivated solely by profit. A small outfit, they couldn't afford the luxury of turning down jobs out of respect for some hazy criminal ethic—a stance that had made them outcasts even among their own kind.

Headquartered in an underground base deep in Dorvalla's unpopulated northern wastes, the clan received routine payoffs from both Lommite Limited and InterGalactic Ore, to ensure the safety of their shuttles and ore barges. The Tooms used much of the funds to bribe the commanders of Dorvalla's volunteer space corps to ensure the clan's own safety—with the understanding that the clan would refrain from operating within the Videnda sector.

Because Eriadu was outside the sector—and notwithstanding the fact that they were already receiving payoffs from InterGalactic—the clan had accepted Lommite Limited's generous offer of Republic credits to perform a bit of sabotage work. InterGalactic would simply have to understand that the nature of their arrangement with the Toom clan had changed. More important, the contract with LL didn't preclude the possibility of the clan's entering into a similar contract with InterGal—as certainly might be the case after the Eriadu operation. In fact, the clan had every intention of contacting InterGal to suggest as much.

No one in the clan had expected InterGalactic to contact them before Eriadu.

A leather-faced Weequay, Nort Toom himself accepted the holotransmission from Caba'Zan, head of security for InterGalactic Ore. The clan was mostly made up of far-from-home Weequay and Nikto humanoids, but Aqualish, Abyssin, Barabels, and Gamorreans also numbered among the mix.

"I want to discuss the most recent offer you tendered," Caba'Zan's holopresence began. He was a near-human Falleen, burly and green complexioned.

"Our most recent offer," Nort Toom said carefully.

"About destroying Lommite Limited's ships at Eriadu."

Toom's deep-set eyes darted between the holoprojector and one of his Weequay confederates, who was standing nearby. "Oh, that offer. We have so many operations in the works, it's sometimes hard to keep track."

"I'm glad to hear that business is good," Caba'Zan said disingenuously.

"I've a feeling it's about to get even better."

The Falleen came directly to the point. "We're willing to pay one hundred thousand Republic credits."

Toom tried to keep from celebrating. The offer was twice what Patch Bruit had paid. "You'll have to go to two hundred thousand."

Caba'Zan shook his hairless head. "We can go as high as one fifty—if you can guarantee results."

"Done," Toom said. "When we see that the credits have been transferred, we'll make the necessary arrangements."

Caba'Zan looked dubious. "You're certain about the reentry coordinates for LL's ships, and the time of their decanting at Eriadu?"

"Maybe we should go over that one more time," Toom said.

"You said Rimma 18, at 1300 Eriadu local—unless something has changed."

"Only for the better," Toom said reassuringly. "Only for the better."

"And you'll make it look like an accident."

"That's probably the best way of handling it, don't you think?"

"We don't want InterGalactic implicated."

"We'll make certain."

Toom deactivated the holoprojector and sat back, clamping his huge hands behind his head.

"Do you think they know about LL's hiring us?" his confederate asked in obvious incredulity.

"It didn't sound that way to me."

"InterGalactic is offering three times as much as Lommite. Are we going to return Bruit's money?"

Toom sat forward with determination. "I don't see any reason for that. We just have to make sure we can execute both contracts." He grinned broadly. "I have to admit that this appeals to my sense of unfair play."

"You mean—"

"Exactly. We sabotage everyone's ships."

Eriadu was an up-and-coming world in the outlying star systems. Situated close to the intersection of the Rimma Trade Route and the Hydian Way, Eriadu demonstrated a fierce devotion to industry, in the hope of achieving its goal of becoming the most important planet in the sector. To that end Eriadu had even developed a small shipbuilding enterprise, owned and operated by distant cousins of Supreme Chancellor Valorum, who chaired the Galactic Senate on Coruscant.

Eriadu's orbital facilities paled in comparison to similar ones at Corellia and Kuat, but among the smaller shipyards, Eriadu's were second only to those at Sluis Van, rimward and just off the principal trade routes.

Eriadu's lieutenant governor had done much to facilitate the burgeoning partnership between Eriadu and Dorvalla, emphasizing the senselessness of Eriadu's importing lommite from the Inner Rim when Dorvalla was practically a celestial neighbor. The quantities of ore required by Eriadu Manufacturing and

Valorum Shipping were such that neither LL nor Inter-Gal could have filled the orders on their own, but Lieutenant Governor Tarkin saw no dilemma in that. He insisted that he hadn't set things up as a contest, but there was no denying that it was anything but. Tarkin was even on record as saying that the company awarded the lucrative contract would probably be able to effect a financial takeover of the loser.

Tarkin had arranged for one of Eriadu's orbital habitats to host a ceremony to endorse the potential partnership, with all the cardinal players present: Jurnel Arrant and his counterpart at InterGalactic, the executive officers of Eriadu Manufacturing and Valorum Shipping, a plethora of business personnel who stood to gain from the new partnership, and, of course, Tarkin himself, representing Eriadu's political interests.

Sporting the finest in robes and tunics, everyone was gathered on the esplanade level of the orbital facility, awaiting the arrival of the ore barges LL and InterGal had dispatched. The separate flotillas were scheduled to arrive within an hour of each other, local time.

"I'm certain that this will be an auspicious day for all of us," the lieutenant governor was telling Arrant and the head of Eriadu Manufacturing. Tarkin was a slight man, with a quick mind and an even quicker temper. He stood as rigidly as a military commander, and his blue eyes held neither humor nor empathy.

"Tell me, Arrant," the manufacturing executive said, "do you foresee a time when Lommite Limited, on its own, could supply enough ore to meet the demands we're projecting for the near future?"

"Of course," Arrant answered confidently. "It's

simply a matter of expanding our operations." He turned and tugged Patch Bruit into the conversation. "Bruit, here, is our field supervisor, among other things. He has just notified me of a rich find, not a hundred kilometers from our present headquarters."

Bruit nodded. "Our survey teams—" he started to say, when one of LL's security agents cut him off.

"Chief, I'm sorry to bust in, but we need to talk in private."

Arrant watched worriedly as Bruit allowed himself to be led away.

"What's going on?" Bruit demanded when he and the security man were just out of earshot.

"Something has yanked the barges out of hyperspace short of their reentry coordinates. We don't know the cause. It might be a problem with the hyperspace generators, or maybe an uncharted mass shadow."

Bruit heard people gasp behind him. When he turned, everyone's attention was fixed on the huge monitor screens that displayed views of the orbital shipyards. Some distance from the shipyards, and way off course, several lackluster space barges were reverting to realspace.

"Bruit, are those our vessels?" Arrant asked in mounting concern.

"Yes, but there has to be a good reason for their decanting early."

"This is most unexpected," Tarkin remarked. "Most unexpected."

The well-bedecked crowd gasped again. Bruit watched in shock as a second group of ships began to emerge from hyperspace.

"InterGalactic," his security man said in disbelief.

"They're going to collide!" someone said.

"Bruit!" Arrant screamed, as the color drained from his face. "Do something!"

What Bruit did was look away.

The screams and cries, the groans and sobs, the strobes of explosive light flashing across the polished floor of the habitat's esplanade deck told him everything he needed to know. LL's and InterGal's barges had been manipulated into mass collisions. Without looking, Bruit could see the lommite ore streaming from fractured hulls, turning local space as white as the molten anger that seethed behind Bruit's tightly shut eyelids.

"The Toom clan," he barked to his security man. "They've double-crossed us."

Someone collided with Bruit from behind. It was Jurnel Arrant, backing away from the display screens in numb horror.

"We're ruined," he mumbled. "We're ruined."

Bruit cleared his head with a shake and clamped his hands on the shoulders of the security man. "Send a message to Caba'Zan at InterGalactic," he ordered. "Tell him that we need to meet as soon as possible."

Lovingly crafted, the listening device was a perfect facsimile of a fire flitter. It sat between Bruit and Caba'Zan on a low table in Bruit's living room, singing its song:

"Here's the long and short of it. Arrant has decided to move against InterGalactic Ore shipments. No petitioning the senate. He's letting loose a shooting war. That much has already been decided . . ."

Caba'Zan ran a hand over his bald pate. "Strange. It almost sounds like your voice."

Bruit squeezed his eyes shut, then opened them and looked the Falleen in the eye. "That's because underneath the warping, it is my voice. I spoke those words—most of them anyway—right in this room."

Caba'Zan's forehead wrinkled. "I don't understand."

"I was briefing my men about the plan for InterGal's ships at Eriadu. Someone recorded the conversation."

"One of your men?"

Bruit shook his head in dismay. "I don't know."

"One of the Toom clan, then."

Bruit took his lower lip between his teeth. "Then why the need to warp the recording, and put on a song-and-dance show for your people in the cantina? Besides, there's no way the Tooms could have gained access to LL's database and gotten the reentry coordinates for our ships. They're not that clever. It has to have been one of your men."

"They're not that clever," Caba'Zan said. "Or that industrious. We wouldn't have known anything about your plans if it wasn't for the bug."

Bruit silenced the facsimile flitter and worked his jaw in vexation. "I'll figure out who it was later on. After I deal with the Toom clan."

Caba'Zan narrowed his eyes. "They played us both for fools, Bruit. If you're implying vengeance, I want some of the action."

Secreted beneath the stilted dwelling, Darth Maul smiled to himself, dropped to the ground, and hurried into the darkness.

* * *

Maul never doubted that the Toom clan would enter into contracts with both mining companies. Nor did he think that the clan would fail to deliver on its promise to sabotage the ships. Thus he had had no need to go to Eriadu to witness the fatal collisions. Instead he had passed the time watching members of the Toom clan shut down and abandon the base on Dorvalla. Surmising correctly that their betrayal would unite LL and InterGal against them—even briefly—the mercenaries had decided to abscond while they could.

Maul had trailed them to Riome, a small, ice-covered world deeper in the Dorvalla system, where the clan already had established a secret base.

A more astute group of outlaws might have elected to put as much distance as possible between themselves and Dorvalla. But perhaps the Toom clan was convinced that even the combined security forces of Lommite Limited and InterGalactic Ore wouldn't be a match for them. Whichever, Maul's next task was to make certain that Bruit learned the location of the Riome sanctuary by planting evidence at the site of the clan's former base.

Maul spent a full day in frigid temperatures and howling winds, waiting for Bruit and his men to arrive. Armed with blasters and an assortment of more powerful weapons, they raced from the shuttle that had delivered them from Dorvalla's equator and stormed the underground base. Accompanying them was a male Falleen and several aliens who answered to him, including the four saboteurs Maul had deceived in the cantina.

Frustrated to find the base deserted, they began a

search for clues as to the mercenaries' whereabouts. For too long Maul was convinced that he would have to intrude on their sloppy search and rub their noses in the evidence he had so artfully sown. But ultimately they discovered it on their own.

Maul was inside his ship when Bruit and the rest reboarded the shuttle and launched, presumably for Riome. The thought of the impending contest invigorated him. He thrilled at the prospect of being able to participate.

Riome loomed white as death in the blackness of space.

In his smaller and faster craft, Maul arrived ahead of Bruit's mixed squad of would-be avengers. His ship hugged the snow-covered terrain, racing over rolling foothills and skirting the edge of a turbulent gray sea studded with islands of craggy ice. Maul had seen no sign of the clan's Interdictor ship in orbit, and assumed that the mercenaries had concealed it in the asteroid field coreward of Riome.

In establishing a base, the mercenaries had found the warmest spot on the small world. It was an area of active volcanism, with immense glaciers pocked with ice-blue light, and patches of coarse grassland, through which bubbled dark pools of magma-heated water. The base itself was a series of interlinked semicylindrical bunkers that had once sheltered a team of scientists. Through the long intervening years, the scientists' abandoned droids and equipment had become outlandish ice sculptures.

Maul landed his ship a kilometer from the base. As on his first visit, he found no evidence of a radar installation. He watched Bruit's shuttle drop from azure skies, fly over the complex, and set down on a circle of permacrete, alongside a disk-shaped Corellian freighter and a gunship of equal size.

The Toom clan could not have been unaware of the shuttle's arrival, but Bruit had managed to catch the mercenaries unprepared nevertheless. His force of twenty emerged from the shuttle aboard a troop carrier equipped with both repulsorlift engines and weighty tracks for surface-effect locomotion. The clan rallied a quick defense, loosing blaster bolts from retrofitted firing holes and a self-contained laser cannon emplacement. The aggressors answered with the troop carrier's top-mounted repeater blasters and rocket launchers, making it abundantly clear that they were resolved to win the day.

Cyan laser bolts clipped the carrier's repulsorlifts and sent it coiling deeply into the snow. Clothed in cold-weather gear and helmets fitted with tinted face bowls, Bruit's legion leapt from ranks of bench seats. A direct hit from the laser cannon blew the carrier to pieces. Molten bits of alloy fountained into the thin air, sizzling as they showered to the frozen ground.

The forces of the mining companies fanned out and began a methodical advance on the bunkers, finding shelter behind boulders that had been carried down the mountainsides by glaciers. What Bruit didn't know, however, was that the base couldn't be taken by a frontal assault—not, in any case, by a mere handful of men wielding twenty-year-old weapons. The lead bunker had been fortified with blast doors, and the coarse grass apron that fronted it was impregnated with fragmentation mines and other traps.

Maul decided that he had to show himself.

He appeared briefly on a rise, east of the base, a

two-legged stranger dressed in a long cloak, deep black against the snowfield. The assailants took him for one of the clan and immediately opened fire. Maul propelled himself over the rise with leaps and bounds, though scarcely of the sort of which he was capable. Bruit did the wise thing and split his team, figuring, as Maul predicted he would, that the lone enemy knew another way into the base.

Maul kept himself in plain sight, dodging the blaster bolts fired by his pursuers, without using his lightsaber. He couldn't have been a better guide if he had been one of them. Briefly hidden by a snowdrift, he called on the Force to twirl himself deeply into the white wave. From the depths of his self-excavated tomb, he heard Bruit's men dash for the relatively undefended entrance to which he had led them.

Maul waited until he was certain that the last of them had disappeared through the entrance. Then he corkscrewed out of the ice cavity and followed them inside. The sibilant reports of blasters and the acrid smell of fire and cauterized flesh had brought his blood to a near boil, and he came close to drawing his lightsaber and rushing headlong into the fray. But slaughter was not his intent. His Master's plans would be better served if the miners and the mercenaries killed each other—though Maul might yet have to dispose of the ultimate victors.

Judging by the way the assault was progressing, it was Bruit's forces that would be left standing at the end. Despite being outgunned and outnumbered, the miners' assault was invigorated by the wrath of the betrayed. Even with a third of their group already wounded or dead, Bruit and his InterGalactic analog persevered, continuing to bring the fight to the Toom clan, which held the rear of the bunker, behind overturned laboratory counters and assorted pieces of instrumentation.

Explosions from the front bunker indicated that Bruit's teammates had blundered their way into the minefield. Shortly, the survivors were turning their weapons loose against the blast doors in an attempt to burn their way through.

Maul scampered along the long wall of the central bunker and found a place from which he could observe the fighting. To contain his eagerness, he gave himself over to evaluating the combat techniques of one contestant or another, making something of a game of anticipating who would be killed by whom, and at just what moment. His predictions grew more and more accurate as the opposing sides drew closer together.

A powerful detonation rocked the front bunker. The blast doors slid open with a prolonged grating sound, and five assailants stormed through a swirling cloud of dense smoke. Two were cut down before they had gone ten meters. The rest angled for the sides of the bunker and began to work their way forward.

The ferocity of the fighting made it apparent that neither side would tolerate surrender. It was a battle to the death—as Maul preferred it, in any case. His attention was drawn time and again to Patch Bruit. For all the disorder in his life, Bruit's displays of daring made him deserving of the lofty position he held in Lommite Limited. Maul was impressed. He didn't want to see Bruit fall to the mercenaries, who were nothing more than the blasters they cowered behind.

Bruit and the Falleen led the final charge, their combined forces going hand to hand with Weequay and Aqualish members of the clan, whose weapons were exhausted. The miners showed them no mercy, and in moments the battle was over, with Bruit, the Falleen, and five others left standing amid the carnage.

Maul wondered briefly if he could leave things as they stood. Bruit would report back to Lommite Limited's executive officer that the Toom clan had double-crossed both companies, and that they had paid with their lives for their betrayal. But it was unlikely that Bruit would let it rest at that. He would want to know who had assembled the adulterated recording, and he might even learn that the information about LL's shipping route to Eriadu had been accessed through his personal computer. Then he would begin to think again about the cantina bug, and perhaps he would scrutinize whatever surveillance recordings were available. For all Maul knew, images of an Iridonian with a face full of red and black tattoos might appear in one them.

Of course, there was no danger of his being traced to Coruscant, much less to his Master's lair. But the last thing he wanted was for Darth Sidious to see his apprentice's face turn up on some HoloNet most-wanted list.

Maul had to finish what he had begun.

He drew his lightsaber, ignited it at both ends, and leapt down to the floor of the prefab bunker.

Bruit, the Falleen, and the others spun around when they heard the resonant thrumming of his weapon, which Maul whirled over his head and around his shoulders. But no one fired. They stood staring at him, as if he were some hallucination born of bloodlust or snow blindness.

Maul realized that he would have to goad them into doing what he needed them to do. He began to march forward, glowering at them with his yellow eyes and showing his teeth, and at last someone fired—the Rodian from the cantina. Maul deflected the bolt straight back at him with the lower of his blades and kept coming.

"We have no fight with you, Jedi," the Falleen yelled.

The remark brought Maul up short.

"This is our business," the humanoid went on. "It doesn't concern Coruscant."

Maul growled and advanced.

Crouching suddenly, a Twi'lek fired, and Maul twirled, deflecting the bolts with his twin crimson blades. The Twi'lek and another security man dropped.

Then the rest opened fire at once. Maul leapt and jinked, spun and rolled, an acrobatic wonder, impossible to target. He stopped once to raise his hand and pepper his opponents with a flurry of Force-hurled glassware and sharp instruments. He turned blasters against each other and wrenched one fighter down onto a table with enough force to snap the man's spine.

His hand weapon depleted, the Falleen rushed him. Maul spun through a fleet kick, breaking the Falleen's arm. Then, without lowering his leg, he broke the security chief's neck.

Only Bruit remained. Gaping at Maul in disbelief, he let his blaster drop from his rigid hand. Maul continued to approach, the lightsaber held off to one side, its blades horizontal to the floor.

"I don't know how, and I don't know why," Bruit

began, "but I know that you must be responsible for everything that's happened."

Maul decided to hear him out.

"You recorded my conversations. Then you altered the recordings to trick the saboteurs you had identified in the cantina. You probably arranged for us to find this place." Bruit gestured broadly. "Can I at least know why before you kill me?"

"It is something that had to be done—for a larger purpose."

Bruit cocked his head, as if he hadn't heard Maul correctly.

Maul gazed at him. "You needn't dwell on it."

He raised his energy blade, preparing to thrust it into Bruit's chest, then restrained himself. A lightsaber wound wouldn't do, not at all. Deactivating the blade, he raised his right hand and made a vise of his gloved fingers. Bruit's hands flew to his windpipe, and he began to gasp for breath.

Jurnel Arrant was in his office when he received the details of Bruit's death on Riome. The messenger was a judicial agent, who had been dispatched from Coruscant at Arrant's request.

"I'm to blame for this entire business," Arrant said in a tone of anguished confession. "I'm guilty of ordering Bruit to bring in outsiders to do the dirty work. I escalated this conflict."

The lommite ore could still be mined, but LL no longer had enough barges to transport it. Replacing them would cost more than the company was currently worth. From what Arrant had learned, InterGalactic was in the same fix.

Anger gripped him. "I'm convinced that the

Neimoidians with the Trade Federation got to the Toom clan and paid them to sabotage our ships, along with InterGalactic's."

"That will be difficult to prove," the judicial said. "The Toom clan has been effectively wiped out, and unless you can produce evidence to support your theory, we can't show good cause for interrogating the Neimoidians." He was about to add something when Arrant cut him off.

"Bruit was a good man. He shouldn't have died as he did."

The judicial frowned, then prized a wafer-thin audio device from the pocket of his tunic and placed it on Arrant's desk. "Before you beat yourself to a pulp, you might want to listen to this."

Arrant picked up the device. "What is it?"

"A recording found at the Toom clan's base, here on Dorvalla. It's incomplete, but there's enough to warrant your attention."

Arrant activated the wafer's play function.

"I wish to see both Lommite and InterGal brought down," a male voice said, "so that someone with real foresight could build a better organization from the dregs."

Arrant's eyes widened in nervous astonishment. "That's Bruit!"

"I understand," a second male voice was saying. "I want some of the action."

Arrant paused the playback. "Who's—"

"Caba'Zan," the judicial supplied. "Former head of security for InterGalactic Ore."

Reluctantly, Arrant reactivated the device.

"We need to team up to accomplish this," Bruit said.

"No one will suspect us, and Arrant doesn't need to know any more than he has to."

"He's not that clever."

"The Toom's have the means to get the job done. We're going to make a move against everyone at Eriadu—"

Arrant silenced the device and pushed it away from him. "I don't know what to say."

The judicial agent nodded, tight-lipped.

Arrant got to his feet and spent a long moment gazing out the window. When he turned, his expression was bleak. He touched a key on the intercom pad, and seconds later his protocol droid secretary entered the office.

"How may I be of service, sir?"

Arrant glanced up at the droid. "I need to make two holocalls. The first will be to the chief executive of InterGalactic Ore, to discuss terms of a possible merger."

"And the second, sir?"

Arrant took a moment to reply. "The second call will be to Viceroy Nute Gunray, to discuss terms of granting the Trade Federation exclusive rights to the shipping and distribution of Dorvalla's lommite ore."

In a dank, fungus-encrusted grotto on the Neimoidian homeworld, Hath Monchar and Viceroy Nute Gunray received a startlingly sudden holovisit from Darth Sidious. First to reach the holoprojector and the cloaked apparition that was the Dark Lord of the Sith, Monchar inclined his lumpish head in a servile bow and spread his thick-fingered hands.

"Welcome, Lord Sidious," he said.

Though his eyes remained concealed by the cloak's raised hood, Sidious seemed to be gazing through Monchar at Gunray, who was perched atop his claw-footed mechno-chair a few meters away.

"Viceroy," Sidious rasped. "Dismiss your underling, so that we may speak in private about recent events on Dorvalla."

Monchar stared openly at Sidious, then whirled on Gunray. "But, Viceroy, I was the one who made contact with Lommite Limited. I deserve at least some of the credit for what has occurred."

"Viceroy," Sidious said, with a bit more menace, "advise your underling that his contributions in this matter were inconsequential."

Gunray glanced nervously at Monchar. "You had better leave."

"But—"

"Now—before he gets angry."

Monchar's gut sack made a sickening growl as he hurried from the grotto.

Gunray slid off the mechno-chair and approached the holoprojector. He had a jutting lower jaw, and his thick lower lip was uncompanioned. A deep fissure separated his bulging forehead into two lateral lobes. His skin was kept a healthy gray-blue by means of frequent meals of the finest fungus. Red and orange robes of exquisite hand fell from his narrow shoulders, along with a round-collared brown surplice that reached his knees.

"I apologize for the indiscretion of my deputy," he said. "He is high-strung from too many rich foods."

Sidious's face betrayed nothing. "Apology accepted, Viceroy."

"Hath Monchar regards me much as I regard you, Lord Sidious: with a mix of awe and fear."

"You need fear me only if you fail me, Viceroy."

Gunray seemed to take the remark under advisement. "I have been anticipating your visit, Lord Sidious. Though I confess that I had no idea you were aware of events on Dorvalla—much less that the Trade Federation had an interest in the planet."

"You will find that there are few matters of which I am unaware, Viceroy. What's more, we have not seen the last of Dorvalla. There is something we will need to attend to in due course."

"But, Lord Sidious, the matter has been resolved. Lommite Limited and InterGalactic Ore have merged to become Dorvalla Mining, but the Trade Federation will transport the ore, and will now represent Dorvalla in the Galactic Senate."

"More important, you have a permanent place on the directorate."

Gunray bowed his head. "That, too, Lord Sidious."

"Then the stage is set for the next act."

"May I ask what that will entail?"

"I will inform you at the appropriate time. Until then, there are other matters I will see to, to secure the power base of the Trade Federation and to strengthen your personal position."

"We are not deserving of your attention."

"Then strive to make yourself deserving, Viceroy, so that our partnership will continue to prosper."

Gunray gulped loudly. "I will do little else, Lord Sidious."

In his lair on Coruscant, Darth Sidious deactivated the holoprojector and turned to face Darth Maul.

"Do you find them any more trustworthy than before?"

"More frightened, Master," Maul said from his cross-legged posture on the floor, "which may achieve the same end result."

Sidious made an affirmative sound. "We are not through with them yet—not for some time to come."

"I begin to understand, Master."

Sidious's mouth approximated a grin of approval. "You did not disappoint me at Dorvalla, Darth Maul."

"My Master," Maul said, slightly bowing his head.

Sidious studied him for a moment. "I sense that you enjoyed being out on your own."

Maul lifted his face. "My thoughts are open to you, Master."

"I see," Sidious said slowly. "Temper your enthusiasm, my young apprentice. Soon I will have another task for you to discharge."

Maul waited.

"Familiarize yourself with the workings of the criminal organization known as Black Sun. And while you're doing that, return to your warrior training. Your lightsaber may very well come in handy for what I require next."